SEP 22 20

P9-DHK-462

FORTRESS
OF
DRAGONS

By C.J. Cherryh

C.J. CHERRYH

FORTRESS

OF

DRAGONS

3 1336 05216 2980

An Imprint of HarperCollinsPublishers

EOS

This is a work of fiction. Names, characters, places and incidents
either are the product of the author's imagination or are used fictitiously and are
not to be construed as real. Any resemblance to actual events, locales,
organizations, or persons, living or dead, is entirely coincidental.

EOS
An Imprint of HarperCollins*Publishers*
10 East 53rd Street
New York, New York 10022-5299

Copyright © 2000 by C.J. Cherryh
ISBN: 0-06-105055-5

All rights reserved. No part of this book may be used or reproduced in any
manner whatsoever without written permission, except in the case of brief
quotations embodied in critical articles and reviews. For information address
Eos, an imprint of HarperCollins Publishers, Inc.

Library of Congress Cataloging in Publication Data:

Cherryh, C.J.
Fortress of dragons / C.J. Cherryh.—1st ed.
p. cm.
I. Title.
PS3553.H358F73 2000
813'.54—dc21   00-25811

First Eos Printing: May 2000

Eos Trademark Reg. U.S. Pat. Off. and in Other Countries, Marca Registrada, Hecho en U.S.A.
HarperCollins® is a trademark of HarperCollins Publishers, Inc.

Printed in the U.S.A.

FIRST EDITION

RRD 10 9 8 7 6 5 4 3

www.avonbooks.com/eos
www.cherryh.com

PROLOGUE

There is magic.
There is wizardry.
There is sorcery.
They are not now, nor were then, the same.
Nine hundred years in the past, in a tower, in a place called
Galasien, a prince named Hasufin Heltain had an inordinate fear of
death. That fear led him from honest study of wizardry to the darker
practice of sorcery.

His teacher in the craft, Mauryl Gestaurien, seeing his student
about to outstrip his knowledge in a forbidden direction, brought
allies from the fabled northland, allies whose magic was not taught,
but innate. These were the five Sihhë-lords.

In the storm of conflict that followed, not only Hasufin perished,
but also ancient Galasien and all its works. Of all that city, only the
tower in which Mauryl stood survived.

Ynefel, for so later generations named the tower, became a
haunted place, isolated within Marna Wood, its walls holding intact
the horrified faces of lost Galasien's people. The old tower was
Mauryl's point of power, and so he remained bound to it through
passing centuries, although he sometimes intervened outside the
tower in the struggles that followed in the lands the Galasieni had
ruled.

The Sihhë took on themselves the task of ruling the southern
lands . . . not the Galasieni, who had become bound to Ynefel, but
other newcomers . . . notably the race of Men, who also had crept
down from the north. The Sihhë swept across the land, subduing
and building, conquering and changing all that the Galasieni had

made, creating new authorities and powers to reward their subordinates and dealing harshly with their enemies.

The five true Sihhë lived long, after the nature of their kind, and they left a thin presence of halfling descendants among Men before their passing. The kingdom of Men rapidly spread and populated the lands nearest Ynefel, with that halfling dynasty ruling from the Sihhë hall at unwalled Althalen.

Unchallenged lord of Ynefel's haunted tower, Mauryl continued in a life by now drawn thin and long, whether by wizardry or by nature: he had now outlasted even the long-lived Sihhë, and watched changes and ominous shifts of power as the blood and the innate Sihhë magic alike ran thinner and thinner in the line of halfling High Kings.

For, of all the old powers, Shadows lingered, and haunted certain places in the land. One of these was Hasufin Heltain.

One day, in the Sihhë capital, within the tributary kingdom of Amefel, and in the rule of the halfling Elfwyn Sihhë, a queen gave birth to a stillborn babe. The queen was inconsolable—but the babe miraculously drew breath and lived, warmed to life, as she thought, by Sihhë magic and a mother's love.

To the queen the child was a wonderful gift. But that second life was not the first life, and it was not the mother's innate Sihhë magic, but a Shadow's darkest sorcery that had brought breath into the child—for what lived in the babe was a soul neither Sihhë nor Man: it was Hasufin Heltain, in his second bid for life and power.

So now Hasufin nestled in the heart of the Sihhë aristocracy, still a child, at a time when Mauryl, who might have realized what he was, had shut himself away in his tower at Ynefel, rarely venturing as far as Althalen—for Mauryl felt the weakness of the ages Hasufin had not lived.

Other children of the royal house died mysteriously as that fey, ingratiating princeling grew stronger. Now alarmed, warned by his arts and full of fury and advice, Mauryl came to court to confront the danger he recognized. But the queen would not hear a wizard's warning, far less dispose of a son of the house, her favorite, her dearest and most magical darling—a child who now, by the deaths of all elder princes, was near the throne.

The day that child should attain his majority, and the hour that prince should rule, Mauryl warned them, the house and the dynasty would perish. But even that plain warning failed to persuade the queen; and the King, Elfwyn, took his grieving queen's side, refusing Mauryl's unthinkable command to destroy their own son.

Foreseeing ruin, Mauryl turned not to the halfling Sihhë of the court, but to the Men who served them. He conspired with the war-lord Selwyn Marhanen, the Sihhë's trusted general, and thus encouraged Selwyn and other Men to bring down the halfling dynasty and take the throne for themselves. So Mauryl betrayed the descendants of the very lords he had raised up to prevent Hasufin's sorcery, and for that reason Men called Mauryl both Kingmaker, and Kingsbane.

Mauryl insinuated both the Marhanen and his men and a band of wizards into the royal palace. Mauryl and the majority of his circle held magic at bay while a younger wizard, Emuin, killed the sleeping prince in his chambers—a terrible and a bloody deed, and only the first act of bloodshed that night.

Hasufin's death was the limit of Mauryl's interest in the matter. The fate of the Sihhë in the hands of Selwyn and his men, and even the fate of the wizards who had aided him, was all beyond his capability to govern, and Mauryl again retreated to his tower, weary and sick with age. Young Emuin took holy orders, seeking to forget his terrible deed and to find some salvation for himself as a Man and a cleric in an age of Men.

In those years Selwyn's own ambition and Men's religious fear of a magic they did not wield led them to rise in earnest against Sihhë rule: province after province fell to the Marhanen, and their followers destroyed all that lay outside the approval of their priests . . . demolishing even the work of wizards who had aided their rise.

But the district of Elwynor across the river from Althalen, though populated with Men, attempted to remain loyal to the Sihhë-lords and to maintain wizards in safety. They even raised an army to bring against the Marhanen, but dissent and claims and counterclaims of kingship within Elwynor precluded that army from ever taking the field. The Marhanen thus were able to seize the entire tributary kingdom of Amefel (in which the capital of Althalen had stood) and treat it as a province, right across the river from Elwynor.

But Selwyn Marhanen—rather than rule from Althalen, remote from the heart of his power, and equally claimed by all the lords of Men—instead established a capital in the center of his home territory. He declared himself king, though not High King, and by his own cleverness and ruthlessness set his own allies under his heel. The lords of districts became barons of a new court at Guelemara, in Selwyn's own district of Guelessar.

From that new capital at Guelemara, Selwyn dominated all the provinces southward. He as well as his subjects, mostly Guelenfolk *and Ryssandish, being true Men with no gift for wizardry, had no love of it either—Selwyn because he feared wizards might challenge him, and his people because they saw magic and wizardry alike as a challenge to the gods . . . so priests of the Quinalt and Teranthine sects had taught them. For both reasons, Selwyn raised a great shrine next his palace, the Quinaltine, and favored the Quinalt Patriarch, who set a religious seal on all his acts of domination. But Selwyn trusted the Quinalt sect no more than he trusted wizards, and established none other than Emuin, now a Teranthine brother, as his advisor. This he did to balance the power of the Quinaltine.*

By now, of all Men loyal to the Sihhë, only the Elwynim had successfully held their border against the Guelenmen . . . for that border was on the one hand a broad river, the Lenúalim, and on the other, the haunted precincts of Marna Wood, near the old tower of Ynefel, and beyond the always restive district of Amefel.

So, with that border established, the matter settled . . . save only the troublesome question of Amefel, the province on the Guelen-held side of the Lenúalim River, the population of which was not Guelenish, but close kin to the Elwynim. Selwyn's hope of holding his lands firm against the Elwynim rested on not allowing an Elwynim presence on that side of the river . . . within a population virtually the same in accent, religion, and customs.

Now the history of Amefel was this: Amefel had been an independent kingdom of Men when the first Sihhë-lords walked up to the walls of its capital of Hen Amas and demanded entry. The kings of Amefel, the Aswyddim, flung open their gates and helped the Sihhë in their mission to conquer Guelessar, a fact no Guelen and no Guelen king could quite forget. In return for this treachery, the local Aswydd house had always enjoyed a unique status under the Sihhë authority, and, alone of Men, styled themselves as kings, as opposed to High Kings, the title the Sihhë reserved for themselves and their successors.

So now Selwyn had severed Amefel from Elwynor and claimed it . . . but at least for this approaching fall season, he foresaw that his own uneasily joined kingdom of Ylesuin, with barons at least two of whom had already tried to claim rule over the Guelens, would fall to internal quarrels the moment he looked elsewhere. If he became embroiled in a dispute with the Aswydds over their prerogatives, that would lead to his own barons scheming and plotting while he was distracted, and that situation might encourage Elwynor to break the unofficial truce . . . leading to war next spring from one end to the other of the lands of Men.

So Selwyn Marhanen quietly accorded the Aswydds guarantees of many of their ancient rights, including their religion, and including their titles. By that agreement, while the Aswydds became vassals of the kings of Ylesuin, and were called dukes, they were also styled aethelings, that was to say, royal—but only within their own province of Amefel. This purposely left aside the question of whether the other earls of Amefel bore rank equivalent to the dukes of Guelen and Ryssandish lands.

Selwyn thus had Amefel . . . or at least the consent of its aetheling . . . by the first winter of his rule, and he still had ambitions to go further. But the opposing district of Elwynor formed a region almost as large as Ylesuin was with Amefel attached, and, undeceived by the apparent truce, Elwynor's lords used that winter to gather forces. By the next spring, with Selwyn in Amefel and Elwynor armed and strong enough to make invasion costly, both sides assessed their chances and declined battle. The river Lenúalim thus became the tacitly unquestioned but still unsettled border.

The Elwynim meanwhile, declared a Regency in place of the lost High King at Althalen. They chose one of their earls, himself with a glimmering of Sihhë blood, who styled himself Lord Regent, and waited, taking it on stubborn faith that not all the royal house of the Sihhë-lords had perished, that within their lifetimes a new Sihhë-lord, some surviving prince they called the King To Come, would emerge from hiding or come down from the fabled northern ice to overthrow the Marhanen and reestablish the Sihhë kingdom. This time the Sihhë kingdom would have faithful Elwynor at its heart, and all the loyal subjects, foremost the Elwynim, would live in peace and Sihhë-blessed prosperity in a new golden age of wizardry.

The Elwynim, therefore, cherished magic, and prized the wizard-gift where it appeared. But outside the Lord Regent's line there were far too few Elwynim who could practice wizardry in any appreciable degree. Certainly no one in the land possessed such magic as the Sihhë had used, and there were few enough wizards left who would even speak of the King To Come . . . for the wizards of this age had had firsthand experience of Hasufin Heltain, and they remained aloof from the various lords of the Elwynim who wished to employ them. Those few Elwynim who had any Sihhë blood whatsoever were likewise reticent, for fear of becoming the center of some rising against the Regency that could only end in disaster.

So the Elwynim, deserted by their wizards and by those who did carry the blood, became too little wary of magic and those who promised it. They failed to ask the essential question: why the wiz-

5

ards remained silent and why Mauryl and Emuin both remained aloof from them, and thus they failed to know the danger that still existed in the shadows and among the Shadows.

So the years passed into decades without a credible claimant to the throne in Elwynor, and without the rise of another great wizard.

Selwyn died. Ylesuin's rule passed to Selwyn's son Ináreddrin, who was a middle-aged man with two previous marriages and two grown sons.

Now Ináreddrin was Guelen to the core, which meant devoutly, blindly Quinalt. That was his mother's influence. As a young prince, he had had no love of his uncivil warlord father, but had a great deal of fear of him. And under this dual influence of his mother's faith and his father's disinterest, Ináreddrin grew up with no tolerance for other faiths, despite the exigencies of the Amefin treaty . . . and with a superstitious fear of wizardry, based on his observation of his father Selwyn's terrors in his declining years. Ináreddrin fell more and more under the influence of the Quinaltine, and exercised little patience with his wild eldest son, Cefwyn—for Cefwyn took his grandfather's example and clung to the Teranthine tutor, Emuin (that same Emuin who had aided Mauryl at Althalen), whom Selwyn had appointed royal tutor for both his grandsons.

This was no accident, first because of wizardry, where little was accidental at all; and secondly because Selwyn saw superstition rising in his son and wished to stop it in the next generation. If Selwyn as a reigning king had found priests and the Quinalt a convenient resource, and to that end had supported them, he never forgot what he had faced at Althalen. Selwyn knew he had lost his son to the priests' influence, but he wanted his grandsons never to dread priests or wizards—rather to understand them, and to keep the best on their side.

This matter of the royal tutor was a source of bitter argument within the royal house: the queen died, Ináreddrin grew more and more alienated from his father, and the very year Selwyn died and Ináreddrin became king, Ináreddrin persuaded his younger son Efanor into the strictest Quinalt faith—lavishing on him all the affection he now angrily denied the elder son.

So did the highest barons—notably the dukes of the provinces of Ryssand and Murandys—lavish attention on the younger prince, Efanor. There was even talk of overturning the succession—for the more religious and proper Efanor became, the more Cefwyn, the crown prince and heir, consoled himself with wild escapades, sorties on the border, and women . . . very many women.

Still, by Guelen law and custom, even by the tenets of the Quinalt itself, Cefwyn was, incontrovertibly, the heir, and it was no light matter to set Cefwyn aside: in that, even the most conservative of priests hesitated.

So Ináreddrin, either in hopes that administrative responsibility would temper Cefwyn—or, it was whispered, in hopes some assassin or border skirmish would settle the matter and make Efanor his heir—sent Cefwyn to administer the Amefin garrison. To do that, Ináreddrin bestowed on Prince Cefwyn the courtesy title of viceroy, thus keeping a firmer Marhanen hand on that curiously independent province and insinuating a closer Marhanen presence into a very troublesome district.

Now, since ordinarily and by the treaty, there was no such thing as a viceroy in Amefel, the duke of Amefel, Heryn Aswydd, was not at all pleased by this gesture, but Heryn dared not protest and give the Marhanen an excuse to send a larger garrison. So Duke Heryn kept his discontent to himself, even agreeing to report to Ináreddrin regarding the prince's behavior, and on the worsening situation across the river.

The duties Cefwyn had, however, were not a sham. Ináreddrin had indeed felt a need for a firmer Guelen presence in Amefel, for the Regent in Elwynor had no children but a daughter of his extreme old age, and now the lords of Elwynor, weary of waiting for the appearance of a High King, were now saying the Regent should choose one of them to be king. They saw that the only way for one earl of all the earls to gain any legitimate connection with royalty was by marrying the Lord Regent's daughter.

The Regent of Elwynor, Uleman Syrillas, refused all offers from his earls, swearing that his only child, his daughter Ninévrisë, would wield the power of Regent herself. It was unprecedented among the Elwynim and by chance unprecedented among the Sihhë Kings themselves that a woman should rule in her own right. Uleman had nevertheless prepared his daughter to rule . . . and when the day came that a suitor tried to enforce his demands with arms and carry Ninévrisë away, the Regent refused to yield.

But the earls' guards were the army, the only army, that the Regent could draw on, and now some earls sided with the suitor and some sued for themselves while others sided with the Regent.

Elwynor sank into civil war . . . and that war insinuated itself across the river into Amefel, where Elwynim families had historical ties and relatives.

So it was into this situation that Ináreddrin sent Prince Cefwyn.

And it was entirely characteristic of Ináreddrin that he told Heryn he was to watch Cefwyn and told Cefwyn to watch Heryn, who was, after all, a heretic Bryaltine and a man with ties to the Elwynim earls.

Unbeknownst to the king, in fact, Duke Heryn was in league with the rebel earl Caswyddian, in Elwynor . . . and that gave the edge to Caswyddian over his own chief rival, Aséyneddin.

And Hasufin Heltain, once again dead, as Men knew death, was waiting only for such a moment of crisis and a condition in the stars. Through the situation in Elwynor, that ancient spirit found his way closer and closer to life . . . he saw Aséyneddin as his ally.

Mauryl, however, had foreseen the hour Hasufin would make another bid for life, and had saved his strength for one grand, un-precedented spell, a Summoning and a Shaping. So he brought forth his creation from the fire of his hearth—not a perfect effort, however, nor mature nor threatening. To Mauryl's distress the young man thus Summoned lacked all memory of what or who he had been.

Mauryl gave his Summoning a name—Tristen—and taught him with more patience than Mauryl had accorded any other student, until the day Mauryl lost his struggle with Hasufin once and for all.

So Tristen, a young man with the innocence of the newly born, set forth into the world to do the things Mauryl intended . . . if only he could guess what those things were.

He came not to a wizard, who would teach him, as Tristen had hoped, but to Prince Cefwyn, on the very night when, despising his host, Heryn Aswydd, Prince Cefwyn was sleeping with Heryn's twin sisters, Orien and Tarien.

Now Tristen was as innocent a soul as ever Cefwyn had met . . . a youth seeming incapable of anger, feckless, and utterly outspoken, but wizardous in his origins at the very least, for he confessed he was Mauryl's.

Cefwyn's curiosity was immediately snared; and once Cefwyn began to deal with Tristen personally, he found himself snared in-deed—for having suffered his grandfather's angers and his own fa-ther's cold dislike of him, after the northern lords' wish for Efanor and Efanor's desertion toward religion, this was the only offer of an utter stranger's friendship he had ever encountered, and from a kind and innocent heart.

Meanwhile Tristen continued to learn . . . for he was a blank slate on which Mauryl's spell was still writing, Unfolding new things in wizardous fashion, at need; and providing him knowledge unpre-dictable both in its scope and in its deficiency. Tristen wondered at butterflies . . . and asked questions that shot straight to the prince's much-scarred heart.

Cefwyn's affection toward this wizardous stranger made Duke Heryn Aswydd hasten his plans for war . . . for Cefwyn was growing fey and difficult. Heryn used King Ináreddrin's suspicion of his son to lure both the king and Prince Efanor to Amefel . . . hoping then to do away with Cefwyn and the younger prince in the same stroke as King Ináreddrin. Thus he would overthrow the Marhanen dynasty, end Guelen rule as the Guelens fell to fighting each other, aid Caswyddian to become High King in Elwynor, and establish himself as a ruling aetheling, a power in the new Elwynim court.

Prince Efanor, however, had not ridden with the king. Fearing for his father's life if the accusations were true, yet willing to give his brother a last chance to confess, he had ridden straight to Cefwyn to find out for himself the truth ahead of their father's arrival, to spring any trap upon himself if one existed. It was a brave act of a religious man, and of a brother Cefwyn had once loved.

And when Cefwyn knew his father had listened to Lord Heryn and was proceeding with Heryn's full confidence into Amefin territory, he was horrified, and rode at once to prevent the ambush he foresaw, no matter the danger.

He arrived too late, and was almost overwhelmed by the force that had killed the king. Heryn's plan would have come to fruition but for one thing: the knowledge of warfare Unfolded to Tristen that day, on that battlefield, and in that knowledge and with a sword in his hands, the gentle stranger turned warrior. He rescued both the princes and defeated Heryn's allies.

When Cefwyn reached Henas'amef not only unexpectedly alive, but king of Ylesuin, Heryn paid with his life for his treason. Tristen, however, wounded by his own self-knowledge and by witnessing Cefwyn's justice, strayed into the hills, where he fell in with the Lord Regent of Elwynor. Lord Uleman was dying, and in hiding from his rebel earls. The old Regent's last wish was to bring his daughter Ninévrisë to Cefwyn Marhanen, as his bride . . . for the only hope for the Regency was peace with Ylesuin. The Regent died, his spirit possessing the ruins of Althalen, and he was buried there.

So Tristen brought Lady Ninévrisë to Cefwyn, and the new king of Ylesuin fell headlong in love with the new Regent of Elwynor.

Tristen, for his services to the Crown, became a lord of Ylesuin, no longer mocked for his simplicity, but rather feared by the Guelenfolk, for no one who had seen him fight could discount him. The townsfolk and countryfolk of Amefel, on the other hand, adored him, and saw in him the fulfillment of the prophecy of the King To Come—a fulfillment Cefwyn himself foresaw, and did not attempt to fight. "Win his friendship," was Emuin's sage advice regarding his dealings with Tristen, and so he had; and now Cefwyn saw before him the chance for that friendship to settle the whole world at peace, for he did not see Tristen as a reigning king, but as a king in symbol, a reconciliation with the Sihhë. As he declared to Ninévrisë, nothing would be more cruel than to settle on Tristen's glad spirit all the daily obligations of a reigning king.

Meanwhile Heryn's sister Orien became duchess of Amefel, since Cefwyn was not ready to set aside the entire dynasty, and had seen none but the ordinary Aswydd flaws in Orien. He hoped to content the people of Amefel with that appointment and thought that a woman with no martial skills and no command of an army would be a more biddable ruler in the troublesome district.

Orien, however, was bent on revenge, and lied in her oaths. Lacking armies, lacking skill in war, she sought another means to power . . . and with her earliest attempts at the wizardous legacy of her house, found her answer in sorcerous whispers from the enemy, Hasufin Heltain.

She was not a great wizard, not even a moderately great one, but she deceived herself that she was. Hasufin's immediate goal was an entry into the fortress of Henas'amef, but because of Tristen and Emuin, he could not breach the wards. It was no difficulty at all to move his pawn Orien to make an attempt on Cefwyn's life and another pawn to make an attempt on Emuin's life. Meanwhile he drew the rebel army across the river to all-out war: Aséyneddin invaded Amefel in force.

The first two attempts fell useless: Cefwyn and Emuin both survived.

The third, Aséyneddin's, was the real one, aimed not at kingship—Aséyneddin's purpose—but specifically at Tristen, whom Hasufin recognized as Mauryl's last and most effective weapon, and who must go down if Hasufin was to prevent Tristen's rise as a Sihhë-lord.

Sorcery, a wizardous art reliant on chaos, was strongest in a moment of chance and upheaval, and there was no moment of upheaval among Men greater than the shifting tides of a battlefield. So Hasufin made his strongest bid to destroy Tristen, who stood between him and the life and substance he could gain through Aséyneddin.

In the world of Men, at a place called Lewenbrook, near Ynefel, the Elwynim rebels, under Lord Aséyneddin, met Cefwyn Marha-nen's opposing army. That was the conflict Men fought.

But when Aséyneddin faltered, Hasufin sent out tides of sorcery in reckless disregard. A wall of Shadow rolled down on the field, and those it touched it took and did not give up. It was Hasufin's manifestation, and all aimed at Tristen's destruction.

Tristen, however, took up magic as he took up his weapons, when the challenge came. When Hasufin Heltain loosed his sorcery, Tristen rode into the Shadow, penetrated into Ynefel itself, and drove Hasufin from his Place in the world.

Cefwyn meanwhile had prevailed in the unnatural darkness, and when the sun broke free of the Shadow, he had managed to hold his army together and continue the assault. Aséyneddin's forces, such as survived, shattered and ran in panic.

It was a long way back to the world, however, from where Tristen had gone to fight. Exhausted, hurt, at the end of his purpose, Tristen all but resigned his wizard-made life, finished with Mauryl's purpose, too weary to wake to the world of Men.

But he had once given his shieldman Uwen, an ordinary Man with not a shred of magic in him, the power to call his name. This Uwen did, the devotion of a simple man seeking his lost lord on the battlefield, and Tristen came.

There was a moment, then, when Cefwyn stood victorious over the rebels, that he might have launched forward into Elwynor: the southern lords had rallied to the new king, and would have followed him. But Cefwyn saw his army badly battered and in need of re-grouping. He knew the enemy was on the run, meaning they would sink invisibly into Elwynor's forested depths—and he knew, as a new king, that he had left matters uncertain behind him. The majority of his kingdom did not even know they had changed one king for an-other, and the treaty he had made with Ninévrisë had never reached his people. He stood in the situation his grandfather had faced, at the end of summer, with a winter before him.

Good campaigning weather still remained, but harsh northern winters and the Elwynim woods could make fighting impossible. So for good or for ill, Cefwyn opted not to plunge his exhausted army, lacking maps or any sort of preparation, into the unknown situation inside Elwynor, which had been several years in anarchy and still had rival claimants to the Regency. Instead he chose to regroup, settle his domestic affairs, marry the Lady Regent, ratify the marriage treaty, and rally the rest of his kingdom behind him in a campaign to begin in the spring. It seemed unlikely that any great power could *rise in Elwynor during autumn and a winter, given that the rebels were now fighting among themselves and that his army and Tristen had already defeated the two strongest forces Elwynor could field.*

So Cefwyn went home, trusting his father's trusted men, gathering up his brother Efanor, to take up the power of the monarchy as it had been.

So he thought. But when he reached his capital, he discovered his father's closest friends among the barons meant to wrest the real power into their own hands, for his father had let them do much as they pleased for years—had taken their decisions and put his royal seal on them. The clerics had preferred Efanor: that was a known difficulty. But the barons had for the last decade had a king they could rule. They meant to have another one, and in their minds and by all prior reports, Cefwyn was a wastrel prince who would be a weak king if they simply provided him diversions and women. He could be managed, they had said among themselves.

That was not, however, the nature of the king who came home to them: Cefwyn arrived surrounded by their southern rivals, who were clearly in favor, and allied to Mauryl's heir, betrothed to the Elwynim Regent, advised by a wizard, and proposing war on the Elwynim rebels. The barons quickly realized they were not facing Ináreddrin's dissolute son: it was Selwyn's hard-handed grandson, and the barons, accustomed to dictating to the father, were set down hard.

So the most powerful barons of the north took a new tactic . . . they were older, cannier, more experienced in court politics: they already had the good will of the most conservative priests. They would use the Quinaltine and the people's faith, prevent the marriage, treat the lady Regent as a captive—and seize land in Elwynor.

Cefwyn determined just as resolutely to bring them into line and shake the kingdom into order. He sent the southern barons home to attend their harvests and to prepare for war, all but Lord Cevulirn of Ivanor, whose horsemen had less reliance on such seasons, and who stayed as a shadowy observer for southern interests.

In Elwynor, meanwhile, the wars had come to a swifter conclusion than anyone expected. One rebel lord brought a largely hired army out of the hills, supplied it off the resources of the peasants, besieged his own capital of Ilefínian, and declared the Lady Regent a helpless captive in the hands of the Marhanen king. This brought the situation Cefwyn had left in Elwynor to a state of crisis, and Cefwyn took immediate steps to set elite cavalry at the bridges that

12

faced Elwynor. This both stabilized the border and removed some of the force on which the Crown maintained its authority.

Cefwyn took immediate measures to assure that the Quinalt would approve both the marriage and the treaty that recognized Ninévrisë as Lady Regent of Elwynor, independent of the Crown of Ylesuin, and renounced all claims to each other's kingdoms.

The barons retaliated with an attempt to limit the monarchy over them, and to reject both the marriage treaty and their king's associates.

Tristen and Emuin both had kept to themselves since their arrival . . . for Cefwyn, fighting for his right to wed the woman he loved and trying to wrest back greater sovereignty in his own capital, wished to obscure the presence of wizardry in his court.

Obscurity, however, only increased the mystery surrounding Tristen. The barons saw him and Emuin as an influence on Cefwyn that must be eliminated, and on a night when lightning, whether by chance or wizardry, struck the Quinalt roof, a penny in the offering in the Quinaltine was found to be Sihhë coinage, with forbidden symbols on it.

The charge against Tristen was to be sacrilege, wizardry attacking the Quinalt and the gods.

Cefwyn suspected that His Holiness the Patriarch himself was devious enough to have substituted the damning coin, and Cefwyn moved quickly to compel the Patriarch into his camp. But the rumors were so rife that Cefwyn felt compelled to remove Tristen further from controversy and from the site of rumors. In what he thought a clever and protective stroke, he sent Tristen back to Amefel not as a refugee in disgrace, but as duke of Amefel . . . a replacement for the viceroy he had left to replace the disgraced Orien Aswydd.

Now this viceroy was Parsynan, a minor noble appointed on the advice of some of these same troublesome barons, notably Murandys and Ryssand . . . for Cefwyn had exiled Orien Aswydd and her sister to a Teranthine nunnery for their betrayal, and had never appointed another duke, until now.

Hearing that Tristen was going to Amefel, and that Parsynan was recalled, Corswyndam Lord Ryssand panicked, for he feared certain records might fall into Tristen's hands and thus into Cefwyn's. He sent a rider to advise Parsynan of his imminent replacement.

Corswyndam's courier rode hard enough to reach the Amefin capital ahead of Cefwyn's messenger. Receiving the message, Parsynan quite naively brought his local ally Lord Cuthan, an Aswydd by remote kinship, into his confidence, since this man had supported him against his brother earls before.

Cuthan, however, was in on a plot to create war in Amefel, a distraction for Cefwyn. If Amefin earls rebelled and seized the citadel, Elwynim troops would then invade and engage with the king's forces: this was what was promised, and Cuthan not only failed to warn Parsynan it was coming . . . but he also said nothing to warn his brother lords that a detachment of king's forces was about to arrive along with a new duke, one they might approve. One or the other would happen first, and Cuthan meant to stay safe.

So, ignorant of such vital information, certain Amefin, led by Earl Edwyll of Meiden, seized the South Court of the fortress of Amefel and settled in to wait for Elwynim support.

In the same hour, losing courage, Cuthan told the other earls that the king's forces were coming.

And there were as yet no forces from Elwynor: Tasmôrden's forces had not arrived.

The other earls consequently sat still . . . which suited Cuthan well: he and Edwyll were old rivals, and now Edwyll was patently guilty of treason, sitting alone in the fortress with the Marhanen king's forces approaching. And none of the rest of them were yet guilty of anything, as long as they kept their secret. The one most apt to betray it—was Edwyll himself.

Then in a thunderstroke, before anyone had thought, Tristen arrived and moved swiftly uphill to the fortress to take possession. The commons turned out to cheer. The earls of Amefel rapidly set themselves on the winning side.

Edwyll meanwhile died, having enjoyed a cup of wine—out of Orien Aswydd's cups, untouched since the place was sealed at her exile. Whether Edwyll's death was latent wizardry attached to Orien's property, or simple bad luck, the command of the rebels now devolved to Edwyll's son, thane Crissand, who was forced to surrender. Tristen now had the fortress in his hands.

Not satisfied with the death of earl Edwyll, however, or possibly at the instigation of some party to the guilty secret, Parsynan, in command of the garrison troops, seized the prisoners from Tristen's officers and began executing them.

Tristen found out in time to save Crissand . . . and summarily dismissed Lord Parsynan from the town in the middle of the night and without his possessions.

It was scandalous treatment of a noble king's officer, but if there was anything wanting to make Tristen the hero of Henas'amef, this *settled matters. The commons were delighted, wildly cheering their new lord. Crissand, Edwyll's son, himself of remote Aswydd lineage, swore fealty to Tristen in such absolute terms it scandalized the Guelen clerks who had come with Tristen—for Crissand owned Tristen as his overlord after the Aswydd kind, aetheling, a royal lord.*

The oath reopened all the old controversy about the status of Amefel as a sovereign kingdom. Crissand had become Tristen's friend and most fervent ally among the earls of Amefel . . . who, given a lord they respected, came rapidly into line, united for the first time in decades, under terms forever influenced by Crissand's oath.

In the succeeding hours Tristen gained both the burned remnant of Mauryl's letters, and Lord Ryssand's letter to Parsynan. The first told him that certain correspondence Mauryl had had with the lords of Amefel might have some modern relevancy . . . one archivist had murdered the other and run with the letters. The second letter revealed Corswyndam's connivance with Parsynan.

Tristen sent Lord Ryssand's letter posthaste to Guelessar, while Cuthan, revealed for a traitor to both sides, and possibly guilty of more than anyone knew, took advantage of Tristen's leniency to flee to Elwynor.

In the capital, Corswyndam Lord Ryssand knew he had to move quickly to lessen the king's power or lose his own. It happened that one of his clerks had reported that the office of Regent of Elwynor, which Ninévrisë claimed, included priestly functions. So at Ryssand's instigation, certain conservatives in the Holy Quinalt rose up in protest of a woman in priestly rites. This objection would break the marriage treaty.

Cefwyn countered with another compromise and a trade of favors with the Holy Father: Ninévrisë agreed to state that she was and had always been of the Bryaltine sect—that recognized, though scantly respectable, Amefin religion. She agreed to accept a priest of that faith as her priest, leaving aside other difficult questions, and on that understanding, the Quinalt would perform the wedding.

The barons now came with the last and worst attack on Ninévrisë: charges of infidelity, Ninévrisë's with Tristen, laughable if one knew them. But Ryssand's daughter Artisane was prepared to perjure herself to bring Ninévrisë down. So Cefwyn learned when Ryssand's son Brugan brought the charges to him secretly—along with a document giving much of his power to the barons, which was clearly the alternative this young lordling presented his king.

Therein Ryssand overstepped himself: it gave an excuse for a loyal baron, Cevulirn of Ivanor, to challenge Brugan. By killing

Brugan, by popular belief, Cevulirn proved Ninévrisë's innocence. If Ryssand should make public the attack on Ninévrisë, that fact would come out to counter it: Brugan had died a liar.

But if it should come to public knowledge, someone would surely challenge Cevulirn, and if he won again, another and another would challenge him until they could cast the result in doubt. Cefwyn still hoped to deal with the other barons, and would trade silence for silence, casting the killing as a private quarrel to prevent the destructive chain of challenges and feuds that would tear the court apart.

But that meant Cevulirn had to leave court, avoiding Ryssand's presence, and Cefwyn girded himself for a confrontation in court with a powerful baron who had just lost his son to a man who had not stayed to face challenges.

Into this situation Ryssand's incriminating letter arrived secretly into Cefwyn's hands . . . and Cefwyn thus had the means to suggest Ryssand also retire to his estates immediately, or have all his actions made public to the other barons.

So the treaty stood firm, Cefwyn and Ninévrisë married, and Tristen settled in to rule in the south as lord of Amefel, lord of the province containing old Althalen and bordering Ynefel and Elwynor across the river.

But on a day that Tristen, with Earl Crissand and Uwen, set out to visit the villages, they came across an old shrine, where the apparition of the Witch of Emwy, Auld Syes, appeared as the precursor to a terrible storm. Lord of Amefel and the aetheling, she hailed them, as if those titles were not one and the same thing. She bade them ride south to find friends, and then to feed her sparrows.

Further, she asked permission to visit Tristen at some time in the future—in effect, asked passage through the magical wards of the Zeide of Henas'amef. Tristen granted it, to his guards' great distress.

South they rode, then, in the rising storm, and encountered Cevulirn, who had turned banishment to good use, riding north to inform Tristen of those matters too delicate to be entrusted to couriers.

The two of them took counsel how to use their resources to help Cefwyn in the spring, and agreed to call in all the other lords of the south—which Cefwyn could not dare. Their plan was to set a camp across the river and divert Tasmôrden's attention southward. Cefwyn had forbidden them to win the war, because the Quinaltine northern barons were already distressed about his reliance on the Teranthine south . . . but together Tristen and Cevulirn saw what they could do to bolster Cefwyn's cause without violating the letter of their king's orders.

Tristen and Cevulirn set out then toward the river to view the situation firsthand. On the way they made a stop in the village of Modeyneth, where Tristen raised the local thane, Drusenan, to the rank of earl in Cuthan's place, and commanded the raising of an old Sihhë wall to hold the road. In so doing, they found that Drusenan had concealed a number of Elwynim who had fled the war. For want of any other safe place to settle them in his lands, Tristen authorized them to build a refuge within the vacant ruins of Althalen . . . where no settlement was permitted, under Crown law, but where they were out of the way of traffic coming up and down the vital road to Elwynor.

Having done those things, Tristen and Cevulirn rode on, and were at the river when Tristen realized, through that gray world only wizards could touch, that the Elwynim capital, Ilefínian, had fallen.

So there would not be a winter's grace to prepare: the situation was immediately more grave.

Meanwhile in Guelemara, and to the discomfiture of Murandys and Ryssand alike, Cefwyn invited his former lover, Luriel, Murandys' niece, back to court. With considerable inducements of land and favor, he arranged her marriage to the son of Duke Maudyn, lord of Panys, his commander on the riverside.

In this manner and at one stroke he shone a light on his consort's generosity and his own reformed habits . . . and undermined the confidence of his opponents in each other. This marriage allied Murandys' interests with those of the lord of Panys, who firmly supported the Crown.

In Amefel, meanwhile, in a reunion of a far different sort, Tristen rescued from prison a young thief, Paisi. This was a street boy who had once guided him to Cefwyn's justice: Paisi's fate, he was convinced, was linked to his own, simply because the whole web of incidents leading him to his present allies was a series of linkages, and those linkages were a likely target of hostile wizardry—simply put, those once connected to him at points of critical decision could connect to him again, at points of critical decision, for good or for ill.

This one looked already to have a taint of ill about it—for in saving Paisi, Tristen had a falling out with the Guelen Guard, the garrison in Henas'amef, for it was from them that Paisi had stolen, and Tristen would not see him hanged. Instead, Paisi went to Emuin's tower to become his assistant . . . and certain guardsmen and even the patriarch of the local Quinalt left Tristen's court in anger. Tristen had been right: the boy once involved at a crisis of decision was involved again, and whatever would have happened had Paisi *hanged, would not now happen. Some other event was now in progress in which Paisi had some part to play, and he trusted Emuin to keep as much order in that event as anyone could keep.*

The disgruntled soldiers and the patriarch went to Guelemara, and their reports when they reached Guelemara created a storm in the Quinalt. They accused Tristen of serious breaches of Crown law, usurpation of royal authority, and the promotion of wizardry in Amefel. Strict northern priests, supported by Ryssand, had already preached doom in the streets, and as this further attack gained momentum, Cefwyn moved secretly to silence the most outspoken of these priests, one Udryn, as one of Ryssand's men.

Meanwhile, regarding the charges now made public, he could do nothing but declare the laws themselves outdated, since his only other choice was to agree that Tristen was a lawbreaker. This in no wise comforted the orthodoxy, but the open expression of opposition to the king was a little quieter since the disappearance of the priest.

Tristen and Cevulirn parted company, swearing to meet next with all the lords of their former alliance, on Midwinter Eve, in Henas'-amef. And for his part Tristen settled in earnest to the preparation of a winter camp for an army.

That same Midwinter was to mark the marriage of Luriel to Lord Panys' younger son—in a capital seething with dissenting priests and fears of wizardry.

And in the middle of the ceremony the Quinalt Patriarch was found murdered, with Bryaltine symbols about his person.

The wedding fell apart in riot and religious frenzy, in which Ninévrisë's unfortunate priest fell afoul of a mob and lost his life.

Cefwyn countered quickly to gain the favor of the mob by diverting suspicion toward Tasmôrden's agents . . . though he himself suspected the zealot priests and an act of very local revenge. He took clear command of the capital and of the situation, at least for the day, and moved to counter Ryssand, whom he blamed above all others.

Back in Ynefel, Tristen's guests had come, every one of them, and they settled to feast on a night Emuin had warned Tristen was the hinge not only of the year, but of a magical age of ages.

At the stroke of midnight Auld Syes entered the hall in queenly guise and danced one dance with Tristen . . . after which the lights went out and the old haunt in the lower hall broke wide open.

Tristen entered into it, in defense of all the rest, and found himself not in battle against shadows and dead wizards, but walking in Ynefel of old, himself a shadow in the life of the Tristen who had been.

There he met Owl, companion of his early days with Mauryl, his guide through Marna Wood on the road that led him to Cefwyn, and his harbinger of war at the battle of Lewen field.

And Owl came with him when he crossed that bridge again, back to the haunted mews at heart of the Zeide. Owl was on his arm when he returned, to the distress of all around him . . . who knew now that they dealt with magic and that the war Tristen proposed was not only of iron and edges.

But rather than reject that war and their magic-wielding ally, they gave thanks to have Tristen on their side and pledged their support anew.

Owl was not the only venturer out into the world that night.

Orien and Tarien Aswydd fled their exile as armed men descended on the defenseless nuns who sheltered them . . . Quinalt men, attacking a Teranthine order. Reflection of the riots in the capital, religious conflict had come to the countryside of Guelessar.

And the outlawed Aswydds turned to the only home they knew, to Henas'amef, hoping for shelter.

Elements once part of wizardry were participant again, rewoven into the design.

BOOK ONE

CHAPTER 1

A slow procession passed by night, little disturbing the sleep of Henas'amef. Tristen on bay Petelly, two ladies on horses the lords of Ivanor had lent them, with Captain Uwen Lewen's-son and Tristen's bodyguard attending, all climbed the hill in a lazy fall of fat lumps of snow.

That families were asleep and shutters were drawn and latched up and down the streets lent welcome anonymity to their passage . . . for by day the sight of the duke of Amefel riding in company with the red-haired former duchess and her sister would have alarmed the town.

As it was, their small party reached the Zeide's West Gate and dismounted with little fuss. The stableboys turned out dutifully, bleary-eyed with sleep—until they discovered their lord had brought two visitors they never wished to see again. Then young eyes grew wide, and the boys moved fearfully and quickly about their business.

The gate-guards, who had come inward bearing torches to light the stable yard, also recognized the visitors by that light and seemed utterly confounded to know who the women were. So with the west stairs guards, who came down in their turn and stopped in their tracks.

"Here's your own lord!" Uwen Lewen's-son said to the gawkers. "An' he's gi'en refuge to these ladies, on account of some damn godless bandits has burned down the nunnery at Anwyfar. They walked here in the storm, half-dead and near frozen, which ain't their choice, nor His Grace's. Don't gawp, there, man! Help their ladyships inside! An' you, Edas! Run up to master Tassand an' tell him come down an' get 'is orders! Haste about it!"

Tristen himself was only too glad to have turned over Petelly's reins to a stableboy. Now he climbed the west stairs, taking charge of his guests.

"Where shall we lodge?" Orien Aswydd asked him haughtily, turning and standing fast at the landing a step above him, and only a breath later did Tristen realize she was none so subtly inquiring after her former rooms. Those rooms happened to be the ducal apartment—*his* apartment.

And little as he liked his lodgings, green velvet draperies and all the heraldry of the Aswydds into the bargain, he had no intention whatsoever of allowing these women that symbolic honor of place. The ducal apartments were not merely rooms: they were an appurtenance of high office, a place from which the duke's orders flowed to all Amefel, and *no*, and twice no, Orien Aswydd should not have them.

Nor should she have any other such stately rooms, now that she made a demand of it, not a decision of spite, but rather of realization that nothing he granted her was without consequence in the view of those watching him. Her deserts were in fact the West Gate guardhouse and the headsman's block: king Cefwyn had stripped title and lands from her, but spared her life, despite the fact her crimes included attempted regicide. Cefwyn had spared her life and sent her off to the nunnery instead on the understanding she would never return to Henas'amef or set claim on the duchy.

And now, now so very soon after the new year, here she stopped at the west doors of her former hall, drew herself up straight and defiant despite the ravages of weather and a body lately failing from exhaustion, and strongly suggested she be given the honors of her birth and recent office.

One could—almost—admire her . . . but one could never, never yield to her.

"We'll find a place suitable," Tristen said curtly. "Rooms better than the guardhouse, at least." He knew the outrage he provoked by adding that last remark, but it made his point. And turning to Lusin, his chief bodyguard: "Tell Cook to come." Cook, like many of the servants, had served the Aswydd lords before he had taken the dukedom, which was to say only last year; but now he relied on her and trusted Cook as the only woman of his close acquaintance. More, Cook had children, several of them, and might understand Lady Tarien's condition better than a man would.

Regarding that condition, however, Cook's was not the only advice he needed now. Master Emuin was awake, and knew, and had known about the ladies even before they reached the town gates.

—What shall I do? he asked Emuin now within the gray space wizards used. *The Aswydd women might hear him, this close, but in this moment he did not care.* **Where do you say should I put them?**

—I'm sure I don't know, Emuin said, and as the gray place opened wide, they stood, in their wizardous aspect, in a place of cloud and wind, equally wary of the Aswydds—who were there, unabashedly eavesdropping on them. **This is inconvenient.**

They had feared the stars, had gotten through the perilous time of change with no worse calamity than the arrival of Owl, who was somewhere about, and they had hoped that Owl was the end of the last troubled epoch and the beginning of a more auspicious age.

But, perhaps on the same night, counting the time it took to travel so far—for so it turned out—Orien and Tarien had left their exile and set out to reach Henas'amef and their former home.

—With child, no less, Emuin said, and turned a fierce and forbidding question toward Tarien Aswydd.—*Whose, woman?*

It was harshly, even brutally demanded, so uncharacteristically forceful that Tristen flinched. In the same instant Orien flung an arm about her sister, who shied from answering and winked out of the gray space like a candle in the wind.

Orien's was a swift, defiant retreat.

Emuin's abrupt question rid them, if only momentarily, of the Aswydds' wizardous eavesdropping, and for Tristen's part, he was no little chagrined that he had never asked so important a question in all the long walk back with the women. In his own defense, his attention in those hours had all been to the simple struggle with the snow, and with Orien's challenge to him . . . and then with the dismay his allied lords, down in the camps about the town wall, had felt very keenly, simply to see Orien back in Amefel. That Tarien was with child had seemed to him one of those things women could arrange, and one of those states women at times maintained—consequently had he, a wizard's Shaping, born of fire on a hearth, asked himself that one simple, essential question before bringing the women here?

No, he had not.

Whose child, indeed, begun in a nunnery, where, as he understood, there were only women?

Or perhaps not in the nunnery.

He felt a shadow pass in the gray space, and at the same moment, in the world, felt the wind of Owl's wings pass him and sweep on.

So Owl, who had guided him to find the sisters in the storm, was still abroad in the world. And magic was. And everything that had seemed simple now became a series of choices, each one with consequences.

"The west wing," he said to the men waiting for their orders. "Lodge them there." He knew the house had at least one set of rooms vacant in that wing, since Cevulirn had chosen to camp with his men. And no one lodged in rooms fit for the duke of Ivanor could complain of being slighted; but anything less than her former state as duchess of Amefel was too little in the estimation of Orien Aswydd, who had attempted Cefwyn's life and on that dice throw, lost everything. He thought twice and made a firm choice. "*Cefwyn's* rooms."

"*His Majesty*'s old apartments," Uwen repeated to the servants, as a row of frightened maids and men met them at the inside stairs. "An' hurry about it. Careful on them marble steps. Mind the ladies' boots is wet."

A slip on the stairs, Tristen thought, an untimely, fatal accident would not happen to a wizard outside of wizardry . . . he had no fear either would slip. But a true accident might save the whole kingdom the consequences of his charity. He had brought them here. He had acquiesced to whatever sent them, and being what he was—a lord and a wizard who could wish harm on the ladies and perhaps ought to—he had never learned to do such things. He nevertheless warred in his own thoughts about the wisdom of having brought them into the citadel at all, and had a frowning look from Lady Orien, back from the stairs.

Orien knew he was thinking about harm, at least, she who could wish harm back at him, and perhaps had, often. He feared warfare was inevitable if she would not accept less than her former honors—his magic opposed her sorcery, for sorcery it was. She knew it, she had already met it, and he hoped she might come to reconcile with the situation as it was—but he did not readily see how that might be.

He regretted his act of mercy now, and he wished, if not harm on Orien, at least safety for his staff and all the friends, allies and townsfolk his charity had set at risk by bringing her here. Fool, he was ready to think, as often he had been a fool: but Owl had led him, and Owl, that chancy bird, knew nothing of reason.

Lives had been at risk already, among those he loved. Uwen had come out into the storm searching for his foolish lord, trailing after him Lusin and the rest of his bodyguard, honest men immeasurably distressed to have lost track of their charge outside safe town walls.

And not only his household had ridden out to search for him. Crissand Earl of Meiden and the duke of Ivanor had both come searching, the latter two having wizard-gift enough to find him in any storm . . . and wizard-gift enough to know for a truth what dangerous guests he had brought home.

From those two he was sure that by now the word of the As-wydds' return would have slowly, discreetly spread among the lords encamped near the walls. From the servants here on the hill, it would go like wildfire through the staff, some of whom had served the ladies and their brother Heryn. And word would leap from there into the Bryaltine shrine, too, a random thought informed him, to the nuns, who had been maids to Lady Orien and who now repented their lady's war with the Marhanen through their charitable acts and pious prayers.

From there, for very little good and a great deal of ill . . . rumor of the Aswydds' arrival in Henas'amef would reach every corner of the province, from the border with Guelessar, which had sent the ladies to him, to the borders with the other lords, and northward to those who already distrusted Amefel.

And it would go northward in Amefel, too, to Captain Anwyll's camp, Guelenmen, Dragon Guard, who would wonder what to make of it. Anwyll well knew the ladies were supposed to be under ban, and was sworn to uphold the royal decree that kept them so. Word would run to Modeyneth, where the men of Bryn built a wall; and to Althalen, where fugitives out of Elwynor established a settlement under his protection—and was the lord of Amefel's power that sure, the fugitives must ask themselves, if he housed the sisters of Heryn Aswydd?

The news would go to their enemy, Tasmôrden, sitting in his newly won capital of Ilefínian, up in Elwynor. He had tried to stir the Amefin to rebel against Cefwyn, with the promise of reestablish-ing the Aswydds and supporting them in war. What must he think?

And not last or least, word would reach Cefwyn, telling him that wizardry or the malice of Men had overturned his sentence and freed the two most dangerous prisoners in his kingdom . . . for they were that. They certainly were that. *Sorcery* was their crime, not to men-tion an attempt on Cefwyn's very life, and on his kingdom.

Forgive me, should he write to Cefwyn, but I could think of nowhere else to send them?

The only place he could think of to send them, indeed, at this hour, was to hasten them upstairs, into rooms fit for the royalty they claimed to be . . . *aethelings,* of the old noble house of Amefel, with wizard-gift strong in their blood.

They were not the only survivors of that line, to be sure. His friend, his foremost supporter in council, Earl Crissand, was kin of theirs, *and* heir to the name . . . so he had sworn to himself, so Auld Syes herself had said, in an appearance as curious and ominous as he had ever seen—and no, these women would not take what was Crissand's: whatever came of his constrained charity, Crissand's heirship could not be challenged, not while these stones stood one on the other. It was that certain in his thoughts.

"What's Emuin say?" Uwen asked. They were still standing in the lower hall, Uwen and his guard all deaf to magic and wizardry alike, but Uwen knew his resources, and knew that Master Emuin tended to be awake at night; and knew by experience that his lord's moments of woolgathering were often conversations.

"He's not pleased," Tristen said, blinking the ordinary world into being. His sight centered on Uwen's gray-stubbled, earnest face. "Nor am I pleased, but what can I do?"

"I'm sure I don't know," Uwen said, and bit his lip, which usually presaged his saying something anyway. "Except as His Majesty might ha' had their heads on the South Gate, and didn't, on account of ye told 'im they'd be worse threats to us all if they was ghosts. And, ye know, m'lord, I ain't so sure on that, now."

"I'm not sure on that point either," he said, not in jest, and added: "But I don't think I can kill them, Uwen."

Uwen's look was the more distressed. "Ye ain't o' the mind, nor ever were, m'lord. An' her sister bein' with child, an' all—what's to happen? Ask Emuin. Ask Emuin, m'lord. This is beyond me."

"I fear it's beyond him, too." Uwen was right: he had never been willing to exercise a lord's cold justice, nor had done. But despite his thinking on slippery steps, something felt so utterly wrong in the notion of killing the women, he could not compass arguments about it, could not consider it—whether it was wrong in the magical sense or wrong because it was terrible to kill at all, he had no way to sort out. He only knew he shuddered at it. "Emuin's as surprised as the rest of us."

" 'At there," Uwen said, with an upward glance, the way the women had gone, "looks to be seven, eight months she's carryin'."

"Can you say so?"

"Summat," Uwen said, as they began to walk their own direction, toward the other stairs. "Looks to be. Nine's the term of a child that'll live, an' by the look, that 'un ain't far from it. That 'un's bloomed in the nunnery, gods save us all, but I'll wager she didn't get it there."

Being not born, himself, and never a child, and never intimate with a woman, he had only uncertain questions where ordinary men had sure knowledge. He felt helpless in his ignorance, and so many things had converged in the last few days . . . magical things, dreadful things, hopeful things, and now, it turned out, Tarien's child, which it seemed would come sooner rather than later. He had feared Midwinter, just past, and the turning of the year, when a conjunction of the stars that Emuin said had been his birth had ended, and a new cycle had begun.

"When?" he asked. "How will we know?"

"She ain't immediate, I don't think," Uwen said, who had had a wife, once, and children. "A hellish far walk, she's been, if they come from Anwyfar, an' in the snow, and a-horseback before that. If she was near, that might ha' brought it on. And it didn't."

"Eight months?"

"Seven or eight, maybe."

In magic and wizardry, more particularly in sorcery . . . there were no coincidences. Seven or eight months . . . from its beginning, which was also to reckon.

"Could she have gotten the child in the summer, and no one know?"

"Damn sure she did," Uwen said somberly, "an' all that time, and her bein' a witch an' all, I'd about wager she knew right well, m'lord, that I would."

His thoughts grew vague and frightened and darted here and there in distracted fashion as he walked. His shoulders had felt the burden of armor for hours, as his cloak and his boots were soaked through with snowmelt. He had been scant of sleep for far too long, had walked, letting Tarien ride on the way home—and he thought now, after a month of striving and wrestling with Amefel's danger and Ylesuin's, now that he had done something so irretrievably foolish as this, he might rest . . . he might finally rest, as if he had done what folly his restlessness had aimed toward, and as he faced the stairs upward all the remaining strength was flowing out of him like blood from a wound.

Tarien knew about the child, he kept thinking to himself. When she went to Anwyfar, she knew. When they dealt with Hasufin Heltain, and bargained with him—*Orien knew.*

"M'lord?" Uwen asked, for he had faltered on the first step. All the accumulated hard days and wakeful nights came down on his shoulders at once, and he found he could not set his foot to the step.

"Are ye hurt, m'lord?"

Uwen's arm came about him, bearing him up, and with that help he essayed the first step. Another arm caught him from the right, Lusin, he thought, and he made the next, telling himself that he must, and that rest was at the top of the stairs, just a little distance down the hall.

"Are ye hurt?" Uwen insisted to know.

"No," he said. "Tired. Very tired, Uwen."

" 'At's good, then, m'lord. Just walk."

He climbed up and up the right-hand steps, those that ascended above the great hall, leaning on two good friends . . . and there he paused, drawn to turn and look down on that staircase, on that lower hall lit as it was from a mere handful of sconces. There burned but a single candle in each at this dim hour.

He had come up this stairs from the great hall the one night he had come very close to believing Orien and falling into her hands . . . and then, too, Uwen had seen him home.

He had run these steps the night Parsynan had murdered Crissand's men . . . and the shadows of those men haunted the whole lower hall, all but palpable at this hour.

He had gone down these steps toward the great hall as a new-made lord, and there faced a haunt that now was all but under his feet, the old mews, out of which Owl had come.

And did it stir, tonight, that power, knowing these twin sisters had come home?

He willed *not*. Trembling in the support of two strong men, he willed strength into the wards that kept the fortress safe. He willed that nothing within these walls, no spirit and no living soul, should obey Lady Orien, accustomed as this house might have been to her commands.

He did all that on three breaths, and was at his weakest, but he was sure then that the haunt below in the mews had not broken out or answered to Orien's presence, and that most of all reassured him, for of all dangers in the fortress, it was the chanciest and the greatest.

"Shall we take him on up, then?" Lusin asked, tightening his arm about his ribs, clearly supposing his lord had lost his way.

" 'E's stopped on 'is own," Uwen said pragmatically, against the other side, and shifted his grip on his wrist and about his waist. "An' 'e'll start on 'is own. 'Is Grace is thinkin' on somethin' worth 'is time, and I ain't askin' what till he's through."

"I'm very well," Tristen said then, although for the life in him he could not think of what he had just been doing.

"Lean on me, lad," Uwen said then—neither Uwen nor Lusin was as tall as he, but they had their leather-clad shoulders beneath his arms, and a firm grip around him, and bore him up the last step and down the corridor. His head drooped. He was next aware of his own foyer, outside Uwen's room.

And could not bear to go back into the bedchamber.

"I'll sit by the fire," he said.

"The fire an' not your bed, m'lord?" Uwen asked. "Your bed's waitin'."

"Not now." It was an effort for him to speak, now, not that it was hard to draw breath, but that his thoughts wanted to wander off, and the firelight seemed safer than the dark in the rooms beyond.

Time was when he would fall sound asleep at moments of revelation, at any moment when new things poured in on him so fiercely and so fast that his wits failed to keep up. For hours and hours he would sleep afterward, no physician availing to wake him, and when he would wake—when he would wake, then he would have remembered something he never knew.

But such sound sleeps no longer happened, not since the summer, when War had Unfolded to him in all its terror. He no longer had that grace, nor dared leave his servants and his men a day and more unadvised. He fought to wake, and make his limbs answer him—and yet it was so much effort. If he could only sit by the fire, he thought, and see the light, then he would not fall asleep.

"Will ye take food, lad?" Uwen asked.

"Hot tea," he said.

"Tea an' honey," Uwen said, and a distant murmur went on a time, then a small, distant clatter of cups until one arrived in Tristen's hand.

He drank, and the fragile cup weighed like iron, an effort even to lift. There was no strength in him, and he supported one hand with the other to have a sip without spilling it.

Uwen hovered, waiting for him, perhaps expecting to drop it. Uwen had ridden through drifts the same as he—but was not half so tired.

"Petelly," Tristen said. He did not remember now where he had left his horse. His last memory of Petelly was of his shaggy coat snow-plastered and his head hanging.

"Havin' all the grooms make over 'im," Uwen said, "an' 'e's sleepin' by now, as you should be doin', m'lord."

He gave a small shake of his head. "Not now. I daren't, now. I've things to do."

He failed to remember where Owl had gone . . . Owl had gone

off to kill mice, perhaps, or flown off to some place more ominous, but at least Owl had gone, and nothing worse would come tonight.

"What d' ye wish, m'lord?"

That was a fair question, one to which he as yet had no answer.

"Ye want to post a guard up there wi' the ladies," Uwen reminded him. "There's servants in this house that served the Aswydds."

"Do that," he said, and then heard, in the great distance, Uwen naming names to Lusin, choosing Guelenmen, Quinalt men, men least likely to listen to the Aswydds' requests or to flee their threats.

He had another sip of honeyed tea, sitting before a fire that had been Orien's, in an apartment that had been Orien's, green velvet and bronze dragons and all. It had been Orien's apartment, and Lord Heryn's before her, and on the best of nights he never felt quite safe here. He watched it, guarded it as much as lived in it, and of all places in the Zeide where he could bestow the twins, he would not cede this one to Lady Orien.

The old mews was virtually under his feet here, that rift in the wards out of which Owl had come, and which he had not been able to shut, since.

"Tassand's gone to see to the guests," the next-senior of his servants came to report to him . . . Drys, the man's name was. "Your Grace, would you have another cup? Or will you have the armor off?"

He had lost his cloak somewhere, or Uwen had taken it. The brigandine's metal joinings scarred the chair, and the padding beneath it was much too warm.

He must have assented. Drys knelt and began to undo buckles about his person, and two others helped him from the boots. He stood, then, with Uwen's help, and shed the brigandine, piece by piece. It was light armor, and lighter still the padding beneath, but the very absence of its weight was enough to send him asleep on his feet.

" 'Ere, m'lord," Uwen said. "You ain't stayin' awake. Best ye go on to your bed an' sleep. The ladies is under guard an' dawn's comin' afore ye know it. Ain't a thing in the wide world ye can do else for anyone, but to sleep."

He was defeated. Drys set a cup of mulled wine in his hand, and the mere pungent smell of it sent his thoughts reeling toward the pillows and the warmed soft covers. Whatever he had tried to think of before he stood up to shed the armor went fleeting into the dark.

" 'At's good," he heard Uwen say, realized he was abed, and felt Uwen draw the coverlet up over his shoulder.

Mauryl had used to do that small kindness for him. Uwen had done it most nights, from the time Uwen had begun his service . . . only this summer. So quickly he had sped from youth to manhood— and missed so much, never having the ordinary things a man might know. Summer seemed long ago, an autumn ago, a winter ago. He was wiser now, and knew there were dangers in the world he had never reckoned in the summer.

But he was not unguarded. He had Uwen. Owl was somewhere about. Emuin was awake and wary. Even knowing the quality of the guests he had brought beneath his roof he could draw himself smaller and smaller and smaller, until he could finally wrap himself up in a small dark ball of awareness, and gather to him his hard-won memories.

For memories he did have now, not many, but vivid ones that spread themselves like shadowy curtains. He saw visions of battle- fields and forest, he smelled the stone of Ynefel's rain-swept tower, and faced Mauryl's rain-soaked indignation.

He met Uwen's gray-stubbled face by evening candlelight, saying to him, "Lad, ye mean well. 'At's worth somethin'."

And Emuin's face, gray-streaked beard gone whiter and whiter at the roots, and eyes sunk deep in wells of shadow: "*Mean* well, young lord? *Do* well, there's the challenge!"

He saw Owl, sitting in a leafless, ghostly tree in Marna Wood. Owl dived away and flew before him through the night, his self- appointed guide, above a white stone path that was the Road into the world.

He saw Owl, shining with wizard-light, fly before him through an unnatural night of sorcery, amid the clash of iron and the cries of dying men.

He saw Cefwyn, standing by a tattered banner, saying to him, "We've won!" as if it were true for all time.

He curled tight against the dark, holding fast to these things that bounded the spring and summer of his single year of life, too weary to be as afraid as he ought.

He sank so deep he saw the dark before him.

Then, not in fear, but in sober realization of his danger, he began to travel away from that Edge, resolute instead on reaching the world, determinedly gathering up his resources. He bent all his will on opening his eyes, and on being alive.

He lay still a moment, counting what he had brought back with him, for his dreams were not like Uwen's dreams. Where he went in his dreams was not, perhaps, memory: he had begun to fear so, at least. He remembered not dreams, but efforts; and what he remembered of his ventures told him things.

It told him that all the books in the archive of Henas'amef, all the accumulated wisdom of the kings and dukes of Amefel arrayed on those dusty shelves, was less knowledge of time past than what he could draw to the surface, if the Unfolding came on him again.

But he resisted it. Perhaps that was the reason the Unfolding happened less often now . . . he feared to know. He wished not to know. Men said that he was Barrakkêth, first of the warlords of the Sihhë. But he did not know it. He refused to know it. The Book of that knowledge he had burned in fire, the night before the battle at Lewen field, but the knowledge of the Book that Barrakkêth had written he had stored away as too fearsome, too inimical to all he wished to know. Waking, he tucked that away, and carefully remade his world without that knowlege, testing every part of it, renewing his ties to those he loved. He slept seldom, and waked relieved to remember he did have Uwen, who always slept near him.

He had Emuin. Not Mauryl. Emuin . . . though the width of the fortress lay between them.

He had Cefwyn, who was his friend, though the width of a province and the distrust of all the court lay between them.

He waked by dim daylight cast from outer windows through the archway of his bedchamber. He waked in the great bed beneath the brazen dragons of Aswydd heraldry, and recalled that these things were so.

And in rare luxury of absolute abandon he drew deep, grateful breaths into his chest, finding everything well under his roof, even given their guests, and Orien Aswydd, who would never own this bed again, and never rest where he had slept.

This part of the world he remade, too, and made it sure in his mind, for doubt was a breach, and doubts he refused to entertain. He was safe, abed, suffering the aches of last night's long ride.

His servants moved about. They needed nothing from him. Out in the yard the whole fortress had waked to life without him. The garrison had begun its drills. The town had spread open its shops and gone about its trades. The camp outside had waked, stirred its fires to life, and the tavern help from inside the walls had bustled out with hot porridge to feed the men gathered there. Far across the fields, in pens they had established for the army that would gather there, stablehands tended their charges. Down by Modeyneth men set to their day's work on a wall he had ordered restored, and as far as the Lenúalim's banks, soldiers watched and warded the border. All these things happened this morning without his guidance, or rather, within the compass of his care but without his oversight; and the progress of those unwatched matters reassured him that the sun reliably rose and the roof under which he slept was safe even when he let his attention fall.

He found great pleasure in unaccustomed idleness, in fact: in the small sounds of his servants laying out breakfast for him . . . things also happening quite without his guidance, quite pleasantly without his orders or his will. Indeed, the bulk of things that happened would go on without him, or around him, or in spite of his cautions—and he need not govern every drawing of breath as he had grown accustomed to do since Cefwyn had set him in charge of Amefel.

He had been giving too much, and managing too much, and over-seeing far too much.

Folly, he said to himself.

As if Uwen, who had guided him this summer, needed his guidance now.

As if Tassand, who had come along with him to manage his small household in campaign tents and in palaces alike, could not protect this place and manage the staff without his niggling daily concern and his abundant, constant questions.

He lay, deliciously imagining this morning what each sound meant, as he had seen them do the tasks scores of times.

He imagined that Uwen would be in soon, and that Uwen would be in his ordinary gear and ready to go about his peaceful business. He knew the look of Uwen Lewen's-son of a morning down to the gray of his hair and the freshly scrubbed look of his face . . . and when he rose and dressed, Uwen indeed had joined him in just such a condition, and declared he was going down to the stables and the camps as soon as they finished breakfast.

So despite his guests, he drew a leisured breath, and another one.

It was a fine morning, in very truth—a peaceful, a glorious, a safe morning, leisured instead of idle . . . he had never before understood the distinction in those two Words, until he had found time to draw breath.

"No alarms," Uwen said cheerfully, over buttered bread, "and Her Grace ain't seduced the guards yet."

Tristen knew the power of Orien's persuasions. She had bent her thoughts on him once, though to little result.

And it was indeed worth his concern, regarding anyone set to watch her.

Also the lords had all seen her arrival . . . and they had had few questions last night, considering his long ride, but they would have them before the morning was over. That Orien reported an assault on a shrine in Guelessar, just across the border, seemed credible, but it was still to doubt.

And they had not even heard the matter Tarien brought.

So, breakfasted, dressed, with Uwen off about his duties, he resolved to gain some of those answers from the question that was Orien. He was sure of himself, at least, that she could not charm him into compliance, or overwhelm him with sorcery: she had tried both when he was far more innocent, even then to no avail. If he had fear for his men, he had none at all for himself, nor in the least doubted he could deal with the ladies.

Emuin was asleep, like Owl. So was Paisi. Outside was snow, remnant of the storm that had blown white and thick while it lasted. Now the sun was bright, and the weather seemed to have spent its momentary tantrum. Midwinter, the hinge of the year, as Emuin called it, had passed with a fury.

And just last night they had finally gotten into shelter all the contingents of their muster that had been at risk on the road: Umanon's heavy horse and Cevulirn's light horsemen, both accustomed to sleep under canvas: they were safe in the camp, while Pelumer's rangers out of Lanfarnesse would camp wherever they were. Lord Sovrag doubted the storm would have greatly delayed his boats on their journey south, for the storm wind had blown from the north, and his men, he declared, would manage come what might. So the storm that heralded Orien's return had done nothing to disarrange his plans, and things regarding the camp were in order.

He did not trust, however, that that was true in lands beyond his reach—clearly not so where men had assailed a nunnery and sent the twins toward his hospitality.

"News'd come welcome, out of Guelessar," Uwen had remarked at breakfast, and in putting it that way, laid his finger on the most worrisome thing: an attack on such harmless religious women under Cefwyn's rule, in Cefwyn's own central province, hinted at unrest in the heart of Guelen lands, perhaps even in the capital itself. Welcome, indeed, would be the knowledge that Cefwyn was safe and taking firm, swift action there.

There was the chance, of course, that Orien had made up the story. There remained a chance that she had done the damage to the nuns, or drawn baneful events to them for the sole purpose of setting herself and her sister free of Cefwyn's guards.

But whose if not Orien's was the storm that had so cast things into confusion, and posed Orien and him alike an obstacle? The snow had begun on Midwinter Day, had gathered strength and gathered violence for days—then vanished without fuss once he had found Orien and her sister. Was she so powerful as that? She never had been . . . not alone.

And whose was Owl? *His,* for what he could tell, but he had not planned Owl's arrival. He had not planned the storm. He had not planned Auld Syes' arrival in his hall on Midwinter, or the darkness and all the events and omens which had followed.

And most of all he had not planned Tarien's baby.

So what Uwen had said about Guelessar and the lack of news from Cefwyn settled into his heart with a cold, persistent worry . . . for there was no safe way to send or receive a message in that quarter. If Cefwyn had sent any message to him in recent days, he had not received it . . . and his last messenger had had to come back like a fugitive, in fear of his life from such elements as Orien blamed for the destruction of the nunnery: in fact, it all fit together in very disquieting agreement, the last messenger's story with Orien's tale of the nunnery burned.

And if the king's law did not prevail out into the countryside, not protecting the king's messages, and now, evidently, not protecting houses of worship, of a sect the Quinaltines accepted as respectable . . . as they did not deem respectable the Bryalt faith of the Amefin . . . how then did they regard the lady Regent, Cefwyn's bride? And how did they take their king's other orders?

And was *Ninévrisë* safe, if men were hunting the king's messengers and burning nunneries?

He wondered that with a great deal of concern—and furtively thought he might gain Ninévrisë's attention in the gray space, even at such great distance. She had the wizard-gift, a weak gift, unpracticed, but his certainly was not: after the dire news of last night and Uwen's remark this morning he found himself lingering over a last cup of tea and wondering if, one-sided in the effort, *he* might reach *her.*

He thought so, and wished he had her advice regarding the Aswydds, for that matter: but the risk was far greater than the gain, much as he was tempted to try. She was small and quiet in that aspect: she might enter the gray space unnoticed; *he,* Emuin assured him, could not, and reaching to her, he might well draw unwanted attention—Orien's, for one. But it was only one.

The weather breaking free of his wishes, Orien's arrival, all these things advised him his was not the only will at work even in Amefel. He was far more subtle these days, and knew a wizard-wish need not be thunder and lightning and the overthrow of oak trees. It might be far, far subtler than that . . . wizard-work was, in fact, more effective when it did not flail about and raise storms and blast holes in roofs. Such attacks did not frighten him. The subtle ones did; and if he acted rashly, trusting he could deal with every subtle attack that might come, when the truth was, no, he could not—where would hostile wizardry aim its deadly shots, but straight at his heart?

And where was his heart, but with Ninévrisë and Cefwyn, with Uwen and Crissand and Cevulirn and Emuin himself—all those he held most dear; and those who touched the gray themselves were not most defended: they were instead more vulnerable to such attacks.

Such possibilities Orien brought with her under his roof.

That there were other wishes at work, he was certain.

Whether Tasmôrden, his enemy across the river, had worked this maneuver on him, or whether it was some other force, that he did not know. Eight months, Uwen had said, looking at Tarien Aswydd. And eight months ago Tasmôrden had not even been a cloud on the horizon.

But other enemies had been.

And Orien Aswydd had been hand in hand with them.

CHAPTER 2

Irst it was the kitchens, down in the warm, firelit domain of baking bread and wash water: Cook's maids were scrubbing away flour when Tristen arrived, the scullery lads washing pots, while the open door, braced with a bucket, only gave a welcome, snow-flavored draft to the hardworking staff. Daylight shafted through a haze of steam in an amazing glory of white and old, scarred surfaces. He could not but give a glance to it, despite the sober purpose of his visit.

"M'lord," Cook said, not surprised to find him in the kitchens, or his four day guards outside her domain, finding converse with the maids. The kitchens were one of his favorite places from summer. Cook was one who had been kind to him before others had, and among the very first acts of his rule here, he had set Cook back in her domain. He took tribute now and again in the form of hot bread and the occasional sweet.

This time, however, he was straight from a good breakfast, had delayed only to toss the remnant of bread to the pigeons, and had come down here on matters he hoped Cook had observed last night.

"Seven, eight months along," Cook said to him, confirming Uwen's guess, and added with a shake of her head, as she folded her stout, floury arms: "And wandering in the storm, they say, clear from Anwyfar."

"Lady Orien said they began with a horse and lost it.—But might they have walked that far, do you think? Orien might. But Tarien—"

Cook set her hands on her hips and wiped a strand of blowing hair. They stood in the draft, and Cook was sweating, even so. "To tell the truth, m'lord, I hain't the least notion where Anwyfar is, except it's in Guelessar, which is far enough for a body in high summer and with the roads fair and dry. With the storm, and the drifts and all . . ."

"Was it impossible for them, since, say, Midwinter Eve?"

"I don't know as to impossible, m'lord, but . . ." Cook had an unaccustomedly fearful look, and added with a shift of her eyes toward the upstairs, and back again: "Their ladyships has a gift, don't they?"

"They do," he said. "Both.—So it had to be before that."

"I don't know," Cook said. "I've never traveled by horse. I hain't the least idea. Was it Midwinter, m'lord?"

"Or before. It might have been before. They might have tried to be *here* on Midwinter, and come late."

"For wizardous reasons, m'lord?" Cook's eyes narrowed. Little frightened her, but she ventured her question in a hushed and respectful tone.

"I don't know," he said.

Cook said not a thing to that. She was a discreet soul, in her way, and not a word would she say to the maids that she knew she was saying, but the gossip was bound to fly, and had already flown. He saw the looks from the staff all about them. At a certain point the rattle of a spoon sounded like doom, and swiftly hushed.

"Get back to your work!" Cook said sharply, and: "M'lord, there's sweets, there."

He took one. It was honey and fine flour, and stuck to his fingers. The lord of Amefel licked fingertips on the way out, and then turned back and took two more, which he saved as he climbed the rebuilt scullery stairs.

He ascended to the west stairs, and up to an area of the Zeide which had had a very different feeling for him this summer past, when Cefwyn had been in residence.

Not Cefwyn's bodyguard, now, but Guelen guards from the town garrison stood at that door, and more in Guelen colors stood down the hall. Guards guarding the guards: that was the seriousness of Uwen's precaution where it regarded Orien Aswydd and her sister.

The guards on watch opened the foyer door for him, not advising those within; and at a wave of his hand, he set his own watch on that threshold, a ward, a pass of his hand, and a wish, whether the guards knew it or not . . . but Orien knew it. He felt her attention, and her anger: she had set her own ward on the door, and he violated it with hardly more than a chill.

Her precaution was reasonable and he was hardly angry, but he was sorry not to have set his own last night, for the guards' safety.

His two nunnish guests, clad all in gray, sat at the snowy window, and as he entered, Orien rose straight as a candleflame to defy him, gray habit, red hair unveiled in its cropped despoilment. She had been a lord's sister, accustomed to luxury, sought after for her beauty, her birth, her access to power, even before she had been duchess of Amefel.

Now instead of the glittering court gowns, the velvets and jewels and the circlet on her wealth of autumn hair, she wore a travel-stained gray robe. They had both cast off the nun's wimple, and the red hair—that she had cut to spite Cefwyn—stood in stark, untidy disorder. It was her twin sister, seated in the white window light, who still kept that glory about her shoulders.

From a lush, luxurious woman to this lean, harsh creature that was now Orien—it astonished him how dreadfully the more powerful of the twins had changed, even while the white light that fell on Lady Tarien's seated form found softer edges. Tarien's pale face lacked any of the anger that suffused Orien's: a young face, a bosom modestly robed in gray, a body grown strange and potent with the child inside. Orien stood with her hands on Tarien's shoulders, as if her sister were some sort of barrier to him—and for the first time without the cloak and in the daylight from the window he faced a woman far along with child. He saw in her not one change but an alchemy of changes, the scope of which he did not clearly imagine, and which spun wildly through the gray space, fraught with possibilities. *Power* was there, power over the powerful, in the hand that rested on Tarien's robed belly.

"How may we please your lordship?" Orien asked, and, oh, there was thick irony in that salutation, to the lord who had title now to all that had been hers and her sister's.

"I came," he began, "to see how you fared, and whether you needed anything." He proffered the sweets. "From the kitchens."

He knew Orien would not take them. He saw, however, that Tarien wanted them, and he set them on the table near him. "At your convenience," he said.

"Where are our servants?" Orien asked in ringing tones. "Surely the great Marhanen won't have been so petty as to harm *them*. Where are my sister's maids?"

"Most of your servants fled across the river when Cefwyn came. The others are my servants now . . . or the gods'."

"I demand my servants!"

"And I say they aren't here any longer."

"And our gowns?" Tarien asked. "*Surely* Your Grace has no use for our gowns."

"I've no idea where they are." In fact he had never wondered where the ladies' wardrobe had gone: he had supposed it had gone with them to Anwyfar, in all the chests. The gowns they had worn in their days of power here had been gloriously beautiful, and with all the jewels, he supposed they were as valuable as Lord Heryn's dinner plates—which he had in the treasury. "I've seen no store of clothes, not a stitch of them."

"And our jewels?"

The whereabouts of certain of the Aswydd jewelry he did know, and was sure in his heart that the province's need for grain was far greater than their need for adornment. But he regretted the beauty and the sparkle of the stones, too, all shut up in the dark treasury.

"I shall send up some of the jewels," he said, and then added, because they took every gift as their right: "I lend them, understand, until we need them for grain."

"For grain!" Orien cried. "These are the history, the glory of Amefel! These are the treasure of the Aswydds, *my property!* How dare you sell them for grain?"

"If you were duchess of Amefel, I would agree you own them. But you aren't. And I give them to the treasury."

"I am *still* duchess of Amefel, and damn the Marhanen! If you hold me here prisoner in my own hall, then look to yourself, sir!"

"I'm sorry about the gowns. I don't know where they went. I'll ask; and if I can't find them, I'll find you others. It's all I can do."

Orien drew a deep breath, and perhaps reconsidered her position. "You were always good-hearted, always kind to us before. I see you still have a kind heart."

"I wish you no harm, and ask you wish none."

"Harm to the bloody Marhanen!"

"I ask you not do that." He felt her anger in the gray space and rebuffed it strongly, refusing to encounter her there. In the world her face seemed all eyes, and the eyes a window into a place he chose not to go. He remembered how Cefwyn had wished to kill the twins, at least Lady Orien, and he had pleaded otherwise—not even so much out of mercy, although that had been in his heart—but rather the fear of Orien's spirit let loose among the Shadows in the Zeide, set unbarriered within the wards and the Lines of Henas'amef, in those days when the sorcerous ally she had dealt with still threatened them.

Now they had defeated that ally of hers, at Lewenbrook. And if

Cefwyn had now proposed it, he did not know whether he would have been so quick to save her life, or Cefwyn to hear him: to that extent they both had changed.

—*Is it so? Orien asked him, a voice as sharp and cold as a dagger. Is it so? Did you save us? And had the bloody Marhanen not a shred of remorse?*

"Can you keep us in this prison?" Tarien asked, assailing him from the other side. "We have *nothing,* not even a change of clothes. My sister is the *aetheling.* Whatever else, she is the aetheling, and no one should forget it, least of all under this roof!" Tarien's eyes glistened as she confronted him. A handkerchief suffered murder in her clenched hands.

"Aethelings, yes," Tristen corrected her gently. "Both of you. But Crissand of Meiden is *the* aetheling now, and there's no changing that."

Orien's eyes flared. "By whose appointment? *Cefwyn's?* He has no right!"

"By mine, lady." He could be obstinate. He had learned it of Emuin. And he had every right, beyond Cefwyn's grant of power to him. He was suddenly as sure of that as if it had Unfolded to him: their power had ebbed here, and ebbed further as he gave it away to others.

More, Orien knew it, and fear insinuated itself into all her dealings.

"For my sister's sake," Orien said, past tight lips, "we require a lady or two—a *lady,* mind you. Shall a lady of our rank give birth with the cook and the scullery maids in attendance?"

That was unkind. Cook had never affronted Orien that he knew of. But he had no wish to provoke a quarrel that might bring harm to someone. "If you object to Cook, I might ask Lord Drumman's sister to assist you."

"Lady Criselle? That preening crow!"

Now it was Crissand's mother Orien slandered. "Lady Orien," Tristen said with measured patience. "No one pleases you. You may not have your servants. You refuse all others. I don't know what more there is."

"I wish my own nurse," Tarien cried, and burst into tears. "They *murdered* her, at Anwyfar. They killed all the nuns, and Dosyll with them. She was sixty years old, and she never threatened them!"

"I'm sorry." He was honestly afflicted by her report. "Who did it, and why?"

"Brave soldiers of the Guelen Guard," Orien interposed harshly. "Heroes of the same company the bloody Marhanen garrisoned in my town, the same company as these hulking men you post at my door! The Marhanen's best bandits! Murderers! Mercenaries!"

"Are you sure they were of the Guard?"

"And should I not be sure, with the Guelens garrisoned at Amefel all my life? I know what I saw. I know their badges and their ranks and of one of them I knew the face!"

"Do you know the name?" he asked, with a sinking heart recalling the men he had dismissed home because of their discontent in his service, men guilty of malfeasance and murders that should have sent them to the hangman, if they had not acted under Crown authority, in the person of Lord Parsynan.

"Essan," she said, and he had to bow to the truth.

"I doubt your eyes deceived you, then," he said, "since I dismissed him, with a handful of others, for crimes here. The others, I sent to Cefwyn. He and his sergeant slipped away rather than answer my summons to accounting."

"Gods bless the Holy Quinalt, then! They shouted that, you know, while they burned down a Teranthine shrine, and murdered old women! I don't know what they were looking for besides the wine and the treasury, but they weren't shy about their cause."

"No," he said, "clearly not. I'm sorry for your nurse and I'm sorry for the nuns. And I know Cefwyn didn't send them."

"You know *nothing*. You said yourself, you sent these murderers to him! He sent them back again, to Anwyfar!"

"Not Captain Essan. He and his sergeant took shelter in the Quinaltine, so I understand."

"Oh, so it was the Patriarch himself who sent them to burn Teranthine nuns!"

"I doubt it, and you doubt it, lady. And if you'll give me answers, I can send to Cefwyn. I know he'll find these men. Can you tell me any reason for what they did? Were they looking for you? Were they angry with the nuns?"

"Look to yourself, Tristen of Ynefel! Look to yourself! Yes, it was us they wanted, and do you think common soldiers imagined this? Do you think the drunkards and ne'er-do-wells of the garrison traveled all the way to Anwyfar to raid the wine cellars in the nunnery and assault old women? It was hate for us, and these were soldiers! Someone sent them! Someone put the idea in their heads, and it was the hate they bear all of us who have wizard-gift—it was fear of my sister and me! So look to yourself, Tristen of Ynefel. If they hate us, a hundred times more they hate you, and now you shelter us!"

"That may be true," he said. "But Henas'amef is stronger than Anwyfar."

"A great deal stronger. And have they come for you? Is *that* the cause of the army outside these walls? There were Ivanim we spoke to last night. I saw Sovrag's pirates."

"You did see Olmernmen," he said, letting her shafts rain about him, none landing, for she knew nothing, and struck none home. "And Ivanim. But none of these have to do with the nuns and Essan's men."

"The rumor reached us," Orien said haughtily, with her hands on her sister's shoulders, "even in our rustic exile, it reached us— that Cefwyn has married the Lord Regent's daughter and intends war against Elwynor this spring. And is *that* what we see outside the walls? Will you wage his war for him? Tristen, the innocent? Tristen, the wizard, Tristen, Mauryl's heir, the defender of the king? Does the Marhanen not wield his own sword, these days?—Or does he wield magic, through you? And is *that* what came down on us at Anwyfar?"

It was a fair question, however unkindly put.

"What he calls on me to do, I'll do. And I've wished nothing against you."

Barbs had flown. Now Orien seemed to pause for thought, and heaved a sigh and walked a few paces from Tarien's side. "And do you wish anything against us?"

"Not for yourselves. Not except as you wish harm here, or to Cefwyn."

"Have we sanctuary here?"

Sanctuary was a Word. It meant safety no matter what, justice and all other considerations notwithstanding. It was a strong Word, and Unfolded with magical force.

"Do you wish harm to Cefwyn?"

"Am I required to wish him well?"

"No. Nor would I ask it, nor would he. And I don't offer sanctuary, but if you deserve safety, I promise you'll be safe in this room." A coldness wafted to him out of the gray place, fraught with time, and change. "No more can I do."

"What? You have limits?" Scorn edged her voice. "Or do you set them for yourself?"

"If you work mischief here or anywhere, Lady Orien, I will prevent it. If you work any mischief against Cefwyn or anyone else, you won't be safe here, or anywhere."

"I am your prisoner."

"Yes."

"I demanded my rights of my liege lord, my rights by oath, and Cefwyn denied me them and sent me and my sister away in a common cart in the mid of the night, like offal from the kitchens! Was that just? Was that justice? Better he had killed us!"

"He thought it mercy," he said in all honestly. "And said it was a risk."

"And how long will this arrest go on?" Orien cried indignantly. "Are we to live here forever?"

"As long as you wish to oppose Cefwyn. I won't ever permit that. And I *know* that you do."

Clearly this had taken a turn the ladies Aswydd did not like. Tears brimmed in Tarien's eyes.

"And shall we never leave this room? Shall we not at least have the freedom of the halls?"

He had pity on them in that regard, if not his sense of the danger in them were not so great. He had had his own fill of locked doors and silent guards.

"Not while you intend harm. Think and change your minds if you can. Intend better if you can."

There was a moment of silence, in which Lady Orien gazed at him with heaving breast and fire in her eyes. But then the glance lowered, all but a bowed head, a meek clasping of hands—an implied acceptance he did not trust.

"We have no choice," Tarien said in a low voice. "And we have no chance if we go on as we are." Orien's anger flared, scenting the very air of the room, but Tarien persisted: "Good sir, we did hear in the convent that you had been given Henas'amef, else we wouldn't have dared come here. You were the kindest of the Marhanen's friends. I expect nothing good of him, but you would never harm us."

"Cefwyn didn't harm you," he returned. "And you tried to kill him."

"To win him," Tarien said, but he knew that for a lie, and Tarien perhaps knew he knew, for the gray space grew dark and troubled.

"Emuin's here, too, isn't he?" Orien asked. "I heard him quite clearly."

"He's here."

"Dry old Emuin," Orien said. "Hypocrite."

"He says very ill things of you, too," Tristen said, "and I regard his opinion as far more fair."

It was perhaps more subtle a sting than Orien had expected. Her nostrils flared, but she did not glare. Rather she seemed to grow smaller, and more pliant.

"We shouldn't quarrel. I never held any resentment for you, none at all. You never had a chance but to fall into the Marhanen's hands,

46

the same as we, and you have far more right to be here: I shouldn't chide you."

He felt a subtle wizardry as she said it, and he wondered what she was attempting now.

He broke off the blandishments and the weaving of a spell with a wave of his hand, and she flinched. So did Tarien, for that matter.

"Don't," he said, to Tarien as much as to Orien. "Don't press against the walls. You're in danger, and you're far safer here than anywhere else if you'll accept it."

"Accept it!" Orien said in scorn.

"Accept safety here. It's my best advice."

"I need nothing from you *or* that dry stick of a wizard!"

"But you do," he said. "You need it very much." Orien turned her shoulder to him, but he went on trying to reach her, in the World and in the gray space alike. "Lady, you didn't only open the wards and the window, you opened yourself and your sister to Hasufin. You thought it might give you a way to rule here and be rid of Cefwyn, but all Hasufin wanted was a way inside the wards."

"And an end of the Marhanen!"

"Lady Orien, the truth is, if you had died and if everyone had died, Hasufin didn't care. It didn't matter to him. It doesn't matter to him now—if there's anything left of him. If sorcery finds a way inside the wards, it won't give you back what you had. Cefwyn might have, but Hasufin Heltain never would and never intended to. If you don't know that, you don't know what he was."

She was angry at what he said, but she might think on it. Perhaps she had already thought on it. Doubtless she had had ample time to think, sitting in a Teranthine nunnery in Guelessar with no fine gowns, no servants, no books, and no one who cared to please her.

And in this moment of her retreat, he pursued, with a question which had troubled him since summer.

"You tried to kill Emuin," he asked her, for someone at summer's end had attacked Emuin and left him lying in a pool of blood. He could think of no one more likely than Orien Aswydd, who had commanded all the resources of Henas'amef. "Didn't you?"

She gave him no answer, but he had the notion he had come very near the truth: Orien or someone sworn to her. And he could think of many, many connections she had had among the servants and the nobility of the province, one of whom had perhaps stayed more loyal than most.

"Lord Cuthan's gone to Elwynor," he said. "Did you know that?"

Perhaps she had not known it. Perhaps she was dismayed to learn that particular resource was no longer within her reach, when he was sure Cuthan had something to do with Orien Aswydd. Perhaps through Cuthan she had even known about the proposed rising against the king, and the Elwynim's promised help.

But she said nothing.

He tried a third question. "Did *you* bring the attack on the nuns?"

It was as much as if to ask: *Did you wish your freedom from the nuns, and, Did you grow desperate because the plan had failed?*

And: *Did it work finally as you wished?*

It all might have shot home, but Orien never met his eyes, and he somewhat doubted she heard . . . or that she knew any other thing. He only wished that if it were possible she could find another path for her gift, she would do differently. He wished it on her with gentle force, and with kindness, and she stepped back as if he had grossly assaulted her. The white showed all around her eyes.

"I wish you well," he said in the face of her temper, and included Tarien in the circle of his will. "I assure you I do, as Hasufin never did."

"You take my lands," Orien cried, "and wish me well in my poverty! How dare you!"

It was a question, and he knew the answer with an assurance that, yes, he dared, and had the right, and did. The gray space intruded, roiled and full of storm; and in it, he did not retreat: Orien did. In the World, she recoiled a step, and another, and a third, until she met the wall. Tarien rose from her chair, awkward in the heaviness of her body, and turned to reach her sister, still holding to the chair.

"If Aséyneddin had won," Orien said. "If you had died—"

"You promised Cefwyn loyalty," Tristen said, "and you never meant it. Do you think you'd lie to *Hasufin,* and have what you wanted? If you lied and he lied—what in the world were you expecting to happen?"

She had no idea, he decided sadly. Nothing at all Unfolded to him to make sense of Orien, but he suspected Orien's thoughts constantly soared over the stepping-stones to the far bank of her desires, never reckoning where she had to set her feet to take her there.

Flesh and bone as well as spirit, Mauryl had said to him, when he had been about to plunge down a step while looking at something across the room. He could hear the crack of Mauryl's staff on incontrovertible stone, to this very hour. Look where you're going, Mauryl would say.

It was in some part sad that Orien had had no Mauryl to advise her.

But on a deeper reflection, perhaps it was as well for all of them that Hasufin's counsel had never been other than self-serving.

And she never answered him now, never confessed her expectations, possibly never knew quite what they were or why she continually fell short of her mark.

"What do you hope I should do?" he asked them. "I might send you to Elwynor."

"Send us to Elwynor?" Orien echoed him, and drew herself up with a breath, a shake of her head, a spark in the eye. "Oh, do. *Do*, and you send king Cefwyn's child to Tasmôrden!"

Cefwyn's child, he said to himself.

A man and a woman made a child together, and would it be with one of the stableboys Tarien had done this magic?

No. It made perfect sense. Now her defiance assumed a purpose, and her coming here disclosed a reason. So did the nuns' deaths, at a far remove: whatever men had killed those hapless women, he knew that greater currents were moving in the world, and that none of them was safe.

"And when will the child be born?" he asked, already having clues to that answer.

"I'm eight months now," Tarien said, and settled into her chair like a queen onto her throne.

Nine was the term of a child that would live. So Uwen had said. Three times wizards' three, this term of a child. Wizardry set great store by numbers, and moments, and times.

"And have you sent this news to Cefwyn?"

"No," Orien said. And Tarien:

"We kept it our secret. *My* secret. Even when he sent us away. It never showed until fall, and under all these robes, and then the winter cloaks . . . only my nurse knew."

"Yet the Guelens came," Orien said with a bitter edge. "So perhaps the nuns did see, and perhaps he does know, this good, this honest king of yours, despite all you say."

Tristen shook his head. They were back to that, never resolved. "No. I know he wouldn't."

"What, a Marhanen king refuse a murder? To prevent an Amefin claim on the throne, to keep our secret a secret—come now, what might not our Cefwyn do?"

"He didn't do this," he said with unshaken confidence. "He doesn't know. He wouldn't harm you."

"Come now. If he knew—oh, indeed, if he knew. You," Orien said, "who *are* good, and honest—all these things . . . you'd stick at murder. You have virtues. But three generations of the Marhanen has taught this province the Marhanen do *not!*"

"And this is his child."

She gave him a startled, uncertain look at that saying.

"A child with the wizard-gift," he added, for in the storm he had heard sometimes two lives, and sometimes and faintly, three.

"An Aswydd child," Orien said, "with *Marhanen* blood."

"My child." It was a small voice. A near whisper from Tarien, that still managed a hint of defiance. "And he's right. I think he *is* right; they didn't come from Cefwyn."

"Oh," Orien hissed, "now we believe him again. Now we think him full of virtue and chivalry, this lover of ours. A Marhanen *king* would not hesitate to rip that child from your womb and destroy it, never doubt it. But not here. Not from Lord Tristen's hands. Tristen would never allow it, our gentle Tristen . . ."

He liked nothing he heard, least of all Orien Aswydd appealing to his kindness, and now he wished he had called Emuin to this conference. But it was too late. He saw Orien's confidence far from diminished and her malevolence far from chastened.

"You think *you've* done all this," Tristen said, for she seemed to have no grasp of any other state of affairs. "You let Hasufin Heltain past the wards, you dealt with wizardry, and you think it was all yours? The child has the gift. If he's Cefwyn's, he might be king. And you dealt with Hasufin Heltain! You know what he did at Althalen, you know Emuin cast him out then, and you know what he wants most of all—is that what you want? This child is his best chance since Althalen!"

Tarien had her hand on her belly, and she understood his meaning—at last and very least one of the Aswydds heard his warning, she, who held within herself all the consequence of Hasufin's ambition, and could not escape it, could not on her own prevent Hasufin's taking the child as his way into the world of Men.

"Don't listen to him!" Orien said. "Pay no attention. It's only Cefwyn's interest he cares for, nothing, nothing at all for the babe's sake! Your child will be *king!*"

Tarien pulled away and leaned against her chair, arms folded protectively over her belly..

"Tarien!" Orien insisted, but Tristen drew Tarien's eyes to him.

"Don't listen," he said.

"Amefel is *ours!*" Orien hissed. "*We* are the aethelings. We are the royals and we *were* royal before the Sihhë came down from the Hafsandyr! This land *belongs* to her son!"

It was indeed her claim, and a claim with some justice. Tristen considered that, considered the angry determination in Orien's eyes, and her wishes, and the strength they had. "You can't," he said, to all her wishes. "Not alone. I wish not. Emuin wishes not. *Mauryl* wished not, and I don't think you can wish otherwise to any good at all, Lady Orien. Your servants have gone, Lord Cuthan's across the river—Lord Edwyll's dead, and his heir *is* the aetheling now."

"Crissand!" The voice shuddered with scorn.

"The Witch of Emwy said it, and I say it. Did Tasmôrden promise you what he promised Cuthan? There was no army. There never was an army. He lied to Cuthan. He lied to all the earls, and Edwyll died of the cups in your cupboard . . . or was it your wish?"

Orien's eyes had widened somewhat, at least in some inner recognition.

"Was it your wish?" Tristen asked her. "Your wish, and not the cups?"

Orien's brows lifted somewhat. "The wine. My sister and I had no inclination to die as our brother died. We preferred *that* to exile."

It was not all she preferred to exile: death here, death in her Place, as the Zeide was: foreseeing that danger, even then, he had advised Cefwyn to banish her and the Aswydds of the name. Both dead and alive they had gone out the gate, to prison and burial elsewhere.

"And Cuthan is in Elwynor," Orien said, "with the latest usurper. And *you* sit here. The mooncalf, they called you. The fool. Mauryl's hatchling."

"I was," he said.

"And Bryn?" she asked.

She knew, he was sure now, that Tasmôrden had promised invasion: she likely knew everything Cuthan had done. Messages *had* gotten to Anwyfar, and she *had* expected a rising against the Crown. But she had not known anything since Cuthan's flight: that said something of her sources, and of Cuthan's slight wizard-gift, remote now from her. It was clear that whispers had gone on in the gray space that neither he nor Emuin had heard. In Guelessar, in the autumn, he had rarely reached out to Amefel. Emuin had forbidden it.

"What of Bryn?" she demanded to know.

"Drusenan of Modeyneth is Lord Bryn now."

It did not please her. But she turned her face elsewhere and wrapped her wishes inward, tightly held, and he left them unpursued.

51

"So busy you've been," she said, gazing into distance. "Gathering an army in Amefel, all those tents arrayed outside my walls . . . a winter campaign, is it to be? All for Cefwyn. For Cefwyn's *heir*." Her eyes lanced toward him, direct and challenging. "For his first-born son—his firstborn *Aswydd* son—a kingdom."

"It is a son," he said, for Tarien's child was male, and would be firstborn. That was the truth, and only then knew with full force how it would hurt Ninévrisë.

And that son, not Ninévrisë's, would harm the treaty with Elwynor.

It would harm Cefwyn—the northern lords would reject a child of Aswydd and Marhanen blood out of hand. So would the Elwynim.

"A son," Orien said. One set of plans dashed in what he told her, she gathered up others, and recovered herself. "A bastard, he may be, but a *royal, firstborn* bastard."

Bastard was a child without ceremony, unrecognized. Bastard was a child no one would own.

But that was not so. Someone owned this child. *Tarien* did. Tarien already held it protected in her arms, her eyes wide with alarm while Orien's flashed with defiance of him. They were twins, of one mind until that moment: of one ambition, until that heartbeat. He had divided them. The child had. *Cefwyn* had, for Tarien's feeling was not Orien's, and the realization of that shivered through the gray space with the kiss of a knife's sharp edge.

He was sorry for their pain, but he was not sorry for Orien.

And he sealed himself against all their entreaties and their objections. If anyone could bend Orien Aswydd, it might be Tarien. If anyone could sway her, it might be her twin, given time, and a quieter hour. There was the hope for them: Cefwyn's son he could not reach, not now, not without harm.

"I'll ask about the gowns," he said, intending to leave.

"Servants," Orien said. Her lips made a thin white line. Her eyes held storm that, prudently, did not break.

"Respect the wards," he said, "and respect the guards."

"And if we don't? Would you harm my sister and the child?" she asked, with the clear expectation he would not.

It was the truth. She expected to have won the argument, and to have her way, and she would not.

"I don't intend her harm," he said with a glance toward Tarien, whose eyes met his in dread. "I can't say what *she* means to do," he said directly to Tarien. "Take care. Take care for yourself."

And with that he walked out, sealed against the roiling confusion they made in the gray space.

He realized now that Emuin had been listening for the last few moments, subtle and stealthy as Emuin was. But he did not acknowledge that he knew, not this close to the twins' apartment. He gathered up Uwen and his own guard, who had been talking with the Guelens at the nearer station.

"They ask for their gowns," he said to Uwen. "Do you know what happened to them?"

"I fear they've gone, m'lord, I'd imagine they have."

"The servants?"

"I'd say. His Majesty was at Lewenbrook, His Highness bein' here didn't know one man from another, comin' an' goin'—" When Efanor had been in charge of Henas'amef, Uwen meant, and sure enough there had been no few of the servants fled when Cefwyn came back. "I'll imagine the pearls an' such on those gowns just walked out o' town in purses and tucked in bosoms, and went all the way to Elwynor, or even into noble ladies' dower chests, closer to home."

There had been ladies of various houses near enough the Aswydds to have had access to a wardrobe.

Without the Aswydd sisters in their red-haired glory, the gowns, the jeweled cups, the gold plate on the tables, the hall would never be as fine or as glorious as he had seen it in Heryn Aswydd's reign. He was sad to miss the beauty of it, but not at all sad about the grain it bought for the hungry families, or the army it fed, until hands could let go the bow in favor of the shepherd's staff. Cefwyn had used to say Lord Heryn's court outdid Guelemara for luxury . . . and that was not true in size, but in sheer brightness, it might well have been so.

"I did promise them jewelry, at least. I thought of the necklaces we found in Parsynan's room. I think those were likely theirs."

" 'At were generous," Uwen said. "But a woman's jewelry is money if she took to the road, an' off to Elwynor, as these two might if one of the guards don't watch sharp. An' one of them jewels is three years' wage to these men."

"They won't leave this place," he said, and it had the ring of truth in it as the words came out. "Tarien's afraid." He considered who was near them, and knew of a certainty that Emuin was listening, remote in his tower as he told Uwen the simple, the important truth. "Tarien's child is Cefwyn's son."

"Gods save us, I was afeared so. Ye're sure?"

"A son, and a wizard."

". . . An' His Majesty's. Gods save us all."

"They think the nuns didn't know anything, not even that Tarien was with child . . . but if the nuns did know, word might have gotten to the Quinalt, and to Ryssand, mightn't it?"

Uwen gave a soft whistle. "A chain of ifs, m'lord, but it's a damn short chain, and none of 'em's impossible."

"Ryssand would want them."

"Damn sure he would."

—*To say the least,* Emuin said within the gray space, where he had been lurking the last several moments in utter quiet. *Cefwyn took chances. Now one of them's come home.*

—*What should I do?* Tristen asked Emuin, since Emuin had remarked on the situation. And: "What shall I do?" he asked Uwen, aloud, attention divided, distracted in two conversations at once.

"Tell His Majesty," Uwen said. "This 'un's worth a letter."

—*Write to Cefwyn,* Emuin said, in the same instant. *If Ryssand is behind the raid on Anwyfar, gods save us all, then he's gone far beyond retreat. This is deadly, if he alleges it. And above all else, Cefwyn needs to know before the rumor reaches the streets.*

He had no wish to bear that news—but Emuin was right: the rumor spreading was inevitable. The babe would be born in its due course, with all that he was and might become, and would no one know? It was impossible to keep that secret, impossible to keep it with all the wizardous currents running through the world. Tarien, with her sister, had tried to kill Cefwyn this summer—but was that in fact all they had aimed at?

And did that matter now to the truth that grew inside her, a creature, like himself, with its own presence and own will within the gray space?

Mauryl had made him. What had Tarien Aswydd made?

—*The child is a wizard,* he said to Emuin. *And has he not his own reasons?*

—*Weak yet,* Emuin said, which in some measure comforted him. But not wholly.

Not so much as to give him ease of mind or spirit.

And when they reached the stairs, he and Uwen together, and went down, as one must, to go up again to his wing, it cast him momentarily within reach of traffic in the lower hall—in sight, as it chanced, of the master carpenter, who hurried over with the report of a leak in the archive window, which must be dealt with.

"As it's endangering the books, Your Lordship . . ."

"I'll attend it," Lusin said, Lusin, chief of his bodyguard, whose business had nothing to do with the master carpenter; but ice forced snowmelt through cracks, and the woes of the world went on.

He hourly—even at this hour—expected the report from Modeyneth, of grain headed for storage, safe from Tasmôrden's reach.

He expected another report from Haman, tomorrow, of the horses in pasture. Cefwyn had a child of whom Cefwyn knew nothing, and grain moved, and the library window leaked.

Meanwhile the boy Paisi, who, a former felon, marshaled two servants to carry firewood for him, passed on his way to Master Emuin's tower. Paisi bowed, and the servants bowed, but Tristen had already set his foot on the step before he even gave a thought to the courtesy, or thought of Paisi as a messenger to bear a quiet word to Emuin, one the twins would not hear.

"Tell him I'll see him this afternoon," he said, and Paisi turned, eyes wide, and bobbed a courtesy, knowing well which *he* he meant: his lord would meet with his master in what quiet and privacy they could arrange in the fortress, but hereafter such moments were difficult to achieve, and all they did in the gray space might flow through it to other interested souls.

Emuin was right. He had to write to Cefwyn. The more understanding of such a child Unfolded to him, the more he knew that Cefwyn must not be caught by surprise with this news. Cefwyn had to break it to Ninévrisë, and to the lords in his own court: Cefwyn had to tell his friends, and break it to them early and with all the facts in hand . . . before Ryssand heard it and whispered it piecemeal and had the lords forming a dozen different opinions, each at odds with the other.

To two lords at least he had no need to send a messenger. At the top of the stairs he slipped quietly into a gray space momentarily untroubled by the Aswydds and whispered to Cevulirn of Ivanor, — *Come. Bring all the lords. There's a matter to discuss.*

Likewise he sought Crissand Adiran.

But he did not find him, not in the Zeide, nor in the confines of Henas'amef, or yet in the camp outside the walls. Perhaps he was asleep . . . but the hour argued against it.

He grew troubled, then, and made his presence bolder, and stronger, and went searching more noisily through the gray space, seeking whether Crissand was indeed simply sleeping, and near at hand, or whether something dire had befallen him.

He did not expect to find Crissand's presence far, far north of the town, struggling through drifts. But there he was.

He did not expect, given all the untoward things that had happened last night, to meet evasions, or to know that Crissand had slipped his guards and risked his life escaping him and his notice.

He did not expect to meet the pitch of anguish, or the fear that shut Crissand off from him.

It was not the action of a reasonable man, but that of a man pressed to the limits of his endurance. And he knew nothing that might have sent Crissand out and away from him in that state— except his bringing Crissand's cousins into Henas'amef, and settling them in the Zeide.

That was the fear. That was the anger and the anguish.

He stopped on the stairs, his hand clenched on the stonework, and looked away past the walls of the stairwell. He was heart-struck that Crissand had hidden his feelings from him so well until now, and never disturbed him in leaving.

—*Are you well? he asked. Are you safe? Come back. Where are your guards?*

Crissand failed to answer him . . . too far a thought for Crissand's scant ability, it might be. And now he did dread the Aswydds' attention, and feared to make too great a thing of it.

It might be that Crissand had no inclination to listen: the lord of Meiden rode northerly, toward Anwyll's garrison and, in between, the village of Modeyneth, and the building of a defensive wall . . . all these things were in that direction. There were ample things in which Crissand had a legitimate interest, in his lord's name.

But nothing about Crissand's self-appointed mission gave Tristen any sense of quiet or surety. He felt only the keen awareness that Crissand was Aswydd himself, and that the quarrels that had split the Aswydd house and brought it down might not be done—for if there was a lord in Henas'amef who had reason to take strong exception to the return of Orien Aswydd to this hall and to the shelter of this roof, Crissand had that reason. He had buried a father thanks to her.

—*Be safe,* Tristen wished Crissand, and continued up the stairs, more than distressed: worried to the depth and breadth of his heart. And he wished Crissand's welfare whether or not Crissand heard him, and whether or not it accorded with other matters he cared for.

—*Be sensible. Trust Modeyneth and go no farther . . . above all not to Althalen. And come back to me when you've done what you set out to do. Be assured I am your friend.*

That, he wished Crissand to know most of all.

CHAPTER 3

The lords came to the summons with snow still unmelted on their cloaks, tracking icemelt through the lower hall and into the great hall itself and delaying not at all for conversation or for ceremony. No one pleaded excuses, except Crissand, who did not appear at all.

It needed no magic to know why they had been so quick and why the summons had met with immediate compliance. Cevulirn would have come, regardless, out of friendship, and Sovrag, who detested to be left out of any proceedings, would have come, for one thing, to be sure he was not the object of the council.

But Umanon, the stiff, Quinalt lord of Imor, had come with as great a haste, and so had Pelumer, who viewed schedules as mutable at need.

Together with Amefel these four comprised the muster of the south. War was their agreement, war with the rebels in Elwynor, supporting Cefwyn's intended attack from the east.

And now with neither preface nor prologue the exiled duchess of Amefel had turned up and gained admittance to the center of their preparations?

Folly, they might well be saying among themselves.

Certainly they were due an accounting.

In all sober consideration of that fact, Tristen took his seat on the dais that dominated the great hall, that seat which had been the throne of Amefel when Amefel had been a petty kingdom. Around him hung the tapestries that portrayed the triumphs of the Aswydd line, figures stitched in stiff rows, conspicuous in the Aswydd personal heraldry of gold and emerald. He was conscious of that, too: the Aswydds' long dominance in this hall—and in that consciousness he wore the red of the province of Amefel itself, with the black Eagle crest, the colors of the people, not the Aswydd house.

He had Uwen by him on the one side, Uwen being his captain of the guard, and he had master Emuin, who generally held to his tower. That Emuin had come down was in itself remarkable, and a sure sign of the seriousness of the situation—but Crissand, who should have been here, on his right, was at least a day away by now, a perpetual, worrisome silence.

Crissand was not the only absent earl of Amefel—there was in fact a general scarcity of local faces, not that the earldoms had no interest in the current matter: indeed, they had a more acute concern in Orien Aswydd's return than did the dukes of the southern provinces, who had never been under her rule. But most of the Amefin court had gone out to see to their lands and villages after Midwinter Day, attending ordinary needs and necessities, and traditional observances—in truth, more than one of them simply disappearing from court much as Crissand had done, with no more leave: Tristen reminded himself it was the habit of the court, that no one had ever held them to any different courtesy, and that it was not so different with Crissand—but he knew and Crissand knew that there was an assumption between them that demanded a leave-taking, and that had not been satisfied.

So, too, likely Crissand and likely the other absent earls would be slower returning than they had planned, thanks to the unexpectedly heavy snow: and there was serious business to do out in the villages, plans to make for the spring, justice to hear, even winter weddings . . . all such things the earls had under their hand, and reasonable enough they rode out after the Midwinter festival to see to their duties—if Crissand had ridden to his own lands, to Meiden.

He had not.

So now with Crissand and Drumman both out among the snowdrifts and the wretched roads, it fell to old Earl Prushan to stand by his duke's right hand, an honor usually several degrees of precedence removed from that good old man . . . in fact, beside Prushan, next, were only a handful of the lesser earls and the ealdormen of the town, a set of faces all grave and curious, all come to hear the circumstances of Lady Orien's uninvited return . . . but not the representation of the highest lords in Amefel that Tristen would have wished. It was instead the gathering from Lewenbrook, the southern army, the neighbors, who came to him at his call.

How many of the earls had gotten wind of Orien Aswydd and absented themselves?

Fearing what? Had they not seen Auld Syes enter the hall on Midwinter Eve? Had they not seen enough strange things in this turning of the year to send them uneasy sleep?

A whisper of wind wafted past Tristen's head. Owl swooped down and lit on his forearm, piercing his flesh with sharp talons, caring not a whit for his discomfort, it was certain. He was more and more distressed, and yet refrained from a general call into the gray space, a shout to rouse all that was his against all that was Orien Aswydd's.

"Last night," Tristen began, addressing those who had come, the locals, and the southerners, "last night I heard travelers in the storm, and I found Orien and Tarien Aswydd walking toward the town. They say armed men burned the convent at Anwyfar, and killed their nurse along with the nuns there. They say they had a horse at first, and lost it, and walked the rest of the way, hoping for shelter here. I don't think it's a lie, how they came here. But they're not welcome guests. They're still under Cefwyn's law. I had nowhere to send them, but I don't set them free."

"Send them to Elwynor," was the immediate suggestion, from more than one voice, and others had a more direct suggestion: "Better if they'd burned."

"Point o' that—who burned Anwyfar?" Sovrag asked, above the rest, and that was the question.

"Who burned Anwyfar?" Tristen echoed the question. "Orien said it was Guelen Guard, Cefwyn's men—that it was Captain Essan."

"Essan!" old Prushan exclaimed, and no few with him. The earls knew the name, if the dukes of the south did not, and for a moment there was a general murmur.

"There's another should have hanged," someone said. "Turned right to banditry."

"I know Cefwyn didn't order it," Tristen said. "If he wanted to kill them, he certainly didn't need to send men to burn a Teranthine shrine and kill all the nuns, who never did him any harm."

"Ryssand," said the Bryaltine abbot, standing forward, hands tucked in sleeves. "Ryssandish, it might well be. Parsynan was Ryssand's man, and every other trouble he visited on us Captain Essan had a hand in. And why not this?"

The ealdormen thought so. There were nods of heads, a small, unhappy stir.

"And what when the king in Guelessar finds it out?" Prushan

asked, and Earl Drusallyn, who was almost as old: "And what when the king blames us?"

"Send 'em to Elwynor!" an ealdorman said.

And Sovrag: "Hell, send 'em to the Marhanen, done up in ribbons!"

"No," Tristen said. "No. Not Elwynor, and not Guelessar." He drew a breath, not happy in what he had to tell. "Lady Tarien's with child. Cefwyn's."

"Blessed gods," Umanon said, under the gasp and murmur of the assembly, and a deep hush fell.

"I haven't told Cefwyn yet," Tristen said. "I have to write to him, and my last messenger to Guelemara came and went in fear of his life. I don't know what's happened there, with Guelen Guard burning shrines and killing nuns. I don't know if Cefwyn knows what they did."

"His Majesty doesn't know about the child?" asked Umanon.

"He last saw the lady this summer," Cevulirn said. "So did we all."

"There's the gift in both of them," Emuin said in the low murmur of voices. "What they didn't want noticed, even the ladies of the convent might not have noticed. The king *doesn't* know. But someone may."

"Cuthan," Tristen said, provoking another hush. "I think Cuthan kept her informed, and informed himself."

"Then Parsynan might know," Prushan said.

It was true. It was entirely possible.

"Marhanen issue with an Aswydd and a witch to boot," Pelumer murmured. "The Quinalt will be aghast."

"Not only the Quinaltine," Umanon said, who was Quinalt himself. "Any man of sense is aghast. How many months is she gone?"

"Eight," Emuin said.

"Gods save us," Umanon said, letting go his breath. "Gods save Ylesuin."

"And gods save Her Grace," Sovrag muttered, for Sovrag adored Ninévrisë. "*There's* a damn tangle for us."

What indeed would Ninévrisë say? Tristen asked himself in deep distress. What indeed could she say? She loved Cefwyn, and eight months was before they were married and before Cefwyn ever laid eyes on her—from that far back a folly arrived to confound them all.

And folly it was. Cefwyn had not done it on his own, he was surer and surer of that: Cefwyn, who had not a shred of wizard-gift, was utterly deaf and blind to the workings of wizardry, but not immune: no man was immune, and there was every reason in the world these two women had worked to snare him and cause this.

"The legitimate succession in Ylesuin," Cevulirn said, "was already in question, with the Quinalt contesting Her Grace at every turn, and them wanting to refuse the war if they can't have the land they take. The unhappy result is that there is no settlement on an heir in the marriage agreement. And *that* is unfortunate."

No one had thought of that. Tristen had not. The stares of those present were at first puzzled, then alarmed.

"We're to fight a war to bring the Elwynim under Her Grace's hand," Umanon said, "and now Tarien Aswydd bears a pretender to Ylesuin?"

"No legal claim," Pelumer said, "since there was no legal union, no matter the vagueness of the marriage treaty. In either case, there is an heir: Efanor."

"But the Aswydds claim royalty," Umanon said, "and royalty on both sides of the blanket, as it were. It's not as if our good king found some maid in a haystack. This is troublesome."

"A witch," Sovrag said, "no less; a sorceress. And what's our blessed chance it's a daughter?"

"Small," Emuin said, hedging the point.

"It is a son," Tristen said bluntly. "And he has the gift."

Another murmur broke out, with no few pious gestures against harm. Blow after blow he had delivered to the alliance, with no amelioration, and he had nothing good to offer except that the lady and Cefwyn's son were not at this moment in Elwynor, in Tasmôrden's hands.

"There's some as'd drop the Aswyddim both down a deep well," Sovrag said. "And solve our problems at one stroke."

Tristen shook his head, lifted his hand to appeal for silence, and Owl bated and settled again on his shoulder. "No," he said in the stillness he obtained.

"Ye're too good," Sovrag said. "Give 'me to my charge. My lads'll take 'em downriver, an' they'll go overboard with no qualms at all."

"No," Tristen said again, and the gray space came to life. The hall seemed a hall of statues, everything set, the very pillars of the roof and the occupants of the hall one substance, set and sure and warded against the queasiness just next to this hall, that one place of slippage and weakness in the wards which he could not continue to ignore. "I've thought of our choices. I've asked myself whether it's wise to be good, or good to be wise and, aside from all I can think of, or all I can do, the truth is that the Aswydds built this place. Their wizardry is in these stones. It makes them part of the defenses of the Zeide and Henas'amef. Emuin can tell you so."

"Woven into its defenses like ribs in a basket," Emuin said in the attention that came to him. "The stay and support of it, and every chink and weakness in it, they know in their bones. Wisest was what Cefwyn did, sending them to Anwyfar. They were as safe there as it was possible for them to be, given it was nuns watching them and not an armed guard or a half a dozen wizards. Now someone's made a move to free them, and they've come here not only because they *had* to come here rather than Guelemara, but because they know the same as I their protections are here. They're bound to Henas'amef. That's one point, and never forget it. The second: Ryssand may have burned down a Teranthine shrine, but if Ryssand, not *only* Ryssand was in on it. The man's too canny to do something like this openly, or recklessly. He has concealment he believes will hold, or he has overwhelming reason to do something so rash."

"What reason, then?" Umanon asked.

Tristen tried to answer, and in Emuin's silence he could only shake his head, eyes widely focused, taking in all the room at once, on all levels, as the gray winds tugged and pulled at his attention. "A wizard doesn't even need to be alive," he said, determined to be honest with his hearers as Emuin had never been honest with him.

But once he had said it he felt fear coursing through his hearers. He felt the courage of some, the apprehension of most. *Hasufin* was his fear; it had now to be theirs, and every man who had stood at Lewenbrook knew what he meant: that a wizard need not be alive. Hasufin Heltain had not been alive when he had cost so many lives, when the dark had rolled down on the field like a living wave, and no man among them forgot that hour.

In that general dismay Emuin came to the center of the steps and stood with arms folded in his sleeves, waiting, waiting, silently commanding the assembly's attention.

"His Grace is telling you difficult things," Emuin said when quiet came and every eye was on him. "He means to say that the Aswydd sisters aren't strong enough to have released *themselves* from the bindings I set on them—yes, I! But if they move with currents already moving they might well have done it themselves, and without the knowledge or help of our enemy. But be assured there *are* such currents. There are currents in waters that have been moving for some time, and now these two have cast themselves and Cefwyn's son into that flow, if not with their attempt to free themselves—which hasn't, in fact, gained them their freedom—then certainly early last summer, when they worked petty hedge-witchery to get a child."

"Saying what?" old Prushan asked. "What does your honor mean? That there's some other wizard? The wizard from last summer?"

"Do you mean this is all foredoomed?" Umanon asked uneasily.

Emuin held up a finger. "Not foredoomed as to outcome." The hand flourished, vanished again into tucked sleeves, to reappear with a silver ball, that again vanished. "Say that a wizardous river is in spring flood, and the shore's become damned uncertain. The Aswydds and the usurper are deep in the waters. Hear the lord of Amefel. Hear him! He's the only swimmer in the lot."

Tristen cast Emuin an uneasy look of his own in the murmur of the assembly, not wishing to hear what he had heard, not taking it for any more solid truth than the maneuvering of the ball, and wondering why at long last Emuin, who shied from discussing wizardry directly even with him, had suddenly spoken in council and employed this trickery of the eye.

Was it because *he* had resolved to speak out the truth to these men, and Emuin followed him?

Emuin made a final flourish, hurled the ball at the wall, making the assembly at that side flinch.

Nothing hit. Nothing happened.

"Don't trust your eyes," Emuin said, serenely passing the silver ball from finger to finger, to the assembly's disquiet. A glow possessed his hand, which vanished. So did the ball. "Don't believe what you see. Don't believe what you suspect. Listen to your lord."

A stillness followed.

"Your Grace," old Pelumer said then, "what about Orien Aswydd in our midst, telling whoever might want to know all she can see here? There's the depths of cellars. I'm sure the town itself has a number of them that could host the lady. I'm sure the Zeide has."

"I'd rather have her here," Tristen said, "over all, I'd rather have her where master Emuin can keep an eye on her."

Master Emuin snorted. "Great good that will do."

"But while they're here, Tasmörden can't get his hands on His Majesty's child," Cevulirn said, "which would be disaster if it happened. And if we place the Aswydds somewhere we can't watch, there's a greater chance he might reach them."

"When he does know," Umanon said, "he's bound to be sure the whole world knows. Her Grace of Elwynor a bride, and a queen without a title, and now there's a bastard in the Marhanen line, out of an Aswydd sorceress, no less, and will the Quinalt abide it? I don't think so."

"Sink 'er," Sovrag said. "I tell ye, that's the way out o' this muddle."

"Oh, aye," Emuin said. "We have that choice: kill the child, or let it live: two choices more: kill the sisters or let them live; and again, two choices: keep them prisoner or let them free. The child is male, and has the wizard-gift, and she *claims* it's His Majesty's. Again two choices: believe her or don't believe. Those are your choices, lords of the south, eight choices we all have, but not a precious one else can I think of."

"Do you doubt her?" Umanon asked.

"I believe her," Tristen said, "and I know her son has the gift. In the storm I thought there were three; and there were only Orien and Tarien when I found them. I felt it again when I spoke with them. I have no doubt at all."

"And doubt as to the father?"

"I never felt they were lying." Tristen watched Owl wander down to his hand and he lifted it to oblige Owl, as claws pricked uncomfortably through the fabric of his sleeve. Owl arrived at his fingers, and swiveled his head about to regard him with a mad, ruffled stare, as if utterly astonished by the things he heard—before he bent and bit, cruelly hard.

He tossed Owl aloft, and Owl fluttered and flew for a ledge.

The eight choices Emuin named, whether those present thought of it or not, were the same choices Emuin had had in Selwyn's time— the choices Emuin had had when he killed a prince of the house of Elfwyn, the last High King, the last reigning descendant of the Sihhë.

Gentle Emuin had killed a child.

And Mauryl, the Mauryl who had fostered him, had ordered it.

He stared at the wound Owl had made, blood, that smeared his fingertips: he worked them back and forth, and looked up where Owl had settled.

Wake, Owl seemed to say to him. Rule. Decide. Blood will attend either choice.

He drew a breath, looked at the solemn, shocked faces of the assembly, with the blood sticky on his fingertips . . . and knew that the question was Orien Aswydd.

"She won't rule here again," he told the assembly. "Cefwyn set her aside. Now I do." And as he said it he made that doom certain with all his force, all the might that was in him. Emuin turned in alarm and mouthed a caution, half lifting a warding hand, for Emuin above all others felt the currents shift, much as if he had cast a mountain into the flow.

And half the fortress removed and upstairs, Orien and Tarien surely felt it—for something like a cry went through the very stones of the Zeide and the rock of its hill.

Owl took to his wings, and flew off across the hall to settle on the finial of the ducal throne.

"Amefel," Cevulirn said—Cevulirn, who alone of all of them but Emuin could hear that protest of the wards—"What of the child? What for it?"

He was less sure of that. On few things he was certain. On the matter of Tarien's child and Amefel, he was not.

"I say what I can," he answered Cevulirn.

"So what does His Grace think is coming down on us?" Pelumer asked. "We've Marna on our borders, and an uneasy neighbor it always is, but this winter nothing goes right near it . . . fires die, bowstrings break, men who know the paths lose their way. Is something coming, the like of what we saw this summer?"

"Not only Marna," Sovrag said. "Haunts here. The servants in the halls is saying there's haunts in the downstairs and a cold spot right next the great hall—and in sight of all of us ye went into the dark and come out with that owl at that very spot, did ye not, Amefel? Spooks in Marna I can swear to, and so can my neighbor here who sailed in with me. We come here to fight Tasmôrden. So what are we makin' war on? I ask the same question. Is it Lewenbrook all over again?"

Emuin, too, had heard that shriek through the stones. In him was no fear of haunts in the hall, only a calm assessment that, yes, there was risk.

And it was his assessment.

And all these men knew now what sided with them, and if they were not willing to face what arrayed itself against them, they above all others, knew what it was to face it—they had stood on Lewen field. He did not count any man in this hall as other than brave.

And oh, he missed Crissand's presence now—missed the assessment of the other presence who might read the gray space and steady him.

"You want to know what we make war on," he answered Sovrag's question. "And I wish there were a simple answer. I don't know what may happen. I know what I have to do. Tasmôrden claims the banner of Althalen."

That dismayed them. No, they had not known.

"Well," said Sovrag, "that man's a fool, ain't he?"

There was a small breath of laughter, a relief, in the hall.

"The camp at the river is secure," Cevulirn said in his quiet, customary calm. "The roads are not so badly drifted. The grain supplies are secure. Our enemy has resources. We trust Your Grace has better. Your Grace proved the stronger at Lewenbrook . . . and will again."

"I've no easy feeling," he said honestly. Among Guelenfolk he had so carefully tried to be like everyone else; but these, his allies, had drawn away all the concealment and spoken to him frankly until now he felt compelled to give them all he knew, an exchange of honesty, a revelation so private and so profound in this room it was all but painful. "None from the riverside nor anywhere about, either. I can usually hear things if I listen hard, and there's only Earl Crissand, who's chosen to ride out that way, but it worries me. Everything along that road worries me, and I wish he may come back safely."

"Does Your Grace see any stir out of Elwynor?" Pelumer asked. "—Counting that the owl might, as 't were, fly abroad."

"Where Owl goes I don't myself know. Nor the pigeons." They saw the birds as spies, he was aware, and were wrong in that, attributing to Owl what he might learn from the gift. But that Owl guided him in his dreams, and that his dreams were less fair than the condition of the land he knew around him . . . that he still kept secret until he knew what to make of it. "I don't know their number, daily at Althalen, but I know it's defended. Aeself and his men have my leave to guard the camp, and they do; and Drusenan guards Modeyneth."

"Nothing's troubled them," said Cevulirn.

"Not that I know. None of Tasmôrden's men have tried the bridges that I know, either. And Tasmôrden himself is still in Ilefínian, but a great many who survived have left it and come toward our border villages. This I'm sure of."

A silence had attended his words. It persisted, a little fear, and a hopeful confidence.

"And Your Grace knows this," Pelumer said, the third attempt on his secrecy.

"I know," Tristen said, more than knowing—*aware* of the gift, though a very small one, in Pelumer himself, and Pelumer's asking as an uncertainty perhaps keenly self-directed.

"Far less a trouble than riders and horses," Sovrag said under his breath.

"Is Your Grace ever mistaken?" Umanon asked: Umanon did not have a shred of the gift, the only one among the lords who had not the least glimmering of it.

"Yes," he said, "I've made mistakes. A great many of them. But not so many now."

"Wizardry or magic," Emuin said, "alike has its weaknesses, and worst when one commits one's entire plan to them. Lean on a single staff . . . and another wizard or some traveling tinker can tip it right aside in a heartbeat. That there are more settlers at Althalen, yes, that's so, and he knows, does His Grace, who put them there. That they're a resource, yes, I have no doubt. That they're any sort of an answer to Tasmôrden and his army, no. If they were strong enough to fight him, they'd not have lost Ilefínian in the first place."

"But the weather," Pelumer said. "There's some that have weather-luck . . . as the Sihhë Kings had. Is that so? And that great storm and the Aswydds—was that in Your Grace's intentions?"

"I wished good weather for us," he said, keenly aware that the land lay deep in snow, and that at this very moment Crissand struggled through a windblown drift, remnant of the Aswydds' storm, leading a strange horse, fearful and berating himself for his plight. *Now* he heard the thought in Crissand's heart—or perhaps Crissand had heard him a moment ago. "I didn't wish the storm, no, and I don't think Orien could."

"Then who?"

"I don't know. It might have just needed to snow. The weather's like that. It lasted a fair time, but whether the snow would have its way or just what turned it, I don't know. I think I can turn the weather good again. But so very much has happened since yesterday I haven't wanted to confuse things further."

"Wise notion," Emuin muttered.

"It can snow a while," Pelumer said, "so long as it snows hard in Elwynor."

"If you enter on that," Emuin muttered, "be advised of the danger. Wish for good."

"Pray for it," said Umanon, the Quinalt among them.

"That, too," Emuin said, laying a hand to the Teranthine sigil he wore. "Prayers. Wishes. Many of them. Candles by the gross. Gods bless all of us."

Gods remained a mystery to Tristen, but no one had flinched from the questions or the answers.

And he had never depended on mastering the weather.

"The granaries are full," he said. "I can't say whether the river may freeze; but we have the wall at Modeyneth if it lets the enemy across. I can't say whether Tasmôrden may turn east or south, but there's Cefwyn to one side of the hills and us to the other, and when the weather does serve, we'll not receive an attack: we'll bring one."

"And camp that night in Elwynor!" Sovrag shouted out. "There's the word! In Elwynor!"

"In Elwynor," others echoed, and, *In Elwynor* became the word throughout the hall.

Then Owl let out an eerie cry that came from every place and no place. Some laughed nervously. Umanon blessed himself.

Tristen wished the recreant bird back to him, and Owl plummeted down and settled onto his arm, turning his head backward to look at the assembly.

He had intended to quiet Owl and make him less a disturbance. But he doubted his effort had had that effect.

As for the lords' wishes for the weather to improve, he hoped, no, wished with all his might for fair skies and a warm wind out of the south—and he wished that Cefwyn might begin to move against Tasmôrden sooner if the weather bettered itself.

It was time. It was indeed time.

And Sovrag was right: a camp just the other side, by the riverside and still within the compass of his orders not to undertake to win the war, could discomfit Tasmôrden.

More than that, considering rumors of internal weakness in the steady arrival of fugitives at Althalen . . . he hoped his disturbance at the edge of Elwynor might search out the hollow heart in Tasmôrden's power, the ones only marginally loyal to the usurper, most in fear for their lives. Those Elwynim who would turn again and swear to Ninévrisë Syrillas as liege lady might in such a presence find a place to stand, and Tasmôrden then would find his strength melting away, as the commons found the Lady Regent more to their liking.

In point of fact, it was not alone the weather he wished to change, and had no compunction at all about wishing Elwynim to serve Ninévrisë Syrillas. She had the right to their allegiance, and the good heart to mend the land after its years of war and waiting. There could be no better fate for the Elwynim.

"Time, then," he said aloud, "time for us all to set to work."

So the lords agreed. They were pleased when they left. He had accomplished that.

He remained seated a moment, Owl spreading his broad wings and settling claws into his flesh. "Go," he wished the recalcitrant bird, and encouraged him with a toss, but Owl only moved to his hand, and drew blood, and clung.

"You were very plain, young lord," Emuin advised him, neither approving nor disapproving. Emuin had stayed, along with Uwen; and Lusin and his men. "Some of your army might be afraid. Not the great lords, perhaps, but some of your ealdormen looked green as new apples."

"Cefwyn says I'm a poor liar." Wind brushed his cheek, distracting him with a flap of wings as Owl flew up to his other favored perch, up on the cornice. "When should they discover the danger, master Emuin? On the field?"

"And what will you? When will you make up your own mind?"

"To what?" He was genuinely bewildered.

Emuin's glance followed Owl's course, and came back to him, dark and direct under his snowy brows. "That you lead this army."

"I know I lead it."

"That you rule this province."

"The man who *should* rule is freezing in a snowdrift right now, between here and Modeyneth."

"Crissand."

"Yes, Crissand. In this one thing I'm certain. About the war itself I won't wish. I observe caution. I learn, you see, I do learn, master Emuin."

"That you do." Emuin walked a few paces to the left, and turned again. "So now the truth is out. Cefwyn's child. Gods save us. A Marhanen Aswydd. A white crow. A black dove. And ours to deal with."

"Ours. And hers." He still felt Emuin's disapproval. "I did the best I knew, bringing them here. I still think it's safest. I think it was best to tell the lords."

"Safest, yes. Safer than most dispositions."

"We could *not* send Cefwyn's son to Elwynor. Nor have him in Ryssand's hands."

"I agree. He'll be born here, under all the auspices of this place— and if I read the stars aright—he aims for your birth night."

"For mine." He had not remotely thought.

"Wizardry, wizardry, *wizardry*, young lord! Wizardry is an art of *time* and *place*. We have the place, we've missed the turn of the Great Year . . . what *time* shall we suspect is coming?"

He was appalled. It cast everything in a new and threatening light.

"And we need a midwife," Emuin said. "A woman skilled in

childbirth—a woman with the gift—and proof against Orien Aswydd."

"Are there such women in the Zeide?"

"The best is in town. Sedlyn. Paisi's gran, so he calls her, though no more kin to our young jackanapes than Cefwyn is. And she may serve. The date of birth is the question. Sedlyn might help us. A child can be encouraged to come into the world, or held out of it."

He had only book knowledge of births. He sat on the ducal throne of Amefel, empowered to dispose life and death over a province.

But to change a birth, to hasten, to delay, to meddle with what a child in his very existence wanted to be—the sort of meddling Emuin proposed troubled him.

"Was I wise or unwise to obey Mauryl?" the old man asked him, apropos of no question he had asked aloud, and walked away without another word—more, left without a whisper or a breath of wind in the gray space.

No one else could be so silent, or so secret.

No one in his knowledge had done such a deed as Emuin had done—no one carried such a wound as Emuin carried, having murdered the last prince of Althalen, a child he knew . . . or had known. That was what Emuin meant.

And in the silence Emuin wrapped about him like a mantle, in his secret going, cloaked even from him, for the first time Tristen knew why Mauryl must have chosen this one wizard, of all the others, and sent him to kill Hasufin Heltain—for the silence Emuin could wrap about himself was so great, so deep, that he had never realized it was uncommon among wizards.

He had never truly known, in his reckless, innate magic, that not every wizard could tell him no.

And now that he saw into that silence, he found himself grateful for master Emuin, deeply, profoundly grateful that his first venture into the world had brought him into Emuin's hands. It seemed now no chance had directed him.

And all this time there had been a warm, soft blanket wrapped about him, protecting him, shielding him, containing him in every sense.

Now, in this moment, Emuin quietly folded it and took it away, and left him feeling the cold winds of wizardry in all its reach.

Behold the world, young lord.

Behold the choices of those who choose for others, and who hold life and death of thousands in their hands.

"Ye ain't quarrelin' wi' master Emuin," Uwen said uneasily.

"No," he said, finding it difficult even to speak in master Emuin's silence. But the mortal world went on. "He just now challenged me. A lesson."

"A wee bit late for learnin'," Uwen said, "by me."

"He contains the Aswydds. They can't work while he holds them in. I don't know they even know it. He contains what *I* can do. I see now how much harder that is. And now he's let me go, to do what I wish to do."

A clatter startled the silence, right by him. Syllan had dropped a spear, and was red-faced, gathering it up.

Dropped, perhaps. There were small, darting movements, as the servants quietly snuffed all candles on the far side. Darkness advanced, flowed along the channels of the pavings, spread soft grays from its harsher dominion over the deep, curtained corners of the hall. It chased under tables, at the side of the hall. It divided itself and extended tendrils of dark along the joining of wall with floor, and ran between the paving stones, reminding one that within the wall, all was dark.

Tristen saw movement within that dark from the utmost tail of his eye. He felt a draft from some source that might not be the opening of the robing room and its corridor. The drapery there did not stir. Nor did the great green velvet curtains near the front of the dais.

"We've Shadows in the hall tonight," he said to his guards in the faintest of voices. "Listening. But there's no harm meant."

"Ghosts, m'lord?" Lusin looked anxiously at those dark corners, and Syllan and all his guards gripped their weapons the more tightly.

"Something like. Some were Crissand's men, not bad men at all." He drew a deep breath, and stood, listening. "The hall's been threatened."

"Tasmôrden?"

"I think it comes from outside, and far." He could see the little shadows moving, back among the pillars, and the littlest of all running along the masonwork, like darts of dark fire, flickering like flame. "They're uneasy. They listen. Something's trying to get in."

"Into *your* hall, my lord?" Lusin seemed to take it in indignation, regarding a hall he was charged with guarding.

"The candles don't truly dispel them," Tristen said. "They're always here. They're part of the wards, or they're tangled with them: but they're harmless. Don't wish them harm. Especially the Shadows in the great hall. They're all our Shadows, honest Amefin Shadows, and a few Guelen. They're guards, standing their own watch."

"And elsewhere?" Lusin dared ask. "Elsewhere, m'lord? The old mews . . . what's that place?"

"The old mews leads places. I don't know how many."

"To Ynefel," Uwen said.

He nodded slowly, thinking on that place of strange light and bating wings, row on row of perches, for Ynefel had indeed been within that light and he had been in Ynefel. He recalled the high, rickety stairs and wooden balconies, all bathed in the blue, strange light.

But he had explored them in all their brown, dusty webwork when he was new and when the light was the leakage of daylight through the cracks and the soft glow of candles, casting a shifting, wind-driven light along balconies and out into impenetrable dark of further distances. He had had no idea in those days that dark spots and cold spots and bumps in the night could mean ruin. His fears had been all surmise in those days . . . Mauryl's anger, the whisperings of the wind, the surprise of a carving on the stairs—such things he had feared.

Had the old mews always led there?

He had never discovered any other place *from* Ynefel. He had run amongst the Shadows in Ynefel and not known to fear them— at least not the little ones that came out and went back again in the trickery of candlelight. The stone faces within the walls of Ynefel . . . they were Shadows, themselves, of a sort, that seemed to change and shift on uneasy nights.

And were they destroyed when he drove out Hasufin? Or did they still stand?

"The mews leads to Ynefel, and leads from," he said to Uwen. "And it's a cold spot in this hall. It's the cold spots I like least. Shadows there always are, but the cold ones are never happy."

"What *is* that place?" Uwen asked. "We saw the light, things flutterin' and movin', leastwise we thought we saw. We agreed we might ha' seen.—And I could see you, almost, but for the life o' me, all I touched was solid stone."

"Could you see that much?" Tristen asked, surprised and all attention, now.

"I don't know ye could quite call it seein'," Uwen said. "It wasn't like I was lookin' with me eyes."

"You saw into the gray place. Into the haunt. If it opens to you, don't go in, no matter what. Stand on solid ground, and call to me if you find reason to take alarm."

"Take alarm, lad!" Uwen laughed. "I was cold scairt!"

"Did *you* see it?" Tristen asked the other guards, Lusin and Syllan, Tawwys and Aran. "What did you see?"

"Like the cap'n," Lusin said. "Not at first, but the longer we stood there, we all saw a blue light, cold-like. It weren't fire and it didn't burn. And ye come walking toward us like a movin' bright light, and ye had this owl wi' ye."

"Which hadn't any place it come from, that any of us could see," Tawwys said. "He scares the lot of us, perchin' outside your door, starin' while we're on watch."

"Does he? I'd thought he was in the stables."

"He comes an' goes," Tawwys said, and Aran:

"An' he ain't friendly. He bit Syllan's finger."

"I offered 'im a tidbit," Syllan said, "but 'e weren't grateful."

"He's not," Tristen said, and considered the wounds Owl had dealt him, with the stain on his fingertips. "I fear he'll eat the pigeons. But I can't wish him away."

"Why not?" Uwen asked.

"For one thing, I don't think it would do any good and for another I don't think I ought to. He lived in the loft when I was at Ynefel. When I lost my way in Marna Wood he guided me. And on Lewen field he flew ahead of me. He's always there when I don't know where to go."

"Then he has a use," Uwen said.

"He seems to. At least when he flies I'm not lost. He's here now, and I don't see my way through, but he's here." He had not thought of Owl's presence as a comfort, but he began to think that way. "Someday he'll fly, and I'll know it's time to follow him."

"Don't ye talk of goin' after that bird!" Uwen said. "Or of followin' 'im. I don't trust 'im, not a bit. An' if he goes to Ynefel or worse, don't ye dare go wi'out me. There's roads. We can take 'em, the lot of us."

He was silent. He dared not promise that. He looked at Uwen's honest, worried face. "I can't promise you," he said, and looked away again with a shake of his head, as honest with Uwen in return.

CHAPTER 4

There seemed no courteous way to write the letter that circumstances required. Two pieces of paper, three, four, and five Tristen used, and cast each attempt away into the fire of the hearth near his desk. He had every confidence in Tassand and his servant staff, but he found the letters too painful to have lying about, and he would not leave them a moment on his desk—or send them to his friend.

Orien Aswydd came with her sister Tarien. Tarien is with child, which is yours, and a wizard . . .

. . . Orien and Tarien Aswydd fled Anwyfar when men attacked it. Tarien has your child, a son, and he has the wizard-gift . . .

With the Aswydds in residence a few stone walls away it was folly to carry difficult consultation to the gray space, and he feared he was growing so distraught with the letters he had become easy to overhear. He felt alone, abandoned by his friend, by his advisor. He had somehow to say a thing which he knew would bring pain to two he loved, and which might, in the wrong hands, bring bloodshed and war, and he could not find the words to take away the sting of that unanticipated revelation.

Tarien Aswydd came here for refuge and will bear a child in perhaps a month, which . . .

The sixth attempt went into the fire. He rested his head against his hands, checked his fingers belatedly for ink—they were clean—and at that one practical thought knew that his later attempts at gentle advisement were worse, not better.

At that point he left his desk in his apartment, gathered only Lusin and Syllan to guard him, and went to Emuin's tower.

He rapped, pushed the latch, and discovered the old man, far from having lain sleepless during his hours of flailing about the edges of the gray space, had fallen sound asleep in his chair. Young Paisi was curled by the fire like a young hound, and their supper dishes stood empty on a table cluttered with charts.

He eased the door shut. The latch went down, and stung, doing so.

Emuin's head came up. Eyes blinked, as if trying to resolve what they saw.

"Well, well," Emuin said. "Is there trouble? Or more trouble?"

"Forgive me. I need words, master Emuin."

Two blinks more. "Words for Cefwyn?"

"Yes, sir."

"Oh, try *folly* and *prodigious fool.*"

"You don't mean that, sir."

At this point Paisi waked, looking exhausted and startled at once.

"Oh, I mean it," Emuin said, ignoring the boy. "I said it then, damn his stubborn ways, and I say it again."

"But I can't. Do I say to him . . . Tarien Aswydd has your child, a son? That's what I've written."

"That's fair enough. That should inform a thoughtful young man he's been a fool. That's the essence of the report, isn't it? Maybe he'll hear it from you."

"He listens to you."

"Not in this."

"Ninévrisë will be upset with him, won't she?"

"Oh, I imagine she'll be somewhat upset. She's a lady capable of setting aside her heart's feeling to serve her common sense, but this will test the limit, I rather think."

There had been a time he had not understood Emuin's humors, or his ironies. Now they cut keenly, but he knew that they shielded a worried and fond heart.

"What will she do when she knows?"

"All of that is Cefwyn's to deal with," Emuin said brusquely, "not yours. You're not the keeper of his conscience, nor am I. Just deliver him what he needs to know, and let him find the way through this maze. It's enough we have the lady in keeping and she's not making pilgrimage to Guelemara this winter. At very *least* we'll deal with the birth. I don't know what more we can do with the plain, unpleasant truth."

"Am I not to be his friend? Wasn't that your advice? And shouldn't a friend give him something more than just . . . the plain truth, on a paper? Shouldn't I have something else to say? Shouldn't I be wise enough to have advice?"

Emuin's frown eased, and the fierce scowl revised itself into a more pensive, wounded look.

"Or can't *you* advise him, sir?" Tristen leaned both hands on the table, on the welter of charts and dishes. "You came here with me, and you left him to fend for himself. Idrys is clever, and Her Grace is wise, and Annas is kind, but *you* aren't there, and I think he'd truly wish you were with him when he reads this letter. He needs your advice. He needs it most of all."

"I can't travel in this weather. I'm old. My bones won't stand the saddle, I can't ride through such drifts, and by the time a carriage made the trip the news would have walked to Guelemara, drifts and all. I can't advise him! Too many people know this. *Someone* is going to tell the wrong person, if they haven't already run to the capital to shout it in the streets, and the longer we wait, the more certain that is. We don't know we're not already too late to keep it out of Ryssand's hands . . . particularly if those blackguards of Essan's attacked the nuns because someone had found out about Tarien. Tarien might have been their reason, more fool they—someone's hope to keep her *and* the babe when it's born. And if that was the case and if they lost her, they'd have run straight to the capital and reported to whoever set them on."

"Or they'd run for the far hills and not come at all."

"There is that hope."

"Orien thought it might be because Cefwyn found out. I don't think so. If he knew, he didn't need to send the Guelen Guard: Idrys, maybe, but not soldiers to attack the nuns. I think they could be Ryssand's. Maybe Orien said what she did about Cefwyn finding out because she suspected *someone* had found out, but I don't think that someone is Cefwyn. He wouldn't kill the nuns."

"He would not," Emuin mused, raking tangles from his beard. "I can think of two reasons there was an attack on Anwyfar in the first place: first, the one you name, that someone knew there was a child and wanted Tarien in his hands. Ryssand could do gods know what at that point, none good. So could Tasmôrden, if Cuthan spilled what he knows in that quarter, and if he knows too much. That's well possible.—Or it could be someone's blind ill working that bounced off us like a rock off a shield and rebounded on the closest and most vulnerable of our precautions. Our confinement of the Aswydds was always chancy."

"There's a third," he said, taking very seriously what Emuin said.

"That the working was Orien's, to arrange an escape, and to come here. She surely wished it. Ordinarily she couldn't manage it. But she found a current already moving—and maybe she found help."

"Certainly she'd like to be involved," Emuin said. "And think, too: the gainer in what's happened is Orien. She's here. The great loser thus far in what happened is Ryssand: he'd have been so pleased to have Tarien in his hands. The scandal will still break: there's no hiding it forever. But if *we*'re very lucky we might conceal the child until after the attack across the bridges. If Cefwyn wins the war and sets Ninévrisë on the throne, he can do no wrong in her people's eyes and if Ninévrisë has her kingdom back, she may forgive him his old sins. Maybe *we* wished too hard for Cefwyn's safety and something we've done is looking out for his interests . . . preventing the rumor reaching home, in fact."

"And those women died for *that?*" He was appalled by the thought.

"Oh, don't count it our fault: it may be no one's particular fault—except the scoundrels who killed the nuns, of course. They have the fault. The rest is blind chance. Water breaks out where the dike is lowest, young lord, never the strongest point. And by now, after what Mauryl's done, what I've done, what other agencies have done—there's a lot of water flowing."

"Are they guilty, without knowing what they did?"

"Oh, they knew what they did. And it may even have been Orien they were after. These were Quinalt men. They served in Amefel when she ruled here. They knew her for a sorceress and they hate sorcery. As for the nuns, they were nuns of *my* sect, not the Quinalt, and these men were Ryssand's. Maybe they were looking for nothing more than some charge of latent witch-work to lay against the Teranthines. Ryssand's failed in one assault on Cefwyn's rule; he may be looking for another weak point, and never forget that Cefwyn is Teranthine, and that I am. A sorceress sent among Teranthine nuns to hide her and keep her head on her shoulders—how will that sound among the orthodox and doctrinist Quinaltines?—Ah, me, write you must, but we have to keep this news out of Guelessar in general, if that's possible, yet be sure Cefwyn knows. We've sheltered these women, we have them, all to our advantage now, and whatever wizardry opposes us will go straight for that babe. Rely on it."

Much of it seemed conjecture, none leading anywhere.

But the part about wizardry and the baby sounded all too reasonable.

"So we," Emuin concluded, "must do something about it."

"What can we do, sir?"

Emuin rose from his chair at the table and picked up a rod that was at the moment weighing down a half a score of scattered parchments. He waved it at Tristen, waved again in what seemed an instruction to stand on the other side of the table.

Tristen did so. Emuin pushed the rod end-on toward him across that scatter of charts.

"Now push it back to me."

Tristen obliged. Emuin received the end, and mildly pushed the other end again toward Tristen's side of the table, while Paisi came and stared dubiously at the proceedings.

"Push it back to me," Emuin said, and as Tristen slid it toward him, Emuin placed a thin, arthritic finger in the path of the rod, with a tap diverting it to the side.

"What?" said Emuin. "Are you suddenly weak? Push it to me, I say."

Tristen drew back the rod.

"Push with all your strength this time."

"It would not," Tristen said. "No more than a sword past an opposing blade. It will miss, no matter how much strength I have."

"A child's finger could do the same."

"At the right point, likely so, sir."

"Paisi?"

"Oh, no, sir," Paisi said, tucking both his hands behind him and backing up a step. "I ain't tryin' to stop m'lor' wi' me finger."

"Paisi sees the lesson," Emuin said, "—don't you, boy?"

"As I ain't puttin' my finger in m'lor's way, 'at's sure."

"But you would *win*," Emuin said.

"As I ain't puttin' meself in m'lor's way by winnin' again' 'im, either."

Tristen smiled, but the lesson was not lost.

"And that's what a boy learns," master Emuin said. "What does the lord learn?"

"That if you set your finger in the way of the rod too late, you lose. And if you have your finger in the way at the right time, the rod can't reach you. And it's not about rods . . . or swords. It's about wizardry." The grim thought Unfolded itself and cast a gloom over him. "The point of diverting this wizardry isn't now. It was this summer."

"In the early summer, when a prince shared a bed with Tarien Aswydd. If you will know, he was abed with her the night you arrived."

It was like a dousing with cold water. "Me, sir?"

"You came, you diverted his attention, various things changed, and he had no further time for the ladies Aswydd, but not *in* time, since by then the deed was very clearly done." Emuin picked up one of the scattered charts and cast it heavily onto the table. "Does that Unfold to you?"

Tristen turned it, looked at it, and turned it again in hope it would make some sort of sense. It might have been upside down or sideways for what he made of the scratchings and circles and numbers and intersecting lines. "No, sir. It doesn't."

"Likely because it's wizardry, and not magic. The Sihhë-lords never needed such meticulous proceedings."

"It's to do with the stars and the moon, I see that much. Has it to do with the Great Year?" That was just past, and it had long occupied Emuin's attention in the heavens.

"It's to do with calamity," Emuin said. "Mind, no such chart is infallible. It marks opportunities, moments of vulnerability, moments of power, and, the Nineteen witness! the Sihhë can create their own moments outside of wizardry and throw all our meticulous plans and times askew—gods, but you can, young lord! But I suspect even you find magic easier at certain times and in certain places—or that what you loose flows more readily in certain directions than in others: the river finds the lowest, easiest course, does it not?"

He understood how it explained the twisted course certain of his wishes took, or why he saw some things as easy and direct and some things not.

But he was not diverted by any sleight of hand, not now. His thoughts ceased to skip and turn, and went straight to a single question. He did not even ask it aloud. He *wished* an answer, and Emuin's chin went up, and he frowned, opposing Emuin's will.

"Forgive me," Tristen said. "I wish to know, and not to oppose you . . . not at all to oppose you. I know how hard you've tried to keep all your plans in shape around me, no matter how often I cast them all down. But now I want the truth, master Emuin, with all good will. Inform me, and perhaps you'll have less patching to do. I *might* agree."

Emuin let out a slow breath. "Cefwyn proposes to set out this spring against Tasmôrden. Before the trees break their buds, there is an hour, a day, on which what Men call luck will more than ebb: it will turn utterly against him. That is written in the events he himself set in motion, and written in the stars."

"Then I should be with him!" Tristen said.

"Or—perhaps you shouldn't. Perhaps you can do more from a distance, where you have a better view of what's happening, and where you can lay hands on the very things that threaten him. Possibly you're doing exactly what you should do. Before the trees break their buds, too, that child will be born, here, in Amefel."

He had thought only of weapons. What Emuin said appalled him. "The child."

"Here, I say, the child will be born."

"And I brought her here!"

"Perhaps it was the best of intentions. She's not in a worse place. Parsynan isn't in charge here, Cuthan's not here to help Orien, and Tasmôrden's men aren't pouring across the border to raise the whole province in rebellion. All the things you've done have put her in your hands, not the other way about. I don't say this child's the only danger. What Cefwyn may do when once he hears the news: that is a danger. What Her Grace may do is likewise a danger, and what her people may do is a danger, all approaching that moment Cefwyn's luck—luck! so men call it, and nothing further from the truth—his luck will turn. The flow will all go against him, for a certain number of hours. I confess that all along, I've thought constantly of the battle with Tasmôrden, and that manner of threat. But again, the river may have taken the easiest course. It was natural these women come to their home, to their people. They say the nuns didn't know. And there's a fifth possible agent of the situation at Anwyfar . . . *you*, young lord."

"I would never wish what happened!"

"But you know that you have effect."

"I know that I do, sir."

"We aren't masters of *how* a thing happens. So likewise we must be careful how our letters will inform Cefwyn *and* Her Grace, and do it well. You're quite right to come to me. You're quite right to approach this with caution."

"You know how to tell him. You see the danger. Twice over, it should be you that writes that letter."

Emuin's brows lowered. "Oh, I know these things, I know them too well. Mauryl called on *me* to kill a young prince in his sleep. And I did, young lord, and have bad dreams all my life. Now I see that dream one more time."

"Hasufin Heltain." Tristen drew a great breath, knowing well how their enemy—Mauryl's enemy—had entered a dead babe in Althalen, King Elfwyn's son . . . and nothing might have prevented him, except he had grown too sure of himself, too early . . . a boy's faults of haste, betraying a very, very dangerous spirit to the only wizard capable of dealing with him . . . of killing him, before his adulthood.

"He's dead," Emuin said. "But he was *dead* before he fought you at Lewenbrook. That's only mild inconvenience to him. A woman dabbles in sorcery, far past her knowledge. A foolish woman lets down the wards, in all senses, and bargains for power . . . and what better chance has a wandering spirit? You caught Orien at her sorcery once. We don't know how often and to what ends she opened that window in your apartments. We know Hasufin used Aséyneddin on the battlefield, but that was the right hand of his effort, and it fell too quickly, far too quickly. I suspect this babe for the left, his second and surer gateway, one he already knew he had, and which he didn't risk at Lewenbrook. That babe is half-Aswydd and half-Marhanen . . . wizard-gift matched with all the Marhanen faults—and strengths."

"I hear the child in the gray space. Surely you do."

"I hear him. A son, I do agree with all you said, below in the hall, though I'm a little less reckless in inquiring."

"There seems no harm in him."

"Oh, indeed there isn't. Right now he's Tarien's child . . . an innocent. What better way to breach our defenses? What better way to gain entry to this warded fortress? What better way to defend himself, than by our virtue, and our scruples, and our reluctance to do harm to innocence? If we harm him . . . we damn the virtue that's in us, and we turn ourselves down a bloody dark path. If we kill this child.—*Hush,* boy!" It was Paisi he meant, for a startled shiver had leapt into the gray space, and Emuin whirled about and seized Paisi by the shoulder.

"We ain't to kill it!" Paisi cried, wincing from Emuin's grip, and the danger of flying into the gray space with Orien and Tarien only a few stone barriers away from them brought Tristen's sharp *no!* and with it he imposed a hush so deep Paisi struggled for his next breath, mouth open, eyes wide.

"Be calm," Tristen said, and made his wish gentler, so the boy could get his wind. "Be calm. You mustn't go *there* with what we say here. Be very quiet. Listen to what Emuin's saying to us. Listen. Understand him."

"I brung Gran Sedlyn up th' hill, an' she had a look at the lady, an' she says it's an Aswydd babby an' a wizard. But she ain't sayin' it's evil!"

"Gran Sedlyn is the midwife," Emuin reminded him. "And canny as they come. No, boy—" This, to Paisi, whose eyes were round as moons. "—we haven't any ill intent: that's the point. Wizardry. *Wizardry,* lad, is a matter of seasons and timing, and this . . . this one event is set. That child will be born in his time, and as much as Gran Sedlyn can assure it, it will be the child's time, not Tarien

Aswydd's wishing. It won't please her, but it pleases me, and it gives the child his best chance."

Tristen had misgivings of his own, but none that he chose to discuss in Paisi's hearing. He laid his hand on Paisi's other shoulder, wishing him calm and steady and confident. "Trust Emuin," he said to Paisi. "And don't talk about this. Don't think it in the gray space where the Aswydds might hear you."

"Oh, gods," Paisi said, and his eyes rolled toward the west wing, where the women were.

"Do you understand your lord?" Emuin said sternly, drawing his attention back. "Look at me, boy! Think of filching apples."

"Apples, sir?"

"I'm sure you've stolen apples in the market. In fact I know you have."

"Aye, master."

"And didn't get caught."

"No, master."

"Why weren't you caught?"

"I was careful."

"And slipped in very quietly and didn't disturb anyone. Is that it?"

"Wi' my hands," Paisi said, making a flourish of his fingers, and a twist of the wrist that tucked an imaginary apple up his sleeve.

"Clever lad. Well, now you're the merchant, and you don't want some clever lad making off with any apples. So what do you do?"

"I watch wi'out seemin' to watch. Old Esen down in market, 'e's a canny 'un. He always looks as if 'e's watchin' somethin' else, an' 'e'll nab ye quick as ye can say—"

"*So can Orien Aswydd.* Do you understand me?"

Paisi's head bobbed slowly. "Aye, master, that I do."

"Think as if you were going to steal something from her apartment."

"Oh, no, sir, I ain't."

"As if you were, wretched boy. As if! Pretend that's what you're about, and go very, very quietly, because she's the merchant and you're the thief, and she's very, very dangerous."

"Aye, sir. Aye master. *Yes,* m'lor'." This, with a bob of his head first to Emuin, then to Tristen. "M'lord."

"He's learning," Emuin said. "The fair mother tongue suffers less every day, and he's learned to wash his hands *and* the vessels, and not in the same water." Emuin reached out a hand and tousled Paisi's unruly hair. "I kept you here to hear this, boy, because I'll not have you overhearing half we say and then wondering about it or peeking and prying about the gray space, which, gods know, is the worst thing you could do. Salubrious fear. Do you know the word salubrious?"

"No, master Emuin."

"It means healthful. *Good* for you. Trust that now you know everything there is to know, or at least as much as your lord and your master together know, and don't try to find out anything *except* from me: it wouldn't at all be helpful or *salubrious* for you to pry into Lady Orien's affairs. So don't!"

"Not salubrious, sir. I understand."

"Good!" Emuin said, and to Tristen: "I'll write to Cefwyn, and you write whatever you find to write. The sooner Cefwyn knows, the safer for us all."

The Aswydd ladies walked to Henas'amef for safety, Tristen wrote, with the brazen dragons looming over his desk and Aswydd green draperies open on a blood red sky. *Men attacked the convent at Anwyfar. Lady Tarien is with child, a boy, and yours, which I do not know otherwise how to inform you, except that Emuin and I are taking care here and you should also take care.*

With the help of all the southern lords and the earls of Amefel I hope soon to release the Dragon Guard from their watch at the river. I hope also to be sending the Guelens as soon as the weather permits. I know I have many of your best men. You can trust the officers Uwen put over the Guelens, but not the ones I sent away. I hope you will not restore them to their office. Orien says it was Essan who attacked the nuns at Anwyfar, and I think she is telling the truth in that.

I hope that you are well. All the lords with me wish you well. So does Uwen. Master Emuin is writing his own letter to go with this one. Be careful for your safety. We are doing everything we can here to carry out your orders, which I have never forgotten.

He put the pen in its holder, out of words, at least of those he would write. He heated wax and made the seal.

But on an impulse of the heart he took a fresh sheet of paper and wrote: *To Her Grace of Elwynor, a wish.* And he wrote it only with his finger, with no ink, but in the manner of a ward, and sealed it with his seal and with a ward. He had no idea whether a wizard could receive it, but he thought one could. Most particularly he thought Ninévrisë might have gift enough, and that no one handling it would understand the message: *Cefwyn is in danger. Here is refuge if you need it.*

CHAPTER 5

Snow, and snow: that was the view from the windows of Tristen's apartment, as persistently depressing a sight every morning as the Aswydds' brazen dragons and green draperies within . . . not that he failed to see the beauty in it, piled high and white across the land; yet with all the monotony of it, the beauty of the ice had never palled. He wondered at the new traceries of frost on the windows every morning, meticulous and fine as the work of some fine expert craftsman. The sun in the afternoon melted it, and a miracle renewed it in the morning: he was sorry when he fed his pigeons that their flapping and fluttering at the window spoiled the patterns on the little side pane, where he put out the bread.

Yet every morning it was new, and every morning there was a little more snow sifting down from the heavens, after a fall at night. The sight of it all still seemed marvelous to him, this changing of the seasons and the confidence of ordinary Men that they would see the land change back to what it had been before. This was the last of seasons that he had not seen in his life and between concerns, he enjoyed it absolutely for what it was, wondering what every day would show him, expecting new patterns in the frost.

But nothing about the weather had changed in a number of days now, and the skies that had once appeared to obey his lightest wish now seemed obstinate and ominous in their resistence. The storms that came at night grew worse with every effort he made to change the weather.

And it was now three days since Crissand, among other lords, had left him—certain lords to their holdings, all without a by your leave, m'lord—but Crissand *not* to his own land and with no more request than the others.

Crissand's absence, which had been a niggling concern the first day, had become a worry in the two days since, and last night the silence from that quarter had urged him to venture the gray space in earnest—to no avail.

Now, with the weather resisting him, with the sky dawned gray again, the doubts that had begun to assail him niggled away at his confidence in all else that he knew as certainties.

He regretted his folly in seeking after Crissand, telling himself that when Crissand would, Crissand would hear him—and this morning, in this pearl-colored morning like the last three, he could only remind himself how much harm he could do if he reached out recklessly and drew sorcerous attention to Crissand when he was near the enemy's territory.

In his venture last night he had learned only that Crissand was asleep somewhere . . . and what else did he hope for, at night, and in a snowstorm that sent down thick, fat lumps of snow, that obliterated tracks and buried fences?.

He had slept very little after that. Sleep had eluded him—so, too, had the dreams that sometimes sent him winging over the land on Owl's wings, dreams that might have found Crissand, dreams that might have discovered whether Crissand was snugged down warm and well fed at Modeyneth or fallen in some ditch along the way— whether the lack of urgent danger he had felt in that sleep was the safety of a friendly roof and hearth, or the peace of a mind too frozen and faded to worry.

Too, the gray space was not the place of light and cloud it had been, but a place as leaden and violent as the heavens. It was as if he fought the weather in that realm, too, and could make no headway in it with Orien and her sister close at hand.

Whether Orien knew he tried to find someone close to him, she never confronted him there. Whether Crissand might be attempting to reach him through it—he never heard. And now, as of yesterday, so Uwen said, Crissand's men had set out down the north road looking for him, to ride as far as Modeyneth or the river if they must. And he took that for his comfort this morning: if Crissand were in danger, injured on the road, they would find him.

And if it was otherwise . . . he could only think that it was no accident that Crissand had gone into the land of Bryn, and down the track that Cuthan Lord of Bryn had taken in his exile.

But toward the holding of the new lord of Bryn, too—equally

troublesome. Crissand was a young man of high passions and sudden impulse—agreeable to young Drusenan's appointment to the honor, but the feuds and contentions of the lords in this ancient province had cropped up in unexpected ways before now. Tristen thought there was no resentment there and no possibility of a feud, but he was not utterly certain.

And the snow sifted down and the worry of it gnawed at his peace. He wished better weather to speed Crissand home, and wished it to ease the suffering of townsfolk and shepherds, those whom Crissand had *not* ridden out to visit, in the village of Levey, among others; and farmers across the land, and craftsmen and householders, and the humblest ragpicker in the town, for they all were his responsibility, hapless folk who had done nothing to involve themselves in the quarrels of wizards and kings.

Last night Lusin had reported a roof in the town market had given way, and a man's goods were all damaged: today the man had sent begging intercession with his creditors, for nothing had gone well for him, even before his roof came crashing down. Tristen wished it might go better for him, but he feared even to wish for that, his wishes for weather having gone so far opposite to his intention. He stood at his window looking out over the snowy, weight-laden roofs, the ledges, sparsely tracked by wandering pigeons near at hand, and asked himself had he harmed all those he wished to benefit.

He knew that down in the stable yard Master Haman's boys clambered up to the shed roofs twice a day to shovel them clear for fear of their collapsing. He knew that Haman himself must go out to the meadows where the horses of the assembled army were sheltered, to be sure of the older boys and men who cared for those more remote sites—stablehands whose plight was perhaps worst of all the hardships the army suffered in its winter camp at Henas'amef. Out there it was a lonely and cold duty of breaking ice for the horses to drink, hauling hay from the stacks, and generally keeping their charges from suffering in the cold, while at night their small hearths and their small shelters were beacons to vermin and true shadows that prowled the night.

The soldiers had the cold to fight—beyond the walls, and under canvas, the muster of Amefel, of Ivanor, Imor, and a handful of rangers from Lanfarnesse had all come here in better weather, which his wishes had maintained. But now they suffered from the cold, and endured misery of frozen ground.

He could at least relieve the soldiers of some of their hardship:

at his own charge, the taverns near the gates had set up kettles in their kitchens, for hot suppers. It incidentally used less wood, which cost heavy, snowy labor to get more of. But prodigious quantities of wood fed the camps' other needs: warmth, and the laundry kettles. Reasonable cleanliness for so many men required another small camp of attendants, where kettles sent up steam that froze on any nearby surface—a man needed not bathe all winter, one of the Lanfarnesse-men was heard to remark, only stand downwind of the washing kettles, and be drenched to the skin. And in that vicinity the laun-drymen battled ice: clothes and blankets froze rather than dried, and had to be hung in the smoke downwind to dry at all—so that anyone with a nose could tell which men had come from the camps: the men, the tents, and their blankets smelled of woodsmoke: so did the lords who lived with their men.

Yet—one of the day's good reports—the men were in good spir-its, by reason of the abundance of food and the moderate but cheer-ful quantity of ale: the men needed not stay on hard watch, so Uwen said, and they might have the ale to keep them happy. And the ground being frozen so hard at least meant that mud, that bane of soldiers, was all but absent from clothes and tents—except the mud-holes around the laundry, in which pigs might be content.

They managed, with this continued assault of winter on the army he had gathered. But he could not improve it. And this was yet another iron gray day, with snow veiling all but the nearest towers. Neither he nor Emuin nor both of them together with all the grand-mothers in the lower town had been able to change it . . . and, what was far worse for wizardry, he was beginning to doubt he could. He longed to stretch out, search the gray space, *meet* his enemy if he could find one . . .

But, oh, there was risk in that, mortal risk to all who depended on him. There were so many things at hazard, so many lives, so many things he did not yet understand. If someone had the better of him in the matter of the weather, it was because that wizard had the better of him in other ways, and knew things he did not, and outmaneuvered him with sheer knowledge and experience—as Emuin had done, while Emuin sufficed.

This . . . this opposition . . . was stronger than Emuin.

It was stronger than Mauryl—at least that it had caught Mauryl at his weakest.

But had not Mauryl had to go to the north and bring down the Sihhë-lords to have a chance at subduing it?

And had not the Sihhë-lords failed, ultimately, to contain it?

He hesitated to say that evil was out at the back of this storm. He had read about evil in Efanor's little book, and how it permeated the doings of Men, but he had never found such doings evil, rather good and bad . . . but none without self-interest, none he could not understand even in terms of his own will to have his way. Misguided and foolish governed most actions he had met: spiteful and selfish. These were bad traits; but none quite descended to that worst word in Efanor's book.

Was selfish enough to say for the creature that had stolen one child's life and that might have caused this one to exist?

Was foolish enough to say for the creature who had overthrown all the good that was Mauryl—all the kindness, all the wit, all the learning, all the skill—was foolish and spiteful and selfish enough to compass Mauryl's enemy?

And was selfish enough to describe the desire that had wrecked Elwynor and slaughtered the innocent and driven hapless peasants into the snow?

It might be. Wicked might describe his enemy. But had he not killed? Had he not driven Parsynan out onto the road, and Cuthan across the river? And did not the soldiers who fell to him have kindness of their own, and wit, and learning, and skill?

The sword had found its place to stand in this fortress, too. It lurked by hearthsides, the alternative to peace and reason.

Truth it said on one side. *Illusion* was engraved on the other, and the Edge was the answer to the riddle it posed. It was the answer to the riddle *he* posed. It answered all he was, and there was no word for him but the Edge of that riddle.

Perhaps there was such a word for his enemy, neither evil, nor wicked, nor even selfish, but some edge between absolutes. Perhaps that was why wizards could not compass it.

Not even Hasufin Heltain had compassed it . . . only listened to its whispers and its unreasoning reason. What would a man *need* with the whole world? What would a Man need with absolute power?

If he could understand that, he thought he might understand his enemy, and how Hasufin had fallen to him.

"M'lord." Tassand was brisk and cheerful, arriving in the room, disturbing his thoughts as freely as if something good had happened. "M'lord! Lord Crissand's back. He's here."

"*Is* he?" Tristen reached on the instant for the gray space and restrained himself from that folly. "Where is he?"

But in that moment Crissand answered his question by appearing behind Tassand in the short foyer. Dark-haired Amefin, and dour as the Amefin could be, Crissand was all fair skies and brave ventures on most days . . . but now he was muddy, travel-worn, and exhausted.

"My lord," Crissand said in a thread of a voice.

"Sit down," Tristen urged him, and scurrying about at the back of his mind was the realization that Crissand was never yet a presence in the gray space: he simply could not find him; and had not found him, even with him here, in the same room. *That* alarmed him. "Tassand, hot tea and bricks."

Crissand had surely come straight up from his arrival, coming to him still in mud-flecked boots, lacking a cloak which might have been sorrier than the boots, and all but out of strength.

"Forgive me. Forgive me, my lord. I knew before I was the first night on the road that I was doing something foolish."

"Where *were* you?" Crissand was a candleflame of a wizard as yet, and he had known and master Emuin had known where Crissand was . . . but not precisely *where* he was.

But still not to know *where* he was when he was in the same room with him: that was the inconceivable thing.

He searched with great care, investigated more and more of the gray space in concern for Crissand's welfare, and at last found a very quiet, very small presence, all wrapped in on itself, all knotted up and resisting.

In that condition, Crissand had ridden home again, through this weather.

"I thought it better for Amefel," Crissand said in the voice he had left, "if I went to Lord Drusenan and spoke to him directly."

It was a minuscule part of the reason Crissand had gone and a minuscule part of what must have sent him back in such a state, but at least it was a start on the rest of the tale, and now that he was safe and here, Tristen was willing to use infinite patience. He sat down opposite Crissand beside the warm fire, waiting for the part that might explain why Crissand had left on such a journey on the night his remote cousins—and Drusenan's—had suddenly turned up destitute, escaped from Guelen vengeance, one of them with child . . . and both of them breaking the terms of their exile.

He understood entirely what Crissand had likely wanted to do, which was to set distance between himself and Orien Aswydd. He even understood why Crissand had gone to speak to the new Lord Bryn, successor to the man who had done so much harm to Crissand's father and his people. But the silence in the gray space even now kept Crissand at distance from him, and he waited to hear those reasons from Crissand's own lips.

And waited, and waited. The silence went on between them what seemed an eternity; so he ventured his own opening.

"So did you make peace with Drusenan?" Tristen asked.

"With a will." Crissand seemed relieved to be asked that question and not others: his whole body relaxed toward his habitual easy grace . . . but that motion ended in a wince, an injury he had not made otherwise evident. "He was as glad as I was, to settle all grudges. He wasn't glad to hear the news about Lady Orien and her sister being here. He's not her man. We agreed together, that our quarrel is all with Cuthan, across the river, and I know now in my own heart and for certain he's not Cuthan's man, nor ever was or will be. He received me very graciously, he and his lady."

Crissand finished. The silence resumed.

Then with a deep breath, Crissand added, "My lord, my patient, good lord, I should have asked leave, considering the state of things. Other men come and go. But you've given me duties; I thought I was seeing to those duties—I persuaded myself I was doing that— but before I was halfway to Modeyneth I knew I was a fool."

"I would have granted leave for you to go anywhere. But you left without your guard, and without my hearing you. You were a night on the road before I knew you were gone," Tristen said, "and then I dared not call you too loudly, not with the Aswydds so close. If *they* urged you to do such a thing, they were very quiet about it."

"I'd do nothing they asked!"

"If you knew they asked it."

Crissand was silent, and troubled of countenance, thinking on that, and at no time had he unfurled from the tight, small presence he was.

"I searched for you," Tristen said.

"I didn't hear you, my lord. Unless you were telling me I was a fool—I knew before the night was half-done that that was the truth. I came the rest of the way to my senses when the sun came up and I was trying to find the road in the snowfall. But by then I realized Modeyneth was hardly over the next hill, and my poor horse couldn't have carried me back without foundering. So I went ahead, hoping to borrow a horse, and I presented myself to Lord Drusenan. I wanted to bring you *some* profit for my foolishness."

"I needed no gifts," Tristen said. "I need nothing but your loy-alty—and your safety."

It was not his intent to cause pain, only to urge caution, but

Crissand's color rose and he looked away, surely knowing how he had risked all that they hoped to accomplish.

But it was not just foolishness, and that he had somehow to make Crissand understand . . . and that he could not avow a clear reason for his actions made a frighteningly clear sense, for Crissand had ridden out in the very hour the Aswydd sisters had ridden into Henas'amef, and while on the one hand he did not know what exact thought had seized Crissand to send him out, he was as sure now as he was sure of the next sunrise that Crissand's actions had directly to do with the sisters' arrival, and all of it directly to do with the currents in the magical wind—for Crissand was Aswydd.

And Crissand being Aswydd, head of that lineage in Henas'amef until Orien set foot in the town, he had a strong sense for those currents in the wind. He might have left under direct urging of his own wizard-gift, protecting him or leading him astray . . . completely without understanding it, completely without directing it.

It was no straight course—the last lord of Bryn, Earl Cuthan, who had betrayed Crissand's father, was Orien Aswydd's man, exiled now and the lands gone to Lord Drusenan, but Cuthan was in Elwynor—in *Elwynor,* where their enemy sat.

And with Orien back under the roof where she had been duchess of Amefel, small wonder if that presence stirred the winds of the gray space, and small wonder a man with the gift had done reckless acts, not knowing why they did them. That Crissand had rushed in some direction was entirely understandable.

But that it was toward Bryn, and toward Elwynor, and that, in the gray space, Crissand remained that tight, unassailable ball . . . that alarmed him.

To their mutual relief, Tassand brought the tea, and made some little ado over it. One of the servants pulled a heated brick from the hearth, and Crissand set one booted, sodden foot on it and tucked the other against it for the warmth.

"You might do with dry boots," Tristen said. "You've not yet been home?"

"I met with my guard on the road. They know; they've passed the word to my household. But no, I came straight here."

"Tassand, send a page for another pair of His Grace's boots. And tell his servants make his bed ready."

"Yes, m'lord." Tassand was off, at a good clip.

"So tell me what you did," Tristen said then, and bent another small thought into the gray space. Still it told him nothing. But his eyes had seen. "You're hurt."

"Nothing mortal."

"A fall?"

"Elwynim. I—" Crissand took a sip of the tea and his hands shook. "I should set it out in order."

"Do," Tristen urged him..

"I left without a word to my guard—just rode away from the camp in the night. And I rode, as I've told you—I reached Modeyneth . . . I think sometime after midday, by the time I dealt with the drifts. I took a light meal. I met with Lord Drusenan—that was a long matter; but he was gracious—more than gracious. I slept only a few hours, then left my horse there and took another, by his good will, his best and favorite . . . I owe him the worth of that beast. And I was coming home, as soon as I could, my lord. I took your warning about venturing into the wizard-place, and I feared to try to reach you there, but I knew I'd been a fool, and I feared that concern for a fool might divert you from far more important matters. I'm sorry, my lord. I can't express how I regret it."

Tristen reached again for that knotted presence, touched it briefly, felt it contract, flinching from that contact. "But the wound," he said. "The Elwynim."

"The roads are drifted worse to the north than here. And in the blowing snow and the evening light, I saw riders. I thought at first they were yours, or maybe my own, as did happen, but later than this. When I saw these men . . . they weren't coming on the road at all, and I knew all the border was at risk, so I held back, and saw them go toward the open land and toward Althalen, where Lord Drusenan told me Aeself has his men under arms day and night— Drusenan says—says the same way Aeself and his men crossed without the garrison seeing, over to the rough hills to the north and east, other men come that way, intent on spying out whatever they can see, just looking about and hoping to find a weakness. So I knew this. I hid. I could see them very clearly, just at the edge of night as it was . . ."

"And they were Elwynim?"

"No doubt," Crissand said. "They came across my tracks in the snow. I saw them look around. I had to judge whether to run back for Drusenan's holding or ahead to home, and I ran for home, because I didn't know but that more had come in behind me. I took one arrow, shallow, no great injury; Drusenan's horse will carry a scar worse than that, and still carried me, brave fellow that he is. The snow was coming down again, and with the dark and the trees, they seemed to lose me, by then, I had to wait a time, for the horse's sake, and then I waited a little longer to be sure I didn't run back into them by mistake, because by then I wasn't completely sure where I was. I moved a very little, until dawn, in what I thought was the right direction, but without the stars and with the snow coming down I couldn't tell what was the right way even after I came on the road again. But when the sun came up I had my bearings again and I'd chosen right. Then I met up with my guard, who was out searching for me. And we talked about going back to catch the band that shot at me. But my captain persuaded me we might risk telling them more than we might learn if we lost a man."

"You were right to retreat."

Crissand ducked his head and sipped his tea, two-handed, exhausted, and still withdrawn from him.

"So I came home. My guard at least had the foresight to bring provisions, and I think the horse will be as good as he was; but I never thought to use him so, or to stir up so much trouble. Now the Elwynim know they're seen. I might have managed far more cleverly than that . . ."

"Yet we do know they're inquiring of the state of affairs here for themselves, which may mean that they're not hearing all they'd wish from the villagers. That's good news."

"Yet I am ashamed of what I did."

"Why did you do it? Because I took in Lady Orien? Was that it?"

He asked, no longer believing that that was the answer, but it was a place to start. The answer was not immediate, and Crissand did not immediately meet his eyes, but took another sip, and gazed across the ornate chamber, with its green velvet draperies and brazen dragons.

"My father died in this room, my lord, of Orien Aswydd's poison. It appears I have the wizard-gift, and if that's what sends me dreams, my lord, I could wish it *gone,* but while I have it—while I have it, I beg my lord not to trust that woman."

"It takes no wizard-gift to see harm in Orien Aswydd. I assure you I do."

"I was halfway to Modeyneth before I knew the thing I feared most was not her under this roof, but my lord in these rooms within her reach. And then I wished twice over that I were back here."

Never had he doubted Crissand's heart in his disappearance—but in his silence he found very much to concern him. In very truth, as he had told Crissand himself when *he* had been the one riding off northward and Crissand had protested it, wizard-gift never left them out of reach of one another . . . or it should not have.

Yet Crissand had crept up on him, even in the hall a few moments ago, following Tassand in. He had grown accustomed to knowing just who moved where in the Zeide, and few could surprise him . . . except Emuin.

Except, just now, Crissand, who huddled in the corners of the gray space, seeking utter anonymity, even from him: Crissand, who had found in the gray space that which he could not face.

But he hushed all use of the gift, himself, for he began to suspect what was at least the source of Crissand's fear—for as Crissand had been deaf to his gift before he came, now he increasingly did hear; and now came two women, his enemies, with wizard-gift and hostility toward him. Nothing was coincidence in wizardry. Wizardry thrived on accidents and moments of panic fear or happy recklessness.

And something had found a gap in their defenses, and in his, and in Crissand's.

"When the gift begins to Unfold," he said gently to Crissand, "it's hard to find one's balance. It was dangerous for you to ride out. But it was dangerous for you to stay here with the gift Unfolding and Unfolding with no end to it. There was a time I took Petelly and did something very like."

Crissand looked at him, questioning that, hoping for respect, perhaps.

"Too," Tristen said, "you were amazingly quiet. Master Emuin is no quieter. I never heard you, and I hear most things."

"I don't know about that," Crissand said. "But I took care you didn't hear, my lord. I stole away like a thief in the night and without a word, and I take no honor from that."

"Yet it's a skill."

"None I can claim for an honor, my lord. And if things were going wrong, I failed to ask those who might know." Crissand held the teacup still in both hands, his fingers white on its curve. "I feared being here, I feared going, and I was on the road before I thought my way through it. Then I could have come back, but I hadn't a thought in my head until morning. I don't to this hour know why I went in the first place."

"I do," Tristen said quietly. "That's the simplest thing of all to answer."

"My lord?"

"Danger entered the house—and having the gift, you moved. The gift moves you. It's wizardry. That's what it *is*."

"To be on the road to Bryn before I had my wits clear? To be such a fool? Is that wizardry?"

"Yes."

"Master Emuin didn't take horse in the middle of the night."

"He might have, once, when he was new to it. I've been such a fool," Tristen said, "very often, in the beginning. At times I found myself in very unlikely places . . . the guardhouse at the stable-court gate, for one: Her Grace's camp for another, and in the next moment surrounded by her soldiers, which led me to think I'd been a very great fool. Things Unfold. Wizardry moved you, beyond your thinking about it. My wish brought you back, perhaps, and not against your will, but perhaps faster than you needed come. Perhaps it governed your choice which way to ride and when to leave. I wished you safe at the same time I wished you back, and then I feared— too late—that my very wish might put you in danger. You see? You aren't the only fool. I regret Lord Drusenan's horse. I wish the horse well, with all my might."

"Thank you for that, my lord. I'll return him with one of my father's best mares, and my utmost gratitude; but if you have a hand in it, then he'll mend better than he was foaled."

"I hope that's so," he said. "I hope the arrow troubles you little. I wish you might let Emuin see it."

"It's nothing," Crissand said, and flushed, even while he put a hand to the wound. "It's nothing at all."

Yet the fear persisted, the retreat within the gray space. Nothing they had said had drawn Crissand out of it.

"Yet it is something," Tristen said. "It's a warning. But don't think it was all Orien's doing. Wizardry isn't anyone's. It's patterns. There and here are the same thing. Now and then are the same thing—left and right to the same design."

"I don't understand."

"Why did you go to Drusenan?"

Crissand blinked.

"Why to Drusenan," Tristen asked, "and not to, say, Levey, or somewhere within your own lands?"

Crissand shook his head slowly. "It seemed that was where I had to go."

"So we look instead for those who might have sent you there," Tristen said. "Emuin might have had something to do with your going there. I might. For that matter, Paisi has the gift, and Cevulirn. Even Drusenan himself does, though very little; and certainly Lady Orien and Lady Tarien have gift enough, but I doubt Drusenan was in their thoughts at all. You didn't fall in a ditch in the drifts and you escaped alive, and you come back with news about Tasmôrden's movements, which is something we all desire. So however it was— it wasn't that bad a venture."

A wry smile touched Crissand's mouth, and that knot in the gray eased the slightest hint. "As always, my lord sees the pure snow, not the mire."

"I see the mud, too. But it's the snow that's marvelous. Isn't it? I see the mud, and the ill my wishes can cause; but I wish better than that.—Yet leave wishing to me. I ask you believe me in this, and think about it at your leisure: what brought me to Henas'amef isn't a little pattern, and that means a great many men move to it. All the lords camped outside the walls, and Lady Orien in her nunnery before it burned, and Cuthan and all the rest . . . Everything. Everything is in the pattern around *me,* for good for ill, help or harm. My coming here—harmed your household. It was nothing I wished. But it happened."

"Even my father dying?"

It was a thought on which he had spent no little pain, and no little doubt.

"It might have been . . . because *you* have to be where you are. It's nothing I willed or intended. It's nothing you willed. That's the point. Orien wanted to be here, I very much believe it. Cuthan wished harm; both of them have the gift. Most of all Mauryl Gestaurien did, and he set me on the Road I followed. The pattern sent me here. Do you see? I wished nothing but my safety and Cefwyn's friendship. Nothing was intended. But your father was in the pattern, and when it moved . . . he drank from Lady Orien's cup. There's danger in my company. There's *danger* in my wishes. And because you stand near me—with the gift—there's danger in what you do, and danger in what you wish."

Crissand left his seat as if the vicinity had grown too close, action preferable to the pain his wound cost him. Or perhaps it was the distraction of the pain he sought.

"Parsynan killing my men and my cousins, and Orien's cup poisoning my father . . . and Cuthan betraying him . . . these were all foredoomed?"

"No. Nothing was foredoomed. But we two have to be here, as we are right now, in this room." It was a terrible truth that he had to tell, but he trusted Crissand to withstand it, as he trusted only his closest and dearest friends. "Emuin says that what I will and will not is dangerous. It took me a long while to understand that, but I do. He's very much afraid of me, and he ought to be. He tells me very little, I suspect so I won't make up my mind too early. He says I don't have wizard-gift, but magic. And that means I don't depend on times and seasons: I can wish at any time, for anything. And that's terrible. That is *terrible,* do you see? No seasons govern me. No *times* limit me. I learn wizardry not because I have those limits, but because I want to learn what those limits are—of my friends, and of my enemies. You are the Aswydd, and you will be the Aswydd, no matter Lady Orien's demands. Auld Syes said it; and you *are* my ally."

"Beyond a doubt in that, my lord."

"Yet everyone I love, everyone who loves me, is in danger . . . from my wishes, my mistakes, my idlest thoughts . . . and most of all, in danger from my enemies, especially when they venture outside the bounds. Tasmôrden has the gift. If he can't strike me, the wizard-gift that helps him will try to harm something dear to me. I can protect only what's close to me. Like warding a window. Like making the Lines on the earth. Inside is safe. Outside is dangerous.— Don't leave me again."

In the world of Men the things he tried to explain were all but inexplicable, difficult even for a man with his wits about him. Crissand trembled with exhaustion, and his fear of the gray space and what was Unfolding within him even now kept him balled and silent there. . . small wonder he had a distracted look, and seemed lost.

Tristen reached to the tea tray and moved one cup, which nudged the pot, the other cups, and the spirit bottle.

"Move this, it moves that. That's wizardry. It's that simple."

"It's mad!" Crissand protested. "How do you know what moves the right thing? How does anyone deal with it?"

"I left on such a ride as yours," Tristen said, "and came back with Ninévrisë. I didn't know she was there. But *someone* had to bring her to Cefwyn. I was able to, and I was there. But she would have come, by one way or another. When things need to happen, they happen."

"Yet you say it's not foredoomed."

"It's not. She would have come not because it was foredoomed, but because wizards wished her to be with Cefwyn. Even I, perhaps, since I wished Cefwyn well, and certainly he's happiest with Ninévrisë. The wishes of all those with the gift wishing at once shape patterns, and within those patterns we can move. Within the design, we can choose what we do, and by our choices, shift the pattern that is and change the choices of what can be." So he hoped, who

97

had met himself in Marna Wood, and again at Ynefel, or at least had come fearfully close to it: how mutable time-to-come might be was of vital interest to him. "Only, being Sihhë, as Emuin supposes, it seems I can go counter to that pattern and throw it all into confusion again. I can change what wizards have set and I can do it even contrary to the pattern of the world itself. That's magic, as best I understand it. Magic, as opposed to wizardry. And I think that frightens wizards most of all. Ask Emuin. He explained these things to me. I learn wizardry, because it shows me how to work within the patterns Emuin sees, and not overthrow things. It's hard to be patient. But it's safest for everyone."

"I don't understand," Crissand said earnestly. "But I do hear, my lord, with all my heart, and I do know I do my lord no service by acting the fool—least of all by flinging myself into Tasmôrden's hands. But—"

"But?"

"I thought I was right!"

"Within the pattern, you were."

"But how—if these fits come on blindly . . . how can I know what's truly right? How can I say no to them?"

It was a question, one he had had to answer for himself, by having Emuin in his tower, and always within reach.

"Come to me. Not to Uwen, not to Tassand, no messages by way of Lusin. Come to me and tell me what you feel in the least moved to do, at whatever hour. That's the only way."

He had flaws of his own, he knew: latest of them, he had brought the Aswyddim into Henas'amef, endangering people who loved and trusted him, and never consulted Emuin. It was much the same as Crissand's riding off to the river. He found no difference, at least.

But Crissand was too weary to reason further. The ball that he had made of himself stayed tightly furled. There was only hope he would remember it.

"Go home," Tristen said, "sleep. Come back. *I need you.*"

It echoed through the gray space, that truth that overrode all others. In the Pattern magic made, Crissand's presence was no matter of chance: it was a necessity to him, and Crissand did not remotely comprehend his danger.

—*Crissand! he said, and startled that knot into unfurling, at least a little. Crissand! he said again, and this time the knot came undone.*

—*My lord! Crissand said, and faced him uncertainly. But the gray winds blew and blew, and that grayness about him whitened to pearl, if not to the sun of his presence before.*

—Wake! Tristen said, *and the light shone through, and Crissand shone in the gray space, clear and pale as the morning sun. There you are, Tristen said then. There you are. Look at me. Keep looking at me, he said as Crissand began to cast a look over his shoulder. Here is where you need to be.*

The Edge was beyond them, that dangerous slide into dark. He knew, and perhaps Crissand had seen it, but Crissand had his bearings now, and stood beside him and turned a calm face outward, toward the deeper shadows.

—Don't go there alone, Tristen said to him. *Promise me.*

—I swear it, Crissand said to him, *and drew another, a whole breath. The things he could not learn in the world of Men he seemed to learn by seeing, and feeling the currents of the wind, where it blew, and where it tried to take him.*

So Tristen led him out of the gray and into the candlelight of the room in which they sat.

And a small portion of the light Tristen kept with him, and held in his hand, and let it slowly fade.

"Gods," Crissand said.

"So you know it's not that far," Tristen said. "So you know I can always reach that place, wherever I am. And you can. You don't need to ride to the river to find it, or to inquire what our enemy is doing. Go home. Go to bed."

"My lord." Crissand was at the end of his strength, and yet moved to the wish he made: he rose, and took his leave, regretting what he had done . . . but the need to have done it was stronger than all regret, as if a fire burned, and only going and moving could extinguish it: and it was a true fire. Tristen knew it, as he knew the Aswydd, and only hoped to govern it, for Crissand's sake.

But as Crissand stumbled home, safe in the hands of his own guard, the gray space was clear at last, the tie that was between them was safe, and the warmth that was Crissand shone again on his right hand.

He had gotten Crissand back—in spite of the weather and in spite of all ill wishes to the contrary, he had recovered Crissand, in all senses, and that was a victory.

As for what Crissand had learned at such risk—he already knew. Tasmôrden feared what was going on at his southern frontier, and hoped to slip his own men in among the Amefin, where they could mingle with like speech and stature and coloring.

And now that Tasmôrden knew about Aeself's band of expatriates at Althalen, he surely hoped to lodge his own men among them, to betray them at some advantageous moment. That was the risk inherent in mercy: he read it in his books, but had no need to read it: common sense advised him that he had run that risk in allowing the fugitives to cross and to establish a force there.

He felt the currents Crissand had felt without ever going to the river, as he had said. And for Aeself's sake, for so many other reasons he yearned to draw the main attack south, where he could reach it. But Cefwyn had expressly forbidden him to do that, saying that the northern barons of Ylesuin must have their moment of glory—the very barons that betrayed their king. Yet Cefwyn's orders stood, and the situation within Ylesuin had reached a complexity which had somehow to reach its own resolution: when the south was part of the action, then the northern barons acted together, jealously, against the south. Whenever they had to act together, they also acted separately, jealously, against one another. It was Cefwyn's attempt to make them act together that had done this—and bringing the south in to steal their war and present them a victory could never do what Cefwyn dreamed of doing: that was the difficulty in all this, and considering the attack on his messenger and the attack on the nuns at Anwyfar, he saw the state of affairs in Ylesuin, as clearly as if it, too, were within the gray space.

Tasmôrden's ventures south, this arrow launched at Crissand, offered him an excuse: he might strike back, within the scope of Cefwyn's orders. But if he did move, no small strike would serve any purpose but to draw another small assault, and more harm. What would deal with Tasmôrden's incursions was a hammerblow; no mere chase from a border camp and back, but an answering presence at the edge of Elwynor, on Elwynim soil. *That* he could construe as within his orders . . . while Cefwyn was in danger from within his own kingdom.

His message regarding Tarien had sped, but other messages might have gone astray.

And what then? What then, when the north divided itself again into quarreling factions?

What when the news broke, that Cefwyn had, not an Elwynim heir, but an Aswydd son—a *southern* heir, and a wizard to boot?

Tasmôrden likely knew: Cuthan would have told him. And he would hear about the arrival of Orien and Tarien: it was in the gray space, as the child was, once one knew to look; and would the birth of such a child be silent? Tristen thought not.

Captain Anwyll, wintered in at the riverside garrison, would know once the rumor limped its narrow channels to reach him.

And then what must Anwyll think, a Guelenman, loyal to his king?

Why should Tasmôrden move east, against the heart of Ylesuin, where scandal might do the work of armies, dividing his enemies?

No. It was Amefel Tasmôrden had to fear, where he knew walls were going up and fortifications were rising despite the bitter weather. Tasmôrden was not blind, Tristen was sure, nor ignorant of both trouble in Guelessar and threat to the south. If anything drove Tasmôrden east—it would not be Tasmôrden's own interests.

Did Tasmôrden know that?

Or would Tasmôrden go east, like Crissand toward the river, because irresistible currents moved him?

Tristen sat, the cup cooled in his hand.

Outside the windows, for some reason beyond his wishes, the snow continued to fall.

CHAPTER 6

A gentle snow veiled the banners, snow falling on snow, cooling the passions, hiding the blackened beams of the Bryalt shrine across the square from the Quinalt, so that Luriel's second wedding processional had no such ill-omened sight as it wended its way to the steps of the Quinaltine. Lay brothers swept the steps, which in Cefwyn's estimation only made them chancier, and he held his consort's hand with attentive caution on the climb. Trumpets blared about them, all the bright display of the houses of Panys and Murandys, colors of gold and green and blue and white billowing out in streamers from the drafty doorway above.

The choir began, eerie echoing of voices within the stone sanctuary. Cefwyn had always found it unnervingly evocative of funerals, of souls trapped in the shrine that was the holiest of all Quinalt shrines, all the dead buried in the vaults below. He had seen more funerals than festivals when he was a boy: the old guard of the Marhanen court had been dying; then his cousins dying; his mother and then Efanor's mother dying. He had come to detest the Quinalt liturgy, as he had come to detest the Quinalt's influence over his father. From boyhood he had far preferred the Teranthines . . . partly since it was his grandfather's choice and annoyed his father; but mostly because the Teranthines had more cheerful music and talked less about sin.

But that alliance had been a boy's liberty to choose. The man was king of Ylesuin, the Quinalt was the order that dominated the court and held most power in the kingdom, and to that faith the king must show due and solemn observance.

Especially that was so since he had appointed the new Patriarch, and had to uphold the man in his office. But on the brighter side, he had very good cause to expect cooperation: Father Jormys, now

Patriarch of the Holy Quinalt, was a devout religionist, but no fool, and not unaccustomed to politics, having been Efanor's spiritual advisor since Efanor had left the Teranthines. He had encouraged a little too much devotion on Efanor's part, perhaps, but that had been the extravagance of green youth—Efanor's—and the enthusiasm of a young priest with a willing hearer; and that, too, was settling to sober good sense as the boy became a man courted by dangerous men, and as the priest found himself enmeshed in the court.

And if there was a miracle to be had, some divine blessing to mark the accession of Jormys and the confirming vote in the Quinaltine, it was . . . thank the gods of both faiths . . . the snow. Riots and murder were far less likely when the weather closed in like this. Snow was more efficient than troops of the Guard in dispersing the crowds and lowering the voices that had lately cried out in anger. Men drunk on wine and the last Patriarch's murder had burned and looted the Bryaltines just across the square, convinced that the Bryaltines had sheltered assassins and wizards.

But now the populace had seen a body displayed as evidence of the king's justice on the impious—not that the man was guilty, to be sure. His sole recommendation was that he was already dead, unidentifiable, and a convenient recourse when the mob demanded justice. They had hung the unfortunate posthumously . . . and in that very hour the snow had started to fall, and fall, and fall with no letup.

Hard to maintain the will to riot when fingers and toes were numb. Hard to gather in great drunken numbers when the streets were slippery with ice.

Today, even for a court wedding, he had provided no unbounded largesse of ale in the square, and consequently the majority of those onlookers who came to watch this processional were sober, intent on the spectacle, not the excess of good cheer flowing in the Quinaltine square, which had been the most grievous mistake of the last attempt at this wedding.

And without the drunken crowd, the troublemakers in the town who had escaped having their crowns cracked by the Guard were lying low and quiet. The ordinary folk of the capital who were not standing to cheer the procession were busy sweeping the snow off their steps or struggling with frozen cisterns and ice dams on their roofs.

So in the safety of the snow Lady Luriel of Murandys could attempt again to be married. It was an indecently short time after the murder of the Patriarch to be holding a state wedding, but the affairs of state rushed on: the last Patriarch was three days in the vaults beneath the Quinaltine following a fortnight of extravagant ritual, the blood was cleared off the stones, the shrine was purified, and Lady Luriel and the second son of Panys were back for another attempt at married bliss.

The banners swept in, the procession followed, and in the pageantry of the banners and the trumpets to either hand, Cefwyn marched down the aisle and took his place in the first row of seats, standing with the Royal Consort to await the rest of the court.

His brother Efanor arrived next, and Lord Murandys and Lord Panys . . . the Lord Commander should have been there, too, but Idrys, he noted, had disappeared.

"Where is Idrys?" Ninévrisë whispered in some concern. When Idrys was not punctual, there was a reason, and Cefwyn's confidence in the safety of the place was just a little undermined, the sound of the trumpets gone just a little thin in his hearing.

"Seeing to the Guard," Cefwyn guessed, whispering, and thought to himself, *I hope so.*

The recent upheaval left all the land uneasy. Only yesterday came word of a Teranthine shrine attacked, plundered by bandits, rapine and murder on innocent nuns—disturbing enough in itself until he heard the name of the place so afflicted. Anwyfar was also where he had lodged the Aswydd women, and there was no especial word on their fate. He had the least uncomfortable suspicion it might not have been bandits, rather the actions of someone bent on causing trouble. Idrys had sent men to find out. That report might have come in, among other matters Idrys saw to.

The murder of the Patriarch had not settled the struggle inside the Quinalt, between the orthodoxy and the moderate wing. Far from it. The orthodoxy, which was almost certainly to blame for the death of the Patriarch, had tried to set the blame on the hapless Bryaltines, since the murder had left the Patriarch's murdered body in a room filled with heretic Bryaltine charms and imagery—it was far too obvious a lie, but not for the mob: the mob had set fire to the sole Bryaltine shrine in Guelessar, and hung its priest . . . bad enough if that were the end of it. But it was *Ninévrisë's* priest.

She had attached herself to the Bryaltine sect to please the Quinaltine, who could by straining a little accept that faith, all to allay the popular fear of Elwynim as a people steeped in wizardry and godlessness.

So he did not take it for a coincidence that whoever had murdered the Patriarch, his ally in the skirmishes with the Faith, had blamed the Bryaltines, Ninévrisë's . . . no matter that hapless Father Benwyn, a bookish man and nearsighted to the extreme, had been the least likely murderer in all Ylesuin.

Cefwyn did not take any of it for a coincidence, he found it hard to take the business in Anwyfar as a coincidence, and now came the absence of his right-hand man when they were all met again in this place that had been the center of the previous incident in this first trial of the new Patriarchate and the second attempt at this marriage. It was the first major court function since the Holy Father's funeral and interment, and it was the apt occasion for trouble.

He hoped Idrys was only exercising caution—perhaps personally standing by the new Patriarch even as he robed for the event.

Please the gods they made it through this wedding without incident . . . and married off his former lover before she was herself the focus of trouble in the court.

He tightened his grip on the rail before him as, to the wailing of the choir, the bride and groom arrived in their places at the altar. Shortly after came the moment of previous disaster, the moment when the last attempt at matrimony had ended in blood-spattered priests running out to announce the Patriarch's murder. Cefwyn clenched his teeth as the smoke of censers increased, creating smoke through which the Holy Father should make his appearance—and relaxed with a sigh when the shadowy figure of the new Patriarch did appear out of that veil of smoke.

The entire congregation sighed and seemed easier as that fatal moment passed safely. The choir never ceased its haunting, haunted praise, and the new Patriarch lifted his heavily robed arms and pronounced an untrammeled blessing on the congregation and on the couple.

Cefwyn heaved a second and ultimate sigh of relief, feeling as if knotted ropes had loosened about his chest.

Murandys and Panys, two houses of great wealth, one troublesome, one loyal to the Crown, were now joining hands in this marriage. Luriel, who had looked to marry the heir of Ylesuin, and who had found herself instead in virtual exile in Murandys, was redeemed. Panys' second son, a good young man, had by the nuptial agreement secured himself the right of inheritance in Murandys—when heirless Murandys died, he would pass into the line of Murandys and become lord of the province . . . since Prichwarrin Lord Murandys had produced no male heir, and the sibling line had produced no male either. Luriel would inherit as far as the custom of her province allowed: that was to say, she had chosen her husband; and if she was canny and bided her time, she would be essential to her spouse in the administration of the province of her birth.

Patience was certainly not Luriel's best skill, lending some doubt to her help—but after the vows she became her husband's concern, and her uncle's . . . not to cross his path again until Prichwarrin should die (please the gods) a natural death abed, at a goodly and peaceful age.

The new Holy Father reached the final pronouncement of marriage. The trumpet fanfare rang out. The choir soared to hitherto unreached heights, all but painful to the ears, and the high, pure bells began to peal. The whole town seemed joined in relief that the deed was done, the ceremony had come off without an ill omen, and the Patriarchate had survived.

A second fanfare echoed among the shadowy pillars, the signal for the banner-bearers to file toward their departure. The king and royal family must leave first, with their various banners: then the married couple, in precedence over all other lords and ladies for this one day of their lives . . . though Murandys ranked high in the order of things under any circumstances.

The red Marhanen banner with its golden Dragon swept across the light from the doors, then the red banner of the Guelens, translucent against the sun, bearers fanning out to the side against the snow-laden light. The prince's standard followed.

Cefwyn and Ninévrisë swept to one side, with Efanor close beside them: Luriel and Rusyn of Panys swept to the other side in a flow of blue and white and gold and green banners astream in the ice-edged wind and the pure, clear daylight. The bells rang, the trumpets blew, and such of the town as had braved the cold to stand before the steps, respectable folk all, waved kerchiefs and cheered an event of hope in the affairs of their land.

It was a moment for smiles, and for an unrestrained breath and a sigh. Cefwyn lifted a hand and waved, and Ninévrisë waved. The populace waved handkerchiefs and scarves.

And in that moment a shadow slipped close to Cefwyn's side, as only the Lord Commander could without the quick reaction of the king's bodyguard.

"Ryssand's come to the wedding," Idrys said in half a whisper, and Cefwyn swung his head half-about, appalled.

"Here?"

"He's passed midtown . . . ridden Ivanim fashion to get here—doubtless for the wedding."

"Damn him!" Cefwyn's voice escaped discipline, but he lowered it quickly. "At risk of his *head* he comes here! And nothing from the gate-guards?"

"They reached *me,* my lord king. You were already in the processional. Hence my absence. I've alerted the Guard."

"Damn and damn!" Cefwyn said, and unwillingly caught Ninévrisë's attention. "Wave," he said, and did, smiling.

Ryssand risked everything on this return . . . of course before the weather worsened, of course at the worst moment, of course while the union of the Marhanen with his own troublesome but essential house was still under discussion. Here was the man likeliest at the root of all the realm's troubles, strongly urged to absent himself from the court for the season, and he *dared* come back unbidden?

The timing was no accident. Ryssand was a master of public display for his provocations, and would never arrive to attend the wedding, no, but rather just in time take advantage of the crowd thus gathered to force his king to act or fail to act in public.

And a king who had just arranged this marriage at some personal investment and cost to the Crown had to wonder, did Lord Murandys, father of the bride, who had agreed to the wedding to secure his own unstable political ground, know of the return of his erstwhile partner in dissent? Had they possibly conspired to do this?

"Cuthan and Parsynan are with him, my lord king," was Idrys' final caution, as horsemen broke forth into the snowy square, the banner of Ryssand brazenly displayed. A clot of townsfolk accompanied the column, the curious of the lower town swept up in Ryssand's course through the streets. The celebrants who had been cheering Luriel and her groom saw it and deserted the space below the steps to gawk as the unannounced arrival made his procession toward the Quinaltine.

Corswyndam Lord Ryssand reined his fine chestnut in at the steps and made his bow. And with the banner of Ryssand was another, smaller banner, one which most of Ylesuin would not recognize: the banner of the earl of Bryn, out of Amefel.

Never mind the man, still in the saddle as if he headed some invading army—or trusted Ryssand gave him the ducal privilege of staying ahorse in his king's presence—had no longer any right to the display of those colors.

"My lord king," Corswyndam said loudly enough for half the square to hear. "My lady. My lord prince."

Oh, that was calculated, a salute to Ninévrisë, the Royal Consort. Corswyndam had moved heaven and earth to see Ninévrisë treated as an enemy instead of an honored and queenly bride. By the protocols, she being merely the Royal Consort, he might have omitted her from the reckoning entirely, and yet he did not. He saluted her, he saluted Prince Efanor, whom he courted for a son-in-law. There was no piece of mischief in Ylesuin that did not have Lord Ryssand somewhere involved, and all this public courtesy, all this show was a challenge to his king to accuse him of any of it—an attempt to interject the very scandal Cefwyn had avoided into this most happy of moments.

Cefwyn strode to the edge of the Quinaltine steps and set fists on hips. "You left our lands and our court at our express invitation," Cefwyn shouted down at him. "Now you presume to return without so much as asking our leave. Do you come to honor the new bride? If so, I find your timing damned ill considered, to her, to the noble houses here displayed, and to the Crown, sir!"

"Concern for the realm brought me, Your Majesty." Corswyndam swept a second bow. "And the honoring of my oath to Your Majesty, to uphold the king, the realm, and the Holy Quinalt! Things I've learned dictated I ride with scarcely a guard, in all haste, before intemperate influences might bring worse weather on the roads! And forgive my intrusion into this festive occasion, but I ask a hearing, Your Majesty, of utmost urgency. Your Majesty has been misled—"

"*We* have been misled?" It was clear, now, by the colors of Bryn, what Ryssand dared with this public show, and letting the famed Marhanen temper out, Cefwyn strode a step lower and pointed at Earl Cuthan of Bryn and at Lord Parsynan, faces he knew, one from his stay in Amefel and the other because he himself had appointed the scoundrel viceroy of Amefel on Ryssand's recommendation. "There's a pairing straight from hell! The man who would not be duke of Amefel, who betrayed his own people and contrived with traitors, and the scoundrel who slaughtered a nobleman's guard for his own damned petty spite! Are these blackguards under arrest? Is *that* the gift you bring me, two wretches fit for hanging? For *that*, I may be appeased!"

The two in question held back, and Parsynan retreated a step, looking starkly afraid. But no accusation scathed Corswyndam or brought a decent blush or a pallor to his face.

"The gift I bring Your Majesty is the truth, the much-abused truth, that—"

"Oh, come now, *come*, sir! *Ryssand* defends the truth? If you think it resides in these two miscreants, you need to have a lad to guide your steps!"

"Your Majesty, I bring you peace! Peace with Elwynor!"

"*Damn* you, I say! And damn these two traitors!"

But Ryssand had gotten his blade past Cefwyn's guard, and the poison had reached ready ears. Prichwarrin Lord Murandys, at Cefwyn's elbow, rushed to plead, loudly, before all witnesses, noble and common: "I beg Your Majesty hear him."

"Indeed," said Lord Isin, from his other side. "Indeed, *peace* with Elwynor, Your Majesty. Hear him."

"I know the source," Cefwyn began to say, but then Lord Murandys cast himself to his knee on the icy landing and seized Ninévrisë's hand.

"Intercede, Your Grace, for the saving of your subjects and the king's mercy."

Cefwyn was shocked to silence, but Ninévrisë backed a step and tried to rescue her hand, all but slipping on the ice. Isin besought Efanor's arm in similar plea, but Efanor's bodyguard interposed an armored side, diverting the old man in alarm. A man slipped, guards reached for weapons, and all manner of mischief might have broken out, except Idrys called out sharply, "Hold! All hold!" and set an armored presence beside the royal family, arraying the Dragon Guard and all their weapons at his command.

And still Prichwarrin Lord Murandys, father of the forgotten bride, remained on his knees, a public scandal, and Ninévrisë, recovered from her near fall, refusing to grant him grace.

"Get up," Cefwyn said harshly.

Prichwarrin rose stiffly and obediently to his feet, and Cefwyn turned a baleful stare down at the armed company.

Artisane was there, too, that cloaked woman on the piebald mare, riding sidesaddle in her many-petticoated skirts, and she was a presence as unwelcome in Ninévrisë's women's court as her father was in his own. Inside the Guelesfort, out of public view, he could order Ryssand's throat cut, if he wished the breach with the north irrevocable—and Prichwarrin at the head of his enemies.

But such was the tangle of relations between the Marhanen kings and this most powerful of the dukes of Ylesuin that he could not set ducal heads side by side on Guelcmara's gate. He had not formally banished Lord Ryssand: he had sent him forth in private disgrace precisely because he could not afford a public breach; and he had then countenanced Ryssand's pursuit of an alliance with his house, namely Efanor, trying to patch up the northern region's relations with the Crown—because without the north there was damned little left of Ylesuin.

"Peace, of course, is what we all desire," Cefwyn said at last, "and you shall have your hearing—at *my* convenience! Now clear the streets before these good people demand your arrest! You've disrupted the festivities."

"When shall I see Your Majesty?" Ryssand asked.

"Obey your king!" Idrys said. "Withdraw!"

"At Your Majesty's command," Ryssand said, with another deep bow and with a faint smile touching the corners of his mouth. "Shall I camp at the town gate in disgrace? Or shall I have my residence in the Guelesfort at my disposal?"

Camp at the gate, was on Cefwyn's tongue, and, Sweep the steps of them, close behind. But Ryssand was too canny a campaigner, and the presence of the crowd, the hired tongues that would surely wag the instant this confrontation ended and spread whatever rumors Ryssand ordered, all forced control over the Marhanen temper.

"Sleep in the stables, for all I care, but—" Now, he looked beyond, to his people, acknowledging their witness of this unseemly display. "—take heed of rumor, and mind the source! The words of those who have fallen from grace for murder and treason in their own province are not to be trusted in Guelemara! We will listen and we will hear, but we will not be swayed by the interests of murderers!"

He descended then two steps closer to Ryssand:

"You will have your audience," Cefwyn said in no good humor, and for immediate ears only. "And if these two you've brought affront me as they affronted the duke of Amefel, their heads will sit on spikes on the town gate! Let them look to their lives, I say! And I place their behavior at your account, Ryssand! Look to it, and let them not offend me as they offended Amefel!"

"Your Majesty." Ryssand bowed in the saddle, and bowed again, and a third time before he turned his horse about and rode at the head of his small column—the banners of Ryssand and Bryn happening in the process to seize the precedence over the Dragon Banner of the Marhanen.

For that reason and in full consciousness of appearances, Cefwyn did not descend the steps to tail onto the lord of Ryssand's procession to the Guelesfort. He stood fast on the steps, with Idrys beside him, with Ninévrisë, with Efanor, Lord Murandys and Lord Panys and Lord Isin, and the bride and groom.

"Damn him," Cefwyn said.

"This is my wedding!" Luriel cried, in tears. "This is my wedding, does anyone remember? *This is my wedding!*"

"Be still!" her uncle said sharply. It was a wedding already marginally scandalous, not alone since the Patriarch's murder at the last attempt; all the world knew the niece of Lord Murandys had been in the royal bed.

And now at the outburst from Murandys, the young groom, leaving his bride, went several steps aside to confer with his father, Lord Panys, leaving Luriel alone before the scandal-loving crowd at the foot of the steps.

Cefwyn cast a look at Efanor, the while, wondering how Efanor had taken what had just transpired, and whether the marriage proposal between Efanor and Artisane had assumed an extreme advantage at the moment or whether he should take the excuse of his offense against Ryssand to consider the marriage entirely out of the question. It had seemed advantageous from time to time, Efanor being in no wise gullible and having his own notions how to contain Ryssand's ambition; now, among a dozen times else, he doubted the wisdom of it and asked himself how he could have been so foolish.

Ninévrisë's hand sought his, and her fingers pressed on his as if she would drive her own good sense into his hot-tempered Marhanen head: nothing precipitate, nothing foolish, she silently counseled him. The baron foolish enough to challenge his grandfather to that degree would have gone to the block, so he said to himself, but those raw, rough times of beginning a kingdom were done: his own reign was a rule of reason—so he hoped. Yet he asked himself now how the populace saw him, whether he had won this encounter or whether Ryssand had.

But on the thought of his grandfather's methods he left Ninévrisë, took the bride's hand, and brusquely led her to the groom and seized his hand. He held up their joined hands then to the witness of all the crowd, many of whom had by now forgotten they had come to witness a wedding.

That was what they had come to see. Had they forgotten it?

"A king's penny apiece!" he shouted. It was the third penny the wedding had cost the treasury, but it was a grand gesture, it distracted the crowd into wild cheering, and he left it to Idrys and his capable staff to marshal the crowd into order and to the treasury to find pennies enough.

It was cheaper than bloodshed and the entanglements of a ducal execution.

"Kiss the bride," he ordered young Rusyn, the groom, and as Rusyn obliged, there rose cheers and laughter from the crowd. The union of two young nobles was far more understandable to the people, far closer to their hearts than the constant feuds close to the throne. "Give us a diversion," he added, for the young man's ears alone, and Rusyn, nothing loath, gave him that and more, leaving his new bride breathless, to the utter and noisy delight of the crowd. The traditional cheers went up, and when Cefwyn left the bride and groom to their moment of public display, and reached his intimates and his wife, he passed only a glance to Idrys, who understood every order implicit in that moment's stare and went to be sure all the necessary things happened.

The duke of Ryssand's little entourage had meanwhile had time to clear the square by now, the crowd had been entertained, and now the bridal procession could get under way without looking like the tail of Ryssand's.

"Ring the bells!" he said, realizing that the bells were the source of the silence, and a lay brother ran to relay that order.

"Trumpeters!" the Guard sergeant shouted. "Way for His Majesty an' Her Grace!"

They descended the icy steps without mishap, save one of the lay brothers went sliding in unseemly fashion, to the rough laughter of a now good-humored crowd.

For those who gathered omens from ceremonies, however, this one had not had the best beginning. Everything about the marriage of Luriel and Rusyn was second-best, from the choice of mates to the once-worn wedding finery, which had had to be recovered from soot and, one suspected, even traces of blood the common folk now called sacred.

Not the best-omened wedding, but gods, it was a relief all the same to have the matter done with. Panys was assured of a foothold in Murandys, where the Crown needed a loyal man. Ryssand had timed his arrival for after the ceremony, thank the gods, not to have disrupted the wedding altogether, and Lord Murandys was likely of mixed feelings about the choice of Luriel's wedding for Ryssand's return—Ryssand correctly predicting there would be no bloody confrontation and no arrest to mar a wedding.

But since Murandys had made the alliance with Panys as the way out of royal displeasure, during Ryssand's forced retreat from the court . . . Murandys might be asking himself now whether Ryssand's choice of moments might be a veiled threat against him. It might have been premature, Murandys might now think, to have made an alliance with a friend of the monarch: Ryssand must have some secret behind this move.

So Cefwyn thought, too; and that was the *other* reason not to order Ryssand's arrest. There was more to it than appeared, and its name was very likely Cuthan of Bryn, and Tristen, gods save them all.

And peace with Tasmôrden? He began to guess the sum of matters, and said not a word to Ninévrisë on the matter of this *peace* Ryssand spoke of. She had heard as well as he, and knew no more than he, but neither of them could like the source of it: there was no agreement possible with Tasmôrden in Elwynor that did not preclude Ninévrisë's return as lady Regent—and that condition was entirely unacceptable.

Beyond unacceptable—it was foolish even to contemplate it. Tasmôrden was forsworn, a rebel against Ninévrisë's father. What faith could they put in another oath?

Not mentioning the faith in Ryssand.

So they walked over the now well-trampled snow, with evidence of horses roused out from a well-fed evening before: they walked, a royal procession, a wedding, over snow no longer clean, thanks to Ryssand—but becoming so, in the steady fall of white.

Snow veiled the Guelesfort gates into an illusion of distance and mystery.

Snow lay on the ironwork, a magical outlining of the dragons that were the center of the work, on the gates that lay before the second, oaken set of gates.

"He has something," Ninévrisë said in a hushed voice, as they passed outside the hearing of the crowd. "And it's not good."

"I know damned well he has," Cefwyn answered her. "And I know it's not good."

CHAPTER 7

There was no haste to deal with Ryssand . . . no chance, however, to exchange the royal finery for plainer garb, or to bathe away the incense that clung to the Quinaltine and everyone that had been within its walls.

Efanor came on the unspoken understanding that they had matters to discuss—urgent matters.

"Had you foreknowledge of this?" Cefwyn asked, drawing him into the privacy of the Blue Hall, where Ninévrisë waited, and added as he shut the door: "Superfluous to ask, but had you the least hint of this move?"

"None," Efanor said, and Ninévrisë sank down at the small round table where they often sat in their deliberations. "There was in fact every indication he would remain in his province at least until matters were settled between us. And yet he's brought the lady Artisane, when he certainly knows she's not welcome with Her Grace."

"Unwelcome," Ninévrisë said, "indeed, and so she is. But that's not saying I hold that sentiment to the last. If needs be, needs must. If Ryssand regrets the offer he made in favor of this *peace* he talks about—perhaps that alliance with Artisane is that much more important."

"My very wise lady," Cefwyn said, touching her fingers. "I've no doubt. None of you, either, brother." He withdrew his hand from Ninévrisë's and found that hand wished very much to become a fist, which movement he resisted, as he resisted the absolute order he could give at any moment, any hour, on any given day, to arrest the man. Second thoughts were always possible. As the people's blood cooled, they were less and less wise. "Damn him! the effrontery of the man!"

But common sense, which even a monarch possessed, insisted that this man, this extravagantly provocative man, had come with *something* beyond the ordinary, something so strong Ryssand was willing to cast his life and the survival of his house on its validity . . . and Cefwyn was relatively sure of the nature of it.

It was no surprise, the news that Lord Cuthan had come to Ryssand's lands: he had known that already; he had known Parsynan was there, too, both supping at Ryssand's table, Parsynan nightly regaling the man with Tristen's affronts to Quinalt decency, Cuthan complaining of high-handed abuse of power.

Conservative, noble-born Quinaltine in Parsynan's case, and—at most charitable guess in Cuthan's case—liberal Bryaltine, if Cuthan's private beliefs were even that close to the Quinalt. They were an unusual pair of advisors for any northern baron, to say the very least. Cefwyn wondered, did those watching that pair on horseback consider that curiosity? Did the commons have any least idea they were in the presence of an Aswydd, however remote in blood—advising orthodox Lord Ryssand?

Tristen had sent Cuthan to exile in Elwynor, in effect, into Tasmôrden's hands. Damn Cuthan for a traitor—and depend on Tristen to grant him that retreat. It had given him a hellish problem.

"So Ryssand says he brings peace, and has a man lately in Tasmôrden's keeping," he said, out of that thought. "An offer from Tasmôrden, that's the news, no great wit required for us to guess that much. It wants only the details."

"An offer from Tasmôrden," Efanor repeated. "An offer acceptable to the Quinalt zealots. One can only imagine those details."

"None of them acceptable to Elwynor," Ninévrisë said.

"Which goes without saying," Cefwyn replied. "Still, it would help to know the exact nature of the proposal before he brings it within hearing of the court—or has his agents gossip it about. We took damage enough in our encounter on the steps of the Quinaltine this morning—he uttered the word: peace. Peace, in any form that doesn't involve troops, would come welcome to all the barons. The seed's there. We can't unsay it."

"He was too polite," Efanor said slowly.

"Polite?" Cefwyn exclaimed, for politeness had been nowhere in his sight.

"To Her Grace," Efanor said, "he was polite. Everything he's done, every move his zealot followers have made, has been with the intention of lessening her position, and to chastise *you* for having the effrontery first to choose a Bryaltine wife instead of Luriel and then to support Her Grace's claims to lands the barons—particularly those near the river Lenúalim—would have for their own, if you were our grandfather. Now, and for no reason, he acknowledges Her Grace publicly, and Murandys openly courts her favor. I ask why."

Any question of Ryssand, the Quinalt, and Ninévrisë struck so deeply to the heart of his fears he lost all sense of moderation. Most of the Quinalt zealotry which had caused such trouble in Guelessar had its doctrinal origins in the northlands, in Ryssandish territory, where the Quinaltine faith found its most absolute and rigid interpretation. They had seen that small leaven in the loaf rise up to bloody riot involving half the town of Guelemara not a fortnight ago, at Luriel's first wedding. Priests liberally supported by Ryssand's donations preached their conservative doctrine, and disaffected guardsmen Tristen had let go had spun tales of magic and sorcery in Amefel . . . the part about magic at least was true: sorcery Cefwyn did not believe. They had killed Father Benwyn, clandestinely murdered the Patriarch as too moderate, too accommodating to the Crown—he was sure that the Patriarch's accommodation of the royal marriage had cost him his life.

And most of all Ryssand's darts and the zealots' sermons had flown at Ninévrisë . . . Artisane's empty accusations, Ryssand's attempts to rouse the Holy Father to forbid it, even the appearance of a Sihhë coin in the offering box, sending Tristen into exile. All these schemes had aimed at foreign influences in the land, and he could not forget now that the Aswydds' place of exile at Anwyfar was burned to the foundations: even the moderate Teranthines come under attack. The Teranthines were no longer safe. The Bryaltines certainly would not be.

And Efanor was right: Ryssand had not taken the chance to slight Ninévrisë, on the very steps of the Quinaltine, when protocols might have covered that small spite, when in fact Ryssand's zealot priests would have taken amiss his acknowledgment of her—would have disapproved it heartily if they were there to hear, as they might have been.

What manner of game *had* Ryssand set in motion? And what did he intend?

Order something too extreme, and Ryssand might prove to have another, fatal dart in his quiver . . . something that might unsettle the populace, snow or no snow, into another convulsion of religious outrage.

But what was this courtesy toward Ninévrisë?

"He has something," Cefwyn found himself saying, unable to

look his brother in the eye. "He has something that makes him confident enough to return in spite of me, something beyond an offer from Tasmôrden, which needs must include peaceful dealings between Quinaltine and Bryaltine."

"He has some accusations against Tristen almost certainly," Efanor said, "considering the company he brought with him. And I'm sure Tristen will have done something worth our apprehensions in any given fortnight."

"Almost certainly he has." About Tristen he had no illusions, nor fear of him, either. Gods, how he missed him—missed the innocent indirection that could lead a man to question his most dearly held assumptions. *Truth* went where Tristen went, and his court, it seemed, could not withstand that habit of his. "Amefel can break out in plagues and frogs, and I'll still trust him. But you have the right of it. I fear he's not been discreet, not when he banished the earl of Bryn, not when he sent Parsynan out in disgrace."

"What dared we hope?" Efanor asked. "Discretion hasn't yet dawned on him."

"But, damn them, he's an assurance for our safety, if they understand him well enough, where he is. *Mauryl* held the old tower with never a bleat from Ryssand. What's changed?"

"Ryssand's ambition," Efanor said.

"Perhaps Tristen is the reason we hear from Tasmôrden now," Ninévrisë said softly. "Fear of what rises in Amefel. Perhaps Tasmôrden understands the new lord in Amefel very well indeed."

"So would Ryssand fear the new lord in Amefel, though for different reasons. *He* urged me appoint Parsynan to the post, and I never asked. I never had the full accounting of the archive in Henas'amef; I never had the full account of Heryn Aswydd's dealings, or where the gold flowed, and in Ryssand's *uncommon* attachment to Amefel, Ryssand's *uncommon* fear for Parsynan's safety. Gods know whether we'll ever get it out of the records, not since Ryssand's man went through them. But Ryssand can't touch Tristen—even without this army of alliance he's building—and gods help Ryssand if Ryssand ever struck at me: I don't know if I could restrain Tristen. Surely Ryssand knows that."

"But is it to the good of Ylesuin," Efanor persisted, "if we let the old power wake. Yes, Mauryl was in his tower, but he was quiet in his tower. Is it the gods' will . . . or is it some other will that guides this? I confess to you, brother,—I am not wholly at peace with this. I *trust* the lord of Amefel, I trust him for his honor and for his goodwill—but he *is*—"

Efanor broke off, and left it unsaid, what Tristen was, or might be.

Sihhë?

The High King of the Elwynim?

"He is," Cefwyn said with a sigh, "Tristen. That says all. It says all he knows, more to the point."

"Are we sure?" Efanor asked. "Is it the man we know, who drove Parsynan from the town?"

"Oh, yes," Cefwyn said on a long breath. "Beyond any doubt. No temporizing, no debate. It was his best decision. Gods give us all the courage."

"Gods grant us the wisdom," Efanor said pointedly, "to apply it in due season. And thank the gods there's only one Tristen. Two would be—excessive."

"There were five, once," Ninévrisë said in the ensuing silence. "Five, if he is what most think."

"Gods save us from such days," Efanor said. "And I ask, in all honesty, in all regard for one who's served you very well . . . is it wise to lean for safety on this friend of ours, even willing the best for us, as perhaps he does? He *is* Mauryl's, if he is anyone's. And Mauryl, whatever else, was not necessarily a friend of our house."

"An ally of necessity," Cefwyn said. He had not approached Efanor with his own fears in that regard, and perhaps that was a mistake on his part. Efanor was devout; but indeed, Efanor was emerging from a young man's religious innocence to a sober awareness of the power inside the Quinaltine, and its warfare with the Crown. He had seen firsthand the consequences of Lewenbrook, when an army came back after an encounter with sorcery. Efanor understood that sort of warfare, and when they came to a question of Tristen's involvement—the question was there, and it hung silent in the air a moment.

"I trust him," Ninévrisë said. "*I* believe in him."

"So do we all. So do we all," Cefwyn said, and wished to say it, with all his heart. "He won't betray us. We'll have our army yet, damn Ryssand's conniving heart. He's failed in slandering you. Now he'll raise complaints about Tristen. That's exactly where this is going. I can see it, right under the surface. Tristen's in the wrong and these saintly men he brings to argue how they were wronged—"

"Don't set your mind too early," Ninévrisë cautioned. "This peace—"

"This *peace* he claims to bring," Cefwyn began, but a page hovered in the doorway. "Well? *Well?*"

The boy tried to say a word, but Idrys appeared behind him and simply moved the boy aside. "My lord king," Idrys said, and drew in a man in the habit of the Quinalt, a lay brother, a fearful and woebegone young man.

"That's very well, Deisin," Cefwyn said to the page. It was the presence of the priest that the young man very wisely doubted as legitimate or wanted, but the page drew back and Idrys escorted the priest in.

"It's good you came," Cefwyn said peevishly. The lack of warning about Ryssand was not Idrys' best work, by far, but Cefwyn bit back any harsher word.

"My lord king, this is Brother Meigyn. He asks Your Majesty's protection and a recommendation to the Quinaltine, for his service to Your Majesty."

"And that service?"

"Brother Meigyn has been a clerk of the Quinalt in Ryssand. His position there has become difficult, because of the service he's about to render. If he goes back to Ryssand's court, he's a dead man."

"Give him to Annas. Recommend him to Jormys. What's the tale?"

"Let me dispose of the good brother," Idrys said, and escorted the frightened man to the door, where he gave orders to the page waiting outside. "His Majesty's instruction," Idrys said. "A hot meal, a warm place to sit. Wait for me. I may have more questions."

Then Idrys was back, a black, foreboding presence: master crow with news that did not bode well.

"From Lord Ryssand's court?" Ninévrisë prompted him in a faint voice.

"Just so, my lady. Unhappily, this was my last man in Ryssand's court. Two others had to flee, not without delivering useful information. Another died a suicide, or so the official explanation ran. Meigyn remained to the last. He's given to venial sins, a love of ale and women, far better a Teranthine than a Quinalt avocation, but that's his misfortune. Being my last and best source, he had the good sense to come only when there was something worth his life . . . and considerable reward."

"He accompanied Corswyndam here?" Cefwyn asked, wondering how close the clerk might have sat to the duke of Ryssand, and whether there would be a storm over this desertion.

"Fled, rather, on foot, when he knew Corswyndam was coming here and with what news. He's an unobtrusive man—stole a mule at Evas-on-Reyn, and managed to get here two hours behind. What he does say seems well worth his risk, my lord king. It's the essence of what Ryssand will say tonight."

The details. The chance to set their course before the battle. Cefwyn exchanged a look with his brother and his wife.

"Say on, master crow." Cefwyn drew a deep breath and leaned an arm across the back of his chair, waiting. "What does Ryssand think to win?"

CHAPTER 8

The evening was for a state celebration: Luriel's wedding night and all the grand commotion of a noble union, the bride and groom feted in hall, with course after course of food.

It should have been an unbridled festivity, but the undercurrent of matters in the court had Ryssand and Murandys, those traditional allies, doing a dance around each other more delicate than any paselle on the floor . . . the uncle of the bride tending not, as was traditional, to the side of the groom's family, the lord and lady of Panys, but to his old fellow in misdeed, Lord Ryssand.

Consequently the eyes of every experienced courtier in hall were less for Luriel than for Ryssand's daughter Artisane, emerging tonight as a whispered candidate to marry into the royal house. Efanor had loosed that rumor deliberately: far better to be the source than the subject of speculation.

And perhaps Artisane had also let word slip out. Certainly Ryssand had done nothing to restrain her. Her gown outshone the bride's; it all but outglittered the royal regalia, for that matter.

And clearly Luriel did not like the competition on her evening: her stark-set, basilisk stare settled on Artisane at every moment they crossed one another's line of sight.

A wild bedding tonight, Cefwyn said to himself. Luriel's temper was oil on tinder, in that realm . . . he could say so, who had proposed to marry the lady himself. Now he asked himself how he could ever have fallen into Luriel's web of angers and passions, piques and rages and most of all how he could ever have thought her continual upheaval the ordinary way of women. *That* was a basilisk indeed, tonight, stalking the cockatrice.

The lady beside him, in the simple circlet crown of Elwynor, in fine embroidery and a comparative lack of ornament otherwise . . . this was a woman, and she far outshone the pair of combatants on the floor. So Cefwyn leaned across the difference in their seats—Ryssand's damned stone—to whisper to his consort.

"You're the sun and the moon. They're summer lightning, and a dry night at that."

"And what will you be?" Ninévrisë asked with that wry response he so loved. "Ah! The stormy north wind."

"When Ryssand presents us his little play tonight, by the gods, he'll think so. And they could pile the wealth of the southern king-doms on that minx and not improve her disposition."

"Which?" Ninévrisë asked, dagger-sharp.

"What, no love for Luriel either?"

"I *welcome* Artisane. The two of them will not make common cause, not till pigs make poetry. It should keep the two of them busy and provide entertainment for the rest of us."

They never had loved one another, Artisane and Luriel, contrary to the politics of their houses. Luriel's detestations were legion, her uncle among them, and while the ladies warred with glances across the hall, the uncle and father made solemn converse behind a thick column, and tried to pretend no one saw them.

At a reasonable hour in the wedding-night celebration it was the custom for bride and groom to retire with the maids and ladies and young men trooping after them, bearing lit candles and fistfuls of acorns . . . the latter of which posed great annoyance to the marriage bed, when they cast them in. He and Ninévrisë had found the last wandering nuisance in the small hours of their wedding night, and flung it ceremoniously in the fire.

So on this evening, young Rusyn of Panys finished a solitary paselle with his bride. And on the very last notes, with a flourish and squall of pipes, the traditional chase was on, the young couple, warned by the pipes, dashing for the door, the young men and mar-ried women of the court in close pursuit, snatching candles conve-niently in the hands of servants and having brought their own supply of missiles. The couple might be spared the gifts in the bed if they were fleet of foot, but few made it.

Scores of nuts in a marriage bed, open wishes for children cast among ribald comments: a perfectly respectable tradition that roused nothing but laughter. But a man presenting a single acorn to the love of his life on the ballroom floor was a matter for scandal.

No, not a man: a king. And not the love of his life: the ruler of a rival court. And the fruit of that union would be no ordinary child, but would arrive into the world shadowed with political debts and promises he and Ninévrisë between them would have set for all his life to deal with. What a man started in his lifetime, his sons—and his daughters—needs must finish, and in finishing, set the incomplete pattern for their sons and daughters.

A sobering thought as the shrieking festivity departed, the province of the matrons and the young—which left the somber elders to enjoy a round of wine and contemplation . . . or so it should be, in happier times.

As it was, it left all the lords in position for the confrontation Cefwyn expected, Ryssand lurking about, waiting a summons, trying to obtain one by every means short of walking up and asking.

"Master crow," Cefwyn said.

"My lord king." The shadowy eminence hovering at his back and Ninévrisë's came forward on the dais and leaned down near his ear.

"Is there more news, at this last moment for second thoughts?"

"Nothing more than my king already knows. Shall I summon him?"

"Oh, stay, converse about the weather. Let the scoundrel wonder what we say to one another. Frown and laugh. I'll not help his digestion."

"He's talked to Murandys all evening, and Murandys has been passing more than pleasantries to the other lords about the hall tonight, too, which is just as well: otherwise it would have to come from Your Majesty to explain matters."

"I'd not plead his case.—How *is* the weather riverside?"

"Much the same as here . . . cold winds, bitter weather . . ."

"Bluster of priests."

"With thunder and lightning. Much of that."

"Any word on the whereabouts of the Aswydds?"

"Three of their household are dead with the nuns, nurse and two maidservants, that's certain, but no report of the sisters, dead or alive. My wager is they lived: Orien has sorcery to warm her feet. A further wager: that they went to Amefel. Where *else* might they go?"

"Tasmôrden. To ask him to set *Orien* on the throne of Amefel."

"There is that chance, and a very good chance. But reaching Elwynor requires a walk through Amefel, and by my sense of things, my lord king, wizards do tend toward other wizards. Inconveniently so, at times, but it does keep them collected, and largely concerned with each other."

He was not certain he liked that thought any better. "One wonders if Cuthan knows her whereabouts."

Idrys lifted a brow. "Being Aswydd? Might we ask whether Lady Orien herself brought down the disaster on Anwyfar?"

"An alliance with Ryssand, and Cuthan her messenger? Gruesome thought, *all* our enemies in one camp."

"Oh, a good thought, my lord king. One strike and we're rid of them. But I doubt we're so fortunate."

"If she's gone anywhere, I fear you're right about Amefel. She'll have gone right for Tristen's soft heart."

"Worrisome that the heir to the Aswydds might have gone to Mauryl's piece of work, the very man I do recall my lord king wrote his late father was—"

"Hush, crow. Hush! For the gods' sakes!"

"I think Her Grace is no stranger to that surmise."

"Don't press me! Not now, damn you."

"Aye, damn me while you like. But I pray my lord king think on it when you take counsel what you'll do about this barbed proposal Cuthan brings you."

"You're not free of error yourself, master crow."

"I never claimed to be."

"I don't like a damned procession coming into the town before I know it's on the road!"

"The fault is mine and several dead men's. I am *not* possessed of all information, and my sources have no more protection than their own wits and no more speed than a chance-met mule. But since my lord king has abandoned the habits of his wastrel youth, I'm glad to report he's frequently well informed on his own."

It seemed to be both justification and praise of him, of a convolute and twisted sort, and Cefwyn took it as such, nor did he greatly blame Idrys: they had, after all, what they needed, thanks to Idrys. Idrys had rid the streets of the zealot priest Udryn, but they had lost the Patriarch in retaliation—yet on Idrys' advice he had appointed Efanor's priest Jormys to the office, again, a good recommendation, for Jormys, though devout, was not naive in politics, not in proceedings within the court and not matters within the sacred walls. Udryn's silence had not prevented the spate of retribution against the Bryaltines and even the moderate Teranthines, but the zeal of the populace seemed to have spent itself in the cold . . . granted Ryssand was not the next voice he had to silence.

And granted Orien Aswydd did not find some way to have her dainty finger in the stew.

Ryssand was the likeliest next use for master crow's darker talents.

But then again, Ryssand might become useful—if he could be brought to see his own interests as linked with the Crown, for with Brugan's death, everything had changed for Ryssand: he *had* no male heir, no more than Murandys. He was in the same situation, with Artisane the prize. He needed to marry her up the ranks of nobility, not down, and there *was* no one higher than a prince of Ylesuin and inclusion in the royal family.

That would change his interests on the sudden.

And for the sake of the realm and the agreements that bound the kingdom together out of its former separate, kinglike duchies, it was far better to bring Ryssand into line than to destroy the house with all its alliances and resources.

That was surely Efanor's thought in letting slip the rumor of royal interest in Artisane tonight. Last of all possible motives was any love lost in that marriage: it was utterly impossible to conceive that Efanor loved Artisane or even remotely admired her. It was rather that Efanor loved the kingdom and loved the land more than he loved his own comfort, and thought so little of his chances of a bride he could love . . . shy, serious Efanor never having had much converse with women in his sheltered, circumscribed, and pious recent years.

Gods send him enlightenment, Cefwyn thought, hoping the marriage never needed take place.

And to Idrys, leaning close, he said, regarding the compliment, "I take your meaning, master crow."

"Your Majesty is forgiving and generous."

"To the deserving." He never passed Idrys compliments. He did so, after making the unworthy accusation regarding Ryssand's slipping up on them. He felt bad about that, and could not find a way to unsay it, not with Idrys' acerbic wit. "Well, well, do you think it's time? Let's summon the old fox before he has an apoplexy. I'm anxious to hear the performance."

Idrys straightened with his usual sleek, dark grace and Cefwyn turned a silent stare on Ryssand, who had not failed to watch His Majesty's lengthy conversation with the most feared man in royal service—a lengthy conversation on the very night Ryssand meant to beard the king in his lair.

Cefwyn stared thoughtfully at Ryssand, and stared longer, completely expressionless; and when the rest of the hall had noted that fact and conversations all around had ceased, he crooked a finger and beckoned Ryssand forward.

Ryssand came as he must, and bowed, and the musicians faded away into silence.

"You said you had a matter to bring before me," Cefwyn said. "Here I sit. Bring it."

"Your Majesty." Ryssand bowed a second time, and bowed very slightly a third and even a fourth time, perhaps summoning scattered wits. "Your Grace. Your Highness." He included Efanor, the usually silent presence on the peripheries. "Thank you."

"Don't thank me yet. You're entertaining scoundrels who've met a just condemnation . . . *my* condemnation, since I've had the fair report of what they've done, and you have, I trust, some awareness of that condemnation when you bring them to this hall. Do you intend I behead them and save you the bother? Or would that action utterly surprise you?"

"Brother," said Efanor, advancing a step from the side of the dais. They had agreed Efanor would intercede to keep the fire and fuel separate, when the snake had to feel the stick on its right hand—and that Idrys would provoke Ryssand when the snake had to feel the stick on the left: there was indeed a way to shepherd a viper toward an objective. "—Brother, I've heard somewhat of Ryssand's business. Hear him."

"You and all of this court, down to the scullery maids, have *heard* His Grace," Cefwyn said. "We've all heard some version or another. Discretion has not proven one of His Grace's otherwise extensive gifts.—Oh, I'll hear him," Cefwyn said grudgingly and with a limp wave of his hand. All of this they had agreed beforehand as their position, and so had Ninévrisë. "But I don't welcome traitors to my court!" Having acceded, he burst into a tirade in Ryssand's very face. "And I hold backhanded rumormongers in utter contempt! Let us hear this version." He waved his hand, tacit leave for Ryssand to speak, if he could muster calm against the royal storm.

"Your Majesty," Ryssand said, seeming shaken, "I do *not* support any man caught in wrongdoing, as I have no cause to doubt Your Majesty's word, but Earl Cuthan has a tale to tell, and I beg you hear him . . . not for matters in Amefel, which is another matter altogether. He comes straight from Tasmôrden's court with a letter."

"Tasmôrden's court," Ninévrisë said scornfully. "*Tasmôrden* has a court! Indeed!"

"Your Grace." It was the first time Ryssand had turned conciliatory toward Ninévrisë—his desperation was a remarkable sight, and perhaps it was even a true sentiment he expressed, insofar as the lord of Ryssand might have recognized that the Lady Regent of Elwynor represented a potent force in the Crown's camp, one it was more expedient to deal with—certainly should Tasmôrden's proposal see acceptance, he would have to deal with her in the future. And should Artisane marry into the royal family Ninévrisë was the power over the women's court. His reasons were clear enough.

"Your Grace," Ryssand said mildly to Ninévrisë, "he has an army."

"An army bought and paid for," Idrys interjected sharply. "My lord king, this is no respectable lord: they're scoundrels. Mercenaries with no stake in the lands they are stealing, bandits, some of them *within* this so-named court."

"As the Lord Commander objects," Ryssand answered, "there are irregular elements. But an army nonetheless, and with that army Tasmôrden sits in Ilefínian, which is a fact. He holds a court there—whether legitimate or illegitimate, I leave it to others to say."

"I do not admit it," Ninévrisë said, and Ryssand reprised, refusing to be shaken from his point.

"But *that* he held court there enabled him to receive Earl Cuthan when he fled Ylesuin. And through Cuthan, who alone of his resources could pass our borders alive—merely a courier, Your Majesty!—he sends a convincing offer of peace."

"Convincing," Idrys echoed dubiously.

"Hear him," Efanor said, and said so just as Ryssand drew a large breath in anger. He had to let it go and reprise in a mild, a reasonable voice.

"Thank you, Your Highness. I am honor-bound to lay this letter before His Majesty, for the good of Ylesuin, and pray to do so."

"Peace with Tasmôrden?" Cefwyn said. "I think not."

"Your Majesty, I have brought the letter. Only hear it."

"A letter to me?"

Ryssand hesitated. "A letter which Earl Cuthan was authorized to unseal—"

"A letter from a scoundrel, unsealed by a scoundrel!"

"So that I would know its import to bring it to Your Majesty!"

"You allowed the opening of a sealed letter," Idrys said, and by now sweat stood on Ryssand's face.

It was time to have the content of it. Cefwyn waved a negligent hand. "The letter is compromised, but no less so than the source and the letter-bearer. We will *hear* it, since you've read it, in its principle details and as best you remember it. I will not entertain

Earl Cuthan in my hall, a man who has betrayed his own brother lords and connived with a man recommended to *me* as honest—" He had no need to say that it had been Murandys who had recommended the appointment. He only shot Duke Prichwarrin a burningly resentful glance . . . and at the same time found it noteworthy that Prichwarrin did not stand immediately next his former ally in this moment of peril, but rather over against the nearer column, as far as he dared remove himself from the area. "A man who turned out to be a common thief and a liar, besides. A man who ordered the murder of surrendered and disarmed noblemen. What a pedigree for this business!"

"Your Majesty." Ryssand was not finding it easy going, his immediate plan overset, his witnesses disallowed. "I pray you hear the exact words . . ."

"Tasmôrden's? As if they were sacred writ? As if any letter the bearer could unseal at will is proof in itself? I find all our enemy's arrangements curious. If Cuthan could pass our border at will—why come to you, a league and more to the north? Why not send to *me*, for the good gods' love? Why this care to have it in *your* hands, pray?"

"The enemy knows Her Grace's presence in the court and feared lest the letter—"

Well struck. "Don't say it!" Cefwyn burst out. "Don't *dare* to suggest—"

"Your Majesty!" Ryssand cried, "not my suspicion at all, I assure you, but rather the imagination of our enemy—"

"A lie," Ninévrisë said. "Lies and deception are old allies of his."

"Nonetheless, Your Grace, Your Majesty, if you will hear his proposal—Tasmôrden is prepared to make peace with Ylesuin, and to agreed that the Lady Regent rules in the districts east of Ilefínian, granting to her the title of Queen of Elwynor, granting to the king of Ylesuin the district northward, and agreeing for himself to the titles and honors of the King of Ilefínian and High and Lower Saissond."

A woman who was a fool, perhaps, might have leapt up in rage and tears and lost her case with a people never in the least enthusiastic about their king's foreign war and foreign bride, and for such a response Ryssand undoubtedly hoped.

Such a response the man who had raised Artisane would undoubtedly expect.

But Ninévrisë was not such a fool. She sat, chin on fist, staring at this recital.

"Ridiculous," Cefwyn said with a dismissive wave of his hand. "The man consorts with *sorcery!* He claims a kingship, in Elwynor, where prophecy claims a High King will rise against us! Gods save us, Ryssand! To what do you counsel us? To give this snake a lair from which to breed and strike at our heart?"

"By no means sorcery, Your Majesty!"

"Oh?" Cefwyn asked in mock mildness. "And who informs us of that?"

"Your Majesty, his own words . . . if Your Majesty will read his letter . . ."

"Damn his letter! Word from a heretic!"

"Quite the contrary, in a land rife with the old ways, he contends *against* the dark arts which sustained the Regency—"

Now Ninévrisë did move, drew herself up with a breath. "There is a *lie,* sir."

"The Regency depended on wizardry," Ryssand said in a rush, "as the Lord Regent was a wizard, no less than Aséyneddin's ally—"

"A great deal less than Aséyneddin's ally!" Ninévrisë cried. "Who was a sorcerer!"

"Yet this man struggles against the remnants of Aséyneddin's forces *and* Caswyddian's, your enemies, Your Grace, which have kept the land in turmoil. He struggles against a rise of the old powers—against the far greater threat from across the Lenúalim, where contrary to Your Majesty's law, the old Sihhë *walls* are rising and a claimant exists to the High Kingship . . ."

Corswyndam of Ryssand was dangerous and quick. They already knew that. He delivered a telling shot and Cefwyn lost no time in returning fire, with a slam of the royal fist on the arm of the Dragon Throne.

"You are *deceived,* Ryssand. Dangerously deceived. Good gods, I had thought a man of your years would see it!"

"I am not so deceived, Your Majesty!"

"What, and bring me a murderer and a thief to swear to Tasmôrden's character? It seems apt, but hardly persuasive! And you take his word, above your own king's? What are we come to? And wherein do foreign powers write *you* letters and send *you* my messages as if you were—what, a *king?*"

"If Your Majesty please, only listen to an agreement which may save the realm from great, from incalculable danger! The war Her Grace urges can only cast more and more power into the south, where the dukes of Ivanor, Lanfarnesse, Imor, and Amefel have raised an army, and authorized fortifications your grandfather ordered demolished. This new lord in Amefel, this wizard's fetch, this *Sihhë-lord* as they openly hail him in the streets of Henas'amef . . ."

". . . *is not the enemy of this realm!*" Cefwyn shot back, strike and parry, and now with full knowledge how much this rebel duke was willing to risk in public. This *Sihhë-lord,* as you are at such great pains to call him, is the true friend of this court and the fortifications he restores *at my order* are all that stand between our land and that *purchased* army of brigands Tasmôrden has raised against us, no less than Aséyneddin, with no cleaner claim, no less allied with sorcery—silence, sir! I've heard enough of this brigand's letter!"

There was an uneasy stir in the court, all the same, and he had let it through his guard. Tristen's doings in the south were rumored, but not the wall, and not the current adoration of the populace, or its connection with the High Kingship, and now there was a dangerous murmur throughout the hall as all of it came into the open. Cefwyn rose to his feet and let loose the notorious Marhanen temper, letting any waverers in the court know what the stakes were and what he was prepared to do.

"As for you, sir, do you count Tasmôrden your friend? This man, the heir of Aséyneddin? This man who raised war against his lawful lord? A man who insulted Her Grace, murdered her friends and relations? A man who's *purchased* army rapes and murders and robs the very people he would claim to lead? Is that our preferred friend, sir? And you swear to his *honesty?*"

Ryssand had the sense to bow, and bow deeply, and lower his voice. "I swear to nothing, Your Majesty. I only bear the message."

"Receiving the messenger from an enemy of the realm—gods, sir! as if you were *king?*"

That shot had scored the last time. This time it raised a stir, a charge revisited, clearly a threat.

And Ryssand looked afraid. "I received a traveler, Your Majesty, who turned out to have such a message, and who had alarming reports out of Amefel . . . reports of which I had no knowledge Your Majesty already knew."

Dangerous man, subtle as a snake, but there was no escaping the inappropriate nature of his actions and Cuthan's, and on such subtle issues did the support of those listening sway.

"We knew. We *knew* from the source, and we knew the truth of the conditions in the lands to the south and the reasons for the building of those fortifications. We based our judgment of those reasons on our *personal* knowledge of that source. *Have* you personal knowledge of Tasmôrden's character? Of Tasmôrden's actions this past year? Or how long have you received his messages?"

And so, without accusing, he planted his own seeds in the minds of those wine-touched individuals hanging on their every word.

Opinion of those outside these walls, however, had less to do with protocol than with rumor. And Ryssand's resources in that sense went far beyond Cuthan and Parsynan, beyond anything even a king could muster. Rumor spread on the wings of religious fear: they had rid themselves of Udryn, but now they had the Quinalt Patriarch of Amefel newly arrived in the town, complaining in the inner councils of the Quinalt that the old ways were gaining far too firm a foothold in Tristen's lands. Here was a man who had fled his post and a tolerably comfortable living rather than endure Tristen's rule over him—or so the Quinalt would see it. Guelen soldiers, too, Parsynan's men, whom Tristen's soft-handed mercy had let leave his land alive . . . they had talked in the taverns and all the low places, so the rumors were fairly sped.

Oh, there were a dozen ways men of Ryssand's stamp could take any mercy and turn it back as a weapon.

He had known Ryssand would do this, had seen no real way to prevent it, but he had prevented the worst of the damage, and made his case in front of witnesses half-gone with wine, minds on which subtleties and details would be lost.

And so he waited for Efanor to move in, as he at last did, and interposed quiet, personal words to Ryssand. The intervention became a small, urgent conference, the drift of which came to him, anger on Ryssand's part, fear, and Efanor's solicitous promises. Ryssand was not unscathed in the view of the hall, either: his countenance had gone from ruddiness to pallor and back to congested redness that suggested ill health. The man had lost a son to his quest for power, a recent loss, and no sham; but Cefwyn had no pity.

"I beg Your Majesty's pardon," Ryssand said at last, bringing a reluctant silence to the murmur of speculation among the courtiers.

"I urge Your Majesty grant it," Efanor said . . . playing his part.

"I will not hear this," Cefwyn said, playing his, while Idrys loomed over all.

"Your Majesty," Efanor repeated. "I ask it."

It was what they agreed. When the storm had grown too great and become dangerous to the realm, Efanor would ask pardon, and intercede for Ryssand. Efanor would thus widen his own small court, hitherto mostly scholars and priests, include among his debtors a potential father-in-law, and thereby set himself as confessor to receive all the things that an unreasonable king would not hear.

Cefwyn settled back against the throne in his most forbidding manner. "I shall hear *you*, brother. In the meantime, do not consider we entertain this traitorous Amefin earl or any of his connections, Elwynim or otherwise.—Play!" he shouted at the musicians, who had not stirred in this utter stillness of the hall. After brief hesitation they took up the paselle they had been playing, from its beginning.

It was a light, a graceful music, little appropriate to a royal tantrum, but the whole court drew a collective breath. No one moved to dance except two very young folk who hesitated toward that notion, and desisted, frozen in place.

Slowly, very slowly, Ryssand backed and bowed his way to safety, ignoring Murandys in his retreat.

Slowly the court began to murmur and to move, half a hundred statues come to life. The musicians struggled on, and Cefwyn waved a hand at a cluster of the young people and smiled, waving them to the floor. They moved with uncertainty, and the talk broke out among their elders, almost fit to drown the music.

Cefwyn drew a breath and a second, willing to be soothed as Ninévrisë sought his hand across the gap between their seats.

"Well done," Cefwyn said to his small company of conspirators. "Well done."

"Detestable man," Ninévrisë said.

"Is he not?" Cefwyn said acidly. "Is he not, indeed? But he didn't have all he wanted."

"The court knows the royal disposition," Idrys said, "to the good, say I."

They had married Luriel to Panys, and regained Ryssand and his vixenish daughter . . . well, to no great profit, that latter transaction, but inevitable, once Ryssand dared return.

And it was probably best. Ryssand in the country was apt to breed secret ills, rumor and supposition let loose unchecked by fact. Now Ryssand had to mind what he said. He knew he was watched.

And for good or ill, the rumors were abroad tonight, and those who had not heard would hear. The leaven of the zealots was still fermenting, the discontent of the populace with what, in taverns and in higher places, they called Her Grace's war . . . was no less in certain quarters.

So Tasmôrden magnanimously offered Her Grace sovereignty over a third of Elwynor, and Ylesuin a third, with not a blow struck, their mission accomplished, and no Guelen or Ryssandish lads to bury as a consequence. He had no doubt he had given Ryssand a few wounds in kind.

"Ryssand and the zealots," Cefwyn muttered so only his brother and Ninévrisë and Idrys could hear. "Backing Aséyneddin's heir, and him the ally of the sorcerer who brought down Mauryl. What a contortion they made to get everyone into that alliance!—Do you know, Jormys should preach against it. A few good sermons would do great good."

"I'll speak to Jormys," Efanor said. And a moment later: "I'll go speak to Ryssand and his daughter, and smooth his feathers."

"Mind your own," Cefwyn said and, with great misgiving, watched his brother descend the steps.

Ryssand wanted that royal alliance, oh, indeed Ryssand wanted it. It must give him indigestion, considering the situation he was in now.

Clever men could become great fools when what they most wanted dangled in reach of their fingers. And Ryssand might well enter into conspiracy with Efanor, who posed himself to draw the lightning of all the discontents in the court.

"If that marriage goes forward," Ninévrisë said faintly, beneath the music, "that man will wish Efanor to be king. Have you taken account of that?"

It was a thought. It was certainly a thought. But his trust in Efanor was oldest of all trust in the world. *Efanor* would countenance no move against him: that was solid as the rock under the throne.

"The army will move to the river on the first clear day," he said, "and let Tasmôrden make you another offer when you're standing in Ilefínian. When there's no enemy across the river, and the worry of the war is past, *then* let Ryssand consider his position with me, and speak me fair again."

"My lord king." Idrys had moved close, after brief absence, and had that edge to his voice that meant urgency.

Cefwyn turned his head, saw the black eminence of his reign bearing a grim look indeed.

"What is it?" he asked in honest alarm, and Idrys came close, closer, to his very ear, and whispered a handful of words:

"A letter from Amefel: the Aswydds did reach Tristen. Lady Tarien's with child and claims it's yours."

Cefwyn was not certain whether his heart beat the next moment. He did not let his face change: royal demeanor was schooled from far too early to betray him now. He was aware of all the room, all the reach of consequences, and of his lady sitting at his side.

It was possible, on all counts. He had been a fool, defying his father, disdaining his responsibilities. He had done things he now regretted.

"One of Tristen's letters?" he asked, fey attempt at humor, for they all agreed Tristen wrote the worst letters any of them had ever read, letters utterly lacking in detail. If that was the case he truly despaired of learning more than Idrys had just said.

"Master grayfrock wrote, too," Idrys said with uncommon gentleness. "I have the letters safe with me. I don't know how long this will go unrumored. There are witnesses enough in Amefel, where I fear it won't be secret by now."

Cefwyn's fingers were numb. He rubbed fingertips together, feeling very little, and looked at Ninévrisë, who had heard some of it, but not all.

They won the joust with Ryssand, damn the luck, and were hit from ambush—his own doing.

CHAPTER 9

I *advise you so that you may decide the advantageous time to report the news to your court* . . .

So Emuin had written.

There was no advantageous time to report such news to his bride of not many weeks. Cefwyn was painfully conscious of Ninévrisë beside him, in this intimate grouping in the Blue Hall, in privacy even from the pages. She listened as Idrys read the letter aloud. Her face grave and pale, her eyes no longer dancing, but set on her hands in her lap.

"Forgive me," Cefwyn said, taking her hand in his. "Nevris,—I did a great many things in those days, and always escaped the consequences. This one . . . this one . . . with Tarien Aswydd, of all people . . . gods save me . . . I can't explain it to you."

"She has the gift," Ninévrisë said in low voice, and as if she could no longer contain herself, disengaged her hand, rose from her chair, and walked briskly away to a place remote from him, from Idrys, from Annas, whom they had gathered to share this calamity.

There was no real privacy for a reigning monarch. In very fact, there was nothing he did that failed to impinge on others' lives and fortunes, and gods knew he had not done wisely in this.

"She has the gift," Ninévrisë repeated, and turned to face him, fingers laced together before her. "As will *our* child."

In the depths of self-accusation Cefwyn heard it, and heard it twice, and rose to his feet, asking almost silently: "Our child?"

"I don't know," Ninévrisë said. "I've wished. What more can one do with the gift? A great deal more, it seems."

What more might Tarien Aswydd have done? What might you

have expected of these women, fool? Those questions she kindly held unasked.

"At that hour, in those days," he said quietly, not knowing how to interpret her wounded silence, "I had no good appreciation of what wizardry might do or not do. I was used to Emuin. He worked tricks. He refused to do magic. I didn't know what I was dealing with.—And, no, damn it all, that's not true, either. I knew. In my heart I knew. I didn't believe it would come near *me*. Nothing else did. I was young and damnably foolish, a year ago."

Her face was a regal mask. Did a guilty heart only imagine the sheen of tears in the candlelight?

It was after the festivities, late. All fires in the hearths should have burned down and the servants should be down to one candle, replacing the old ones upstairs and down.

But for this late conference, on his order, the servants had built up the fire in the little hearth and lit every sconce, so pretense and falsehood should have no place to hide, and so that afterward he could not hope he had dreamt this night. It was bright as day, and neither of them were likely to sleep afterward.

"I was a fool," Cefwyn repeated heavily. "There's no more to say for it."

Ninévrisë gave a great sigh and looked elsewhere for a space, then lifted her chin and looked at him squarely.

"We'd not even met," she said.

"You're far too kind."

"Can I be otherwise?" Ninévrisë said sharply. "And can I not pity the child? No one loves it. Its mother has no heart. How will it fare in the world?"

"I don't know," he said. Her question struck memories of his own severance from his father, who had never loved him, his mother, who, dying, had not had the chance.

He had not even thought of that burden, had not, in that sense, thought of the child at all, beyond an embarrassment and a disaster.

"And what will be his inheritance?" Ninévrisë pursued him relentlessly. "And who will be his father?"

"I don't know," he said again, left with no other answer. He found himself with no pity to spare for another boy with no father and no hint of a father's love.

"Folly, to give his first years to Tarien Aswydd," Ninévrisë said, counting the difficulties of a child's existence before he was born. "And yet what *shall* we do? Bring him here? Let your gods-fearing Guelenfolk see a son of yours with wizard-gift . . . as Emuin and

Tristen alike think he has? Tristen has no doubt at all it's a son."
She folded her arms beneath her breast, hugged tightly. "I have only
a suspicion and a hope of a child, as yet, one I can't even tell you
is real, and now he'll not be your firstborn."

She had told him they were to have a child, and he had let that
precious moment slide by in an argument over a royal bastard. It
was an unforgivable, irrevocable lapse.

"Our child. To me—"

"Don't disallow this child of the Aswydd woman! He exists!"

"It's none I care to acknowledge!"

"Yet he exists."

"If I could undo it . . ."

"There's no undoing it. My father used to say that if and could
and wish have no effect outside philosophy. But they do in wizardry,
and I won't wish this child harm. I will *not!*"

He was shaken to the core, confronted by an iron determination,
news he was in no wise prepared to have twice in a night, and his
lady's unanticipated defense of her rival's child. He had no notion
which direction to face, and knew Idrys witnessed his discomfiture—
no advice from that quarter, not a word.

"I ask your forgiveness," Cefwyn said. "It's all I can say. It's my
fault. And hers."

"But none of the babe's fault. And *she* will teach him to desire
the throne and to hate me, and perhaps hate you."

He could not deny her fears. They were his.

"There is a remedy," Idrys said, intervening at last, grim master
crow, reminding a king with a threatened kingdom what terrible,
unspeakable deeds he might command, at the lightest word.

And did Idrys dare bring that darkness into Ninévrisë's hearing?
He found himself all but trembling.

"Don't disallow him," Ninévrisë repeated.

It was not hers to command the Lord Commander. It was his,
and he drew a long, steadying breath.

"He's all but born," he said, "considering the time it was possible. The very limited time it could have happened." It was not the
privilege of a king to sink his head into his hands and shut the world
out of his ears. "He's with Tristen, and Emuin. That's something."
Tristen's letter said *he* and *a son.* He fell into it unthinking, and then
realized he had admitted it.

"And *with his mother,*" Idrys said, "who is a sorceress. That's
also something to consider, my lord king."

The Marhanen temper rose up on his next breath, silently railing

137

on fate and wizardry. But his heart refused to lead him where Idrys advised him to go . . . and he knew whom he had made keeper of his heart, and his gentler nature. He knew what terrible, unanswerable force he would contend with if he attempted the babe's life—and knew that he would himself bring prophecy down on his head.

"Tristen wouldn't countenance it," he said with a sense of relief, and then knew his own bearings, as if he had found the daylight in this night. "And gods help me, *I* won't."

"Both Emuin and the Lord of Amefel are potent barriers to a boy," Idrys said, "but when this seed casts a shade, my lord king of Ylesuin, what shape will it have? And, pray,—" It was one of Idrys' most detestable habits, that pause before his worst remarks: "—what heritage and inheritance will this boy claim?"

Cefwyn bit back an angry request for silence: Idrys' value was precisely that he would say what he thought, whether or not it pleased him; and do what had to be done, at times, whether or not his king had the will to act.

But was Idrys to rule Ylesuin, or was he? And were the decisions to be decisions not to decide, and to rein back Idrys?

And should Idrys say such things to him in Ninévrisë's hearing?

He found he was as shaken by that as by the facts themselves, and discovered in himself a sense that Tristen had found and Ninévrisë had tended, until he did not know who was master of his opinions, or where he had passed beyond Idrys' dark counsel, but he knew he had never made a decision he was surer of. He thought how Emuin, when he entertained notions of being rid of Tristen, had counseled him very simply, and in the face of all the danger Tristen posed him: Win his friendship.

And was that it now?

Win this unintended son? Acknowledge a bastard and create a claimant when the barons' damned haggling over the marriage treaty had left Ninévrisë's son no more heir to the throne of Ylesuin than Tarien's son?

He was mad.

He had gone quite mad, and went to his unresisting lady and took her hand, and looked at her eye to eye, no easy deed.

"I don't know what I can do," he said. "I don't know. I only know Tristen has the situation in his hands. And I know what he *won't* do, and won't countenance, and I know you're right."

"I don't," she said. "I don't know that I'm right. But I know what's not right."

"He'll have his mother," Cefwyn said. "And gods save him, his aunt. But at Amefel now he has Tristen and Emuin, and the Aswydds won't have their way, will they?" He wished Idrys would leave. He longed to gather his bride against his heart and attempt to mend things—to talk about *their* son, and make the moment what it ought to be. But no such gesture would mend what now was.

He tried. He extended a hand. Ninévrisë stood with arms tightly folded, protecting her heart, gazing somewhere that was not this room.

"Go," he said to Idrys, trying to signal him that he wanted rapid, silent departure. "I think we know all we need to deal with."

"There is one other letter," Idrys said, ignoring his king, and drew a second folded, sealed missive from his coat.

And what other, more disastrous missive could have arrived, and from whom, and on what damnable misreading of him had Idrys held it back? The anger all but strangled him.

"For Her Grace," Idrys said, "from Lord Tristen."

It was unprecedented that Tristen write to Ninévrisë. But of course—of course, Cefwyn thought, it was a separate consolation from Tristen, and he was a dog to resent it, even with Idrys' abominable timing; even with his own pain and Ninévrisë's. It came, he was sure, out of the devastating kindness Tristen had, so often timed to wring the temper out of him and drive him to distraction. It was, as much as Tristen understood this matter of children and the getting of them—utterly well-meant, and completely upsetting.

Ninévrisë took it, read what seemed only a word or two. Her hand flew to her heart, and, clenched, lifted to her lips.

Then she said to Idrys, "It's nothing. There's nothing here. Please leave us." The last was sudden, anguished, more plea than order, and with only a glance at him to confirm it, Idrys silently bowed and left.

Ninévrisë ebbed into a chair and held the small paper close against her heart, and Cefwyn held his breath, trying with all his might not to pry into what was, until she willed otherwise, her business.

Then Ninévrisë released the paper to her lap, and to his eye there was nothing written on it, nothing at all.

"He's afraid for you," she said in a trembling voice, and a tear traced a path down on a face otherwise tranquil. "And afraid for me, and would defend us both with all his heart. He wishes us both well."

He could only be one man.

But he still saw nothing to tell him those things. Or he saw nothing he wanted to see . . . for he knew Ninévrisë had wizard-gift, a gift kept small and quiet and never wizard-taught, except what she had learned of her father. And if there was something magical written on the blank paper that only wizards could see, then she had just used it.

He forgave. Against the evidence of his sins of the flesh, her good use of the gift she was born with could hardly weigh at all. He was still her debtor: *she* at least was true as gold to her promises, all of them.

"Do you *read* something there?" he asked, and dropped to a knee beside her chair, to gaze at a paper as blank as the day it was made, save only Tristen's signature and red wax seal.

"I know his heart. I know what he wishes me to know, as surely as if I read it."

"We can trust him." That was true, no matter what in the world changed, and the remembrance of that warmed his heart to a stronger, steadier beat. "I *do* trust him, Nevris. He's scared me at times beyond good sense. And he does, now. What does he say about this?"

"That he loves us. He loves us so much, so kindly . . . no one could deserve it."

"We can contest for deserts," he said, "and you would win." He was grateful, desperately so, to find hope of affection and forgiveness in this blank paper, and in her glance. "If anyone can care for Tarien's baby, do you think, it would be Tristen. He won't harm it. It's not in him to harm it. But he won't let it do harm, either."

She gave a desperate small laugh. "Tristen? Gods, to care for a baby? So much comes through. I don't know how." She placed a hand over the paper and inhaled deeply, several times. "It's as if I was there! Emuin's upset with you."

"Gods, upset. Far too small a word."

"And Tristen's confused."

"Tristen's always confused." His spirits soared in this exchange of breathless probabilities, almost as if she could see through a window into Amefel, one shut to him: but he saw it through her eyes, almost now as if he could see it, and could say that it was true. What she saw gave her courage, and she lent it to him. The relief was so great he could all but laugh. "Tell me all you know."

"There's a boy," Ninévrisë said. "Emuin's found a boy to help him. I don't understand his name. But there's some sort of boy."

"I could be jealous," Cefwyn said fervently, who had been the boy in Emuin's care, in days of climbing trees and skinning knees. "But I'm glad for Emuin, and the boy."

"Uwen's well. So are all the others. Captain Anwyll's off at the river and the weather's been wretched, the same as here. I think . . . I think Tristen's doing very well, except for Orien Aswydd and Tarien."

"That's a large exception." The flood of information after Tristen's lamentably terse letters both cheered him like the voice of a friend and then gave him pause, as if perhaps Ninévrisë added to her guesses to please him. "Does he true say all that?—Of course he does. How could you make all that up?"

Ninévrisë pressed the sheet to her heart. "I *hear* him say it, or I don't hear, but it's like a dream, and I'm sure what he meant. He's done so much . . . the changes, and building the walls and the fortresses up, and he's built up at Althalen . . ."

It should be a lance of ice to the heart . . . the Marhanens had risen to power at Althalen's fall: the condition of his dynasty depended on Althalen's ruin.

But he heard it only half-alarmed, for Tristen did it, and he refused to think evil of his friend—least of all for the consolation he had given Ninévrisë. "I don't think the Quinalt will like that," he said, "but damn them."

"He had to have it for the people, for all the people running from Tasmôrden." Her voice was unlike her, trembling. "And he's saved some of them. He's made them welcome in his lands. He's settled protection all up and down the river, despite the snow. And the lords have come to him, Aeself, and others: a cousin of mine is alive!"

"He's done well," Cefwyn said. "He's done very well. But no matter how Tasmôrden provokes him, he mustn't let those folk start fighting on his land. He mustn't attack from there." And on a sudden thought and a soaring hope: "Can you use that paper and talk to *him*?"

She shook her head, dashing the hope before it reached any height at all. "No. I can't. It doesn't work that way. He cast a spell on the paper. I couldn't do it."

"But don't lose it," he said. The hope, however uninformed, modified itself to the thought that the letter might be bespelled to go on spilling things to them as they happened. He longed to touch the paper himself, wondering whether a man as deaf to magic as the nearest ox could possibly gain some sense of Tristen's presence from it. He knew acutely what he had lost when he had had to send

Tristen away: that sense of things possible and magical that had lent him courage to fight all his battles, that sense of a friend at his back that no one but Tristen had ever given him.

And now that steady, reassuring presence came through his lady's voice, and gave him an absurd confidence that they were not alone, no matter how things seemed to close around them.

But he forbore to touch it, in case the enchantment might die in his hands, and thrive only in Ninévrisë's.

"Thank you," he said. And added, "I love you," as he said often: but now he felt constrained to say it in apology for irrevocable and damaging acts. "I love you for your forbearance. I love you a hundred times more now than at the first. And if you still love me through all this, I'll be so far in your debt a hundred years won't see me clear. Once and for all, I had no idea, when I exiled the Aswydds. *She* may have known. But I didn't."

"Why *Tarien*?" was the sole unkind question, and he could only shrug and force himself to look straight into her eyes.

"I ask myself that question, I assure you. I'll ask it so long as I live. And I can't answer it."

"I answer it. Sorcery led you. You couldn't be so foolish."

"I wish that were so," he said, and bowed his head. "I have been that foolish, and was that foolish, and generally I needed no great help at it."

She embraced him where he knelt, leaned her head against his, all the soft perfume of her hair, and the random hard edge of pearls wound into her braids.

"The news of this will get out," she said, her hand against his cheek. "You know you have to deny this son or acknowledge him in some fashion."

"Let Emuin prove what he is first. Then I'll know what to do."

"Word might already have gotten out. If the men who were guilty of the raid on the nunnery didn't know, the nuns might have. She's near her time. They must have seen. And if they missed it, at least everyone in Amefel must know by now, and there might be spies: in everything else we think there might be spies. Wouldn't they report this back to Guelessar?"

The Aswydds were not a presence one could slip unknown into the town, or keep close in a house where every servant knew them. It was a surety that someone would talk. "It's too much to hope Ryssand doesn't learn it within the week, and will bring it into the open at the worst moment."

"If," she said slowly, "he doesn't already know. She is Cuthan's cousin. Might that not be the arrow they're still holding in reserve? Might *Tasmôrden* know and be conspiring with Cuthan on behalf of that child, price for price, for the next step in their plan?" Her fingers sought his on the arm of the chair. "Peace with Tasmôrden. *Peace* with him. I can't grant this. It's a barbed hook. Everyone of sense has to know it. It's not even to Ylesuin's advantage, let alone yours."

All she said was true, the depth of his betrayal of her had filled his heart and warped his thinking, and he grasped at her logic as a drowning man to a life rope.

"When a battle begins," she continued, "the archers go first, don't they?"

"So as not to hit their own men, yes, commonly they go first." He knew it was not archers she meant, but he followed her where she led, and answered honestly and soberly, looking into gray eyes that hinted, to his mind, of violets.

"I think," she said, "I think we are seeing the archers of this spring."

"Precursors to the attack?"

"I think sorcery's not done with us. Lewenbrook was the beginning of it. After the archers, what would you look for?"

"The flying attacks. The cavalry."

"And the battle line behind that. Well screened, not evident."

"Archery," he echoed, thinking that it was like that, bolts seemingly random, but to the advantage of Ryssand, all to Ryssand's and Tasmôrden's advantage. Except Ryssand had lost his son, and perhaps suffered doubts in Efanor's approaches, as if perhaps there was advantage he could gain. His enemies were not unscathed, so not everything had gone their way.

But right now Ryssand hoped only to confuse matters and gather power into his hands in the confusion. Even if he had won the encounter with Ryssand and cast doubts on the offer, his lords were surely still tempted by this peace, this offer of dividing Elwynor into parcels one of which would be theirs, new lands, new honors, new titles. It had been hard enough to lead men to war with no promise of gain . . . and now if their enemy offered peace and a third of the contested lands, the only barb in the bait his own men would see was the fact Tasmôrden was akin to the hated Bryalt and probably employed sorcery.

He had hit that point hard tonight. He had, he hoped, made them see it.

But that meant that his own likeliest allies against this damnable treaty Cuthan brought were, ironically, the same orthodox Guelen priests that had opposed Ninévrisë's marriage in the first place. The orthodoxy that so narrowly had voted to confirm his nomination of Jormys for Patriarch were more than unlikely bedfellows for him: they were snakes in the sheets. Snuggle close to them, and he was sure they still could bite, and would, irrational in their abhorrence of all things foreign . . . and would they find tolerance for foreignness across the river to be rid of foreignness in the royal bed?

And now, at the moment when all these things were true, when he needed be Guelen to the core and most needed to be able to restrain these skittish, volatile barons from a headlong rush toward Tasmôrden's lure of profitable peace, lo! . . . he had a half-sorcerous son about to be born, and rumor about to break forth in Amefel, of all places.

Give it a fortnight, and Ninévrisë was right. If the rumor needed walk barefoot from Amefel, it would reach Lord Ryssand.

Thank the gods he had the letter, he thought. And then, Thank Tristen. They were ahead of the rumor by some few days, if the gods were good; and Ninévrisë had not had to hear the news first in hall, to be assailed by *that* on Ryssand's lips.

"There's one thing I can do," he said, "that will dash cold water on this peace."

"Attack?" She looked at him in puzzlement. "The snow's not stopped."

"The snow will keep my contentious lords busy . . . or have them forsworn, Ryssand with them. I'll have the army on the march and damn the weather, damn the ice, and damn the opposition."

"The loyal will go and suffer. Ryssand and his allies will dispute you, and if you've sent the like of Panys and the loyal men to the river, and have only Ryssand and his friends in court . . ."

There was such shrewd judgment in so sweet a face. He gazed at it in deep consciousness of his good fortune.

"I can deal with Ryssand," he said. "Only so my friends stand by me."

"That I will," Ninévrisë said, "to the gates of Ilefínian."

"No!"

"To my capital."

He had met the Regent of Elwynor at *his* gates when first he laid eyes on her, muddy-skirted, leading men to conference or to certain death, and it was that look she had now. His better sense wanted to deny her, the more so since she spoke of carrying his child. His better sense ached even at the thought of her riding, in the winter, and in hardship, and into war.

But she was no fool: she had proven that at Lewenbrook, obeyed orders like a soldier and kept her post; and could any man who had been on that field deny any heart that had known that danger, no matter the fear he had for her?

"To your capital," he said. "To the promise I made you." He had kept that, at least, and meant to keep the rest he had sworn to her, if it cost him a son.

But Ryssand would do anything to prevent him.

And he was within a very little now of calling Idrys and bidding him do that which he had resisted doing: arranging Ryssand's lasting absence. But he did not.

But now, considering his grandfather's example, a man who had died abed and at an old age, with a kingdom at peace . . . he was not sure whether, in a king, it was not a mortal sin to refrain from that order.

CHAPTER 10

The hills of Amefel north of the
town were utterly changed in their outlines, white and rounded, small
trees covered. The road had become a zigzag of sharp-edged small
drifts, but Dys' great feet thumped through them with ease and enthusiasm, and even on so grim a mission, Tristen found it a rare
pleasure to break through these barriers of winter, he and Uwen,
and the small number of Amefin guard behind them . . . pleasure
amid grimmer intent, for it was Crissand's point of encounter with
trouble they sought, and the band who had fired at him in the dark
and the storm.

That answer might easily lie in error on both sides: they went to
confirm that hope at Althalen—for it was quite possible that Aeself's
men and Crissand had had a near pass, one with the other.

But in case that was not the source of the arrows, and to be sure
of the safety of Modeyneth and Anwyll's camp, at the far end of the
road, Tristen had requested a band of Ivanim light horse, armed and
ready for encounter, to ride out ahead of him and assure themselves
that things were well in that direction.

He rode out himself, then, for he had the gift to know who was
in the land, far better than any scout, and Cevulirn himself had
volunteered to stand by Tassand and Lusin in administering things
in Henas'amef while he was gone . . . for Lusin and his company
had become far too useful there, Crissand was still nursing his
wound, and wished to go, but Emuin called it folly, and it afflicted
him most when he sat a horse, so there he stayed in the town, as-
sisting Cevulirn and overseeing Tassand's oversight.

So Tristen had no doubt at all in his riding out that he had left
the town in good hands—no slight to Uwen, who had not had the

authority Cevulirn had, when the Patriarch had deserted the town: not even Cevulirn could have prevented that disaster.

Uwen was glad to be with him, all the same, and said so.

"As I ain't set to be any town mayor, nor ever will be, and gods save me, I didn't know what I was to do when His Reverence up and went."

"No more than I could have done," Tristen said, "except I used magic, and that wouldn't have been wise, would it?"

"Not if His Reverence knew 't," Uwen said, "but happens as most times folk don't know, do they?"

"I don't," Tristen said as they rode. "I don't wish people to do things or not to do them. It doesn't seem polite."

Uwen laughed. "No," Uwen agreed. "It don't, at that."

They were on the West Road, since other searchers had gone out to the north. It had seemed good to go by the back route toward Althalen, to be sure that no enemy had slipped in to establish a presence in the lesser-traveled west of Amefel. That brought them generally toward Lewenbrook, though they would not go that close to Marna Wood, and it brought them generally toward Emwy village.

Near Emwy was the ruin of the westernmost bridge, the one that had let Aséyneddin across before Lewenbrook, and it had no garrison, only the observance of Pelumer's rangers, who reported that the bridge stonework still stood, but that it had no decking.

That was quick to mend if an enemy dared use it. With a road to guide them and a means by which stealthy small bands could come deep into Amefel, it seemed a weak point—not utterly so, for it was Auld Syes' land, and under wards far stronger than any he had set at Modeyneth.

But now it seemed worth the inquiry. They would ride out to the west and ride back again by the North Road, where the attack on Crissand had taken place. That way they covered both routes, and Cevulirn's riders were further assurance, deeper into the north than they would go. They would set Modeyneth's men to watching and scouring the hills, which shepherds could do far more efficiently than armed riders or anyone but the Lanfarnessemen.

And well knowing that Pelumer's rangers were abroad from here to Modeyneth and into the rough lands beyond, and that Aeself's men maintained patrols, he rode plainly under the banners, the red of Amefel and the black of Althalen and Ynefel, and with all the equipage of war, besides that they wore the red bands of cloth that Pelumer had decreed to distinguish them from intruders.

And if he needed any other distinction to mark his passage through his province, Owl joined him, soaring past now and again as if to be sure he was still where Owl thought—or perhaps to torment them all with his silent approaches, just near enough the horses to startle.

Owl was not given to lengthy flights, and found perches, Tristen was sure, in one and another of the scattered trees . . . but Owl passed by them at times when there seemed to be no perch, when the hills were as bare as eggs and the land was flat under winter white, and his coming and going put the men on edge. No few of the Guelenmen blessed themselves when Owl would pass near, and one of his guards remarked that, "That bird's often ahead o' trouble."

That did not seem to be Owl's purpose in joining them, however, not as he thought today. Owl might presage change, but he also presaged discovery.

Change came of finding new things, however; and sometimes those things were not what one might wish. It was an all-day ride, in increasing cold, this ride they had undertaken, down a road he had ridden more than once in Cefwyn's company, again with Ninévrisë, and last of all toward Lewenbrook and home again.

That last journey had been very different . . . joyous for the victory, solemn for the loss of many, many lives. And that journey stayed most on his mind—the last time he had seen this land, at summer's end, with leaves on the trees that now were bare and snow-coated.

They counted on an overnight stay at Althalen, but in consideration of the difficulty of provisioning the residents there, they carried provisions for two days. It was slower going than usual for riders, on account of the snow impeding progress, and although they had started at first light, they began to ask themselves whether they might not need those supplies tonight, fearing they might not reach Althalen before the last glow of day left the sky.

"There's reputed to be haunts," said Gweyl, of his night guard . . . not that Gweyl or any of his guard would flee if a whole host of Auld Syes' company trooped across the road. The men who served him had all stood their ground under remarkable circumstances. But it was a worried look, all the same.

"We'll miss supper, at least," Uwen said with a sigh, "damn this road and its holes. We can't make speed wi'out ye break your neck, man, so we just keep goin'."

"They'll provide for us," Tristen said. "No need to make camp. We can go as long as there's light and after."

"I don't doubt they'll be glad to see ye," Uwen said, and added with a laugh: "If it was just us metal-coats, we'd have a cold 'un and a foul look from th' landlord . . . but then, it ain't, and the Elwynim ain't goin' to grudge you a late arrival."

Ahead of them the banners made their identity sure, and would do so as long as there was light to show the colors: so Tristen hoped, thinking of arrows and Crissand's misfortune: foul looks from the landlords indeed.

But a hill farther on, they came to a tree the snow did not disguise, a lone tree taller than the snow-covered rocks among which it grew, and there they crossed a frozen stream, a small sheet of ice.

Owl, absent for the last hour, called from among the trees, and sat as a lump of feathers in the fading wintry light.

"Damn that bird!" Uwen said, startled, and then: "Forgive me, but he don't give warning."

"He doesn't," Tristen said. But it was as if the land had gone in disguise under the snow. Suddenly, from that old tree and the rocks he recalled, the land looked altogether familiar. He remembered being here with Petelly, before he had met Ninévrisë. He remembered the grass on the bank, how it had grown, and how Petelly had drunk from water now hard as glass.

The sun was beginning to stain the leaden, sifting clouds, but he pointed to the way he remembered, and led them off the road and into the untracked white of the hills.

Untracked, but as they rode Tristen recognized the path all along, an old road, a broad course through the rounded roughness of the sparsely wooded hills, paved, once. He felt the presence of old stones in his very sense of the land, and guided Dys around a buried wall where the road took a turn.

"Wary o' them stones," Uwen cautioned the men. "There's trenches an' foundations to stumble into."

Indeed it seemed to Tristen as if buildings should stand to left and to right, and there, yes, a fountain had once stood, fed by that very spring. Now there was only snow, and a straggle of gorse.

Old stones soon poked edges up atop the snow; and a wind rose, sporting around the horses, blowing up under their bellies and playing around their faces. Owl, tracking them since the stream, dodged and dived through the gusts.

"Damn!" Uwen said in exasperation, for Owl made Cass shy violently under him, and arrows could scarcely do that.

"Is there ghosts?" Gweyl asked.

"I'm sure," Tristen said, and yet had no alarm about reaching out into the land, listening for living souls . . . and they were there. He had a sense of presence, nothing threatening. He found nothing threatening in the sport the gusts made.

But there, he felt something other than living souls, something which grew as the light faded and the wind rose.

"Spooky place," Uwen said. "Wind's talking."

It did make a sound, a soft sighing across the snow.

"It's a welcome, no more."

The banners flew out, snapped and bucked, trying the strength of the men that held them steady. And now the wind acquired voices, a mournful sound.

"Seen this," Uwen said above the sound. "It's the ol' lady!"

"Don't fear her," Tristen said. "But go quietly, all."

Uwen had seen Auld Syes more than once, and had seen the Shadows of Althalen. The Amefin guard was for the most part new to this, but they went doggedly ahead toward ruins where they would not willingly have ridden, glancing warily about them.

And a turn or two on, they came on a place where something had made old streaks in the snow, and where strange shapes jutted, half-uncovered, from the depth of the drifts.

They came closer, finding the glint of metal overlaid with ice, then the angle of an elbow, a knee, a shoulder, all frozen in the snow.

"Gods bless," the sergeant of the Amefins said. "It's Elwynim."

It was no hapless band of Amefin that lay thus frozen by the winter, armed and armored. He rode by, giving the area a passing glance, and near a ruined wall they found another such clump of frozen remains, well armored, and that armor sheeted with ice. The faces, for a few showed, were openmouthed, as if they cried out against their deaths.

Suddenly the wind sported with them, and skipped, and streaked the snow and tugged at the banners. Owl swooped near, broad, blunt wings atilt on a snow-laden gust.

"Captain," Gweyl said anxiously.

"Stick close," Uwen said, and half turned in his saddle to call out to the guardsmen. "Don't fear the wind, lads! It's on m'lord's side an' always has been."

The banners flew sideways in the gusts, and the blast of ice-edged cold rocked even Dys' huge strength. Oaths escaped some lips: "Hush!" others said.

"Auld Syes!" Tristen called out. "Do you hear? Soft! Speak softly to your folk!"

The wind fell somewhat, and gusts skipped away over the nearest hill, streaking deep tracks in the snow. Snow still blew, and ran in small clouds off the tops of old walls, in the last sinking of the sun.

But now they came to higher walls which partially sheltered them from the wind, and entered a maze of ruins, old stone walls long devoid of plaster, all dark gray against the snow, and liberally dusted with new fall from the roiled heavens.

Then, past a narrow convergence of ruined walls, appeared walls built of wood, structures abutted up against the old stoneworks. They rode through a gap in old stones and smelled fires, and heard the high voices of children at play.

They and the children caught sight of each other at the same moment, a few heavily bundled figures that stood stock-still and stared, then ran shrieking in among the wooden walls.

That brought out the elders, into that strange still time between oncoming storm and evening, a dim, snow-veiled number of cloaked men with weapons, and a handful of women tightly bundled in shawls and cloaks, carrying spears.

Owl flew across Tristen's sight, and came back again, and presumptuously spread his great wings for a landing, with no perch, if Tristen had not put out his gloved hand.

On that, Owl settled. The banners flew straight out in the gusting wind and Owl, feathers clamped tight and still ruffling, shifted his grip, rowing with his wings for balance.

The guard had stopped still about him, and the leader of the folk came through the blowing snow to pay his respects, came earnestly, sweeping off the cowl to show his face.

It was Aeself, bearded, bright-eyed, and cheerful at the sight of them.

"M'lord," Aeself said with a deep reverence, and turned and shouted out to the others. "This is the lord of Althalen and Ynefel! This is himself, the lord Tristen and his men, and our lord's guard out of Amefel! Show him respect!"

The heavily cloaked men and women knelt in the snow, and the elder children uncertainly did as their elders did, the youngest huddling shyly into parental arms. More came out of hiding among the buildings, until around about the area there might have been a hundred, two hundred souls, all kneeling, in a great half circle.

Astonished at so many, Tristen stepped down from the saddle, and raised up Aeself, and another of his men, then a woman who chanced to be near, for this kneeling and reverence was not his, and nothing he sought. Aeself he embraced, and looked him in the eyes, where he saw the pride Aeself had in what he had made of Althalen. Encouraged, the people, too, rose to see, and Uwen and the guard silently dismounted, until they all stood facing one another, a gathering so silent for that moment of assessment that the gusting wind and the restless shifting and blowing of weary horses was the loudest sound in their camp.

"Lord of Althalen," Aeself said against that silence, "you've come to your capital."

"You've done very well," Tristen said, for dull as he was to proprieties, he knew how much Aeself yearned to be in the right of matters. "You've made these people safe."

"My lord," Aeself said, and hastily waved a hand at those standing near. "Bring our lord and his men meat and drink! See to their horses. Hurry there!"

He had forbidden Aeself to hail him king, and Aeself had obeyed that wish, but he knew the thought in Aeself's heart, and he saw it in these people, who welcomed him and his guard and opened up the wide, rough timber doors of their great hall to him.

"Come in, come in," Aeself urged him, and he did so, with Uwen beside him, and Gweyl and his guards, leaving Dys and Cass to the men, with all the horses.

The place was half of that same rough timber and half stone from the ruins. He was anxious to have his men out of the cold, but this place was large enough to receive them, and Aeself left the wide doors open for all to come and go, despite the snow falling outside.

Women, snow-sprinkled and bundled up in shawls and scarves, hurried to bring in trestles and benches, and men brought snowy planks, so that in a moment the barren place had tables. Women hurried back with baskets of hard bread, and men brought bowls, while the chill wind wafted the scent of food around the half-open hall.

"The horses," was all Tristen needed to say to receive Aeself's assurances there was provision for them and that the men had help settling them. In the meanwhile nothing would do but that they sit and accept mulled ale, while onlookers jammed the door, a living wall that cut off much of the wind and made the hall all but snug.

"Are you well here?" Tristen asked, and had Aeself's assurance that they were, and more than that, they thrived: Modeyneth helped them, and they had no sickness in the camp, no lack of warm blankets and dry boots.

Other questions waited on their supper, which waited for the men to come in, and when they did, it was a good thick stew with their hard bread, rough fare which came wonderfully welcome after a long cold ride.

With so many bodies already to block the drafts and a good fire in a chimneyed old hearth giving off a grateful warmth on the right side, still more of Aeself's folk crowded in, a living blanket of well-wishes and earnestness.

"I came to see how you fared," Tristen said, broaching the business on which he came, "and to learn whether there might be Tasmôrden's men across the river, and I found dead men outside your walls, frozen in the snow."

Heads nodded solemnly. No one seemed surprised, but no few blessed themselves.

"Two bands came at us here," Aeself said, "and each time the wind came up, and the snow blew. We said to ourselves it was a ghost wind when first we heard it. And the next day we went out to find whether they'd been back, and there they lay, stiff and frozen, Tasmôrden's men, and up to no good. So it happened the second time, two days after that."

Even among the Amefin men blessed themselves, and Uwen said, softly, "It were the old lady got 'em."

"Your enemies aren't welcome at Althalen."

"Gods bless," Gweyl said, and his men with him, while the Amefin echoed the same.

Tristen said quietly, "The earl of Meiden said he fell in with armed men to the west and south, as he was riding from Modeyneth, and so we sent Ivanim by the north road and came by the west, to see if they had come toward you. We thought we should come see if you needed help. And clearly not."

"As you see . . . no, my lord. We *have* help."

"Do you need anything? Are you in want of anything?"

"We want for nothing but the chance to serve," Aeself said, "to post our own guards along the river, to defend *you*, my lord. We are *your* men to order. And if Tasmôrden's men come into this land, we know them, and we know whom to trust."

"Do it," Tristen said without a qualm, and to Uwen's slight unease in the matter.

"M'lord," Uwen said softly, "the rangers is out, too, an' there might be a misfortune."

Tristen shook his head. "They'll wear the red badge." He had looked Aeself in the eyes and knew this was a loyal man, and that Aeself of all men would countenance no spies.

"Here are three hundred men," Aeself said, "and eleven women who know the bow and who can stand and shoot, and the women can keep a tower, if we raise one, if we have your leave. We can take the field. We have men skilled in woodcraft and in stealth, and we can range up and down the river and be sure who comes and goes here."

"So do the Lanfarnessemen, to the west," Tristen said, "but the land east of Modeyneth, there we have no eyes but the villagers who live there. There you might do us a great deal of good."

"Only so's ye choose good an' loyal men who'll not make off wi' pigs an' th' like from the villages," Uwen said, "them as feed ye."

"That we won't countenance," Aeself said solemnly, to Uwen's blunt concern, and on a second cup of ale, they shared news . . . not a great deal from the camp, but very much from the town, which was as far from Aeself's knowledge as Guelemara itself. Aeself and his two companions having been as far as Henas'amef had told every detail on their snowy evenings, so Aeself confessed—so now these folk born to Elwynor knew the names of no few earls of Amefel, and all the lords of the south, and their devices and colors, knowledge that might be vital in the struggle to come.

And of Henas'amef, they, being many of them countryfolk, wanted to know the sort of shops there were, and the taverns, and food—oh, very much the food: such things fed them while they dined on hard bread and barley stew.

All these things they freely provided, besides the news out of Guelessar and the quarrel of Lord Cevulirn with the lord of Ryssand, and all the doings in both courts, besides the voyage of Umanon with Sovrag, his longtime enemy in the south . . . while Aeself and his lieutenants told them a darker story, of Tasmôrden's connivance with the Saendal, the hill bandits, his marriage with a Saendal daughter and his theft of Aséyneddin's gold, from the time Aséyneddin had gone south to what would become the battle of Lewenbrook. With that gold Tasmôrden had rewarded the Saendal, and well armed and well fed, they had taken advantage of the fall of other leaders to gain the service of masterless men, for hire.

That was the core of Tasmôrden's army.

"Not that they love one another," Aeself observed, "but that they have no other master, and hate one another, but serve him, because not to serve him means to fall to the others—no man walks away from Tasmôrden's army. The dogs find him."

Many among the Elwynim blessed themselves at that, and none of the Amefin had heard the tale, so Aeself provided it.

"The Saendal hunt with dogs," Aeself said, "and Caswyddian when he was claiming the kingship had a large kennel himself, which Aséyneddin took, and let his dogs and Caswyddian's fight, and the ones that lived he had guarding his camp. So Tasmôrden had a number of Saendal hounds as a gift from his father-in-law, and when he took Aséyneddin's holdings he took all the dogs he found and had them and the hounds fight, and the ones that lived guard his camp. He hunts men with them, and sets them on anyone that defies him. If a man leaves the army, the hounds hunt him down."

Tristen listened in deep distress, thinking of the yellow dog that had used to follow him out on his rides in Guelessar, fond, foolish creature, and thinking that nothing he heard of Tasmôrden recommended him, this not the worst he had done, but nothing savory either.

He wished the men such dogs hunted might escape them. He saw how some of Aeself's men were very quiet and apprehensive as Aeself told the tale, and he wondered whether among these fugitives who listened to him some might have served Tasmôrden, or Aséyneddin, or Caswyddian before now.

"Well, too grim to go to sleep on," Uwen said quietly—indeed, some of the children huddled close to parents' sides at the edges of the gathering, and many a man had a gloomy look, brooding over weapons that Tristen recalled he had forbidden.

But Uwen told the matter of the feast at Midwinter, and how the Lady of Emwy had come to dance, and how Owl, who had found somewhere else to shelter, had flown right out of the walls: it made a good story, Tristen thought, who was part of it—better, in fact, than it had worrying about the rift at the time. But the people were awed to hear about the Lady, and astonished about Owl.

"The Lady watches this place," Tristen said, "and very likely your intruders fell afoul of her. I know at least that the men who ambushed Lord Crissand haven't come here to trouble you thus far, and they're very likely those in the drifts outside the walls. The Lady stopped them."

"Is she a pretty lady?" asked one of the children.

"I think she might be," Tristen said, recalling the gown of golden lace, the gown like cobwebs, and a face that never would stay in the memory, no more than snowflakes in the hand. "She has a daughter. Auld Syes is the Lady's name, and Seddiwy is her daughter, and if you speak kindly to them, I've found they'll be good neighbors."

"I would give her bread," the child said, at which her mother hushed her, and rough men laughed a little.

"That you would, sweet," Uwen said, tousling a small dark head. "And sweet dreams to you tonight."

So all of them began to settle for the night. And there was a nook curtained for warmth and furnished with fine cloth . . . where or how they had come by it, Tristen had no idea, but Aeself gave him and Uwen this finest bed, and all the guard had their bedrolls, so they could lie down in comfort. Aswys reported the horses well fed and settled, and chose, himself, to sleep in the shed nearest his charges, where he was accustomed to rest.

It was in one sense easier to rest here than in the Zeide with all its duties and expectations . . . here Tristen settled, sure he had satisfied every request, and fulfilled everyone's needs, and answered their curiosity, and that now he could close his eyes, with Uwen beside him and ale-bound for sound sleep.

But he had no sooner said as much to himself and attempted rest than he became aware of a furtive presence, a movement on the edge of his sensibilities, and not a comfortable one.

He lifted his ear from the pillow, not certain whether he had heard something or imagined it. But the wind had begun to blow, breathing cold through the cracks and making the curtains move.

"M'lord?" Uwen rose on an elbow in a dark less only by the fire outside the curtains. "M'lord, there's an uneasy sound, sum'meres."

He felt the same, not that they were threatened, but that something untoward had happened out there. Lives were out in the wind, but they went out one by one, and three at one instant, and if he listened he could hear angry voices.

If he listened, he could hear them speak of traitors, and angry retribution; and one there was with a quieter voice, a Shadow . . . not the One he expected, not Uleman, who had rebuilt the old wards here, but a gentler one, one seated far in the recesses of the gray space, who rose, and came forward what seemed a long, long distance, yet remained far from him, and trying to speak.

He wished to know what this one had to say, and strove to close the gap, but every effort turned him aside. He became aware of darkness where that Shadow moved, of strange shapes shifting and flowing, Shadows within shadow.

Then a blue light flared up and ran along the foundations of the old capital. Wards leapt up bright and strong, and he could no longer see the Shadow he had been watching at all. The web of light spread outward from where he stood, bright and clear as he had seen it shine before Lewenbrook.

This was the web that was Uleman's making, so strong now it sang and rippled like harp strings. Outside was dark and danger, but where the web reached, embracing all the sleeping people, was safety.

Yet there were doors within the Pattern: it Unfolded to him that within the weaving there was such an access as existed in the Zeide . . . and had always been.

He could go through that portal and reach Ynefel.

Another path led to the Zeide's lower hall.

A third ran to a place somewhere to the north and east, one as easily within his reach as the other two, but of great peril: a place of muddled sound and strange shapes, yet familiar to him in the way many things he had never seen seemed familiar, and Unfolded to him.

"M'lord."

He could reach that third place. And he could reach Ynefel. And he could take one step and be in the old mews, from which he could walk straight into the lower hall of the Zeide.

And beyond that, from the Zeide's portal, to still other places, places unvisited in very long . . .

"M'lord, will ye hear? The wind's takin' on fit to blow the roof off."

A shape came out of the gray, a woman of grays and gold, gowned in cobweb lace. It was Auld Syes, and the small Shadow of her daughter went after her, skipping and flitting.

But after them ran an entire troop of shadows, less comely, and less dangerous than these two.

He wished them not to cause any harm in Aeself's camp.

Owl came swooping by, and on the edge of his wings the light glowed white, white that blinded.

He blinked, still dazed, and was aware of Uwen in the dark. Through a seam in the curtain, he saw the banked fire that had broken forth into flame where wood jutted from the ash. A gust of wind must have wakened it.

The wind outside moaned around the eaves.

"What a blow!" Uwen said, "It's woke the fire up. Gods!—D' ye see somethin', lad, where ye're lookin'?"

He shook his head, hearing the murmur of the guardsmen wakened from their sleep. He was still dazed from the vision of other places, convinced he could reach the Zeide from here as easily as wishing: he could walk through the old mews; he could stand in

Ynefel's ruined hall between one blink and the next, and truly *be* there, and touch and be touched.

Had he fallen asleep within such a place as the mews in the Zeide, and not known it?

Or was it within his dream that such possibilities existed?

And suddenly his waking mind made sense of the memory of that third place he had seen in his vision, which was the Quinaltine, beside the Guelesfort—and his heart beat fast to think that he could come that near Cefwyn.

It beat faster still to feel the trouble he felt in that place, and to know danger moved in it, danger which Cefwyn might not see. He himself had stood in the Quinaltine before the altar. He had seen the tangled shadows mill behind the Lines the Patriarch had drawn— he had pitied them, unhappy, angry shadows, Quinalt souls laid to rest above Bryaltine and Teranthine, all jumbled together, all within walls raised contrary to the Lines earlier masons had made. The Patriarch had seemed utterly unaware of what screamed and strained at the barriers: it was all silent to him. It was utterly outside the priests' awareness how later masons had laid down contrary Lines, blind to the proper Lines of the earth, blind to what earlier masonwork had stood there—these later builders, Quinalt builders, for whatever reason, had laid their own structure over that place and crossed the Lines in impossible tangles, pockets, dead ends, traps, from which the anguished souls could not escape.

Oh, there was power there, but it was not any power Efanor's little book described as godly power. It was a terrible place, like the hell of Efanor's book.

And far from curing it, the priests before that altar had walked one principal Line, over and over, deaf to the pain and anguish which roiled just behind it, souls in torment, imprisoned for all eternity in spaces too small for their smallest longings.

That was the place that third passage went.

And with a breath and a wish he might cross that distance tonight and find Cefwyn.

But disturbance among the priests would not serve Cefwyn: he foresaw panic among them if he stepped out of the stonework, by magic, in the place these men called holy. He feared to do it, and was unsure, moreover, what he might disturb there.

It was a chance. A risk. It was nothing to undertake inconsiderately.

"It's eased way off," Uwen said with a sigh, meaning the wind.

"At least the roof is stayin'.—Are ye all right, m'lord? Ye wasn't havin' a dream, like?"

"Somewhat of a dream," he said faintly, but he did not say what he had learned, not even to Uwen. He doubted it would reassure Men in the least to know that their wards both intersected Althalen and reached to Henas'amef, though they were leagues apart. He saw possibilities in it. He saw a way he dared not take yet.

He ought to ask Emuin, among other matters he had discovered here.

A blast of wind made the wooden beams groan, and woke the fire to full life in the heart.

"Damn," he heard one of his guards say, and knew honest men were afraid of the violence in the dark. More, he knew in himself the power to mend that fear, and he knew it was time to mend it.

Calm, he wished the heavens. Be calm.

And in his own heart he was sure now, sure that it was time to move the war against Tasmôrden, sure that he must move, even if it made things more difficult for Cefwyn to explain to the other lords . . . and sure now, reaching out through the maze of the wards, that he could reach not one, but three Places and perhaps others.

He had seen the Lady walking the hills hereabouts, and knew the secret traces between the wards: walls were no barrier to the Old Power. She had asked admittance to the wards of Henas'amef, and he had granted it—to the good, he was sure now, for now the Old Power ran as it had been accustomed to run, between here and there, between here and Guelemara, until the priests' Line dammed it—on purpose or otherwise.

He had said he ruled in Henas'amef, and in Althalen, and on that hill above the river, where stood ruined Ynefel: and now, having laid his head on the stones of Althalen, having dreamed here, he had found the Lines as apt to his hands as the reins of his horse. He drew in a deep, deep breath, sitting disheveled in the dark, amid his blankets, knowing all these wards at once, all the work of Masons and all the Lines on the earth, all the lives of common folk at their work and all the nobles and wizards who had ever ruled—

And these Lines, often walked over the generations of Men, often worked, these graven paths of habit and deed . . . all were his. They were not his by Cefwyn's grant, although that had confirmed his lordship for Men; they were not even his because Mauryl had meant him to rule them, though that was so, too.

They were his because they obeyed him. And they did, now. It seemed that the power in them ran through his veins, and stood the hairs on his arms and the hair on his head on end. He could have lived without breathing, for the power that ran through him needed no such thing.

But breath was what he chose, and the solidity of the lives around him. He strove to make out some detail of Uwen's presence in the dark, desperate for it of a sudden, for he had strayed that far, that remote from Men. And when his eyes had searched out the least hint of Uwen's shape, and his hand had found Uwen's solid, strong arm, then he told his heart it could beat again.

"Go back to sleep," he said to Uwen.

It was quiet now, all the moaning of the wind stopped, the wards quiet and not in evidence. Uwen was all shadows, and all loyalty, and all love, and if there was a moderation to the power that ran through the air and through his bones, if there was a caution and a reminder in his heart, it was Uwen's.

Perhaps it was not a good thing to wish too hard, too absolutely.

Perhaps, he thought, considering Uwen, it was well to do his weather-wishing not absolutely, but with regard of Men, and with love of the men around him, and of the men who were his friends: there was his safety. There was the assurance he would do good and not harm.

In that thought alone he could lie back down and let his guard deal with the fire and the questions what that storm might do outside. It would abate. In time it would abate as a storm should, and the weather would moderate, and he would have done no harm with the power that ran through him to the tips of his fingers and the soles of his feet. He would still be Tristen. He remained as Mauryl named him, and as he named himself, and nothing could tempt him out of that choice, no offer of the enemy, no pure sensation, no curiosity.

Tristen, he said to himself, and summoned that youth who ran naked on the battlements of Ynefel, that young man who raced Dys across the pasture, chasing dying leaves.

Being Tristen, and flesh and blood, he could sleep.

And in the morning, in the silence of all the world, Aeself's men opened the doors and they all walked out into a strange sight.

"It ain't snowin'," Uwen exclaimed. "Gods, I forgot what the sun is!"

The sun glanced off the recent fall as if jewel dust had been the last sifting from the heavens. And Tristen looked about him at the still edge of winter and drew a deep breath. When he looked carefully into the gray space, he saw the soft blue fire of wards not only about the old buildings, but the new.

That had happened in the night, and not, he thought, of his doing.

"Lord Uleman," Tristen said softly, for he realized for the first time in the clear light of this morning, and without the driving snow, that Aeself's camp included the tomb they had made. The Lord Regent's burial place stood within the wall just outside their makeshift great hall . . . Ninévrisë's father, walled into his grave by the devotion of his last remaining men, on a night when Caswyddian's hunt was closing on them and all their lives had been in jeopardy.

Tristen walked across the untracked snow and laid his hand on those stones he had last seen the night the old man had died; and within them he felt no threat such as Auld Syes could send, but rather a sense of peace and great strength and safety.

"Sir," Tristen said, just for the two of them. "Is it you who've stopped the snow this morning? I take it very kindly if you have. Your own people live here, now, have you seen? I think you must have. Protect them."

There was no clear answer to his touch, so he thought at first, but when he drew back his hand he saw the blue fire running on his fingers and tracing its way up his arm.

Owl, wretched bird, came and perched on the crest of the ruined wall, and asked his silly, persistent question.

"Foolish bird," he said, not ill meant, and Owl swiveled his head remarkably far about and glared at him from eyes like black-centered moons. He was not a creature of the daylight . . . but he was here, ruffled, looking like Emuin with too little sleep. "Why do you follow me?" he asked, and then knew that was a wrong question: Owl never followed him. Owl preceded him, like a herald.

He turned around again, unaware he was observed, and met the awed faces of the whole of the people that had gathered, marveling at the snow and now at another strange sight.

"This is the Lord Regent's grave," he said, for it was Uleman who deserved their reverence. "Did you know?"

"We chose this place by chance," Aeself said. "Or believed we had. But could we settle in such a place by accident?"

"It was his accident," Tristen said. "The Shadows in this place can be dangerous. He's remade the wards all about your building: I saw them last night, and I couldn't improve them. The Shadows here respect the Lord Regent above all. And if you do see an old woman or a little girl, respect them. They always give good advice."

"My good lord," Aeself said in a hushed voice.

"Might there be breakfast?" he asked then, for he hated the awkwardness of their reverence; he wanted only to have a warm cup and a friendly converse, and to be on their way. He had seen so much he wanted to think about, and so much he thought he should report to Emuin, and now for no reason in particular his thoughts, skittering like mice, had darted toward Tarien and toward Cevulirn and all there was yet to do. "We should be on our way."

There was breakfast first, porridge and honey that lent a comfortable warmth all the way to their fingertips, and the men were glad to be setting out toward their own home in the evening—toward a place, perhaps, where the wind was less noisy and less threatening.

They were glad to saddle up, on this bright morning: even the horses seemed eager to be under way.

But as they were mounted and about to set out, Aeself, reaching up, pressed a small and much-used paper into Tristen's hand. "We had but two scraps of paper, my lord, in all the camp, and forgive me the condition of them. The one is the muster of Althalen, for your use; and the other . . . the other is a letter to Lady Ninévrisë, on our behalf. I know you sometimes send to the king in Guelemara; and if it please Your Grace, send it on to her. The burden of it is the news we have of Ilefínian, such as we put together by all our accounts: you know from last night all we have to report, but read it: I send it unsealed. I'm her remotest cousin. She may know my name; to that end, I signed it. But I ask you put your seal on it, my lord, if you approve it, and recommend me to her."

Aeself had never confessed before that he was in that degree Ninévrisë's kin, never claimed rank in the Regent's house, and in the tangled nature of the noble houses, perhaps he had never held it.

But now he held the post of seneschal of Althalen, at very least, the keeper and the protector of all the loyal Elwynim who made it across the river. He was the defender, and the man who saw to the commonest, most necessary things to keep alive the folk who came to him, against weather and Tasmôrden's men. Auld Syes herself had taken Aeself under her protection, and perhaps safeguarded Crissand, too, against the worst they could do.

"You will have all I can give," he said, "when we come into Elwynor."

"To bring my lord into Elwynor is the honor I want," Aeself said, looking up at him. "Grant me that."

"When you see the fires alight," Tristen said, "then ride to the bridge."

"My lord," Aeself said fervently, and Tristen took the two precious scraps of paper and put them in his belt as he rode away. The well-wishes of all the folk of Althalen were at his back, the banners out in front, and the Amefin guard about him, and a clean, clear sky above all.

" 'At were well done," Uwen said. "Well done, on your own part, m'lord. 'At's a good man, that."

Owl turned up, flying across their path. And Uwen blessed himself, and so, Tristen guessed, did many of the men in his company, but he did not turn to see.

In time, on the way, to Dys' rolling gait, he read the unsealed papers, written with a crude pen in a fine, well-schooled hand.

There were the number of men Aeself had said in the muster, by name and quality, as fairly written as any such account his clerks brought him. The message to Ninévrisë was respectful and sadly informed her of the death of very many of the family, by name, and of the execution or death in battle of friends, by name.

And it told her of the fate of the treasury, put away in cisterns deep in Ilefínian, so, the missive said, *the Usurper will have hard shift to bring it out again in the winter.*

Aeself Endior, your cousin.

Aeself had been right to have given him the letter unsealed, and at his discretion. Knowing what news it had, he might send or not send—and he did not find it prudent to send the original into Guelemara, where his messengers were in danger. He feared the letter might fall into hostile hands, and inform Ryssand where the missing treasury was . . . although Tasmôrden might have guessed, and doubtless Tasmôrden had probed the wells: Cook had thought of a similar stratagem to save her utensils during Parsynan's regime, and it was not the first time such things had been done. But in the winter, and near-freezing water, Aeself was right: it was not secrecy that would keep the treasury safe, it was the bitter cold of the water.

And by the time the water warmed enough to lower a man in, he intended the wells might have changed hands again . . . but not that Ryssand should find some way to the gold first. It was knowledge for Ninévrisë to have, first and foremost. He had a gift to give her, when they met in Ilefínian. He saw the moment clear before him, Cefwyn safe and well, and the Regent's banner flying over the courtyard.

The weather in the Amefin hills around him held clear and the sun warmed his back in a way it had not done since the first of winter. Even the air held a different smell, of moisture and melt, and the snow underfoot lost the crispness of deep cold.

"The weather's taken a turn," Uwen said. "It even smells like spring."

So he imagined, and thought a while, and tried to imagine consequences, as Emuin and Mauryl had taught him.

But at the last he saw there was nothing to gain by waiting.

So gathering up the courage to wish change on the world, and blind to all untried things it meant, he willed that the spring come in earnest and the snow depart.

Nothing seemed to oppose that wish, nothing this near, nothing at this moment opposed him.

He did not trust the ease with which the weather obliged him: he felt his wishes all unfettered, unopposed, unmatched in the world.

Therein, too . . . he had learned to question his own wisdom.

CHAPTER 11

Pigs in a gate, Cefwyn said to himself, kneeling amid a glow of candles, did not squeal louder or wiggle harder than the recalcitrant barons when they heard the order to bring their men to the bridge at Angesey.

Ryssand was doubtless the loudest . . . having Cuthan and Parsynan in hand, all prepared to confront the king in solemn council, after his defeat at the wedding party, and having raised a certain support for the notion of peace among the barons accustomed to support him. Instead, finding his schemes ignored and the order given to march without his having had a second hearing, Ryssand was so wroth he had struck one of his servants to the ground.

So Cefwyn heard, at least, from Efanor, who retained favor with Ryssand's staff. For himself, after passing the order at night, after the wedding party, and with no consultation or counsel with any of his advisors on the matter . . . he had declared to all concerned his need to seek spiritual, not mortal, guidance for this war, and he had barricaded himself in the King's Shrine within the Guelesfort.

He took no counsel but his brother's and the Holy Father's, and fasted . . . was in prayer, seeking the favor of the gods on his holy venture into Elwynor, and could not be disturbed.

Could the barons who carried the banner of orthodoxy and the doctrinists fault him for fasting and prayer?

He knelt and went through the forms of devotion, not that he believed, but that it seemed one thing to create the subterfuge; it was somehow mean and disrespectful, his conscience informed him, to sit in the shrine drinking and eating while he lied to the barons and mocked what good and decent men supporting him thought holy.

So he did go so far as to pray during those long hours, if only

165

the memorized recitals of formal catechism, and as he passed beyond hunger to light-headedness even fancied a certain spiritual elevation . . . he had had not a bite to eat, and no relief from the chill in this drafty little precinct.

He had no relief from thinking, either, in the tedious hours of kneeling, until at last his unaccustomed knees were beyond pain and his shoulders had acquired an ache that traveled from one aggrieved portion of his back to another like the stab of assassins' knives.

For the first time he knew his body had lost the resiliency of his boyish years; for the first time he accounted how he would pay for all the little follies of youth . . . at seven, he had cracked his knee falling through the stable-loft floor: that came back to haunt him. The elbow he had affronted in weapons practice not five years gone, that afflicted his shoulder as well. The time Danvy had pitched him off over his head, the slip on the ice when he was twelve, the times his mother had warned him about leaping off the side of the staircase . . . you'll break your feet, she had said, and he had not remembered his mother's voice clearly in years, but he could now, in this long watch.

In what he fancied was the night he endured a silence so deep he heard echoes he had never heard, as if the Guelesfort itself had a secret life within it, ghosts, perhaps, distant shouts, sharp noises.

It was a shrine his grandfather had dedicated and never used. Efanor had used it, in his childhood, all too often, for a refuge from the shouting and the anger that had filled the royal apartments . . . shouting and anger that had said very many things a son had not wanted to hear about his mother.

To this day Cefwyn wanted not to think about it, not wishing to remember the worse aspects of his father, who had found fault in both the mothers of his sons. In the death of his own mother and his father's preoccupation with a new wife, he had found alternate escapes, Emuin's study among them, and far less savory nooks of the Guelesfort and the upper town. A brother's at first grudging acceptance had sustained Efanor during the quarrels, the reconciliations, the tirades and the sorrows of *his* mother's marriage, for no woman at close range could escape their father's eternal discontent. But when Efanor's mother had died, this echoing silence was the place that had consoled Efanor.

Efanor, the younger, bereft too early of a mother he had adored, and led far too often into sin by his rebellious elder brother, had seemed to lose heart somewhere in the extravagance of mourning afterward, being at that age boys began to think more deeply and ask themselves questions. Efanor had found peace first by retreat to this place of cold stone and then by agreement with their father—finding a father's doting on him a great deal safer than the tirades and angers that came down on his brother's head.

And perhaps he'd just grown tired. Cefwyn could find no way to blame him . . . Efanor, for whatever reason, had spent his adolescent hours in this room, thinking, in a state of mind Cefwyn only now understood. *Thinking,* as no boy who valued his freedom or his reason should have to think, led by the priests into self-doubt and fear. The Quinalt attributed evil to evil actions. Efanor's mother had died, a sister stillborn. Was that not evil? And had Efanor's sin and rebellion not caused it all? And was their father not quieter now, and grieving, and did not their father need him?

Peace ought to come of this self-questioning, so the priests avowed. But that was not what came of Cefwyn's vigil: rather it was anger at their father, understanding of his brother such as no other place had taught him.

He found anger at Ryssand, too, who had seized on Ináreddin's weaknesses, fed his furies, undermined all trust that might ever have existed between Ináreddin and his eldest son, and perhaps—though he could not find the proof—dealt with Heryn Aswydd in the plot that had sent Ináreddin and almost Efanor to ambush and death.

Had not his own letter had a part in it—his revelation to his father that he had found in Tristen the Elwynim King To Come . . . and had bound him in fealty?

Gods, did Ryssand know *that* matter, and could Ryssand keep silent on it if he did?

Doubtless not.

Patently not.

But of causes that had brought Ináreddin to that fatal battlefield, it was not his letter. It was *not* his letter, but Ryssand's undermining his father's trust, it was Heryn Aswydd's feeding that fear, secretly reporting to his father . . .

He felt the numbness growing in his back, as pain passed beyond limits. And pain in his heart diminished. He was not his father's murderer. He had almost saved him. Almost. Fate, or wizardry, or whatever guided the affairs of Ylesuin these days, had snatched responsibility out of his hands, and then snatched Tristen, too.

Unfair, but necessary, perhaps. There was no one less blamable for the ills of the court—ills that would not even reach Tristen's understanding in Amefel—or that might have reached it, to Cuthan's discomfort.

Tristen, unlike his king, had not a second's hesitation in dealing with the unwholesome. Tristen had never learned to negotiate: there was the difference, while He had grown up *negotiating* for his father's affection. Emuin had another boy now. He was glad of that . . . jealous, but glad; and swore if the boy was not grateful, he would bring the wrath down on the lad.

He had had the benefit of Emuin's teaching. Of Annas' patient management. They had saved him from going down Efanor's road.

And there was Idrys. Thinking on it, in this long meditation on those who had shaped his life and brought him to this moment, he was not sure he was fond of Idrys. It was hard to be fond of the man, in the way it was hard to love a honed blade—but rely on it? Absolutely.

One need not grow maudlin, over Idrys least of all.

Yet . . . was there nothing for all the years, all the trust, all the hard duty, and all the concentration of a life bent only on saving his? The Crown and the kingdom owed this man more than he had ever gotten . . . he relied on Idrys, repository of all the unpleasant confidences a monarch could make to no one else, not his pious brother, not his wife, not his best friend's gray-eyed innocence; and thinking on it, damn it all, he *was* fond of Idrys, though he could never say so.

Idrys was out at this very moment, having necessarily extracted his last reliable spy and resource from within Ryssand's house, trying to find out what Ryssand was up to from less dependable, external sources. While the king was at his prayers the king's right hand was at work steering the events his order had set in motion, and if things outside this chamber had been going contrary to his orders, Cefwyn had every confidence that no sanctuary would deter Idrys from reporting.

Efanor came and went, however. As near kin, Efanor brought him the water custom allowed . . . and brought his own reports of the barons' answer to his call to arms, barons who, deprived of access to the king, sought alternative routes of information and protest, barons who, still uncertain as to where Efanor himself stood, revealed more than they knew.

And on this day, too, Efanor came in very softly, still making quiet echoes, and sat down near him on a prayer bench.

"Marisal will march," Efanor relayed to him. "Osanan is contriving excuses and wishes to hear the peace treaty."

Cefwyn heaved a sigh. Of the nineteen provinces of Ylesuin, five were indisputably with Tristen, four were marginally with him, five at least dared stand with Ryssand, and the rest . . . danced an intricate step in place.

"Guelessar?" he asked. Efanor himself was duke of Guelessar.

Efanor hesitated the space of a breath, head bowed. "Guelessar is a title," Efanor said, the truth both of them knew: that his power was not the real power in the province, only a title that gave him estates and honor. He had very little governance over the lesser lords who administered the districts. "The lords *in* Guelessar are meeting and have been meeting and two at least have sent messages to Ryssand. For my word, at my order, they will march, will they, nil they." Then Efanor added, the bitter truth, but honest: "How reliable they will be to go to the fore of a battle, and how reliable to stand . . . that remains to be seen."

"Will we know that of any men on the field, until the moment comes? Relieve yourself of guilt on that account. Gods, gods, that I ever dismissed the south!"

"If you'd kept the southern barons here in court, there'd have been civil war, and you know it."

All too well, though he hadn't known it when he'd called on the south to defend their border before his father's body was cold in his grave.

He had soared at the height of his power when he had stood on Lewen field, victorious over the sorcerous enemy. He had had a tattered and battered army, but five provinces of the nineteen all devoted to a newly crowned king, the likelihood Panys and Marisal and Marisyn would join him in a drive north, and the blessing of the Lady Regent of Elwynor into the bargain, not to mention the likelihood some of her provinces would join them an effort to go straight to her capital and end all the war.

But his southern army had been tired, winter threatened . . . and he had been king in deed only to half his kingdom.

Crowned in the south, heady with the support of barons ready for action, filled with the desire to restore his newfound beloved to her throne—and, he had to admit, to impress her—he had instead come north to claim the heart of his kingdom, this, in the foolish confidence he could take up all his father's alliances intact. Then, he had thought, he would have had power enough in his hands to assure a well-conducted campaign in the spring with minimal losses on either side.

But he had discovered that his father's compromises with the north had been more extensive and more damaging to the Crown's authority than ever he had suspected. Earliest, he, too, had taken the advice of Murandys and Ryssand, his father's trusted advisors, first of all in appointing Parsynan as viceroy over Amefel, and in so doing, he had fallen into the pattern and embroiled himself in his father's compromises.

He had, with the aid of his friends and advisors, old and new, worked his way to real power: he had wagered everything on the matter of his marriage and gained the Quinalt's approval. He had lessened Ryssand's influence. Now after handling the rebel barons roughly, he set a test for all the north: march in a blizzard, march in defiance of all sanity, march in defiance of the enemy's lying peace offer . . . or refuse and stand in rebellion to the Crown while the battle flag was flying.

He would be king in truth, or not at all—that was his determination. He would not spend a lifetime catering to fools or compromising his way into his father's situation. He grew aware of his silence, aware of Efanor's eyes studying him, and when their eyes met, Efanor said:

"They did listen, Cefwyn. They did hear you. Whatever they decide, your arguments for this action were not wasted."

Efanor knew what he gambled, as perhaps no other could—Efanor who, if he went down, would have to deal with Ryssand in his own way—a different way, perhaps, with a necessarily diminished force, in a vastly changed kingdom.

Thus far he had Tristen uniting five provinces in his name, while he as king could claim only three as solid, one of them Llymaryn— Sulriggan's province, gods save him, Sulriggan, as self-serving a pious prig as ever drew breath, a man with no stomach for fighting—but even less for being left without royal protection: he sided with the Crown because Ryssand hated him for his weathercock swings of loyalty. *There* was his sudden source of courage.

Panys he could trust absolutely. He suspected that Marisal might have moved more quickly to join him because Sulriggan had, being a neighbor, but he still gave the lord of Marisal all due credit, as a man who would not break his oath of fealty. It was a sparsely populated province, with fewer men under arms, but the lord being a devout man and a decent one, he gathered himself and marched.

Those three he had, yet he could not even claim the undivided enthusiasm of his own brother's province of Guelessar, in which the capital sat, in which they now were. It was not surprising, perhaps, since Guelessar was the hotbed of politics of every stamp *and* the seat of the Quinaltine, and could no more make a decision than the council and the clergy could.

But, gods, that was difficult to hear, and it was difficult for Efanor to report.

"I would think," Efanor said quietly, "that you have prayed here as long as profits anyone, and it may be time now to come out and hold council. Your captains have readied the army to move. What more can there be? If you ordered such as you have to march now, you might frighten the likes of Osanan into joining you."

He saw his brother in the light of half a hundred candles, modestly dressed as always, but with a certain elegance: whence the gold chain about his neck, that did not support the habitual Quinalt sigil, but rather a fine cabochon ruby? Had he seen Efanor without that sigil in the last year?

And whence the rings on his fingers, and the careful attention to his person? Had this worldliness begun to happen, his brother attiring himself to draw a lady's eye, and he not seen it?

He stared, entranced and curious, seeing in this suddenly handsome and elegant younger brother the flash of wit as well as jewelry, the spark of a man's soul as well as a saint's. This was his successor, if it had to be. This was the continuance of the Marhanen, absent an heir of his own body, staunch in loyalty and awakening to the power he had.

There was hope in his brother.

"Also," Efanor said, "I have some concern for Her Grace."

"She's not fasting!" He would not let her fast, not with the chance she was with child. That had meant she was alone for her devotions, except for Dame Margolis, who ran her household.

Efanor seemed abashed. "Her Grace has reported the morning sickness to her maids."

He was appalled. The maids gossiped in every quarter. Ninévrisë knew better.

Then he was sure she did know better, and intended to break the news unofficially—deliberately, with calculated effect. Rumor would chase rumor through the halls. When Tarien's secret became a whisper, *after* the whispers about Ninévrisë's, it would only be meaningful in the context of Ninévrisë's secret. Women's secrets would battle one another for weeks in the back corridors before they both came to light in council; and lords, again, would take sides.

But before that, the army would march. *That* might be in her mind.

"Likely her stomach's upset," Cefwyn said, trying to make little of what men ought not to take note of—yet. "So is mine, for that matter. Ryssand is a bane to good digestion."

"Whether it's true," Efanor said, "I am no judge. But it must be end to end of town by now. And *in the people's minds* their own prince will be the firstborn. Your lady is a very clever woman."

"Their own prince." He kept his voice muffled. He had his guard outside, but he wanted no report of crows of laughter and loud voices to come out of his solemn retreat. He could not believe it. He had counted up the days since their wedding night, and it was possible, but only scantly so. It was too much to expect, too soon. "But if it's not true . . . if she's made this up only because of the Aswydd woman . . ."

"She surely wouldn't."

"We have scarcely enough time together . . . three months, three months, is it not, to be sure?"

Efanor blushed, actually blushed. "I believe women know signs of it, besides the sickness, and there's a chance she's right. Besides . . ." Efanor added anxiously, "her father was a wizard, no less than the Aswydds. So couldn't she—?"

"I honestly don't know what she could and couldn't. She could be mistaken."

"But if she's deceived herself," Efanor said, "you'll be in Elwynor and maybe in Ilefínian before anyone knows it. Leaves don't go back on the tree. Isn't that what grandfather used to say? You'll *have* Elwynor."

"*She* will have Elwynor," he reminded his brother.

"To the same effect, is it not?"

By the time anyone knew whether there was a prince to come, the war and the outcome of it would have been settled . . . except that knotty question of inheritance. Had Ninévrisë thought of that when she confided in a maid?

Or had the sickness been real, and the confidence in the maids a necessity?

And would not the child remove Efanor and all his line from the succession? Perhaps Efanor hoped for it. Perhaps he saw it as he would, as his chance of freedom.

"It will open a battle in the council," he said to Efanor. "To loose this, on her own advice—"

"There is the chance," Efanor said soberly, "that it was the truth, and the sickness was no sham."

"And if it is, she should not ride!"

"Where shall she stay?"

"I would protect her."

"But the rumors would fly. And there would be danger."

"These are good Guelenmen, most. It's Ryssand who's poisoned the well."

"He still thinks he has the advantage," Cefwyn said. "And damned if he does. He will march. Cuthan's head is in jeopardy, Parsynan's with it. I long to say the same of Ryssand, but his *obedience* would serve me better. I don't need the other two."

"Don't trust him. Never trust him."

Cefwyn laughed, bitterly, and hushed it, because of the still and holy precinct. "Trust? and this the father of your prospective bride? I trust him only to make mischief, and I shall *never* allow you to make that sacrifice, I tell you now. I'll have none of Ryssand in the royal house, in the blood, in the bed, in the intimate counsels. No! don't nay me. I have had unaccustomed time to think, and I will not have that girl attached to you. If I should fall—don't marry her. If I come back, by the gods, you *won't* marry her. I love you too much. "

He surprised Efanor, who looked away and down, and seemed affected by what he had said. He hoped Efanor believed it.

"And I, you," Efanor said at last, "but what other use for a prince who'll never rule?"

"Don't say you'll never rule. War is—"

"Don't say that! And don't talk of falling. The gods listen to us in this place."

"The gods listen to us everywhere or nowhere. It's common sense I make provision. Every farmer who marches with the levy knows to instruct his wife and his underage sons. Shall I do less? She'll ride with me. I know there's no stopping her. And if you rule, promise me Ryssand won't live to see the next day's sun. Marry that chit of his to some farmer. *Break* that house. It will be a detriment to you."

Efanor looked about him as if he feared eavesdroppers. "Not here," Efanor said. "I beg you don't say such things here."

Efanor revered this place, his refuge, his place of peace, the source, Cefwyn suspected, of all Efanor's fancies concerning the gods and the means by which Jormys and then Sulriggan had secured a hold on his brother. And Efanor wished it not to be profaned with talk of killings.

"I respect my brother's wishes," Cefwyn said. "Respect mine. For the good of Ylesuin—promise me."

"I do," Efanor said, and his face was pale when he said it . . . damning himself with the promise of a murder, so Efanor would see it.

"You're no priest. You're a lord of Ylesuin, you're the duke of

Guelessar, my heir, and *justice* is in your hands, a function of the holy gods, the last good advice the Patriarch preached to me. Murder isn't in question. *Justice* is."

"Idrys argues much the same," Efanor said. "And constantly. Yet you will not hear him."

"Caught in my own trap," Cefwyn said.

"Yet if you kill Ryssand—"

"Merry hell," Cefwyn said, and Efanor gasped at the affront. "So to speak," Cefwyn said. "And my wife may be with child. *That* won't please Ryssand either, especially as he wishes me to die childless and his darling Artisane to bear you an heir. Tarien Aswydd, meanwhile, will bring forth my bastard son, a wizard and a prince of the south, an aetheling. I can't think Ryssand will dance for joy at that, either, although who can say what he'll find to object? Any complaint will serve. He brings them like trays of sweetmeats . . . here, pick one you like."

"Pray the gods for help. *Use* the time you have here. Trust them. And come out and lead the kingdom."

"Dear Efanor." It was on his lips to say wake from your dream, but he could not spoil his brother's faith, not when it was bound to lead to quarrels, and he needed quarrels least of all. "Dear Efanor. I trust you. Ask the gods for me. I'm sure you're a voice they know far better than mine."

"I do. Nightly. And have." Efanor glanced down . . . had always had the eyes of a painted saint as a boy, and did now as a man, when he looked up like that. "I hated you when Mother died, and I prayed for forgiveness. I wanted to love my brother, and I prayed for that. I wanted not to be king, and I wanted not to marry, and I prayed for that. By now I must have confused the gods. So they give me Artisane."

It was the most impious utterance of humor Efanor could manage, brave defiance of his fears in this overawing place, and Cefwyn managed to laugh.

"I wanted my freedom and they gave me the crown," Cefwyn said. "Both of us were too wise to *want* to rule, and thus far, you've escaped."

"Only so I go on escaping, and you keep your head on your shoulders, brother. If Ryssand harmed you, yes, I would kill him with my own hands. I have only one brother, and can never get another. I don't care to be king. I care that you have a long, long reign, and I wish Ryssand nothing but misery. I *can* be angry. I *can* be our grandfather."

"Oh, I know you can be angry! I knew you *before* you became a saint."

"Don't laugh at me."

"I never laugh at you. Come, come—" He held out open arms. "As we did before we were jealous. As we did when we were young fools."

"Still fools," Efanor said, and embraced him, long and gently, then gazed eye to eye and in great earnestness. "You need to call the council. You've shown the loyal from the doubtful. Now reward the loyal and chide the rest. And gods save us, master crow reports he doesn't think Ryssand knows yet about the Aswydds."

That was a vast relief. "He's sure."

"He doesn't *think* so. That's as far as he'll go."

"Will you carry a message to Ninévrisë? Can you?"

"I'm a pious, harmless fellow. You know I can go anywhere without scandal."

"Tell her everything we've said. Tell her I love her beyond all telling. Make her understand. Tell her be no more indiscreet than she's been."

"I've no difficulty bearing that message. Will you hold council?"

"Oh, yes," he said. "Our prayers are done. Hers and mine. I need her by me. Tell her . . . tell her I'll see her in the robing room, beforehand. Two hours hence. Make her know I love her. A man belongs with his wife, after all I've done amiss—and what have I had to do? Be here, separate from her! And if she's ill, where am I? Holding council! Reasonable and wise she may be, but when a gut turns, wisdom has nothing to do with it.—Ask her if it's true."

"I can't ask her that!" Efanor was honestly appalled. "Don't ask me to ask her that!"

"The robing room. Two hours. I'll ask her myself." He clapped Efanor on the arm. "Away. Carry messages. And be there, in the robing room, yourself."

The robing room held no privacy, and hardly space to turn, with the Lord Chamberlain and the pages and the state robes on their trees, the king's and the Royal Consort's, stiff with jewels and bullion. It was of necessity the red velvet embroidered with the Dragon in gold, a stiff and uncomfortable Dragon that reminded a man to keep his back straight; and pages buzzed about with this and that ring of significance, the spurs, that were gold, the belt, that was woven gold, and the Sword of office, the belt of which went about him all the while he fretted and had no word yet of Ninévrisë.

Then the door opened, and Ninévrisë came in, wearing the blue of Elwynor, with the Tower in gold for a blazon, like a lord's, on her bodice, and the black-and-white Checker for a scarf about one shoulder. He had never seen it, had no idea by what magic the women's court had created such Elwynim splendor . . . Dame Margolis, perhaps, who arrived close behind her. *There* was the likely one, the one who would have stayed up nights to accomplish it; and nothing of what that array meant was wasted on him, nor would the meaning miss its mark in hall.

She was the authority over Elwynor, damn Ryssand and his peace offers from a traitor. She had few jewels. But she shone in his sight, and he came toward her in the silence of the chamber and took her hands. He knew he ought to say something clever and formal and endearing, but he had no words. He simply held her hands and gazed into the gray-violet of her eyes, and said, in a whisper almost hopeless in the silence:

"Efanor carried me a report . . . are you well, are you able? I'll not risk your health." He kissed her hand, all propriety allowed. "I love you. I love you. I love you."

She carried his hand to her lips, bestowed a kiss of her own, unprecedented in his court as the petticoat; but it was tender and fervent and made him for a moment think of things far different than statecraft. He could not take the time, could not deal with her in the way he wished even with loyal servants present. The lords were waiting, the kingdom was waiting . . . but, damn custom, he said to himself . . . he was the king, damn it all.

"Out!" he said. "Annas, give me a moment. All of you, all of you but Her Grace, out. Dame Margolis, with Annas, if you please."

There were two senior pages, Annas, Margolis, all sensible people, all in his gratitude for their immediate and unquestioning departure. He need not even look away from Ninévrisë's face, need not let go her hands. He kissed her, long and soundly, and held her tightly against him, and whispered against the flower fragrance of her hair, "Gods, half my meditations were on you, how you fared, how you thought of me, what difficulty you might have . . ."

"It was a clever thing to do," she said against his neck. "It was clever and wise and gave them all time to stew and bubble."

"And for good men to obey, leaving me the blackguards and the laggards. But Artisane's loose, and I feared for you, gods! I was afraid. And when Efanor said you were ill and the maids were let loose to talk—"

"I fear I betrayed myself. I didn't intend it."

"The anxiousness of the war? Might it be that? A bad bowl of stew?"

"Don't name food to me. No dishes. Even yet."

He held her hands clasped together, made her look at him. "It's likely?"

"It might be fear. It might be. But I've dreamed . . . I've dreamed since our wedding night, I've thought . . . I've hoped . . . I've feared . . . all these things at once. My son . . . and if my dreams are true, it *is* a son . . . has no inheritance, no place, no people. . . ."

"*My* son has Ylesuin. And yours has Elwynor."

"He doesn't."

"He *will*." He feared wizard-sight. He wanted not to hear it, wished nothing foredoomed or foreboding between them. "I'll reign into my old age and he'll be a bored prince as I was, with both kingdoms in one bloodline, and *peace* for his reign."

So he said, but he saw fear in Ninévrisë's eyes, a fate she believed and kept inside her, secret, with her son.

Her son. His son. His love. His life.

It took all his courage to face that silence and wait for her to speak.

"If he's born," she said in a trembling voice, "all else is possible."

"He will be born. *You*'ll take care. You'll use the good sense you had in Amefel, and keep yourself safe. It's you I love. It's you I can see and have in my hands, and for the gods' good love, don't give our enemies a shot at you. I don't understand wizards, and prophecies, and what's foredoomed and what isn't. I only know what I have to do and that's keep my promise to you. I'll give you your kingdom. And we'll build a great ship, the sort that sails on the sea, and we'll anchor her in the Lenúalim and we'll make her our palace . . ."

"With silken sails," she said faintly, resting her head again against his shoulder, and gave a great sigh. "That we never unfurl."

"Red ones or blue?"

She laughed, and lifted her head, all the bright faith in her eyes. "The left red, the right blue."

"Oh," he said, "we must be facing upstream."

"We should be used to a contrary current by then."

Her face was pale, her skin all but translucent, like light glowing through it. She looked fragile, and immensely strong, all at once. And if an ordinary man could have a vision, he had one then, and knew that all their plans were like the ship, the fancy of their hearts, with nothing certain, nothing but a prophecy of a King To Come that hovered over all their lives . . . and two sons, now, yet to be born, and not under one roof.

Danger to his life had never struck terror into him: fear, but never terror, not even on Lewen field, to this degree. There had been a shadow on that day as dark as night, and memories of memories that never would surface, not for a sane man: he had thought it all in the past, and his life become tame wrangling with his barons; but now he was as good as on that field again, this time having given his heart outside himself, this time with so much to lose, and so much to gain.

"We'd better call Annas and Margolis back," he said. "We have to go make Ryssand miserable. Are you well?"

"A little giddy. No more kisses. I won't have my wits in there."

"Truly. Are you well?"

"Oh, I shan't miss this. I won't. You have a sword. Give me a dagger to wear. If we go to war, I won't be ranked with Artisane and Bonden-on-Wyk."

"There's my love." He gave up her hands, went to the door, having left himself no servants, and called in Annas and Margolis and the pages, catching a glimpse of courtiers prowling like wolves among the columns beyond, a hungry and angry lot of wolves, who until lately had been well fed and complacent in their individual haunts.

The Dragon was about to flex his claws, and the Tower had set her defenses and armed for confrontation.

CHAPTER 12

Captain Anwyll was back in Hen-
as'amef, on his way to Guelessar, and a company of Ivanim and
Lanfarnesse rangers were at the camp on riverside, reporting through
Anwyll that they had met no intruders on their way, nor had report
of them from Modeyneth. The snow was melting, but not yet to
mire, no great impediment to travel, and the men came off the road
not into town, where, Uwen said, they might disgrace themselves in
the taverns, but out in the tents the Ivanim had left, half the Ivanim
camp, where they found a comfort far surpassing that on the border,
all the same: ale kegs set out, and steaming kettles the taverns provided. It was holiday for them, and a merry one.

The Guelens, too, were packing up, to yield their permanent barracks to the Amefin who had been housed in the hastily made second
barracks, in less comfort; and there was both cheer and regret there:
certain of the men had liaisons, even children, in town, and there
were tears and the possibility of desertions.

So Uwen reported.

"Tell them," Tristen said, "I'll speak to Cefwyn for any that
choose to come back, after the summer, and I think he'll grant it;
but they owe their company their service now."

"That's more 'n fair," Uwen said, and went to tell the men.

And for the officers, Anwyll who had spent hard weeks in camp
and for the Guelen captain who had gotten his rank because all
higher had deserted, it seemed right to Tristen to have them into hall
for a good supper and the honor they were due . . . a sword or a
good mail shirt, Uwen said, was a soldier's gift, and Cossun the
armorer had brought the best of both, a ducal gift.

So they met in hall . . . the usual fine fare, for Cook never

179

disappointed them, and the lords were glad to come to the gatherings: and Anwyll and the Guelen captain both sat high at the tables, and stood for all to honor.

"Thank you," Tristen said, presenting Anwyll his gift, a fine sword with a red leather sheath and a goldwork cap, and the silvered mail.

"Your Grace," Anwyll said, and gave him a soldier's salute, blushing as he did.

So with the Guelen captain, a plain man, who had never looked for a captaincy, and while Anwyll was a man of some connections, this man was not, and took his sword and fine armor with stammering gratitude.

"An' for the men," the captain said, "a word to Your Grace, that they've stood guard here and seen duke and duchess and viceroy, and say that Your Grace has done . . . that Your Grace 'as done the best of 'em all."

That brought a little cheer from the Amefin, and there followed a presentation then from Uwen, which was a box for each, and in those boxes, tenscore and more holy medallions the Teranthine father had blessed, "For the men," Uwen said, "luck and the gods' blessin', which the reverend father himself will give out, an' bless every man as served here."

The assembly applauded, from every table, and the captains and their aides took their formal leave in great and heartfelt cheerfulness, Tristen was glad to see . . . he well knew now how great a harm unhappy men could work. He had finally made good his promise to Cefwyn to march the Guelenmen home. He had had to do it all at once, with the uncertainty on that border, but the tents and all merely changed hands, and the gear the Guelens owned was all their armor and their horses. The Dragons had packed up in a day and ridden out on the next, and made as good speed toward Henas'amef as men might who had the comforts of town to lure them.

So too, in their departure, Tristen chose his moment to make other changes.

"Lusin Bowyn's-son will be lieutenant under Uwen," he said to the assembled leaders and nobles and soldiery, "and I set him in charge of the house guard; Syllan Syllan's-son has charge over the fortress and its walls, Aran Gryysaryn over the town defenses, and Tawwys Cyll's-son over the supplies to the camps. My chief of household, Tassand Dabrynan, will be my chancellor, with all the offices of the Zeide under him." None of these offices had existed since Orien's few days as duchess, and he could think of no one more apt.

"My night guard will serve as bodyguard, and men from the Amefin guard will take their place."

Emuin had a sense about ceremonies, and had deftly arranged things so that everyone had his honor and necessary duties found names to describe them. It was not a mistake, Tristen thought, that he had come out from Guelessar with fewer men than he might: he found others here, among the Amefin, overall found less of confusion in his court now, as he sent the Guelenfolk home, than had existed under the garrison before he came.

As important, he kept faith with Cefwyn, and entrusted Anwyll with a message that said simply, *We will soon have a camp settled on Tasmôrden's side of the river. From that we will prevent any force moving to the south or west.*

He had added: *Anwyll has carried out his orders in very hard weather, and so have all his men. I have also sent the Guelens, who are not the men who have done the harm in Amefel. Certain men of the Guelens have wished to settle in Henas'amef and I ask out of our friendship for their release when they have done their duty this summer so they may return to families here.*

Then, from the heart: *In all these matters I hope I do well and hold out hope we may see each other this spring. The lords of the south wish you well and so do the lords of Amefel send all their good will. So do Emuin and all the house.*

It was a message of more sentiment than substance. Anwyll knew the details which he would tell Cefwyn, when they met, details worth days of questions. He sent the message Aeself had given him, too, with Anwyll, who was a harder, sharper-eyed young captain than had gone out to the river: it was a risk, he thought, but he trusted Anwyll would by no means hand over to Ryssand or Ryssand's men the things entrusted to him; his honor had suffered enough in his moment of doubt when Parsynan had set the Guelens on helpless prisoners, and never would he be as easily confused as he had been that night. He could have no better messenger than Anwyll, for being able to come directly to the Lord Commander. A lowly sergeant like Gedd the enemy might hound: but a captain over a province . . . he doubted even Ryssand would dare.

And in a handful of days there would be no Guelen force within the south for the first time since the rising against the Sihhë. Cevulirn's men were there, under Cevulirn's able lieutenant, while Cevulirn himself continued in the camp at Henas'amef, the man of grays, the lord who could obtain the consent of the others so deftly they never seemed to consider refusal. Under Cevulirn, the town had suffered no disasters in his absence; under Cevulirn, the camp ran smoothly, and Cevulirn's presence touched his along with Emuin's and Crissand's, a quiet assurance of things well in order, from the hall, to the barracks, to the town streets and the camp outside the walls. From Crissand he had an awareness of the lords of the town, men Crissand knew well, and knew that they were content—Crissand was an uneasy point of unrealized distress, to have sent his lord on a long, cold ride; but that was Crissand's nature, to wish to be faultless. Cevulirn was an easier presence, seeding less worry, less of everything. Where Crissand was the burning sun of bright day, casting light and examining everything, Cevulirn was the remote moon, changing and the same, content to leave a few shadows so long as the major things moved along as they ought.

Tristen did not think he would ever change either or them, or wish to. He sipped lukewarm wine and his thoughts raced in a hundred directions as he considered the prospects of the changing weather, heard the well-wishes of the various ealdormen of the town directed toward the new officers of the court and the province, considered the resources he knew were setting to work with the replacement of the Dragons at the riverside . . . the Ivanim were no great hands at building, but the rangers of Lanfarnesse were skilled at many crafts, and the Olmernmen vowed to bend their considerable skills with ropes and tackle to move the deckings into place—without oxen, so they claimed, which seemed to him half-magical.

Sovrag was exceedingly confident: Cevulirn's Ivanim were dubious. But the Olmernmen would ready great frames out of ships' masts—weather or no weather, Sovrag had declared—and have them in storage with the rope and the sections of decking over which the Ivanim stood guard. This was the word Anwyll had brought back with him to Sovrag, and in his cups, Sovrag revealed his plan to the company.

"One day," was Sovrag's boast. "One day to see that bridge bear traffic, much as ye like. She'll *carry* oxen; she don't need 'em to rise."

"Believe him," Umanon said.

Tristen hoped, willingly, for it meant a far quicker readiness on the riverside than they could manage with ox teams.

"I wait to see," he said, and lest that imply doubt, added: "I expect it."

And after that the evening rolled, wine-colored, to its cheerful conclusion, the lords of the south delighted in the prospect of bridges, all the lords of the town delighted in the prospect of a town utterly under Amefin authority for the first time since the rise of the Marhanen—it was strictly understood there would be no cheering the

Guelen departure, no disparagement of the Guelens, either, not before they went out and not after.

So Tristen had worried there would be, and Emuin and Uwen alike had passed the word to the officials of the town and the officers of the watch: he hoped it had gone where it needed to go.

"A health!" Crissand stood, lifting his cup, among the last toasts of the evening. "To the bridge!"

"To the bridge!" everyone cried, and drank.

"And a health to the Dragons!" Crissand, whose house had suffered most from the Guelens under their former captain, and an anxious silence fell, for Crissand had nothing to praise in Guelenmen. "These are honest men," Crissand said aloud, "and the scoundrels have gone home, after Parsynan. Here's to the *honest* men of the Guelen Guard!"

"To the Guelens," the others said, and Cevulirn, rising, lifted his cup, and added: "To an honest king."

They all drank. Anwyll blushed red with wine-flushed pleasure, and rose and proposed in his turn: "And a health to the honest, loyal southrons, one and all!"

None of it Tristen found fault with at all. But they had drunk very many rounds and the candles had burned far down, the hour close to midnight. He had learned from the lords of Amefel the formulas by which he dismissed the gathering, and made a proposal of his own:

"To Amefel and the Amefin, good rest."

"To the duke of Amefel, good rest and good fortune," the lords all said to him, drained and upended their cups, and then the company of the evening began its nightly retreat, now with lordly folk speaking respectfully to Tassand as an officer of the household.

"Good night, my lord," Crissand came close to say, and knew his approval of what he had done, cheering the Guelens: he had done it, defying his own bitter hurt, and done it because he thought it support of his lord, and to heal a breach; and now grieved for his father because he had said it—so many things boiled up in Crissand at any one moment he was rarely quiet.

But Tristen touched his arm and wished him well, wished him peace, and caught Crissand's eye for an instant that became a moment. He had no idea himself of what it was to mourn a father, or what it was to hold such anger as Crissand had held: all this violence was beyond his knowledge, except that Crissand governed it, desperately envied the calm of a man like Cevulirn, and in that envy of a man his lord respected, governed himself with a hard hand.

It was for love Crissand did such things, an extravagant, devoted love, that when it was in the ascendant smothered all other things; it was only once he had acted that the anger and the grief came back to confuse his generous heart.

"It was well done," Tristen said in his turn, and was grateful. For a moment the love and the anger ran to and fro, confounded, and each passion doubted the other's honesty: in that much, Crissand bore a wound that had never healed. Wine had perhaps made it the more evident. And it was that healing which Tristen wished tonight, with a touch and a glance. "Well done. Go, sleep. Join me at breakfast."

"My lord." Cheer began to win over the confusion.

The matter of Crissand's adventure to Modeyneth was settled, the Dragons were back from the river, Cevulirn's men and Pelumer's and Sovrag's were all set in place and on watch against the enemy.

And in Crissand's lightening mood Tristen found his own heart lighter: he allowed himself a feeling of accomplishment in a world of intentions, a court at peace and things in better order than before he took the province. Crissand had taken no great harm of his adventure, and showed signs of recovery in a larger sense, as well—nothing, tonight, of the Aswydds, or his fears of the women who languished upstairs, rather he had determined to settle divisions and heal breaches tonight, and had urged the Amefin to generosity no one expected.

It was by no means the full assembly of Amefin nobility. A number of the other lords were out in their own lands tonight, particularly those bordering Bryn, and by now taking good advantage of the sudden turn in the weather, he hoped, and setting their households in order for the spring. The lords who remained in hall tonight were friendly and easy in the company of the southerners, dignified old Pelumer fallen fast asleep in his place, in fact. One of his men waked him and gathered him off to his bed.

For a moment then in leaving Tristen delayed, seeing Lusin and Syllan across the hall, in the foolish thought that he needed to wait for them—but they were about their own business. From now on he had not Lusin and Syllan to guard him, but Gweyl and the men of the night watch, who had come close to him on his left, to see him back to his apartments.

He had them, and he had the four Amefin he had taken to stand night guard in their place: it was another change, one that set men he relied on in better places, and gave them honor, but it made him sad to lose the ready recourse to their friendship, and when he had told them his intention, it had made them sad, too, amid more honor than they had ever looked to have in their lives.

He wished them well, last thought of all before he collected his new guard and Uwen, and left the hall, to the whisk of Owl's wings.

It was change again, and sadness preoccupied him as he left, the knowledge that there were new men with him, and that for the good of Amefel and Lusin and the rest his life had gone past another milestone, another good-bye. He found nothing easy to say to the new men, though he knew it would have pleased them. He tried not to think on Lusin's objections, but he heard them in memory as he walked in silence up the stairs. There was not the irreverent banter between Uwen and these men. Their presence in the gray space was that of servants, remote from him, too respectful for close confidences.

Of other presences—he heard, remarkably, nothing tonight, so much so he extended curiosity to the other wing of the Zeide, and heard sullen silence, a surly temper.

There were two who had not rejoiced in the general festivity. He had not invited the Aswydds to the hall, and he was sure they knew something was proceeding below . . . knew, and were jealous, but Emuin had taken pains to ward that hallway, and kept a close watch over the guards, picked men all, who watched there.

Paisi's Gran Sedlyn the midwife had taken the guard's anteroom in that apartment, besides, and attended most of their wants, except that frequent requests to Cook brought up delicacies for Tarien, who was vexingly fickle in her whims and her appetite—but Cook said she had been so long before she was with child.

Otherwise the ladies had troubled the household very little at all, even during Cevulirn's two-day governance here. There was no news, either good or bad, out of that apartment, and he decided that tomorrow he should concern himself and pay at least a brief visit.

So he thought, setting foot on the topmost step of the stairs, when suddenly the gray place rang to a presence and a threat, and the tone of it was not Tarien.

It was Crissand, and Crissand was in danger.

"M'lord?" a guard asked. He knew Uwen was beside him. He knew Lusin and the accustomed guards were still down in the hall, with Tassand; but Crissand—

Crissand was in the lower hall, where the old mews made a rift in the wards. And suddenly the wards were threatened.

Tristen spun about on the precarious marble steps and ran down them, two steps at a time, startling servants who were changing the candles at the landing, while Uwen and Gweyl and the new guards hastened behind, a clatter of men and metal. He reached the lower hall, passed the broad double doors of the great hall, and there was

Crissand, running headlong toward them—toward *him,* Tristen knew of a certainty, and the thoughts in Crissand now were fear: fear of what might be behind him, fear of what he might have brought into the Zeide, fear that he had breached his promise to come to Tristen before doing something rash.

Lusin and his old guards all arrived at once from out of the great hall, rallying to the commotion in the hall, if not to a danger none of them had perceived.

"Voices," Crissand said, and his was low, for Tristen's ears and Uwen's, alone, as a late straggle of guests and servants gathered to overhear. "Voices came from the storeroom, noble voices, learned voices, and I heard the king's name and Her Grace's, and something about moving before the walls were finished. I feared treason, my lord. And—and when I looked into it, sensibly, so I thought, cautiously—suddenly there were men—there were men . . .''

"In the storeroom, Your Grace?" Uwen was attempting to make sense of the matter. Crissand, the man who had led the defense of the Zeide courtyard and faced death with never a tremor, was shaking as he spoke, and Tristen could sense his efforts to keep his wits and set aside the fear.

"It . . . it was no one I knew, my lord. And there was a room, a table . . . it wasn't *here,* my lord. But the place where Owl came from. Where *you* disappeared."

Tristen set his hand on Crissand's shoulder to calm him, and though he knew the answer said, "Show me where."

And they went to the spot of candlelight beside the great hall, the sconce that hung on the wall where the old mews had been, that stretch of stone wall, at the base of which the pavings were the aged cobbles and fill of the old courtyard instead of the even work of the new.

Crissand laid his hand on the stonework beneath the sconce. "Here," he said.

Tristen had no doubt at all. A storeroom was near, one that served the great hall, but the voices had nothing to do with that.

"They named Modeyneth, my lord. And the wall—and the child.''

"Tarien's child?"

"I think they meant hers. They argued times and seasons, and the birth of a child. One said—one said best strike while the child was yet to come, than to wait until after the birth and risk a stillborn. Another said the child only complicated the issue and they should do as they would do and let the child take his omens from them.

I'm sure of the words, but they don't mean as much to me as they might to you or Emuin, I'm sure, my lord."

They might well make more sense to Emuin. Tristen only guessed it regarded wizard-work, and the Zeide.

But it could not be Ynefel, where the mews had led him.

"You didn't recognize the room."

"No, my lord."

"Did they see you?" he asked in all seriousness.

"See me? I don't think so.—Do you know where it was? Was it where you found Owl?"

Around them were only his guard, Uwen having waved all the curious servants away, and that Crissand could venture through that rift—or at least see what lay beyond—that he had not anticipated.

"I very much doubt it was Ynefel you saw. But this—" He set his hand to the stone next to Crissand's, deceptively solid stone for the moment, as the gray was deceptively quiet. "This place must lead there, and something drew another place close for a moment. It reaches different places. I don't know yet how many or to where. Ynefel is one. Althalen is." He could not but recall the dream he had dreamed within the old Regent's wards. "The Quinaltine in Guelessar is another."

It was that which he most feared, the plots of priests near Cefwyn, no friendlier to him than they had ever been. And in the flickering light from the sconce, Uwen frowned. Crissand's troubled face, however, took on a different, puzzled look.

"It wasn't ruins, and it wasn't holy men," Crissand said, and his eyes widened as if something only then came clear to him. "There was a banner, my lord." And took on a look of outrage. "*Your* banner, my lord, the Tower, with a Crown!" And having said it, Crissand's fist clenched as if he would rip that offending sight from his own memory. "The High King's banner."

"Tasmôrden," he said, in quiet conviction now where Crissand had been, and where the old mews led besides. "There's clearly another place it goes. Wherever in Ilefínian Tasmôrden sits tonight, this place leads."

He wished—almost—to open the rift again, to venture into the room and the council Crissand had seen . . . and seen, but not been. The fact that Crissand had the gift had let him see into the place, but Crissand had not gone further, perhaps had no power to go, alone, for which Tristen was very grateful. The thought of Crissand caught and trapped on that other side, in Tasmôrden's hands, turned his blood cold.

Yet on the thought, the stone beneath his fingers warmed, and he saw the room then, exactly as Crissand had described:

The table, seven men, the banner Tasmôrden had usurped.

And one man was on his feet facing him, shouting at the others: Don't tell me what I saw, damn you! He was there! Eyes widened. Oh, gods!

So at least one of them had seen Crissand in return, and one presence in the gray space leapt to awareness—one, who had sat with his back to him, leapt up and turned in astonishment.

Two, now had seen. And that crowned man who had leapt up was Tasmôrden.

A hound bayed, somewhere in the distance, echoing in unseen halls.

And, sword in hand, Tasmôrden approached the wall, willing to face him, intent on discovering the nature of the rift, and would have no hesitation in breaching it from his own side, to the peril of all the places it led.

Unless someone gave him pause, unless someone gave him reason to fear that which he might find on the far side.

"My lord!" Crissand's voice, and Uwen's: "If you can go wi' him lad, go! Protect his back for us all!"

And Crissand was beside him, in that rift between rooms, with a sword to thrust into his hand, and Owl was before him, so he knew he was meant to go.

"You should have seen their faces," Crissand's lively rendition of the scene far exceeded anything Tristen would have thought to say. "One fell to the floor, praying forgiveness of the gods, another fainted dead away, I swear to you. Another—it must have been Tasmôrden—" Crissand glanced at Tristen and Tristen nodded, fascinated by the account as well as the rest. "Tasmôrden dared raise a hand to my lord, his guard all about him—until my lord raised the sword and *wished* him back!"

Crissand's account, together with the banner that lay folded and somber on the table before them—Crissand's gift to him on their return from that room in Ilefínian—lent substance to the tale—and Uwen and Emuin and all those gathered about him in the ducal apartments had it for evidence.

Emuin, however, was less pleased.

"Well done, on the whole," Emuin said. "To have called *me* was better." And to Paisi, who had been standing next to Emuin when he and Crissand returned and so was of necessity included in this meeting: "You see here the way *not* to satisfy curiosity, boy. Consider the consequences of the lord of Amefel in the midst of Tasmôrden's guards, unarmed and alone."

It was true, at least as he had gone.

"Yet now we can overhear his councils," Crissand said.

"I doubt it. He'll set guards there and take counsel elsewhere."

The excitement faded from Crissand's face. "So if he hadn't seen me, we might have learned much more."

"Possibly," Emuin said, and added, on another thought: "Or they might have discovered it on the other side, and come through, to *our* peril. There is that."

"Something breached the mews," Tristen pointed out. "It *was* Tasmôrden in that room." He had seen Tasmôrden in his dreams and knew by that means, not the most solid of evidence to bring forward, and he hesitated to say so. "But he didn't know they were overheard, so *someone* did it by accident, on his side, on ours . . . someone made a mistake."

Emuin turned a glance toward Crissand, and Crissand shook his head. "I've no such gift," Crissand said.

"On the other hand, perhaps you *do*," Emuin said, "and should have a care, young lord! On that evidence, have a care what you wish! Were you even *thinking* of Ilefínian?"

"I was wishing I might serve my lord," Crissand confessed. "But I was outside the great hall when I heard the whispers to my right."

"Not enough," Emuin judged. "I doubt it was enough. Someone is stronger. If he let fly that casual a wish, it was an unlatched gate, was all. A means by which."

"Tasmôrden himself isn't that strong," Tristen judged.

"I take your word," Emuin said with sobering directness, "and judge you do know, young lord."

"Meaning what, sir?" Crissand asked.

"Meaning wizards were involved," Emuin said sharply, "and a damned strong one, somewhere about, and thanks to you, the barn door was open, young sir, with people going in and out it.—Wish elsewhere, henceforth, but not in the lower hall, which is as haunted a place as one can find this side of Althalen!"

"I shall, sir," Crissand said meekly enough, and meant it with all his heart, Tristen was sure, as much as a young man untaught in wizardry could keep from wishing.

"Still, there's there substance of what we heard," Tristen said. "They know about Tarien."

"Cuthan clearly brought more than stolen parchments across the river," Emuin said.

"If Cuthan hasn't used the mews himself," Tristen said. "And if *Lady Orien* hasn't."

Emuin cast him a glance. "Past my wards, she didn't. Of that I'm certain."

"So would I be," Tristen said, for he had had no sense of Lady Orien's involvement: across in the other wing of the fortress, she *knew* something had disturbed the wards, yes. That fact had gone through the very air, like the reverberations of a beaten bronze, since they had come out of the mews, and it still disturbed the gray space. But the rift opening on Tasmôrden's schemes was not Lady Orien's doing, nor Tarien's.

"So, well," Emuin said, with finality. "Someone's attempt at *our* unlatched door—and I don't mean the portal—didn't go as well as he wished. It all came back on him, twofold."

"An' Tasmôrden ain't that pleased," Uwen said. "But, m'lord, ye shouldn't ha' gone. Two men wi' swords ain't much of a match to men in their own quarters."

"But you haven't heard all," Crissand said, and his voice was low now, and filled with passion. "I said my lord raised his sword, but it wasn't the sword that stopped them, but the light. He *glowed*, so blindingly bright, I'd have fallen in fear myself if I were in front of him. Tasmôrden's guard fell back, Tasmôrden himself ran behind the table— and my lord's voice, his warning against any pursuit whatsoever—still echoes within those walls . . . gods, I hear it to this hour!"

What Crissand modestly failed to mention was his own part. The guards had fallen, and in the frozen confusion, Crissand had swept past Tasmôrden, contempt in every line, had taken the banner, ripped it from its fastenings.

And to Tasmôrden's face as he passed again, Crissand had waved the banner, saying, in a shout of his own that only his lord had the right to those arms. *Woe to any pretender who dares fly this banner! It belongs to my lord!*

Tristen wondered, in the way things about the gray space faded in the light of the world, whether Crissand even recalled saying so, or making that claim for him.

So it was in his dream.

And the banner itself being the substance of the matter, and being such a gift as it was, the substance of his dreams, from the man whom Auld Syes had hailed as the aetheling—could he—dared he— refuse it?

BOOK TWO

INTERLUDE

The drifts were melting, under a clear blue sky and a blazing bright sun, the wondrous change in the weather that had come the very day Cefwyn left his prayers. Some more hopeful and pious folk called it a miracle.

The soldiers at the rear of the column, less reverent, cursed the mud.

And in the matter of miracles, particularly those of his own invocation, Cefwyn was dubious, but he gladly took the good fortune he had, praised the gods in solemn thanksgiving before the whole court, as the people praised their lately pious king.

For himself, he wondered whether Emuin and Tristen had had a hand in the weather, and whether the change indeed presaged a turn in his luck from a completely different source.

Whatever the source and whatever the meaning some might find in it, sunshine was certainly better than gray skies for an omen of setting-forth: the road, which progressively turned from white to brown under the feet of men and horses, still was frozen hard enough to prevent the cart wheels from bogging down. That was miracle enough to encourage any soldier's hope of success in the enterprise.

Cefwyn rode his warhorse, Kanwy, whose big feet made his own way, no matter the weather, and Ninévrisë rode a gray mare likewise of the heavy horse breed, whose sure back and steady disposition made her safer for a lady in her delicate condition, in Cefwyn's estimation.

Behind them came the muster of the Guelens, and those of the Dragon Guard unit which had served the city. Part of the Prince's Guard had come as well, men who had accompanied him to Amefel in the summer, and who were now lent by his brother Efanor, along with their commander, Gwywyn, lately commander of the Dragons under their father. The rest of Panys had marched, no doubt there. Young Rusyn brought the rest of their muster to join his father, Lord Maudyn, and his elder brother. Marisal was coming: Cefwyn had their lord's word. And likewise Sulriggan's province of Llymaryn would come, so he had Sulriggan's early and extravagant promise.

It was less than the army he had envisioned, but not the calamity he had envisioned, either. Move they did, and now all the other lords, from Marisal to Isin, had to reconsider their positions: stand aside in avowed cowardice or in support of Ryssand, or take to the roads and go to the riverside. Tardiness would not serve. Llymaryn had used up that excuse in the last war.

Gods bless the mayor of Guelemara, too, who had sent his house guard, all five of them, but it was symbolic. Guelemara's various lords had sent the rest, and so Efanor stood vindicated in fact and not only in name. Gods bless Panys, never slow to answer the call to arms, and gods bless Marisal, a man of honor, who had stood by his king at an hour when the list of loyal names had been far shorter than it had grown to be.

So the army was on the road, not, again, as Cefwyn had envisioned, as a tide of men marching down a green-sided road, but still with a warm sun beating down and heating armor despite the lingering chill from the snow around them, a sun melting snowbanks and filling the smallest depressions with foot-dampening snowmelt.

It had not been practical to delay to bring Marisal up to the capital before going on to the riverside. It was not practical for any of the rest to muster there and then march west, when the road directly from the provinces was shorter, and he refused to ask it merely for show. At a certain point pageantry was very well for confidence, but practicality said that they should save their wagon axles the added stress and save their marching strength for speed through enemy land.

So in this somewhat gradual gathering of force, let the other duchies ask themselves whether their neighbors might by now have joined the army, and ask themselves was the list of abstainers and the tardy growing shorter by the day, leaving them conspicuously exposed to blame?

He had waited for no debate in council, only declared what conclusion he had reached after his fasting and prayer: he would march at once and asked for the lords to move as quickly to honor their oaths and come with him.

Rusyn had not hesitated a heartbeat. Hard behind him came

Marisal and Llymaryn, and after that the timid and the traitorous had toed the ground and said, well, of course, and yes, they understood the gods' leading, but it was difficult to muster on such short notice, and they were not at all glad of a war or sanguine of the outcome . . .

But dared they let the king go to certain death and the kingdom then go to ruin? Dared they be the laggards, when others were going?

Ryssand had not even gotten his chance to speak—had protested and tried to outshout his king, regarding dire news from the south, by no means his wisest course, for he had lost dignity by it, and moreover, the new Patriarch was on his king's side. Jormys in his new robes of office had come to the dais to declare a holy mission against a sorcerous usurper, a defiler of his oaths of fealty and a despiser of the gods.

The accusations against Tasmôrden were all true, Cefwyn was sure. But the refusal of his king to hear his case sent Ryssand from the hall in blackest fury, and without consulting Efanor he snatched his daughter Artisane up and left the capital without informing his king whether he would march.

He left rumors behind him of sorcerous alliances, a royal bastard among the Aswydds under the malevolent influence of the lord of Amefel, who held court swathed in ill-omened black, kept a familiar about him in the shape of an owl, and had reestablished Althalen as his capital.

It was, perhaps, too much for the populace to hear at once. They were celebrating the rumor of Her Grace bringing forth an heir . . . a rumor that had had days to run before Ryssand blurted out wild charges of bastardy in the south. The Aswydds were no part of the people's experience or recollection. The people had the evidence of a child *within* the bounds of marriage, a king who had fasted and prayed and emerged blessed by the Quinalt, with all pomp and pageantry and calling for holy war against a godless enemy. The people heard the blare of trumpets, saw the muster of troops and colors, and Ryssand's departure went all but unremarked, except as one more movement of lord and guards in a town that saw many lords and many companies.

If *he* had failed to rally the entire army, so had Ryssand failed to draw his supporters after him . . . for they were caught in confusion and doubted where their best advantage might be. The rumor of Tarien's child was unleashed, and far from shocking: it was over the horizon, beyond the border, far away, and young princes committed indiscretions, but the king had married and gotten at least the whisper of an heir. Her Grace riding through the streets found cheers, now, and doubtless scrutiny to see whether she showed signs of her condition, which meant prosperity to a year, to crops, to flocks, to gold and fortune. If there was disapproval of her now, it was that she rode . . . la! she rode astride. It was not appropriate. The king should put his foot down and protect the people's heir, and by no means take Her Grace near a battlefield . . .

Yet she was the Lady Regent, and noble, and noblewomen did such inexplicable things, being made of other stuff than the commons: she rode with authority, and gained cheers as they passed out of the town, and childless women ran up to touch her skirts, which attested how the people believed, both in her condition, and in her royalty, gods-sanctioned to spread blessings.

Ryssand had never counted on the Royal Consort's being with child, never counted on a potential heir between Efanor, Artisane's ambition, and the throne—never counted on the Quinalt-sanctioned potency of a king's turn to piety and fatherhood. And he had lost his bearings, lost his opening, lost all momentum, and found himself in possession of two houseguests, his chief witnesses, Cuthan and Parsynan, both now linked to Tasmôrden, Amefel, and sorcery.

"How do you fare?" Cefwyn asked, glancing at Ninévrisë, who sat bundled in furs on the mare's broad back. He thought he detected discomfort in her shifting about. At the last rest the party had taken she had moved stiffly, and if there was one thing not to his satisfaction in the whole business it was exactly what the people found not to their satisfaction: Ninévrisë's insistence on riding with him. "We can rest again if you like."

"No," she said.

She had ridden with him to the battle against Aséyneddin. She had shown sober good sense in the councils of his officers, where her opinion was worth hearing, and she had taken command of the camp without a demur, keeping that in order and keeping herself out of unwarranted danger. In that sense, riding with him to war was safer than staying in the capital without him.

But the conditions were not the same. Her condition was not the same.

"You're frowning," he said.

"It's the months of sitting that's the matter. It's four months stitching silly little flowers."

"All the same . . ."

"I hate little flowers! I don't want them on my gowns!"

"Four months sitting in a chair," he said, and felt sympathy for the discomfort of the saddle. He had his own share of it. "Sitting and signing and sealing and signing and sealing. I have forests I've never seen. Lands I've never ridden."

"You could have taken time."

"And left you to Artisane?" That conjured too grim thoughts: Brugan dying at the foot of the Guelesfort stairs, and he chased off to other subjects. "No. The dog-boys have the hounds to run: I've even given them a pony, to exercise the dogs at the chase and keep up . . . gods know, maybe this summer we'll hunt . . ." But that was wrong, too. Ninévrisë would not share the sport. She would miss all the summer, and stitch little flowers amid the likes of Artisane and Luriel . . . while he . . .

He grieved at the thought, he discovered. He was appalled to know he was jealous of the child—but he had wished a little time to themselves. He had imagined a year, two, perhaps, for the two of them to be lovers, before the dynastic ambitions of their two nations invaded their bed. Everyone in the kingdom wanted to know the particulars of his wife's condition, and all his courtiers looked at her for every sign of increased girth.

Now they rode out: they leapt from war to war and not a summer to themselves, not even the leisure to grow a child in peace.

But today she had the kiss of the sun on her face, and managed the gray mare with a fine hand, no matter the discomfort of the ride. There was a liveliness in her this morning that he never wanted quenched, no matter the demands others set on them—and he had not seen that fire burn again in her until she was on horseback and under the open sky.

Perhaps she saw the same change in him, mirror into mirror. In the still-snowy land, in the muster of the forces, he found this was a moment to catch, one of those jewel moments of a lifetime to store away against the ravages of enemies and the chances of war.

Wrong to risk coming with him? Wrong not to stay in Guelemara, when her own people's welfare was at risk, in all of this, and Elwynim who thought there was no choice might yet rally to her banner if they saw it?

They were riding out in hope of everything. They might gain. They might lose. Not being sure of either, they were free as birds . . . and he might have won his struggle. He might finally have won . . . for Ryssand had gone and no one had followed: he had boldly set Ryssand the challenge the recalcitrants never once seemed to have expected of a son of his father: march with the army, obey now or be forsworn.

And now did Ryssand's neighbor Isin have second thoughts in his support of Ryssand, and did Nelefreíssan, and did the others of the north? They were the martial barons, the warlike, hard north, and had Ryssand miscalculated? No, of course the king was not supposed to have done what he had done. The king was supposed to act modestly and responsibly and take no such risks with his life and the succession—in short, the king should play their game with their dice, by the rules Ryssand dictated moment by moment. His father had. Would not he?

The king's consort, moreover, surely would stay in the hands of women of the baronial households, in reach of retribution, and needed their support to have any comfort at all—therefore, the king would be cautious.

She had certainly thrown that to the winds—and now lords who had been entirely unwilling to place Ninévrisë's future children in the line of succession now complained she was endangering a king's child with her riding.

The petticoats had never concerned the lords; this did.

Her Grace must take care, old Isin had been bold enough to say, frowning as he saw Ninévrisë ahorse at their riding out. Surely, if nothing else, a carriage . . .

"Thank you, sir," Ninévrisë had returned gaily, riposte and straight to the heart of northern pride, "but I rode to Lewen field with the king and will not desert my husband now."

Ah, such a look as Isin had had when she said those words about deserting.

And the army such as the town contained had stood gathered in the square before the great Quinaltine, with the bright brave show of banners, and the sound of bells ringing, and the trumpets blaring—with all that in the air, could hearts a little less selfish than Ryssand's not be moved?

At the very last moment before they rode out, the lord of Osanan had come to him, afoot like some peasant farmer, pushing his way through the line of Dragon Guard as he sat Kanwy back and the martial trumpets shivered the air in the Quinaltine square.

"Gods for Ylesuin!" the Duke of Osanan had shouted from among the last screen of guardsmen, the old battle cry. "Osanan will be there, Your Majesty!"

Cefwyn believed it, and indeed, before they had cleared the town gates, Osanan's standard-bearer had come, in earnest of his lord. Osanan had a far ride home and the mustering of his men, in order to recover his standard, but that pebble was suddenly in motion.

Ryssand's edifice of pride had crumbled that little bit more, at the stirring of an old warhorse's heart.

Cefwyn gazed ahead of him now, with the heavy flap and snap of the royal banners in his ears, his, and Ninévrisë's colors flying before them. It was his order to display those banners all the way to the river and beyond, to show them in every village as they gathered that ragtag of peasantry that would come to their sovereign's call along the way.

They moved up the long road that passed ultimately through Murandys itself, bound for the bridge that would take them across the Lenúalim and commit them once and for all to keeping his promise to his bride. And the sun shone down on them as they began.

But toward noon, the east shadowed horizon to horizon with cloud, and by midafternoon it was clear that weather-luck was only for their setting-forth.

Soldiers grumbled, seeing rain in the offing.

But the wind that blasted down as the cloud came was bitter cold, buffeting the standards and making it clear that rain was not the threat.

"So, well," Ninévrisë said cheerfully, bringing up her hood. The first snowflakes stood unmelted in her dark hair, and her face bore a wind-stung blush. "It will be better than mud, will it not?"

"So much for weather-luck and fasting," Cefwyn said, so only she heard.

And in very little time winter enfolded them: the sky grew leaden and the air turned gray with flying snow.

"If Tristen managed this," Cefwyn said across the voice of the wind, "could he not have managed to hold the sunshine just until we crossed the river?"

CHAPTER 1

The weather turned back to brutal cold, troubling in itself: Tristen saw it coming on the afternoon after Anwyll's departure and no wish he could make brought back the sun. Gray cloud closed in, and bitter wind, and the drifts lately melted froze hard, a fine dust of snowflakes blowing across it at first, then sticking, with a night's greater fall. And days subsequent were no better.

Beeswax candles by the score lit master Emuin's studies, meanwhile, candles to light the crabbed note-taking that had gone on at any moment of every day, every night. Drafts swept through the tower and down into the guardroom on rare clear nights, and by that, Tristen knew master Emuin peered into the heavens despite his promises to observe the wards and keep the shutters closed.

On the obscured nights there were no such drafts: then Emuin delved into old texts, and by dawn and dusk sent Paisi on this and that mysterious errand to the archive and to the Bryalt shrine, after which the nuns, too, came with texts.

It was precise times master Emuin avowed he sought, the times of Tristen's arrival here, of Tarien's baby's likeliest conception, and of other events months and even centuries past.

Most of all master Emuin sought the very hour of Mauryl's Summoning him. Emuin had guessed it, by gross reckoning, as the first day of spring, but the precision and the sure reckoning—that was the chimera Emuin stalked through the old records, through guardhouse accounts and even Cook's recollections of his arrival: with so many grandchildren to her credit, and the duties she had regarding festivals and solemnities, Cook had a sense of dates and birthdays and feast days, and preserved a better reckoning in her head than the archives did on paper, regarding some events.

All this, Emuin said, was to determine the most auspicious day—and the least—for Cefwyn's son to be born, while the weather raged in rebellion outside the windows.

Books, anecdotes, the stars: such were Emuin's sources, as Emuin sought understanding in ways Tristen himself could not have done—for one thing because nothing of Emuin's knowledge had ever Unfolded to him, and for another because he had not thought to ask the questions Emuin asked. He felt the impulse to magic and chose his moments by some reading of the insubstantial wind of the gray space, while a wizard reckoned and reckoned and consumed ink and paper and kept records it had never remotely occurred to him to keep.

But to know in advance that a moment was coming . . . this seemed valuable, if one could. He sometimes failed to know what men might do, as he had failed to know how the soldiers would behave when he dismissed them; and in this Emuin surpassed him. So, too, Emuin professed to him, could any wizard: hence wizards had bested the Sihhë-lords in the past: let it be a lesson to you, Emuin said.

To know *when* a thing had been in the past was not quite as useful as to know when it would be in time to come, but Emuin could tell him that, too, and fit together the scattered accounts of the Red Chronicle and the Bryalt account. He had read them, read every history he could find—but he had had no awareness of time at the first of his reading and still had a faltering grasp of it. The better part of an hour could slip past while he fed the birds. He could still grow fascinated by some new question and chase it through convolutions, unhearing while one of his advisors spoke to him, patiently telling him what he doubtless did need to know.

In sum, the same faults he had had at the beginning he had, though in lesser measure, and he tried to mend them, where he saw them. He tried to give Emuin answers to his questions now, for instance, since he had been there and Emuin had not been entirely aware of Mauryl's doings, but his own beginnings in particular were a haze to him, and he retained only few keen impressions of that hour—or rather he retained them all, but not the ones Emuin wished.

He recalled fire—his senses had all been overwhelmed by fire . . . and he recalled pain: he still bore a scar on his finger. He remembered getting that.

But most of all, the more he needed to remember the structure by which Men reckoned time, the more keenly he remembered the unbridled extravagance of those days, fire which had never seemed brighter, air which had moved over his skin with a touch like fingers, dusty stone underfoot which had had a texture so curious and so smooth . . . and, oh, the rain, and the thunder . . . the tastes, the smells, all these things that had poured in on his senses, new and wonderful and commanding his utter attention—to Mauryl's distress.

But on what night of all nights this had happened, he had no recollection at all, nor any sense how many suns had risen and set before he first beheld the forest outside Ynefel's walls, or how much of a season had passed before he knew the source of that sighing of leaves which rose to the winds outside the fortress walls.

After he had learned the world from the loft he had known day and night as related to the sun, but he had not known how to count the days—it had never occurred to him that days had a number, or that they would be different one from the other. As a consequence only certain days stood out like signposts, significant to him later, in terms of what would come, but then only days like other days, when miracles of dust and wings and sunlight were all one long vision.

That such times and movements of the stars had been important to Mauryl while he was watching pigeons in the loft, oh, that he could well believe now. He recalled every detail of Mauryl's presence at the sole table. Their dinners had always competed with the charts and the inkpots for room, and he had read none of them, but he recalled how they looked.

And that Emuin, with his books and his charts and his reports from Gran Sedlyn on Lady Tarien's condition could fix one date above others as the time for the child to be born, he could also believe, for he had learned there was a regularity in the heavens beyond the simple repetition of day and night and full moon and new—but he could not help Emuin in the reckoning.

That Orien Aswydd also knew these things he was not wholly certain, for he had never associated her with charts and scribing—and that she might not know the complexities as well as Emuin . . . that failed to comfort him. It reminded him instead that she had relied on an outside source. Having the gift, lacking skill and learning—she had used the gift and listened to whispers from the gray space, whispers which might have told her all those things a better wizard might cipher for himself, whispers which had counseled her to do things which a better wizard would fear even to contemplate.

And that same source of advice was likely at least in the conception of the child—if she lacked it now, as they strongly hoped she did, it meant that her advisor was no longer in the world of Men and had not been since Lewenbrook, but they did not rely on that belief.

She might be cast adrift, ignorant of seasons; but she might have known from the beginning *when* the child had to be born; or the child might have that knowledge within himself—nothing told him how children knew their time, he, who had been Summoned whole from the fire of a hearth.

Certainly Orien would resist any time of Emuin's choosing. That went without saying.

Meanwhile Tarien, who contained the subject of all Master Emuin's reckoning and Orien's wishing, sat with her sister in the apartment that had been Cefwyn's—there was troubling irony in that choice—and stitched and stitched patterns in linen.

So Tristen observed. He visited them daily since the weather had turned contrary, not that he found their presence pleasant, but that he wished them to know he thought of them constantly, with all that meant. And always when he visited, it was the stitching that occupied them.

They were spells, he was sure, these squares of black thread on white, these growing structures like ebon snowflakes. It was a marvelous skill they had, a mystery in itself, but what these things meant, Emuin said he did not know.

Was this the wish for snow, that made their movement of men and supplies so difficult? Did it exist, worked in thread?

And while Orien remained a creature of edges and angles and angers, Tarien waxed like the moon toward full.

They stitched in his presence, while by day and night the wizard that was Orien Aswydd prowled the confines of their condition like a wolf before the fold and wished for freedom and rule.

They stitched, and wore their cherished jewels only for each other's benefit. They had two fine gowns which did little to recover the glory of their appearance in the summer. They dressed in costly cloth in the isolation of their prison, and Orien chose dark Aswydd green against which her skin showed stark, unhealthy white. Her cropped hair flew like a fire about her face, and she took no pains with it, while Tarien wore hers loose, and her laces loose. She only grew more silent, less responsive to his visits, until on the most recent visit she did not respond at all.

They stitched and whenever he came near the wizard that was within Tarien turned and shifted and turned again, innocent and restless, not yet wanting freedom.

But when he was not present, Tarien did speak. She was impatient and full of tempers and storms, so the servants swore . . . so the midwife Gran Sedlyn swore, in the one report he had had directly from her lips: the old woman, Paisi's gran, white-haired and portly, reported most to Emuin, and came and went without fuss.

But Gran Sedlyn hung trinkets about the Aswydds' door: that he saw, and found some foreign virtue in them. He did not oppose them, seeing they strengthened, rather than weakened, the wards, by however little. The sight of them reassured the guards who stood by that door, as his invisible wards did not, and he wished those wards stronger than they were.

And still the weather stayed bitter cold, spitting snow until the drifts piled deep, and the wind howled about the eaves of the fortress at night, rattling shutters and prying at every edge and nook and cranny.

That, he most distrusted. Unlike Ynefel, which had creaked and complained at the wind's assault, the Zeide stood strong and resistant, but he heard the wind's attempts at the roof slates and in his rare dreams he heard it prowling about, looking for weaknesses. It grew bold, and he knew Orien wished counter to his wishes.

For the first time in his memory, he counted days . . . for the letters, his and Aeself's, would just be arriving.

In the same number of days, the southern army was ready and past ready to move, awaiting only the break in the weather that as yet his wishes could not gain them.

In the same set of days, the child was approaching birth—soon, now, the midwife said.

Crissand declared he brooded too much, and urged him to go riding . . . though Crissand himself was busy now with the army, with his lands, with his men, and had no dearth of things to occupy him: and dared he ride out, himself, and leave Orien unguarded in the way that only he and Emuin could watch her?

That was foolishness indeed.

So he waited. And he fed the pigeons.

Until the day when Paisi came to interrupt his breakfast, and to beg his presence in the tower—"As master wishes to speak wi' Your Grace," Paisi said with a bow, gasping for breath the while. The boy rarely walked anywhere, but this was uncommon haste.

"I'll come immediately." And to Uwen who sat at breakfast with him: "No need. I'll take the guard. Feed the pigeons, will you? They expect it."

"Aye," Uwen promised him, and would, as he did, some mornings—indeed, all through the town, so the rumor came to him, the townsfolk had taken to feeding them—for luck, they said, calling them the lord's birds. There was certainly no starvation on his windowsill, but they had their rights.

Even on a day when Emuin might have an answer for him.

He threw on his cloak in the chance that master Emuin had had the shutters thrown wide and hurried on Paisi's heels, following Paisi's quick steps until his own breaths came hard, to what he hoped was the news Emuin had been looking for all these days.

The tower was warm, ablaze with light from all the sconces and from the fire. The table was even in moderate order, the parchments stacked, the inkpots capped.

"Master Emuin?" Tristen said, and unfastened the cloak.

"A date," Emuin said in triumph, and laid a chart atop the other charts, beginning at once to talk to him about the measuring of the heavens, and the calculations of the moon and its motions and the planets' travels through the Great Year.

It was doubtless the proof—useless words, at least to his under-standing of it, but he saw that Emuin had arrived at his answer, and he dutifully observed what Emuin showed him, a crooked finger trac-ing the results on parchment.

"This is the reckoning of the year past," Emuin said, "and here's the hour of Lewenbrook, and *here* is the day, the very day I'll wager Aséyneddin looked to provoke his battle—I had not reckoned this, well, well, lying senseless at the time. But this is the day he would have wanted. But Cefwyn roused his troops out and came for him before things were advantageous to Aséyneddin.—And here's the hour Hasufin would have chosen on the day the battle did take place: noon, the very exactitude of noon; but noon he did not have, because Cefwyn pressed him . . . and you did, gods, yes, you did, having a sense about such things, and never needing ink and pen."

"It was *Cefwyn* who led," Tristen said. "*Cefwyn* who chose the time."

Emuin blinked at him. "But you agreed, did you not? You were there. You urged him forward."

"I went with him, like his soldiers."

"To Aséyneddin's ruin." Emuin seemed a little put out by his dismissal of any part he had had in choosing the hour of the battle—but truthfully, Tristen thought, it seemed to him that all of them had rushed toward it. Even the horses had taken a fever for battle, pace quickening until the thunder rolled through the earth.

Had he guided the hour? Had he wished the horses faster and faster on that morning? Had he willed axles not to break on days before and all that army hastened into each day's gain of ground?

It appalled him if he had done so, not knowing: he thought not.

But if not he, then who?

Emuin's finger traveled back and back through the spidery notes. "Here, the night of your arrival in Henas'amef; I had it from the guard records—my memory I thought was exact, but this has the very hour, as they marked it against the glass. And here, the date of a gift of mine to the Bryaltine shrine . . . they write down such things. Still not precise. The guard is never precise, and the Bryalt abbot has been known to err, but on this matter, I think not, and not both of them together. 'Twill serve. 'Twill serve. This was the hour."

"Of my coming *here*?"

"Why should it matter? Why should it matter, you ask? Because that hour was momentous for your presence, young lord, but not only that. Not only that! In that hour, in that selfsame hour, was this babe's conception. I have my sources among the maids . . . not the moment, alas! but at least a time within three hours."

"That night?"

"Before Cefwyn came down the stairs to answer *my* summons, and would I'd given it earlier—or perhaps I would *not*." Emuin gave a wave of his hand much as if he brushed away a gnat. "We never can guess what might have been. What is, is, and that's what we know. What will be is a fine pursuit, but fraught with too damned many possibilities. Fortune-telling, I tell you, is not what it's surmised to be. But *here* the child was conceived, in the very room where he'll be born—dare you call that placement utter coincidence, eh?"

"It's a fine room. It was vacant."

"Ah, yes. Of course. Perfectly ordinary. Damn, but these things fit together! Nothing out of the way at all. And on this day, and on this hour . . ." Emuin showed him the intersection of a half a score arcs and lines, and suddenly shuffled to another parchment. "This was the hour of *your* birth, do you see? This was Mauryl's best moment, as I reckon it, the new moon, the moon of beginnings! It was the earliest moon of spring, and I think near Mauryl's own moment: the hour of his own birth, perhaps, however long ago, or the hour when he had most to hope for success of his enterprise. This, above all others, was your hour to come back into the world . . . so this day may have been yours already, a natal day, a day of accession, of some auspicious moment in the life you had once. It was your point of correspondence to him, do you see? And no accident that that was so! *Hence,* your power in this venture! On that, Mauryl relied—as he did in our venture at Althalen, that night, that bloody night." Emuin's hand trembled, and moved on among the arcs and bird-track scribings. "There, there, was Hasufin's last death, the realm's rise; your birth; perhaps Mauryl's, all the same day! do you see? And if Hasufin had lived this long, to see this Year of Years—" Again Emuin's hand moved, to the end of the chart. "—at this hour, that midnight of Midwinter Eve, he would have worked a Working to bind the next age. He failed!"

"Did we?"

Emuin looked distraught, as if that had been the wrong question. "What do you expect of me? I'm a wizard, not born to magic!"

"Forgive me."

"But you set your seal on this age. *You.* Yourself. You're still here." Emuin searched amid the stack of parchments, discarding one and the other in increasing frustration, until he had disordered all of it. Then: "Aha! This. This is your answer, young lord. This is your new age. *This, this day* is where we are now. And that babe—that babe of Tarien's—is on both charts, one for his conception, one for his birth. Follow this arc."

Tristen observed, such as he could, the arcane notes. They were all measures of risings and settings.

"And this is your Day in this new cycle of years, this is your beginning—" Emuin's gnarled finger traveled to an intersection. "And we have a babe about to be born. Tell me what you think the hour will be."

Tristen moved his finger toward the intersection of lines Emuin said was his own, and hesitated, for there was a double set of lines— ominously so, to his unlettered perception. He stared at that coincidence of lines, with not a notion in the world what the numbers signified, or which was which, but all that was within him telling him there was something to fear here.

"Just so," Emuin said, and so stood back from the charts—cast a measuring rod down atop them as if they had become negligible to all further reckonings. "Just so. One for midnight, one for dawn. And to that end I've asked Gran Sedlyn to reckon very carefully and keep me advised down to the hour of her estimations, never forgetting wizardry's in question here. Wish, young lord! Wish the world to your own measure. Wish the babe for any hour but midnight and any day of the year but Hasufin's. Wish the heavens to speed the spring and melt the snow so we can be done with this wretched war. Wish a speedy delivery of this child by daylight. And wish *Cefwyn* well, when you do all these things."

"I do," he said fervently. "Above all, I do that."

CHAPTER 2

The storm wind came in the night and howled around the eaves and rattled shutters, a new wind, from a different direction, and singing with a different sound, on this, the night before the anniversary of his first night in the world. Tristen sat up in bed and listened, feeling no threat in it, hearing no ominous voice in it, only the banging of a shutter somewhere distant.

Thunder cracked.

That, he thought, sounded more like rain than snow, and he rose from bed, flung on a robe, and went out to the heart of his apartments, already feeling the air warmer than the bone-deep chill of recent days.

Lightning flared in the seam of the draperies before he touched them. He parted them, and with a loud boom of thunder, light blazed down the clear sides of the windows, lit the Aswydd heraldry in colored glass in the center of the window and flashed repeatedly, bringing the dragons within it to fitful life, casting shadows about the room.

Rain spattered the panes, spotting the colored glass, glistening beads on the clear side panes. Lightning lit the adjacent roofs, and the rain came down hard. Droplets, lightning-lit, crawled down the glass.

In the same way rain had come to Ynefel and made crooked trails over the horn panes of his small window.

So the thunder had walked above Ynefel's broken roofs, and the trees outside the walls had sighed with hundreds of voices. Balconies had creaked and beams had moved. Shadows ran along the seams of the stones.

But there in Ynefel he had not known Uwen's presence . . . as now there was approaching behind his back a very sleepy Uwen, drawn by the sound of the storm, stumbling faithfully from his bed. Emuin, too, was awake at this recasting of the weather, and Paisi had waked, as Tarien and Orien had, as all through the fortress and the town and the camps sleepers waked to the wind and the rain and the thunder that heralded another turn in the fickle, wizard-driven weather.

Uwen came, blanket-cloaked, past the shadows of brazen dragons the lightning made lively with repeated flashes as Tristen looked back at him. Uwen had his hair loose: he raked at it, but achieved little better. In outline he looked like Emuin at his untidiest.

"South wind," Uwen said, and so it was. "It don't sound that cold."

"It doesn't feel cold," Tristen said, turning to put his hand on the glass. As he had gone to bed, frost had patterned the panes. Now these meandering streams of water cast crooked shadows against the lightning.

A prodigious crack of thunder made him jump.

—Rain on the horn-paned window. A hole in the roof of the loft.

—A hole in the Quinaltine roof. Fatal anger of the barons, a threat to Cefwyn that did not go away.

"Oh, 'at were a good 'un," Uwen said. "This is a warmin' rain, this is."

Spring was back. He had gained it once and now gained it back again, as if all influence to the contrary had waned and on this night he reached his ascendancy.

He had all but come full circle now, past sunset and into the night. Morning would bring the anniversary of his beginning, the evening hours, the precise hour of his own origin, likely at sundown.

Tomorrow night, Emuin had said the birth of Tarien's child would be most portentous . . . and now the weather turned.

He listened for disturbance in the gray space, but Tarien's child slept quietly in his mother's womb this stormy night—a week and more away from entering the world, so Gran Sedlyn insisted. It might not, then, happen tomorrow, on that date Emuin called portentous: there were no signs of it happening, and Tarien's time Tristen understood could not be rushed, even by wizardry: the babe was as the babe was, and at the moment it seemed quiet.

So the Zeide, too, rested quietly, anxious as these days were for him.

One more day before the dreaded day.

He had feared the day of his birth as long ago this fall, wondering would the wizardry that had brought him forth from the dark give him yet another year. When he had feared that, he had had no imagining even of winter and all it might bring. Now for all his dread, he was indeed approaching that point, and, lo! the weather turned back again in his favor. After holding the land by fitful bursts of bitter cold, after his wishing day after day for the spring to come, lo! the skies turned violent and rainy as they had been in his first memories: full circle, and tomorrow he would truly be able to say, offhandedly, oh, it was thus *last year,* like any ordinary Man.

" 'Twill wash the snow away before morning," he said.

"If it don't turn all to ice again," Uwen said, "as it did. If old North Wind wins the contest one more time an' comes back in force, there'll be slippin' and slidin' from here to the river."

Let the rain for good and all erase the snow, Tristen wished, passing his hand across the colored glass panes, and this time feeling power leap to his will.

Let the spring come, he said to himself. Winter had had its day and more. It was time for that season of rain and leaves whispering and roaring in the storm.

It was time for the tracery of water on windows and the crack of thunder in the night.

It was time again for the sheer beauty of a green leaf stuck to gray stone, and the terror of Mauryl's staff, like thunder, crack! against the pavings.

He had forgotten his clothes that day, and Mauryl had chided him, patiently, always patiently and with a faint sense of grief and disappointment that had stung so keenly then. It still did.

He had remembered a robe tonight—but his heart yearned toward the outside and the rain and the memory of chill water on his skin, and Mauryl's cloak after, and the fire at Ynefel. If he failed there, Mauryl would forgive him, wrap him in warmth, make all things right.

If he failed here, in his war for Cefwyn's lady, there was no mercy.

He would have come full circle tomorrow evening, but Mauryl would not come back. Had not Uwen told him—that men did not do over the things they had done, but that the seasons did?

So there was both change and sameness, there was progress and endless circles. The Great Year and the Year of Years themselves produced the same result: Men changed; Men died; babes were born, and grew; and died; the seasons varied little.

Thunder rattled the leaded windows, fit to shake the stones.

Owl called.

And elsewhere and to the west a wizardling babe waked, and moved in startlement, heart leaping.

Then pain began, an alarming pain, a sense of sliding inevitability—and change that could not be called back.

Tristen rested his hands on the marble beneath the window, dreaded the thunder he felt imminent, and winced to its rapid crack, feeling it through all his bones at once.

"M'lord?" Uwen said, seizing his arm.

He had felt pain before. This was different. This, this was the pain of a babe attempting to be born in haste, by wizardry.

This was the fear of a woman distraught and alarmed, a woman who well knew the risks.

He heard a voice urging, **Let it be now, let it be now.**

Now was not the time Orien would choose. But the voice continued relentlessly, striving to coax the babe into the world, urging the mother to join her efforts.

—Master Emuin, he called out into the gray space.

Emuin was there, aware and alarmed.

—She's trying to force it, Emuin said. She must not. It must not, young lord.

—It's too early.

—In every way. It wants not to come at all. She begins now to ensure the day of the calendar at least. No,—damn! Midnight! She strives for midnight! And she must not succeed. Make it quiet! Hush! Be still!

He had no idea how to calm the babe and the mother, while the thunder cracked and the winds of chance and wizardry roared.

In the gray space Orien's voice urged haste, urged the babe toward birth, and the pain began, stealing his breath.

"Tassand!"

Uwen called for help, thinking him ill, but he drew in a great breath and willed Tarien still, asleep, if nothing else, and the babe to be well.

He was aware of Orien shaking Tarien's shoulder, encouraging her.

Then she perceived him, and the anger that swept through the gray place was potent as the storm above the roof. Defiance met him. And pain, Tarien's pain . . . that came.

He felt the cold marble table surface under his hand, realizing he had shaken Uwen off, and that Uwen was behind him, concerned and not knowing what to do.

—Be still, he willed the babe, and drew in a breath and straight-

ened back, willed against all Orien's determination that Tarien's pains cease. Her breaths and his came as one, and he slowed them, slowed all that was happening.

But in his hearing Orien was urging her sister now, that Tarien, having the pangs that heralded the birth, must set to it, must deliver the child or lose it, adding panic and fear for the child to Tarien's gray presence.

*—No, he willed. **Neither will happen.***

The gray stilled for a heartbeat, a breath, and another, labored, heartbeat.

"What's happened?" he heard Tassand ask, but he saw Tarien's surroundings, and in one place he stood, and in another sat, aching and out of breath.

"I don't know," Uwen said, " 'cept it's a takin' of some sort, an' he ain't in his own mind. Set 'im down. Here, m'lord. Here's a chair."

He trusted, and sat. Having both bodies doing the same thing made it easier to manage. He gathered his awareness, stretched out fine and far, and found Orien's angry presence in the gray space, elusive, clever, governing her sister in ways mysterious to him.

He had no need to send to Emuin. Emuin had sent for the midwife, both in the gray space and on Paisi's quick feet—for thinking the babe a week away, Gran Sedlyn had gone home tonight, as she did one day in seven. Paisi ran, to bring her up the hill, in the storm and the lightning. He was aware of Paisi racing out the West Gate barefoot as he had lived much of his life, slipping on the cobbles, running in icemelt, rapidly insensible of pain.

And at Emuin's lancing inquiry, he knew Gran Sedlyn's unfamiliar touch, an old woman roused out of a warm bed and searching, he thought, for stockings, even before Paisi was past the first uptown street.

"There we are, m'lord," Uwen said, and pressed a warm cup into his hand. He trusted anything from Uwen, and sipped at it, brought to a realization of soldiers and resources at his command.

"The Aswydds," he said. "Orien's trying to bring the baby. Go tell the abbot." The man's workings were small, but the man knew the Aswydds, too, and the abbot was closer and fleeter of foot than Gran Sedlyn.

He said so, and in the gray space Orien tried to bar him from doing that. So did Tarien, following her sister's lead blindly, desperately, in her pain. For a moment a storm raged, but harm was all too easy if it came to a struggle, and he disarmed himself and kept out of the gray space except the most minuscule awareness, wishing no harm at all to the baby. Orien might assail him and cause him pain, but he sat and sipped hot tea and bore with it, for rage as she would Orien made no gains against his determination to hold things as they were.

It was Tarien that afflicted him worst, Tarien with her pain, and her fear, and her anger: she tore at him and pleaded for everything to be done.

—*Mine! she cried. My son! My baby! Let him alone! Let me alone! You're killing my baby!*

—*Your sister will harm him, Tristen answered her. It's your sister's time, not his. Hear him. Hear him, not Orien!*

But Tarien was blind in her fear and deaf. Orien was her life, and Orien said now was the time. Orien said to wait was to kill her child—and so he wished them all quiet, smothered Orien's dire warnings under stifling silence, smothered Tarien's fears and even the babe's silent struggle.

A distressed guard came to his door to report screams from the Aswydds within the apartment, and that the baby might be coming. And at the same moment Uwen had returned, reporting the abbot was awake.

"As he's prayin', or whatever he can do. Ye want me to go over there?" Uwen asked, meaning the other wing. "A midwife I ain't, but babes an' foals is some alike."

"It won't be tonight," Tristen said into what seemed a great hush. "Orien wishes it. But I wish otherwise."

"M'lord," Uwen said with some evident misgiving. "A baby once't it starts comin' ain't amenable to arguments. Ye stop it, an' ye might kill the baby."

"The babe's alive," he said, staring into that gray distance, "and so is Tarien."

"It ain't good," Uwen said. "It ain't a good thing, m'lord, if there's a choice."

"There isn't," he said, and drew a deep breath, aware of Orien and Tarien and the babe all at once.

"What are they at?" Uwen asked him. "Is it the baby comin'?"

"*Orien* wishes it," he said, and went back to his chair in the study, picked up a just-poured cup of tea as thunder cracked and boomed above the roof, wizardous and uncertain. The gray space opened wide to him, and Orien was there, and Tarien appeared, a hurt, small presence with the child wrapped close, not yet free. "But the time is wrong."

"The babe's?" Uwen asked, "Or master Emuin's?"

"Both," Tristen said, with utter assurance, sipped his tea, and Uwen's expression eased.

He knew others had waked, now. Emuin was there, and from a greater distance, Crissand roused out of a sound sleep, confused and alarmed and half-awake. Cevulirn had sat up, in his bed in the camp outside the walls.

They consented to what he wished so strongly—supported *him*, as if they had set arms about him, not questioning what his wish was. Their trust in him was a heady drink, and gave him strength against Orien.

And not just Orien. He became aware of a presence elsewhere, from far away, from the north, from Tasmôrden's direction, and that presence was thin and subtle and laced with excitement and desire.

He would not have that. He flung himself from the chair with a crash of the teacup, sent a table over as he flung out a hand to the nearest wall and willed the wards to life, strong, stronger than any intrusion.

The wards sprang up blue and strong as he could make them, from here to the town gates: he felt them, and as he turned about, hearing outcries and questions, he saw astonished faces, Tassand's, and one of the guards from upstairs. But Uwen was there, too, calm and steady, saying to the rest, " 'At's all right, His Grace is seein' to what's amiss, just ye stan' still and don't fret."

In that moment violence lanced between the fortress and the heavens, and Emuin's will deflected it. Thunder boomed and shook the very stones, and men cried aloud in fright.

"We're inside," Uwen said, "an' 'Is Grace is watchin' out for us, so the lightnin's ain't to fear. An' if he don't want that babe born tonight, 'e won't be."

Crack! went the thunder above them, and Emuin flung out an angry wish to the heavens, chiding the storm . . . and Orien Aswydd.

So Tristen did, and stood fast while three more sharp cracks pealed and boomed through the stones. The very air seemed charged, and the smell of thunderstorms and wet stone permeated the apartment, as if a window were open.

A woman's voice cried out in agony, and that pain went through the gray space.

—*Bring him into the world!* Orien cried, defying him as the lightning whited the windows. Do nothing they wish!

Lightning flared beyond the window, such as he had never seen, whitening everything in the room, and blinding him, deafening him with the crack of thunder.

The blindness lingered a moment in the gray space, and in the world of Men. His sight cleared slowly on Uwen and the frightened staff, sight shot through with drifting fire. And the wards were under assault, from within and from without.

"I'll go to her," he said, and forgot, as once on the parapets of Ynefel, that he had left his clothing. It was his servants and Uwen who pressed that necessity on him, and dressed him in haste, a few moments' delay while he shivered in the cold, as his sight within the world and within the gray space slowly returned, and all the while the wards rang and echoed to the assault. Emuin held it. He did. He was aware of Cevulirn and Crissand, both dim and far and confused about the source, both in danger.

—*Silence!* he bade them harshly. *Be still! Hold the wards!*

In that, their efforts aided him. The ringing grew more distant. Tarien grew quiet, but he was aware of Orien prowling the wards of a physical room, her room, Cefwyn's room, the room where the babe had begun its life. She attempted the window, and opened it, bringing in a gust of rain-laden air. It did not breach their protection: he would not permit it, and, dressed at least to his servants' insistence, he left his apartment, went down the hall and down the stairs, then up again, to the wing that housed the women, while Orien raged at the barriers of the sisters' prison.

Owl whisked up the stairs, a fleeting Shadow of an Owl, as he came to the floor where the women were. Guards were at sharp attention as he passed them, going toward the doors.

Earl Prushan was waked from his sleep, the Aswydds' neighbor in that hall: the old man had come out in his night robe, with his bodyguard and his servants, and farther down the hall, so had Earl Marmaschen and some of the lesser residents, like shopkeepers gaping at some parade in the streets, for he brought himself, and Uwen, and his guard.

"Open the door," he said to the guards who watched the doors.

Orien had opened every window, to judge by the cold wet blast that met him in the foyer and the windblown flare of drapery as he went into the room. The candles within had all but a few gone out, and in that semidarkness sat Tarien in a chair by the billowing draperies, with Orien leaning over her, arms about her heaving shoulders.

"Let her be!" Tristen ordered Orien.

"She is my *sister!*" Orien cried in indignation. "My sister! The babe is coming! Let her be! This is women's work!"

Tristen strode to the open window vent and shut it, stopping at least that source of draft and harm, and the ringing of the wards grew dim. The thunder still muttered above them, and lightning flashes made the roofs a tangled maze outside the clear and stained panes of the leaded glass.

Then he turned to the women, and willed the child quiet.

Orien willed otherwise, and held to her sister, cornered as they were. They were down to two candles, and those fluttering, the wards he set threatened, if not overwhelmed, until Uwen shut that vent as well.

His guards stood in the doorway. And Orien hated them, opposed them with all her might, as Tarien's face showed pale in the candlelight, and Tarien's hands made fists that battered the chair arms.

"Let me be!" she cried in the grip of renewed pain. "Let him come! Oh, gods!"

She convulsed, but the babe resisted: his time was not yet, and he wanted help not to leave the shelter he had, not to move to Orien Aswydd's bidding. And Tarien breathed in great, rapid gasps, her hands clenched on the chair now like claws, and the breath stopped, as if she could not get another.

"*Out!*" Orien screamed at them, and at him: "Don't touch her! *Don't touch her!*"

"Be easy," he said, and touched Tarien's hand nonetheless. A breath came. "Be still."

"Don't hear him!" Orien said. "Bring the child into the world!"

They were linked, these twins: Tarien's body clenched in pain, answering her sister.

"No," he said. He feared for the guards, and Uwen; and he turned on Orien himself, gathering force, wishing not to harm the one twin, but resolved now to sever them.

—*No! Orien cried, and flung all she had at him.*

But he saw how in the gray space a delicate knot bound them, delicate but strong and of lifelong standing. It was not force that would sever it, or the keenest knife, only a delicate undoing, and both twins resisted, Tarien with sobs and interrupted breath, half-fainting in her sister's arms.

He would *not* that Orien force her sister. He would *not*, and Orien fought back with burning eyes and a grip in this world and the gray that defied him to untangle her.

He began to do so, in the gray space, prying the two apart, but it was agony for Tarien, who clung to her sister, and would not let her go.

Then he knew Emuin was aware, and was on his arthritic way up the stairs toward him, already in this wing. Paisi, too, was hastening Gran Sedlyn out her door. Thunder cracked, the heavens riven and battering the windows with rain.

—*Let him come! Orien cried. This is the mixing of bloods, this is the heir of the High Kings, this is the vessel of the great lord, and in him is the prophecy, greater than Mauryl's working, longer than Mauryl's working!*

—*Hasufin Heltain's vessel, Emuin said, at distance, overcome with a pain in his side. Orien struck at him, intending a mortal wound, struck at Uwen, who could not perceive it, struck at him, at every living thing in her reach, randomly and without reason.*

"No!" Tarien screamed, as a crack of thunder ripped the air. Her back arched away from the chair and Tristen flung himself to his knees, seized Tarien's clawed hand in his, and willed her pain to ebb.

Threat lanced at his back; and Uwen was there, quick as Orien's strike.

A silver knife struck the floor and spun away across the figured carpet, ending under a chest. Orien struggled in Uwen's grip, but Tristen willed her silent and her curses void. Her strength was ebbing, like the thunder that muttered in the distance now, after that last violence. He held Tarien's clammy fingers in his, tenderly, quietly.

"Be still," he said, sorry for her pain. "Hush. Hush."

"My prince," Tarien said between pangs and on sobbing breaths. "He was *my* prince, before he was hers—and I have his son. I have his son! She can't take that away!"

"Hush," Tristen said, and rode the waves of pain with her: he could do that, now, in the quiet that settled around them. He smoothed the waves, stilled them to a flat sameness of discomfort, until she leaned her head against the chair and drew deep breaths, sweat beading her white brow.

The child within grew quiet.

"Your sister wants your child," Emuin said harshly, and he was there in the room, a shadow against the last two candles. "She wants him for Hasufin Heltain, and to be his, the babe must die—open your eyes, woman! You have a little of the craft and a smattering of the wisdom! You'd have more if you didn't blind yourself! See her! *Look* at what she truly wishes!"

217

"Let my sister alone!" Orien cried from across the room, where Uwen and the guards had taken her. "Let me go! *Damn you!*"

She was exhausted now, not an imminent threat. "Shut that window!" Emuin said, and Gweyl moved, shut the last of the window vents, at the far end of the row. That stopped the bitter draft. "Fool!" Emuin said, and meant Orien Aswydd.

"Murderer!" Orien screamed back, and wished Emuin dead, as she had wished him dead at summer's end, and moved one of her servants to murder him. "I *curse* you!" she cried, and tried things she had read in ancient parchments, a treasure trove of Mauryl's letters, but Emuin swept that aside with hardly more effort.

"It's not the words," Emuin said, "it's the wisdom, and that doesn't come by wishing, woman! It doesn't come by spite! Come, gather it up! Can you?"

She could not. All her efforts scattered to the winds. The storm was gone, the violence within it was gone, and what was within Orien ebbed and dissipated like the force of the wind. The air had that feeling.

"Take her to the guardhouse," Emuin said, "and stand guard over her. You, Gweyl, yourself."

"No!" Orien cried, outraged. "Tarien!"

Tristen made no move to intervene. Emuin had the matter in hand, and the wrongness within Tarien's body was the greatest concern, the distress of the child. He dimly heard the commotion of Orien's forcible departure, but he held Tarien's hand and willed her safe and the baby safe until he lost all feeling in his knees—and until finally a more friendly fuss in the room heralded Gran Sedlyn's arrival, a peasant woman with strong, competent hands and a comforting voice.

"Get the lady to bed," was Gran Sedlyn's quick order, and Tristen gathered himself up as Uwen helped Tarien to rise, and between the two of them, one on a side, they took Lady Tarien to her bed in the next room—the same that had been Cefwyn's bed when he was here.

There Gran settled her and tucked pillows beneath her back and made her comfortable. "No place here for men," Uwen said, and drew him back.

But Tarien's hands moved upon those sheets, and he sensed, in that haze to which her mind had retreated as the pain had eased, the memory in her of that bed, her bed, a hint of remembered scent, that was Cefwyn.

There was love, a woman's love, at once foreign to him and

comprehensible: love and loss of a man, and a bond to the child within.

No place here for men, Uwen had said, and he felt strange and lost in Tarien's grief, yet understanding the loss, which was his own loss. Neither of them had kept Cefwyn here. No one could. His Place was elsewhere, his love elsewhere bestowed . . .

"Summat warm to drink," Gran Sedlyn wished, whether for herself or for her charge was unsure. Paisi hovered over his gran, and Cook was there, summoned by the abbot, so she said, but little needed now as a midwife: Cook had made sweet tea, and brought it, but Tarien turned her face away angrily and swore she could take no such thing, even as that real scent chased the beloved, remembered scent away. Her spell was broken. She suffered loss again. Women bedeviled her, her sister, Gran, Cook: they hovered and chided and would not let her lie alone in her grief.

It was women's magic. He felt the soothing influence in the gray space; but elsewhere, at the limits of his awareness, Orien Aswydd raged in her new confinement, full of violence, trying desperately to have Tarien's attention, and attacking her guards.

He feared for Uwen—acutely, in that instant. He cast Emuin only a glance.

"Orien's threatened Uwen."

"Go," Emuin said, and he left matters in the apartment to Emuin's care and went out, almost without a guard, for the ones at the door had no orders regarding him and the ones guarding him had all gone downstairs with Uwen.

The wards lower down rang to Orien's efforts. They had shut her behind an iron door and it did nothing to prevent her curses. He ran to the end of the hall, sped down the west stairs and down and down to the guardroom steps, where Uwen was.

Safe, he was glad to see, but not for any of Orien's wishing.

"There's an unhappy woman," Uwen said with a jerk of his thumb toward the closed door.

"She's done all she can to breach the wards," Tristen said, and went down himself, and laid a firm binding on the door and all about.

Within, Orien flung herself at the door and hammered at it with her fists, cursed him and raged at the barrier until her voice cracked.

But she would not get out and no Shadow would get in. Tristen turned and looked at the corners of the small nook where the guardhouse stairs came down, at the dark places beyond the smoking tallow candles.

Reeking of death and slaughter, Emuin had said in rejecting such candles, and reek they did. This entire stairwell did. The Aswydds had made this a place of pain, and so it was now: Shadows lurked in the seams of the stone and in the nooks beyond the light—murdered Elwynim, some; malefactors, murderers, thieves, and traitors . . . the innocent and the guilty and the unfortunate: all the pain suffered in this place, all the lives that had ended in this small room.

—*Be free,* he said to some, and others he bound, for it Unfolded to him how to do that, as he had not known when he was confined here himself. She might have rallied such Shadows. He removed them from her reach.

Then the place was quieter, save only Orien Aswydd's hoarse shrieks and occasional and faltering strikes at the door.

Last of all he felt a presence, a Shadow among other Shadows, and from the tail of his eye thought he saw one he knew—Heryn Aswydd, bloodied and burned as he had died. Cefwyn had sent away all the Aswydd dead and tried to dispossess them of their Place in the world, but the living Aswydds had come here, and brought the dead ones back, or waked this one from sleep, so he feared.

Heryn he bound to the hallway of this little nook, finding no pity for the man who had sought Cefwyn's life and betrayed so many. A shriek followed; and that was Orien; and silence came after that.

He gazed at Uwen's shocked face, at the guards who had defied sorcery carrying out his orders—scared men, troubled men. He reached out a hand and touched Uwen's arm, and then touched one after the other of the rest of them, wishing them well.

A muffled thump attested Orien's rage at his small magic. Rather than desist he made it a greater one, wishing good to all the soldiers, good to all the house. It was a war of curses and well-wishes, and so it went on for a moment until with a final hammering at the door, Orien desisted.

"Come upstairs," he said then quietly.

"There ain't much comfort in that cell," Uwen said. " 'Cept we left a light an' a pail of water. Shall we fetch a blanket an' a bench?"

The gate-guards had left the same for him once: a candle in an iron cage, that cast great squares of light about ceiling and walls, and straw to ease the cold of the stones. It seemed too cruel, even for Orien; but she had sped wishes for the baby . . . she owned it, in her thinking, and it was too hazardous to open that door and engage with her until the dawn. A banished spirit had found its way into the royal house of Althalen: Hasufin Heltain had made his bid for life in a stillborn babe. He had no wish to see it happen here, to Cefwyn's child.

"Not until dawn," he said. By then it would be *his* day, and *his* evening, and the sun would shine and the darker forces would find less strength. Shadows—and Hasufin was such a Shadow—found the dark far friendlier.

He did not know how long it might be, the watch they had to keep, but Orien had not given up the struggle for the babe's life, Hasufin's threat was not yet abated.

And by his will, they would not open that cell door until both things were so.

CHAPTER 3

Tarien slept fitfully, into the middle of a night that saw the snow washed off the roofs and torrents pouring from the gutters. She lay abed, curls of russet hair clinging to a damp brow, in the light of many candles.

The clepsydra's arm rose to the uppermost, and at that precise instrument's movement, Emuin poured in a carefully measured cup of water, ready for the purpose, instrument and cup alike on the water-circled dining table of the Aswydds' apartment.

"Glass," Emuin said sharply, and Paisi inverted the hourglass that backed their measurements. "Pour the cup."

"Mark on the paper, master, afore ye forget."

"I won't forget! Pour the damned cup! Time's passing!"

Tristen watched askance, wondering would master Emuin indeed remember to make the mark, which accounted of the finer measures of the night, and watching until he did. The drip of water from the water clock was far more accurate a measure than marked candles and more reliable even than the costly glass . . . but only if one poured the water back in quickly. Master Emuin had brought it down from his tower, and set it up on the table, and still fussed over what exact moment it had begun.

A spate of rain hit the windows, and lightning flashed.

Cook and the midwife Gran Sedlyn sat watch; and the nuns, who had served the Aswydds before, ran errands for herbals from Gran Sedlyn's small shop in the lower town. Guards watched. Uwen waited.

So, too, did Orien wait and watch and pace her cell, exhausting herself against unyielding walls and an iron door . . . most of all hurling her anger against the wards that defended the door. So the guards reported, men unnerved by the strength and persistence of the rages and the virulence of the curses. To the guards stationed there, Paisi had brought blessed charms, from master Emuin, and more from the abbot.

"For what good they'll do," Emuin said, "but luck attend them while they stand by that cursed door.—Where's the damned owl?"

"I don't know," Tristen said.

"The bird could make himself of some use," Emuin said peevishly. But of Owl, for the last hour and more, there was no sign.

Now they watched by candlelight, a cluster of men banished from the vicinity of the bedchamber as too noisy and too much disturbance to Lady Tarien's pain, but neither Tristen nor Emuin wished to leave Cook and Gran Sedlyn to watch alone, considering the lady's abilities and ties to her sister. Tarien seemed intent on the child's good health, seemed not to share her sister's insistence on a birth tonight, but had seemed rather to be struggling to keep the babe's own time . . . until she slept, which they all took for a hopeful sign.

But even the iron latch and the iron door below were not utterly trustworthy barriers against her sister, particularly as ordinary men watched it. There were wishes and wards and barriers . . . but that link had had years to work, and it was strong. Orien's will stretched toward her sister, and urged the babe to restlessness.

Yet the hours slipped away, measured by arcane instruments and the patience of Orien's warders. At the very mid of the night Emuin reasoned she would cease to trouble Tarien, for that marked the start of another day, as some reckoned.

But they were not out of the darkness, nor out of Orien's hopes. The efforts kept up, as the arm rose and Paisi turned the glass for midnight.

More moments passed.

"Before dawn would seem to be close enough," Emuin said glumly, "she hasn't given up."

"Perhaps she doesn't know it's midnight."

"One congratulates a man on his birth. We are now, by the stars, at yours."

He had wondered would his life continue past the anniversary of his Summoning. And indeed it had, now, and he sat, substantial, beside another fireside, knowing so much more, and in circumstances he could never have imagined a year ago.

Orien continued her assault.

"Bid the lady in the guardroom know it's midnight," Emuin said sharply, and Paisi sped down to the soldiers.

Paisi was gone a time. There was no point at which the efforts ceased—but there was one at which they grew more fierce, furiously, wildly angry.

"Unreasonable woman," Emuin said. "Disagreeable, unreasonable woman."

Paisi returned at a run, out of breath, wide-eyed with fright and concerned with what seemed at his very heels. But he had been safe, as the guards were safe, below: Tristen had not been unaware the while of anything that went on in the fortress, and he directed Paisi to a warm spot by the fire until the boy could warm the chill from his bones.

So they sat, their small group of men: Uwen, who knew something of births, and master Emuin, who knew little, and the guards, who had heard much and knew only slightly more, Tristen thought, than he did. Paisi, the youngest, seemed to know most of all of them.

Once more the cup spilled and the glass turned. Twice.

But the third time the sand began to run, something happened in the gray place, and it was no longer stable as it had been. Tarien woke, and the babe woke with her, and a moment later a muted scream came from inside the bedroom.

They all glanced that way, as alarm filled the unseen space, then vanished in Orien's sudden leap of satisfaction, her assault on the wards. But the assault failed and she fell back again.

"Two hours till dawn," Emuin said with a heavy breath. "Two hours."

Another hour approached. Paisi hurried back to the bedroom, not the first such errand, and was gone a space, and came back tight-lipped.

"Gran says as the babby's comin' now an' 'e ain't waitin'."

Tristen drew in a breath and paid attention such as he could spare. The gray place had become slate gray cloud, shot through with red like fire—Orien's doing, her wishing grown greater with her fear of failure and loss.

Emuin reversed the glass the third time.

And now the gray space began to show a more and less of pain, as it had been at the beginning. When the pain was more, conversation would become difficult and distracted. Tristen left the table and wandered the border by the windows, with an occasional glance to Emuin's glass and the water clock.

A cry rent the peace, and he could bear no more of it: he left their vigil for that in the bedchamber, where Tarien lay propped on pillows—not the beautiful creature now, but an unhappy and desperate one, caught between their will and her sister's, back and forth, back and forth, until now she looked at him in the gray space, with eyes dark as the cloud that boiled about them. She began to drift away—pulled, not her own doing—and reached out her hand as if she were sinking, drowning and taking another presence with her.

He seized the outstretched hand, and held it, and wished the pain away, and the life within her safe, while the winds howled and the life in her ebbed. She had strayed right to the Edge, and that darkness half-swallowed her, at times less, at times more. He held on.

—*Come this way, he begged her. Come with me.*

—*My sister, she said repeatedly, my sister.*

For another voice called her, and another self was there, within the darkness . . . at least one more was there, and perhaps others. It seemed to Tristen he heard Heryn's voice, full of anger and demands, and he felt Tarien cower. Her hold on his hand slipped and slipped again.

And then the Wind came, sweeping the others away, and whispered, most gently, mostly kindly:

—*Let me be born. Woman, let me be.*

And the cramping pains struck, fierce and strong, carried on Orien's wish, driven by the Wind.

—*Here, my lord, he is yours . . . Orien's voice rang strong and clear. Orien's will drove Tarien's body, and Orien's presence, stronger than ever she had been in the gray place, swallowed Tarien's will like the Edge itself.*

"No!" Tarien cried out as she slipped, and in the World, her nails bit deeply into Tristen's hand. He knelt by her bed and wished the pain away, seeking her presence in the gray world, feeling her sever that connection to Orien strand by strand as it pulled her toward the edge.

Rejecting her sister, preserving the life within her . . . she slipped and he felt her nails pierce his hand.

"It's coming!" the midwife said. "It's comin', ain't no question now, m'lady. It must come."

Emuin leaned into the doorway. "A handful of sand, a handful of sand, woman—*wait that long!* It's too early!"

—*My lord, here's your vessel!*

Tarien screamed, vehement as Orien at her worst, beside herself with pain and lashing out at her sister. —*You'll not have him!*

Orien vanished. Still the child came.

"Wizardry, woman!" Emuin shouted, and wished with a force

225

that might stop a river in its course. "You wanted wizardry! Use it now! Orien wants your son. Your sister wants him for a vessel for her master! Is that your wish? *Is it? Save his life, woman, hold back!*"

"It's comin', it's coming," Gran Sedlyn said.

"I can't!" Tarien screamed, and the baby's drive for the world of Men would not be denied again.

The Edge was all the gray space now, and Tristen held fast, unwilling to relinquish his grip. On Tarien his hold was firm . . . but the presence within her flowed out, whirled away into the dark, and flew out of reach.

"Stillbirth," the midwife said.

"Damn!" he heard Emuin say.

And again in the gray space, and with telling force: **Damn!**

—**Hold to her,** *Tristen said.* **Master Emuin, help me hold her. She'll die.**

—**It's the baby he wants,** *Emuin said to him. His hair and beard and garments alike streamed in the gale that the Edge swallowed up. Tarien was half in it, the babe all the way gone . . .*

But something was in the dark: the Wind that gathered itself for a first breath in the World.

—**Not yours,** *Tristen said to the Wind, with all the force that was in him, and of a sudden he felt the rush of Owl's wings past his hair. Owl soared ahead of him into that gulf and he found himself rushing into it, a familiar place after all, a place of blue light, beating with wings.*

A boy stood there, preoccupied among the hawks, a well-dressed, fair-haired boy who began to look toward him, head turning, until the Wind called him by a name Tristen, hearing, could not hear— would not hear, for it was not the name he knew for the child.

—**Elfwyn,** *Tristen said, commanding attention, and now the boy cast him a dark-eyed glance. With the very next blink the boy was a well-grown youth, straight and tall, with Cefwyn's very look.*

—**Sir?** *said the boy, but the dark within the dark was in his eyes.*

Tristen reached out his hand, wishing the boy to come to him, wishing him safe and his mother and his father safe.

Fire leapt up, spectral red amid the cool blue light as the Wind called to the boy again. Out of that fire a black figure advanced, outlined in Wind-driven flame, and the boy faltered as that Shape held out a commanding, open hand. The wind roared, and the boy stood transfixed, fair hair torn by that Wind, hand all but touching the hand that reached for his.

—**Elfwyn!** *The second time Tristen called, commanding now, and* *the boy's head turned, the hand dropped. The name that was not the boy's Name echoed again in the nameless light and the dark hand seized on the youth's shoulder.*

And in the very teeth of the gale Tristen called a third time, the magical time: **Elfwyn!**

The boy looked at him in startlement and the dark eyes turned cornflower blue, pale and with a hint of gray, until there was nothing of the darkness in them. The boy's hand touched his.

The Wind raged and tore at them. Needles of ice and pain lanced through flesh and bone, and the gulf gaped under them.

Then Owl flashed between, bound away, and with that guidance Tristen turned toward what he knew was home, with the boy in his grasp. They traveled toward the darkness beyond the rows of birds on their perches, and constantly Owl flew ahead of him. Tristen gripped the boy's shoulder, then his hand, and increasingly as he walked the hand he held was smaller and smaller, and the steps faltered, until he must sweep the child up within his arms, and hold him fast as he walked toward the dark circle.

He saw candlelight. He stepped into it . . .

And drew a great, deep breath, flavored with the cold of the downstairs hall at the site of the haunt, that stretch of odd flooring that fronted the old mews. He found himself with a newborn baby in his arms, a wizened, bloody creature with tight-clenched eyes and clenched fists, a babe that suddenly drew breath and let it out in a loud and lusty wail.

He slipped the pin of his cloak, the blood red of Amefel, and wrapped the baby in it against the chill . . . he walked, and guards posted at the stairs stared with misgivings as he passed with the small bundle in his arms.

He climbed the west steps, and passed guards he had not passed going out of Tarien's apartment, men struck with consternation and surely wondering where he had been.

He did not venture the gray space now. He had no idea where that shortcut might send him and the babe both. He had no idea where Owl had gone, but when he reached Tarien's apartment the guards opened the door for him. He carried his small angry charge through the outer chambers into the one where Tarien lay, and Emuin watched, and Gran Sedlyn met him with a face astonished and distraught.

"*You* took it!" Gran Sedlyn said, and behind her, Paisi stared, round-eyed.

He said not a word, but took the baby to Emuin, who sat by

Tarien's bedside, holding her hand, and she all disheveled and with her red hair pasted about her temples.

"We took out the sheets," Gran Sedlyn was saying, a noise in his ears, "an' 't was as if maybe we took out the babby amongst 'em by mistake. We couldn't find 'im, we couldn't find 'im, and Your Grace had 'im all the time . . . and where was Your Grace?" the confused woman asked. "Sittin' here, as I thought, and then . . ."

"He's safe," Tristen said.

"Safe," Emuin echoed him, with meaning, and maintained a fierce ward over the place, over the woman who rested, pale and shrunken, amid the pillows. Only as Tristen unwrapped his small burden and showed her the baby's face did her eyes open wide, and go from grief to wonder. Her hands reached, not as Orien's had reached, but with an urgent, tender desire. He laid the baby on her breast, and Tarien folded her arms around her child, and looked at him as if the very sight poured strength and life into her.

"His name is Elfwyn," Tristen said, and Tarien's eyes flashed wide, lips parted, perhaps to protest she wanted some other name. But she said not a word. Emuin looked at him, too, and with a sharper, worried expression, but without dispute.

"Elfwyn," Emuin said.

"My baby prince," Tarien murmured, with her lips against the infant's pale and matted hair.

"Let's wash 'im," Gran Sedlyn said. "Let's 'ave a look 'ere, m'lady."

"No," Tarien said. "No one will take my baby. *No one will take him!*"

"Hear me, woman," Emuin said harshly, and with a hand on the child and Tarien's arm. "He has his right soul in him. This is truly Cefwyn's child. That *isn't* what your sister wanted. Do you understand?"

"She's dead," Tarien said. Her lips faltered as if they were frozen. "She's dead. She can't have him. My prince loved *me,* and she'll never have him!"

Emuin looked at Tristen, and Tristen at him, with the feeling in his heart that Tarien was not mistaken. He left the room, unwashed and exhausted, and suddenly aware that Uwen was not there, and Uwen would never have left his heels. Gweyl and all his new guards were gone somewhere, but Lusin and Tawwys had come in, among the silent wardens of the Zeide, and Syllan and Aran were outside as if they had never left their former duty to him.

"There was fire," Lusin said, and had no sooner said, than Uwen came through the door, soot smeared about him, and with Gweyl close behind.

"Thank the gods," Uwen said. "They said ye'd come downstairs, an' the fire, an' all—"

"Orien burned," Tristen surmised.

"In her cell," Uwen said, and held his hands as if he wanted a place to wipe them, in this prince's apartment. "Set the pallet alight, the candle to the straw, an' the chokin' smoke afore the flame: it were like an oven in that cell, an' the guards up above didn't know 't till the smoke come up the stairs."

That flaring strength in the gray space . . . Orien's attempt to drive Tarien to birth: in death she had reached for freedom and bound herself to the stones of the Zeide.

"Where was ye, m'lord? Where'd ye go?—An' what's this wi' the babe?"

"In there," Tristen said, still unsure he should have given the child to Tarien, but compelled to it by a magic that spoke to him as strongly as the wind and the earth themselves. "With Lady Tarien."

"Gods bless," Uwen said, and raked his hair back with a sooted hand, leaving streaks on his brow. "Gods bless. An' 'Er Grace dead an 'er ladyship wi' the baby. An' what's to be wi' *him?*"

"He's Cefwyn's," Tristen said. "And Emuin's there. Emuin won't leave him." He felt that as surely as he had felt the strength and the will in Tarien's arms. "He's Cefwyn's son, his name is Elfwyn, and Hasufin won't have him."

There was a new Shadow loose within the wards downstairs. He was sure of that. It was bound to the stones of the place, exactly as he had once feared would happen when he had advised Cefwyn to exile all the Aswydds and not to execute them. An iron door had not been enough to hold Orien Aswydd prisoner: she had proved that well enough.

But in the purpose she held worth her life, she had failed. She was not done with trying for wizardry, perhaps, and Hasufin himself could not fault her effort or her courage . . . but she had failed.

He went back to the door to reassure himself all was well within the room, and saw Emuin and Lady Tarien and the babe, all in the light of a single candle.

He saw a life that had not existed before now. He found that, amid all else, the most remarkable thought, and he took with him the remembrance of the boy and the youth who might someday re-member meeting him, in the maze of the mews.

Owl joined them as he and Uwen left the apartment, and banked away down the stairs, to the startlement of the guards below, he was sure. Whether Owl was satisfied he had no idea.

But on the precise day on which Emuin calculated Mauryl had Summoned him to life, at the very first light of dawn, an entirely new soul had drawn a first breath, and Cefwyn had a son.

CHAPTER 4

Rain and thunder above canvas brought dreams of campaigns past, recollections of mud and hard living far to the south—of days spent waiting and nights spent in far less luxury than a royal pavilion, two cots made into one, and warmth against one's side.

But that warmth gathered herself in the last hours of the rain-drenched night and stole away . . . and over to the baggage piled out of the rain, in a corner of the huge tent. Cefwyn paid slight attention, deciding that Ninévrisë had thought of something undone, or left, or needed, in the way one did in the middle of the night on a journey, with all one's belongings confined to chests and boxes, and had the servants remembered the new boots or packed the writing kit?

Gods knew. There were times one simply had to get up and dispose of the question, and this night of noise and fury in the heavens, with the tent blown hard by the gusts and no great likelihood the army was going to break camp in the morning—this was such a troubled night, on their slow way through the edge of Murandys and to the river camp.

But Ninévrisë, having rummaged up something, or failed to find something, was quiet for a long while after.

Too long, Cefwyn decided. He had made up his mind to sleep late, having waked several times to realize the deluge continued, and still cherished the notion of late sleep until he rolled over to see what she was doing and saw her standing distressedly in the lightning flashes, with something flat and pale pressed to her bosom.

Then he knew that what she had ferreted from the baggage, from her belongings, was a piece of paper, *that* paper, and at this hour.

He shoved an elbow under him, looking at her in concern until he had a glance back.

Then she came back to him, and threw herself on her knees by the bedside.

"The baby's born," she said. "Tonight, the baby's born."

It was certainly not the sort of news to cheer either of them. The letter had told them nothing more till now, until he had ceased to believe it was anything but an inert scrap of unwritten paper.

But now this news broke through the days of silence, at the lightning-shot edge of a dawn that saw the army stalled, the roads surely turned to ponds and rivers.

And now in the dark of the tent he could not judge her expression, whether she wept, or frowned, or had no expression at all.

"More news," she said, and her voice trembled, barely audible above the battering of rain on the canvas walls. "Orien's dead."

"*Orien.*" He was taken aback, and wondered whether she had mistaken the twins and misspoken. Women died in childbirth, and should it not be Tarien who died at this birth?

"She burned to death," Ninévrisë said. "She burned in her cell."

"Good gods." His memory of a glorious, beautiful woman could not fit the image of such a death. He raked his hair back, pushed upright and hauled the blanket around him against the chill of the rain and the unhappy report. "I take it it's that letter," he said. "Is that all he says?"

"The baby's name is Elfwyn," she said. "Tarien called him Maurydd, after the old wizard, I think; but Tristen said he was Elfwyn, so Elfwyn he is, now."

A king's name, for a king's bastard. And not only a king's name, but the name of the last High King. *That* would not go unremarked among his uneasy barons. It was provocative and a trouble to the child and to him. Gods, what was Tristen thinking?

"What more?" he asked, unsettled. Tristen could be feckless at the most damnable times. "What news of Tristen?"

"He . . ." Ninévrisë's breath caught in her throat. She seemed to have caught a chill despite her robe, small wonder, at such news, and he moved quickly to gather her up and into his arms, in the warmth of an occupied bed.

The shivering kept up for a moment, and now he knew the truth, for Ninévrisë had taken the matter of Tarien's baby so entirely worldly-wise and matter-of-factly he had convinced himself she accepted it without a ripple.

Now in a stroke he doubted all his assumptions, about this, about all the other slights she took so calmly. She forgave him in the very embrace of her arms and the inclinations of her heart, but the existence of a child named as, gods help them, Tristen of all people . . . had named this child . . . what could she think?

What could anyone think?

And what did Tristen think, giving *his* son that name? Not a damned thing, was the first conclusion that leapt up in him: Tristen could be the most feckless soul alive, did things because those were the thoughts he said Unfolded to him, thoughts that leapt into a head that otherwise could be utterly absorbed with a hawk's flight or the shape of a leaf.

Yet Tristen, the worst liar in all Ylesuin, was not dealing with a hawk or a leaf in this child . . . this was not something Tristen would treat casually or on a whim, and the other aspect of his flighty concentration was that absolute, terrifying honesty, in which he would leap in where no courtier would tread. He had met that appalling honesty when—gods! when he had left off his folly of lovemaking with the Aswydd women and gone downstairs to look a stranger in the eyes . . . and he had never after been able to avoid that stare, that truth, that honesty. Like a boulder in a brook, it had diverted all his life into a different path.

And now . . . now the result of that moment was a child, and *Tristen* named him. He was deaf to wizardry, but like a deaf man, he could feel the drumbeat in the ground under him: a moment had come back to haunt him and change his life.

Elfwyn Tristen named the boy. So, indeed, Elfwyn he was, the will and word of his unacknowledged father and his father's wife notwithstanding.

And this Elfwyn, this bastard prince, was in fact heir to *nothing*, since his only legitimate claim, Amefel—where a maternal lineage did have legal force—had passed to Tristen's hands. But in his Aswydd and Marhanen blood he had substantial claims to everything in reach, if he one day decided to reach for it and cause a world of trouble.

With that name, the name of the last Sihhë High King, he had claims to gods knew what more.

Is *this,* he asked himself, the King To Come? This child? *Mine?* It was not what he had thought. *Tristen* was what he had thought, and trusted Tristen's complete lack of ambition. But this? Did Tristen name his own heir, in this child?

"It's not all," Ninévrisë said faintly, holding to him, "it's not all. Ryssand's with Tasmôrden."

He laughed, untimely, unseemly given the circumstances. "That's no news."

"He means to kill you."

A second time he laughed, this time because he was already set to laugh and wanted to deny all fears tonight and reassure her . . . but on his next breath he fully heard what she had said, and knew it was part of that letter, and felt cold through and through—not believing, far from disbelieving a warning from Tristen—and in the context of this newborn child, potential heir, potential pretender to more than two thrones.

"*Here?*" he asked.

"Tristen overheard some sort of plot, I don't know how, but I think the way wizards know. Tasmôrden's courting Ryssand—he's persuading Ryssand, with all sorts of promises if you should die, if *we* should die . . . that they'll make peace, for lands, all the bargain to be good no matter who makes it. *Efanor* would have no way to rally an army."

"Does Tristen say that?"

She hesitated. "I think it's been there a while. It doesn't feel part of the rest, but I only heard it tonight. I think it was the disturbance there. And I wasn't sure of it before, but now I know it's there . . . I don't think I thought it was different, thinking you by no means trust Ryssand, or Cuthan, either. But it's different now, and I know, and I don't know how I know, except it's from the letter. But Tristen doesn't know where we are, he doesn't know we've marched—"

"He's not received my message."

"Not yet. It's not yet there. But what Tristen knows, in the letter . . . and what I know in my heart . . . I'm not sure which of us knows it, but between us, I do know, and Ryssand *is* coming. He'll pretend to have a change of heart. He'll count on your welcoming him. And he'll betray you, and I don't know how I know!"

"Do you know it for the truth?" he asked. "Are you absolutely sure?"

"I'm afraid," she said. "And I don't know why, except this letter."

A paper blank except for seal and signature, and no more readable for him than before . . . wizard-work. Magic, Emuin insisted. Perhaps it was even bound to the *truth* of the situation, reporting when the world grew chancy enough and the barriers that divided them from Tristen and from their enemies grew thin.

Lightning made shadow play on the canvas walls, the outline of other tents close at hand. It felt like dawn, but the clouds were so thick and the rain so intense no light reached them. Idrys, Lord Commander, but still in his intentions his bodyguard, slept, or pretended to sleep, in the other chamber of this tent, among the maps and the armor. Waking guards sat duty there, too, out of the rain, men who had been with him even in Amefel. Close by their tent was the entire Dragon Guard, trusted men.

Could he fear for his life and hers tonight, so protected?

So too, he had claimed the mass of the Guelens and the rest of the common levy, and held a camp on its way to war. Osanan had joined them. Marisal was sending men. He had rallied more men than he had hoped.

Were there traitors already insinuated among these men?

They were bogged in a lightning-shot deluge that had followed sun and then snow. The heavens were utterly confused—and that was surely wizardry or the worst weather-luck a campaign ever had: and here they were bound for the river bridge, and as yet had seen nothing of the contingent from Murandys, when Murandys was the land through which they traveled.

Nelefreíssan and Ryssand had farther to march, and it had not been certain they would come, since Ryssand's storming out of court and out of the capital, but would they now, if Ryssand meant some act against him?

There was no one else he could summon. His missives southward he had sent in a bundle, all to Tristen, to give to the lords with him, for he knew now that letters to their capitals would not find them at home, but rallied at Henas'amef, to come by the southern bridge, for the stony hills of Gerath lay between, a wedge of land that had no straight trails, and all too many blind valleys: it had swallowed armed force before now and given nothing back. Tristen could not reach him.

And was the north to betray him?

Thank the gods at least the southerly bridge, the one Tristen held, would not become the sally port for Tasmôrden to start a diversion in Amefel.

"So Ryssand will come," he mused aloud, "with nefarious intent. And dare I say his message with Cuthan passed both ways, and he passes all we do to Tasmôrden? Who knows? Tasmôrden might have such a letter as we have."

"Ryssand intends to kill you," Ninévrisë insisted, more directly, more urgently. "If he does, Tasmôrden will let the army retreat from the field, and Ryssand, and Murandys, and all of them . . . all under truce . . . *they* will deal with him. *They* will sign a peace. The army will march home, owning part of Elwynor. They'll crown Efanor."

This was no idle threat, but a well-formed plot. He found himself perversely intrigued by the mechanisms of what might be his death. Did men often have such a vision of events to follow their impending demise? It was like a taste of wizard-sight.

"No dagger in the dark," he surmised. "Nothing so definite. That leaves witnesses and evidence. But men lose heart on a battlefield. Ryssand takes the field, his heavy horse fails the charge—breaks and falls back. The wing they're in collapses. The enemy sweeps around. Our army makes haste in retreat . . . and the rest follow. Hard for a man to stand when his neighbor's flung down his shield and bolted. Never count the good men that will die in such a maneuver."

"Tell Idrys. *Kill* Ryssand before he even arrives here!"

Ah, for his gentle bride. "Not that simple."

"It *is* that simple. This man will kill you!"

"Out of a dream and a letter with nothing written on it? Gods, all of this is such a flight of ifs!"

"Don't make light of me!"

"I do hear you. I take it in utmost seriousness."

"Is Tarien's baby an *if*? Is Ryssand, then?"

"No."

"If we seem about to win, then what will Ryssand do? Someone may tell more than Ryssand dares have known if you take prisoners of Tasmôrden's side. He daren't have you win! He'll only grow more desperate to strike at you, a knife, or poison—witnesses won't matter then. He'll want to set Efanor on the throne, see him wed to Artisane, and then Efanor's gone. Look at all he's done! He's severed you from the southern army. He's dared bring Cuthan to court. He's affronted you and stormed out. If he comes to join you now, you'll know what he intends. Be rid of him! Gods, be rid of him!"

Idrys advised it. Now Ninévrisë advised him the same.

And yet—and yet he had no evidence to justify himself to the rest of the barons. He had no proof of Ryssand's actions, more than that damning letter to Parsynan Tristen had sent him, and that was old proof. A great deal of water had flowed under the bridge since then . . . most significantly that he had let Efanor court Ryssand's daughter; now if he ordered Ryssand's head on a pike, would the rest of the orthodox north still take the field with good will? Would they fight to the uttermost to support a king who had just killed the foremost of them?

One thing was suddenly very clear to him.

"*You*, love, can't stay in their reach."

"Elwynor is no Guelen prize! My land, *my* crown—"

"My heir," he said in a low, determined voice, and with his arms about her. "My love. My very dear love, you're the foremost hostage they could hold . . . your welfare, above all heirs and all else. I love you. I honor your claim and risk all my kingdom to bring it to you. But this warning, if I believe it, changes everything."

"I am sovereign in Elwynor! You swore—"

"I *deny* you nothing. I admit every claim. I make myself your debtor when I ask you—I plead with you, for my own peace of mind—to take *our* son and *our* heir out of harm's way."

"Back to Efanor, who has enough to do to defend his own interests, let alone mine!"

"Efanor has men enough and guile enough to keep you safe. I know my brother. I know my brother as he was before he took to priests, and I swear to you there's a man there. If he should take the throne, Ryssand wouldn't like it."

"I believe it all, I never doubted it, but I won't leave you."

"Nevris." He pressed her head still with his hand, hugged her tightly against him.

"I'll not go, thinking I'll never see you again!"

"I swear to you I've no intention of dying, love. I'll deal with Ryssand *and* Tasmôrden. But I can't take you onto the field, and most especially I can't defend myself wondering whether you're safe back in my camp, or held hostage in Ryssand's."

"I'm not a fool!"

"Nor am I! And not being one I can't divide my attention—don't argue with me, not in this. You know I'm right. If you're there I'll be thinking of you, no other thing. I know you'll be suffering all the worry I'd suffer if you were there. But that's your part to suffer, mine to ask it, or I won't have my wits about me—Hear me! I'm king, and it's my damned army! Go to Efanor!"

She said nothing. She held to him. He routinely lost arguments when she said nothing. But this time he would not yield, and he waited, and waited.

"I'll go to Amefel," she said, prying herself from his arms, and with a rustle of the paper she had abused with her holding him, spread her hand on it, smoothed it.

He had not thought at first of Amefel. But it was fortified. Its people were Bryaltines. Tristen ruled it, and had the loyalty of the people.

It was a better choice. And hardly farther away. Assurnbrook was a deep and treacherous river, once it received the flow of Arrey-burn on its way north to the Lenúalim—that was one reason no bridge had ever stood in its shifting sands and soft banks, and the other the fact that Murandys had had no interest in linking itself to Amefel. But Assurnford was not that far south of their camp here, and once across that, Ninévrisë would immediately be in a Bryalt land, safe even in the countryside—not risking the mood of Guelen villages, who, no, would not be pleased that the woman for whom Guelenmen went to war was going back to safety.

He did not mention that hazard, knowing how it would sting her pride: it stung his that his own people were so inclined to hate her. But he did know a better choice when she laid it before him: safe from the time she crossed the Assurn, not having to brazen it out with the banners and Idrys' authority or slip into Guelemara cloaked and by night, simply to reach the Guelesfort in safety.

"Idrys will see you there."

"Idrys won't," she said. "For one thing, he won't leave you."

"He'll do it if I order it," he said, "and if he wants Ryssand's head, which he does. More than that—he serves the Marhanen. And you carry the Marhanen heir." Then it crossed his mind that where he sent her, Tarien was, and she had to confront that situation. "Tarien's there."

"So is Tristen. And Emuin. Tarien doesn't frighten me. Nothing there frightens me."

"Then you'll go tonight. Now. We'll make as little fuss about this as we can." Her sickness had troubled her, at the Guelesfort and on the march, and she had endured her misery and forced down soldiers' fare, refusing to have anything more delicate. He had lost all his arguments until now, and he took no chances. "A soldier's tent, a packhorse, Idrys and four men and their gear. Can you do it?"

The rain rushed against the walls of the tent. The river would be up, and the crossing at Assurnford itself an ice-cold flood of snow-melt. He knew what a misery that soaking ford might be. But Idrys knew the crossing in all its treachery, and he would get them to safety.

"I've no doubt," Ninévrisë said, and Cefwyn held her tightly, wanting nothing more than to have her with him and nothing less than to see her in a town where no harm would possibly come near her.

"Before the sun's up," he said. "With no fuss, no delay. Idrys will want to come back, and I won't forbid it. I'll see you after this is over, in Ilefínian."

"In Ilefínian," she said. "Don't worry for me. Guard yourself. Do whatever you need to do. Say I've gone to the capital: there'll be less talk, and if trouble comes after us, it'll take the wrong road."

"Wise lady."

"Promise me: don't let Ryssand's men near you. Set him near any engagement: let him bear the brunt of any encounter.—And carry my banner with you."

They had planned the advance from the river through provinces that might be favorable to Ninévrisë. All those plans were cast to the winds, and her banner by all custom should not fly if she were not there: but custom be damned, he had no difficulty agreeing to it, if it saved them fighting Ninévrisë's loyal subjects and killing honest men.

"I will," he promised her. "All I do, I do in your name."

"I'll launch rumor north from Henas'amef, with Tristen."

"See you don't launch *yourself*," he said, for he had a sudden apprehension of her finding Elwynim forces inside Amefel, and the temptation it would be to her.

"Trust me," she said, "as I trust you to take my capital."

"I've no choice," he said. "And I swear to you that banner will fly."

They made a silent farewell then, a lovers' farewell, with the storm flickering and roaring beyond the tent walls, and the rain pouring down.

After that he waked Idrys, and Idrys listened, expressionless, to the plans they had.

"I'll be riding back," Idrys said, as he had known Idrys would say.

"There'll be no trouble tracking us," Cefwyn said in grim humor. "I trust you'll find me, crow: you never do miss trouble."

CHAPTER 5

After the deluge of rain came the west wind, from the evening of Tristen's day, blowing the clouds from the sky and warming the last piles of snow, drying the fields and banging at loose shutters. The banners atop the South Gate flew straight out, and the pigeons when they came to the window had hard work to maintain their places.

They were still as many as before: Tristen counted them as he did every day, worrying about Owl's appetite, and still they stayed safe.

And still Tarien's babe stayed safe, and slept, as Uwen assured him new babies did, and nursed and slept and slept some more. Gran Sedlyn refused to leave, having mislaid the baby once: she slept close by on the night of that day, and tended Tarien and Elfwyn both. It was passing strange to Tristen that now he must think of a new soul, a creature that had never existed before, but there he was, indisputably a baby.

As for Orien, she lay where she had died, and no one wanted to go into that fire-blackened cell. That very day, and on Emuin's advice, Tristen sent for masons to wall up the guardhouse, from the stairs on down. It was simple work, requiring no great time to accomplish it. And when it was finished, he and Emuin both had warded it, for the sake of Tarien's soul, and Elfwyn's, and to give Orien's spirit what rest it might find—but Tristen doubted she wished peace at all.

Orien had lit her own funeral pyre that night. Shut behind the cell's iron door, guarded by men in the hall above, she had still found an escape, a way for her spirit to go walking, cut free from her bonds—so she had imagined, to seize a new home in Tarien's body, but she had failed in that attempt. She had attempted to escape

240

the wards altogether, riding an intruder spirit's will, and to fly all the way clear; but she had become lost, left behind. The wards had thrust her ambitious soul back into the cell from which it had extended itself—and now with the new wall and the wards, Tristen hoped they had bound it there, bound it and sealed it in such a way it would never escape.

But there was still a danger from the old mews. If some power came in by that and breached the wards there, then Orien might have help to free herself—for she had made herself a Shadow, and a dangerous one, potent and quick—dangerous especially to Tarien.

Tarien had rejected her sister's influence, had defended herself with unexpected strength, and utterly cast her out, terrified at what desire she now saw—but she had weak moments. She had ambitious moments. And she remained vulnerable to Orien's desires, a woman who mothered Cefwyn's son, and on whom they had to rely.

In the meanwhile, however, the contrary weather seemed now not to resist his wishes. The roads were drying, he knew from messages that Cevulirn's men were well established, and now he took it on faith that Cefwyn would do as he said and march to the river.

So he had done. But Tristen lingered here, waiting and waiting for a message from Cefwyn.

For the pride of the northern barons, Cefwyn had said, they must go first across the river.

But for the friendship that was between the two of them, Tristen believed a letter would come, and that from that letter he would learn things he needed to know.

So for two days more he found things to occupy him, the questions of supply, of weather damage, of disputes over scarce resources; and questions, too, of master Emuin, who would not march with the army. Emuin continued his scrutiny of the heavens and his consultation of dice. From time to time he made inquiries of master Haman on the behavior of horses and stable mice—and made them again, while Paisi had caught a mouse in the lower hall, and kept it in a cage: about that matter, Tristen had no understanding, but the mouse ate well, and took water from a silver dish.

The pond thawed, and the fish waked from their winter sleep. Amid all his more serious concerns, Tristen took them bread crumbs, and saw with delight that the small birds had come back to the barren trees in the garden.

Yet all of this filled a time of waiting—waiting for word from Cefwyn, worrying for what he knew of Ryssand's purposes, wondering what use Cefwyn might have made of what he could send to

Ninévrisë . . . or whether Ninévrisë might have heard his messages at all; wondering whether Anwyll had reached the capital yet, and whether he was safe, and whether he had reached Idrys without incident. Of all messengers he could send, *surely* no one would assail a captain of the Dragons at the head of his company—and surely he would have a message soon, telling him he was free to cross the river.

But the third afternoon the gate bell rang, startling the pigeons into flight, a sudden wall of gray wings obscuring the sky, beating aloft; and at that iron sound of the bell his heart rose up, the same, and he quickly shut the window and latched it, caught up his sword and his cloak before his servants closed about him to put both on him, and was out the door of his apartment, papers and signatures and petitions of town nobles forgotten.

He was sure it was the messenger he awaited. He knew that Emuin was in his tower, that Tarien was in her room asleep: all these persons he was always aware of.

But he was suddenly astonished to understand that *Ninévrisë* wanted him, and was thinking of him at this very moment.

He stopped on the stairs in midstride, alarmed, casting about him to know what mischance had let him and Ninévrisë touch, so far apart, and whether dangerous wizardry had hurled them together: she felt so unaccustomedly strong, and distressed, and glad, and close . . .

She was at his own town gate.

He hurried down the stairs with his concomitant racket of guards and weapons overtaking him from behind—Uwen was elsewhere, about his duties, but Gweyl and the others were with him; and letting them follow as best they could he half ran down the lower hall to the west doors and out to the stable yard.

There he spied a stableboy with a sorrel horse at lead.

"Is he fit?" he asked the boy, who stammered yes, and without any regard of ownership or the boy's destination, he took the lead and with both hands vaulted onto the sorrel's bare back. "It's no great concern," he said to Gweyl and the guards, who had caught up. "Wait here!"

Those were certainly not their standing orders from Uwen; but Ninévrisë was already on her way uphill, and Tristen was in no mood to wait for saddles and four more horses. He turned the horse to the gate and rode out on the instant onto the street and down, bareheaded, bannerless, but bound for answers and an appearance he had never looked to see come to him.

At the midtown crossing he saw the weary visitors coming uphill, a rider in a muddy blue cloak—Ninévrisë—in the lead, with, of all men, Idrys, and ten guardsmen in plain armor, mud-spattered to a brown, dusty sameness with their horses.

Had *Cefwyn* come south to join him? he asked himself, with a dizzying flood of hopes and fears—together they could do anything, overcome the north, accomplish all his hopes—but if Cefwyn came south it meant calamity with the northern provinces.

And it was only Ninévrisë, only Idrys, which frightened him beyond words.

He rode up to Ninévrisë's heartfelt and weary gladness to see him, and the gray space opened, pouring out everything to him: her pain, her distress, his letter, his warning; and Cefwyn days advanced on the road to Elwynor . . . none of these things with words, and none in order, and all with her exhaustion and fear. He was as dazed at this Unfolding of dangers as if the sky had opened on him.

"Tristen," she said aloud, reaching out her hand. "Oh, Tristen!"

"Is Cefwyn safe?"

"To our knowledge," Idrys said in his low, calm voice. "He bade me bring Her Grace to Henas'amef for safety, but the roads so delayed us I looked to find you on the road north by now."

"I waited for his message, sir."

"None reached you?"

"No," he said, dismayed.

"One should have. I'll be off," Idrys said, "this hour, with the loan of horses."

"With the gift of anything you need," Tristen said fervently. "But what message should have come? And did Cefwyn not get mine, with Anwyll?"

"None from Anwyll," Idrys said, and by now they were riding side by side, bound uphill, with the curious stares of townfolk all around them. "But His Majesty will be at the river by now, and Anwyll may have to go there."

"Sir, Tasmôrden's plotting with Ryssand!"

"That, he knows."

"The letter told me," Ninévrisë said. "Your letter, the magical one. Only I fear—I fear it didn't tell me everything, and there might have been news there for days that I didn't hear until the news about the baby."

He had never been sure it would tell her anything at all. He was vastly relieved to know that not all his efforts had gone astray, and he saw in what had gone amiss no mere chance, but a hostile wizardry.

And whose wizardry it was, since Elfwyn's birth, he now was sure.

"When we reach the Zeide," he said, "I'll tell you all of it. And I pray you wait, sir, and tell me everything that was in Cefwyn's letter. I'll order horses and supplies, all you need. But I need your advice, what I should do."

Riders were coming toward them at a fair speed, Uwen Lewen's-son, with Gweyl and the rest, and Lusin, all of them astonished to see who had arrived.

But they all knew how to take things in stride, and meeting them, simply reined about calmly and rode with them, without a question, while the townsfolk on the street that stood and watched did so in a certain solemnity, not sure what it all meant, perhaps, but knowing that visitors had come. Enough of them surely recognized Ninévrisë, and even more surely, the Lord Commander; and their arrival in such grim, unlordly guise must start rumors running the streets . . . rumors of danger to the kingdom, perhaps even of defeat in the north and disaster to Cefwyn . . . Tristen had feared the same in his own heart, had no doubt the townsfolk would fear the same—even that Uwen and his guard might guess Ninévrisë's appearance with Idrys portended calamity.

So at the crest of the hill, in the open square, Tristen turned the borrowed horse about to face the straggling curious in the street and gave them the things he could tell them.

"King Cefwyn's army has moved against Earl Tasmôrden! He's requested us to safeguard the Lady Regent, and so we will! Her Grace of Elwynor, our guest and ally, with the Lord Commander, her escort—the Lord Commander will rejoin the king, in Elwynor!"

A cheer went up at that report, relief on all the faces.

"Wise," Idrys said in his low, travel-worn voice, "and a wonder to the people of Henas'amef to be so trusted by His Majesty, to be sure."

That ironic observation might be the underlying truth, but the people waved in unfeigned jubilation, and with the bells ringing and the echoing commotion outside, Tristen brought his small party inside the gates.

"The Lord Commander and his men are riding back immediately," he said to Uwen, and to Lusin, sliding down from the sorrel's bare back. A boy ran up to reclaim the horse, and now Tristen saw Tassand had hurried out into the nippish air and down onto the west door steps, ill dressed for the chill wind: "Her Grace is our guest, Tassand."

Those three he needed tell, and everything else happened—boys running for ponies to ride down after remounts, master Haman shouting, and Tassand hurrying up the steps as fast as his agile legs would carry him. Lusin, too, dispatched messengers with the necessary instructions for others of the staff, all of this in motion before they had reached the steps. Tristen promised supplies, clean clothes, hot baths if the men would wait that long.

"We have no time," was Idrys' protest, but Tristen swept Ninévrisë and the Lord Commander at once up the steps and inside. Down the hall only a short distance he brought them into the old great hall, far more intimate than the newer one the other side of the stairs, and nearer the kitchens. Servants whisked chairs into position, moved a small table, and had a pitcher of wine and a steaming teapot and service ready almost before they could settle in the chairs—and immediately after that a cold meat pie, cold bread, cheese, and sausage. The servants were hard-breathing, his guests a little dazed by the instant flood of amenities, but Cook had learned since Cevulirn had gone to the river that Tristen's messengers and his friends arrived ravenous and left with bags and wallets stuffed with food, and every such arrival met this hospitality unasked and unadvised.

Hot herbal tea and honey met instantaneous approval.

"Her Grace is carrying the heir to the kingdom," Idrys said, first of all, to Tristen's dismay. "And has risked a great deal in coming this far."

"I'm very well," Ninévrisë said shortly, cherishing a warm cup in hands pale-edged beneath the spatters of mud.

Another prince, leapt immediately into Tristen's essential understanding, though why he should think *son* scarcely skimmed his wits. He had not heard the child as he heard Tarien's, but he had no disposition to doubt it.

"This message," she said. "This message of yours, and Cefwyn's . . ."

"Cenas carried it," Idrys said, "with the king's writ and seal. And had ample time to be here."

"He's not come," Tristen reiterated.

Uwen had joined them cautiously: he was bidden listen to all councils. "Gedd," Uwen said now in a quiet voice, and drew a darting glance from Ninévrisë and Idrys.

"Sergeant Gedd carried Cefwyn's last message," Tristen said, well understanding, "and was days late. He had to let go his horses and hide and move by night: he was followed out of Guelemara."

"Two of my men never came back from that ride," Idrys said. "Now Cenas. And he left without fuss."

"Gedd weren't clear of the town before they were on 'im," Uwen said. "I think ye should hear Gedd, sir."

"There's no time," Idrys said, "not an hour.—Send him with me, I'll hear him and send him back again as we ride."

"With no difficulty," Tristen said quietly.

"What's this about Ryssand?" Idrys asked him. "What do you know?"

He began to reply, and only then realized the Lord Commander might believe in his walking through walls, but would not understand it. "There's a doorway of sorts, where the old mews were. And it goes to places. Ynefel is one. But the lord of Meiden overheard a hall in Ilefínian, where wizards and Tasmôrden and his men were holding council."

"The lord of Meiden."

"Crissand," Tristen said. "They know about Lady Tarien's baby; that's one thing. And Hasufin isn't dispelled."

"The wizard." Idrys knew precisely what wizard, what trouble, and that it presaged nothing good. Ninévrisë knew, and it was two troubled looks he had. "Lewenbrook didn't suffice, then."

"It sufficed," Tristen said, "to drive him back, but he tried again, and I think he's with Tasmôrden."

"Grim news," Idrys said.

"But he didn't break through, here," Tristen said, offering the best news he had on that matter. "He tried to take Tarien's baby, the way he did the prince at Althalen . . ."

"Oh, dear gods," Ninévrisë said, and her hand flew to her heart.

"But he didn't," Tristen said quickly, seeing what distress it brought her. "It didn't happen. Orien's dead. She tried to help him, and she tried to get free, but she couldn't, and she died. Hasufin's still in question, but he isn't here. The baby is safe."

"Dear gods," Ninévrisë said again.

"Came here," Idrys said darkly. "How? Like what happened on the field?"

Tristen shook his head. "More quietly. The wards wouldn't let him in. There's the gap in the wards where the old mews were; there's another at Ilefínian . . ."

"And he came from there?"

"Not *from* there," Tristen said, "but he was there, at least . . . he had influence there."

Idrys' face, unwashed, spattered with mud and filmed with dust, seemed carved of stone, the lively flick of a dark eye the only expression.

"He seems to have *influence* many places, Amefel."

"He does."

"And the earl of Meiden overheard this plot."

"He and I," Tristen said. "Tasmôrden knew about Tarien's baby, and sent Lord Cuthan to Ryssand, to make trouble."

"That he did," Idrys said.

"But more than that," Tristen said, "Ryssand's agreed to kill Cefwyn. That's what I sent with Anwyll. Cefwyn mustn't let Ryssand's men near him."

"That the letter told me," Ninévrisë said in anguish. "And Cefwyn knows it . . . but late. I don't know how I know, but I did learn it late, didn't I? I felt it, the farther I rode . . . part of it was late! And if he'd known—if he'd known when Ryssand was in court—"

"Wizardry," Tristen said. "The weather—everything's gone back and forth, from what I wish, what Tasmôrden's wizardry wishes, wherever it comes from."

"Wizardry indeed," Idrys said darkly, "and I belong with my king."

"I don't wish to keep you," Tristen said, "but let Uwen come with Gedd, too, since Uwen's heard all we've done here. They'll ride with you as far as you need. Cevulirn is already at the river, with Sovrag and Umanon. Pelumer's rangers are wherever they need be, not mentioning Aeself's band, Elwynim, who watch up and down the river. All our supplies are in place: we can be across the river in one night and reach Ilefínian in three."

"Do you say so?" Ninévrisë said, as if all the weight of days on the road had lifted. Rarely, too, did Idrys' grim countenance ever show his heart, but his relief in hearing that was visible in every line of him.

"Well done." Then, more sharply, as if a thought had come to him. "*Sovrag's* there, you say. With boats."

"One boat, always, if not others."

"Can he set me ashore at the Murandys bridge? Can he possibly ferry the horses?"

"I don't know. One man, two—with horses. Perhaps."

Idrys gnawed his lip, doubtless weighing the risks involved and the fact that once at Anwyll's camp, there was no other way but the river or the roads on the far side of the bridge—but a vast stony dome and a meander of deep woods lay between the bridge at

Anwyll's camp and that bridge Cefwyn would use to cross into Elwynor: Tristen had seen those hills not in the flesh but in his dreams of Owl, a jagged maze of rock and forest on both sides of the river, rough land that had been the saving of Ninévrisë and her father, and of no few men this winter who had escaped Ilefínian—but nowhere in it were trails fit for horses: Idrys and Ninévrisë had surely come here by the longer way round, down by Assurnford, to make any time at all.

And to escape that long swing south by a fast ride north to the camp and a windblown course upriver to Cefwyn's bridge . . . indeed, if Sovrag could, it would save time.

"The winds I may wish you," Tristen said, "but only as well as I've wished the weather, which is sometimes good and sometimes not—the winds might be foul for days, and I don't know how many horses they can manage, or even if they can. But I know Elwynim have crossed with their horses, northerly, by swimming. It's a great risk."

"If not the boats, then the swim," Idrys said. "Afoot until I can find a horse. Cefwyn expects you to come with all your force, as soon as you can. And to protect Her Grace."

"I'll ride after you as soon as tonight.—Emuin is here," he said to Ninévrisë. "Stay with him. Tassand will take care of anything you wish."

"I have no doubts of either of them," Ninévrisë said.

"Uwen will go as far as need be, then. We've signals among us, for the rangers. He'll show you. And when you come there, sir, tell Cevulirn secure the far side: I'll be there, perhaps before he can cross."

"M'lord," Uwen said faintly, "you'll be takin' only the new lads wi' ye."

"I'll be safe," Tristen said, with no doubt in his mind, and Idrys took the moment, grimy hands and all, to take a quarter cup of wine and a morsel of bread and cheese.

"I'll get me kit," Uwen said, rising, "by 'r leave, m'lord, and I'll bring Gedd."

"Half an hour, Captain," Idrys said.

"Yes, sir," Uwen said, and left quickly. Tassand took that departure for a signal to come in and report Ninévrisë's accommodation ready.

"I'll enjoy the tea so long as it's here," Ninévrisë said, cradling the cup in muddy fingers. "And thank you: I'll be grateful."

She was at the end of the strength she had, and sustaining herself in the gray space: Tristen had been aware of that failing, and lent strength of his own, steadying, wary of Tarien's existence above—and aware suddenly of another presence, nearer, at the door.

Owl flew in, eliciting a motion of fright from Ninévrisë; and immediately after Owl, came Emuin.

Ninévrisë held out a trembling, anticipating hand, and Emuin took it like a courtier, pressed it in his.

"Safe," Emuin said. "You slipped up on us. Slipped up on me, wily that you are, and that's no mild achievement. We had no idea you were coming."

"You know what's happened," Ninévrisë said.

"I've heard," Emuin said. "Unfortunately, so has the Aswydd girl, I fear, but no matter, no matter, you're here and Cefwyn's other advisor . . ." With a glance toward Idrys. ". . . is soon on his way back, I gather."

"You gather the truth," Idrys said, and washed down a bite. "As fast as horses can move us." He rose, a tall, daunting presence. "I fear, Your Grace, someone's followed my men, picked off my messengers, and my lord's couriers, and known in each instance when and where they'd be."

They all looked at him.

"What do you mean?" Ninévrisë asked. "Ryssand?"

"Ryssand's treachery, ultimately. But you say Gedd was followed. Now Cenas hasn't come. It wasn't for lack of secrecy. But secrecy's failed us. Either it's wizardry, which is *not* a talent among my men or Ryssand's, or the culprit doesn't get his knowledge out of thin air, but from councils."

"Who?" Tristen asked.

"Someone within my circles.—If you're the wizard you say, master grayrobe, wizard me this, and tell me who is the traitor."

Tristen stood still. Owl had landed on a chair arm, and folded his wings as Emuin considered the question in the gray space and out. Tristen did so, too, thinking of all the officers who came and went, and all the pages and servants.

"I assure you I'll consider the question, master crow," Emuin said. "If I find an answer I'll send it to Tristen. *He* knows how fast."

"I'll be to a horse," Idrys said shortly, "and do the things I know to do. I'll reach him. Your leave."

Idrys was on his way to gather resources in a fortress he had lived in for a year and more, and where he knew well where to look. Tristen delayed for Emuin, and Ninévrisë.

"I'll just sip my tea," Ninévrisë said. Her hands were trembling.

"A hot bath, a clean gown, and I assure you gentlemen I'll be very well."

"Idrys will reach him," Tristen said.

"I've no doubt of the Lord Commander."

"Best you go upstairs," Emuin said. "Let the servants put you to bed. They'll bring you tea."

"I prefer present company." There was a certain distractedness about Ninévrisë, a fragile grasp of the world around her, a fear of solitude, and of the halls above, where a presence haunted the gray space. "How does Lady Tarien? Is she well?"

"Well," Tristen said. "She won't trouble you."

"A prisoner?"

"Not free," Tristen said, "not free to come and go, but where her choices lie, I've not asked her."

"And the child?"

"Thrives," said Emuin. "The lady dotes on him, will not leave him; I ask Your Grace bear with her and the child under this roof, awkward as it is. There's no place else safe to send them."

The gray space seethed with Ninévrisë's troubled presence, and with a well-banked anger. "She tried to kill Cefwyn; wished me dead; has my husband's son—I take these things, understand, with what feeling you might expect. But likewise I take your meaning. I understand Orien is dead. But dead *here*, within the wards. Is *that* safe?"

"Warded," Emuin said, "as warded as we can manage. But you should know the babe is gifted. And his dreams we also ward and treat gently."

"I bear the baby no ill will at all," Ninévrisë said faintly, a breath across the teacup. She emptied it. "Might there be another cup, if you please? I've suffered from thirst as much as cold—the wind was bitter."

Tristen poured it for her himself, and she warmed her hands with it, after a sip.

"Did you fear anything?" Emuin asked her pointedly. "On the road, did anything threaten you?"

"Not in that way. It was a harder ride than I thought. I wouldn't stop, and Idrys wouldn't, and between us, and as much as the horses could bear, we just kept going." She lifted the cup in both dirty, trembling hands and had a sip. "The women's court in Guelemara had Ryssand's daughter and Murandys' niece. I assure you Tarien Aswydd doesn't daunt me in the least."

"Her Grace also," Tristen said, lest Emuin have failed to know, "has Cefwyn's son."

Ninévrisë cast him up a sudden, sharp glance, the cup clutched between her hands. "A son. *I* think so. Is it certain?"

It was nothing he could define, but he still thought so, and did not even perceive a presence yet. It was in the currents of wizardry that ran strong and deep in all he saw, everywhere about the place. A child of Orien's wizardry had come to be in this place: here was one of the other side—

And yet neither was necessarily an enemy to the other. It was not utter misfortune that he had delayed here to safeguard the one child, instead of waiting for Cefwyn's message with Cevulirn, at the river . . . a message that they now feared was lost. Three months ago he had had difficulty imagining things to come, and now he had diverted the enemy's current into his own hands, and seen far enough down the river he could say—yes, a son, another son, and to know that was acceptable. There was nothing else he could say of it, no word he could use, but *acceptable,* against all other forces loose in the world.

It said nothing, however, of Cefwyn's safety, and Idrys' fear. If Cefwyn had an enemy closer to him than Tasmôrden or Ryssand, that was outside his reach—and inside someone else's, where the old, old current that was Hasufin might after all prove stronger, or quicker, or simply overwhelm him and all he protected there.

He had first discovered fear in Ynefel's maze of walks and shadows. He had first met nameless terror in the loft where he had found Owl, and explored apprehension and unease under Marna's shadow. None of these Words was new to him—but the knowledge that ruin could be so absolute and so sweep everything he loved with it, in one stroke, against one man—this indignation, this *anger* wrapped in fear he had never felt in all his life. Moderation had no place in what he felt, and he did not know the depths in himself this might reach.

But two sets of eyes read more of him than he might wish—both with the gift, both of them reaching into the gray space, and wishing his restraint.

"Young lord," Emuin said, the only man but Mauryl who could chide him and call him a fool, "don't forget yourself. I fear there's more and worse to find. But you know more now than then. You may *be* more now than before. The Year of Years is at its beginning this time. This is your age. The last, I fear, wasn't Mauryl's after all. It wasn't Hasufin's, either, by the narrowest of escapes.—And damned certain, this one isn't mine."

Ninévrisë looked bewildered at this exchange . . . her lineage endmost of all those who had ruled in these lands, the Elwynim and the Guelenfolk.

The Amefin aethelings, Crissand's folk, were older . . . not by much, but older than the Sihhë's presence in the south, Tristen knew it not alone from his books, but from the dark that kept Unfolding under his feet.

Emuin himself in his studies had reached as far as the stars could show him, as far as Mauryl had taught him.

There was Auld Syes, who warded Althalen. She was old as the hills were old, and said almost as little—what could one say, who watched the currents move, for whom the years were a vast and endless stream?

All . . . *all* of that stream flowed past him in the blink of an eye.

"Pity Orien," he said, strangely moved, and drew a breath too large for his body. "She had no knowledge. She never knew anything at all."

Emuin laid a hand on his shoulder, only that.

Ninévrisë said nothing, only looked at both of them, the teacup forgotten in her hands. She was *there*, in the gray space, and heard, but whether any of it at all fell within her understanding Tristen could not tell.

He only had to go, now, and be sure of his defenses, around what he left. He feared more than ever in his life. The enemy had no mercy, and no alternative but to meet him: the enemy feared the same as he, and would strike at anything outside his wards.

The enemy would strike first at those the loss of whom would most damage, most wound him, most drive him to anger.

The enemy, like Cefwyn, had already moved.

CHAPTER 6

Ninévrisë slept. That was best, Tristen thought. Uwen was on his way to the river with Idrys, and that was well, too, for Uwen could only worry, otherwise . . . although in the task at hand he missed Uwen's sure hands and his calming steadiness.

Instead he called on Lusin and Gweyl to arm him. It was an upside-down order of things, arming him before the guard in the barracks was under arms, before midnight, but his bodyguard never questioned, sure that they were riding to the river before dawn, sure that the stable was gathering up horses and that messengers were out to the barracks and the fires were lit on the hills, advising every Amefin lord. It was the call they all had expected since Cevulirn had marched, and expected hourly since Ninévrisë and her party had arrived.

Lusin, who would not go to war with him, looked regretful in that knowledge; but he had his duties. "You'll command the garrison that remains," Tristen said to him. "Prushan will give you all the help you may need," Prushan, a reasonable and sensible man, was too old to ride to the river, even to sit a horse behind the lines, and would provide the lordly authority in town. "And he'll need your advice. Give it to him as you do to me."

"I wish to the gods I was going with ye, m'lord. All of us. We still hoped we would."

"I need you here more than in the line," Tristen said. "You know that I do. Emuin will be at his wizardry and maybe here and maybe there . . . I fear *Paisi* will know more of what's happening downstairs than he will. Worst, if there's danger of wizardry . . . of sorcery breaking out, Emuin will know what to do for that, but he can't watch his own back and he can't settle disputes in the hall. Her Grace is here. She's wise in most things and she has wizardry of her own . . . ask her if you find yourself at a loss, but she mustn't risk herself or draw attention. There's Lady Tarien and the baby, both with the gift . . . you'll have them to watch, and don't trust her: she's an open doorway. Anything can walk through it, and you have *only* master Emuin and Her Grace to deal with what does. Lord Prushan's able to deal with the town, but the Zeide itself—*you* understand it."

"Enough to be cold scairt, m'lord, an' that's the truth."

"Enough to stand your ground," he said. "As you would on the field. You'd fight there. So you will here, protecting what's here. And watching that place in the hall—that most of all. You and Syllan, and Aran and Tawwys—I want one of you four, none else, to be at that place day and night: take turns. And set the abbot to watch the wall at the guardroom stairs, where Orien is, turn about with the Teranthine father. If at any time whoever's on watch doesn't think things are right with those places, send for Emuin, and don't wait."

"As things could break out there."

"As things could break out there," he said. "At any hour. Paisi's not a bad one to have on watch with you, where Emuin can spare him. He has the gift. Just don't let him watch alone. And above all else, don't let Tarien and don't let Her Grace near those two places."

"I'm to tell her no?" Clearly Lusin doubted his ability.

"Say that I said so." He clapped Lusin on the shoulder, no longer servant, but a friend, and a trusted officer. "Go now to Crissand's house. Tell him he'll ride with me in the morning. *Don't* let him in the lower hall."

Lusin's expression grew distressed. He was never inclined to argue with orders, but he understood, then, that he, too, was being sent off to a distance and he liked very little what he guessed.

"Go," Tristen said.

"Aye, m'lord," Lusin said, clearly struggling with the urge to say something. He hesitated on his way to the door. "Ye want us t' be back here, m'lord?"

"No. Don't let Lord Crissand follow me," he said. "Whatever you have to do, see he stays away from the mews.—Send him to Emuin, if he argues."

"Ye ain't goin' after another banner, m'lord."

"No. Not this time." Lusin appealed to him to trust him; and he cast himself on that trust. "It's Efanor I want. I'm going to warn him of the danger to his brother and set him a task the same as I give you. But I mustn't make a mistake in this. If Crissand tries to follow me, I don't know that I can protect us both, or find the way for him. Now go."

"M'lord," Lusin said, and went, well knowing that his lord was at risk, and not happy in being sent away.

But it was necessary, what he did. Tristen knew that as surely as if it had Unfolded, for Cefwyn's back was undefended, and the doors that all led to the mews were undefended. He was not utterly sure a path led into Guelemara, but the gray space was everywhere, one could surely reach it everywhere, and tangled as it might be—where the Lines of a place failed, there the walls between the gray space and the world of Men were weak.

And if a place on the earth had ever afflicted his senses in the same way the mews did, the misaligned Lines within the Quinaltine itself defined that place.

There must be a way through, there; and it was that place he sought, both to warn Efanor, the simple reason he had given Lusin— and to mend those Lines before they afforded a passage for the enemy into the very heart of Cefwyn's capital.

To protect the mews from such an invasion he had taken such precautions as he dared. He had warned Emuin and Ninévrisë of his intention because he was sure they could not prevent him. And now he sent Lusin with his message, so late that by the time Crissand could even reach the mews, he would have done what he set himself to do—for, give or take the war of the weather, and considering the craft and strength of the enemy, he knew he had a remarkable run of that mystery Uwen called Luck, that quantity he saw as a stream of opportunity flowing their way.

That favorable current was back again tonight: the winds in the heavens served *him* and cleared the roads, and Her Grace had warned Cefwyn and reached him. But as with swordplay, the enemy might allow the pattern a while, only to create false confidence . . . and he would not press this *luck* of Uwen's by casting Crissand's rash, brave presence directly into Hasufin's reach, on unfavorable ground.

The new guards by his door at night, Amefin, had one advantage over Lusin and his old friends, and even over Gweyl and his comrades: they were far less forward to charge after him on their own initiative. He went down the hall, down the stairs, and past the closed great hall as if he were going to Emuin's tower, with only two of the Amefin in attendance, and descended into the lower corridor where the servants had left only the single candles burning in the sconces.

Owl came winging past him, from whatever perch he had occupied. He had wondered would Owl agree with him, and Owl evidently did—Owl swooped down the hall ahead of him to the disquiet of the young men of his guard.

He had envisioned willing the Lines into his sight and the wards opening for him in an orderly, careful process; he had envisioned alerting Emuin, in the moments before he went, to keep his intentions out of the gray space as long as possible.

But the instant Owl reached that part of the hall the Lines were there and the old mews showed itself without his will, blue and rustling with wings; and into that vision Owl glided, away and away into the blue depths.

—*Emuin!* *he had time to think.*

But only that. Owl, contrary bird, had chosen a path of his own without his wishing it, and he followed, as follow he must. . . .

The light became gray, sunlight falling aslant through familiar tumbled beams.

He was at Ynefel, not Guelemara . . . and wanting Guelemara, he wandered and stumbled instead through the ruin of Ynefel's lower hall.

He was immediately put out with Owl. He had no imminent sense of the enemy's presence, but he knew the enemy might lurk anywhere and knew if he went delving into one place and the other, it only increased his chances of encountering danger.

Hasufin had held this place . . . had been born here, perhaps, and this shattered hall was more likely a haunt than most. Ynefel was first, a place old, and enchanted long ago, walls more ancient than any existence he had had.

That was the peculiar strangeness the mews evoked. He was never conscious of himself as being old, but he knew in his bones what was older than his presence in this land. And Ynefel was one such Place, a tether for strayed, damned souls.

Shadows ran here, the dead, he had come to understand, of lost Galasien, not of Men. All around him, he saw the faces locked in Ynefel's walls, stone faces that had seemed at night to move in the trick of a passing candle.

Three in particular stood at the corner above, where the stairs had turned. The wooden stairs had fallen, but as he looked up he saw them still watching, one seeming horrified, and one angry, the third at this remove seeming to drowse in disinterest.

He blinked and shivered, and was suddenly in the courtyard of Ynefel, looking back at the door, where Mauryl's face had joined the rest.

Mauryl looked outward and elsewhere, seeming blind to him now, disinterested.

Owl flew past, and he was glad to look away. Any sight was better than Mauryl's disregard of him. He followed Owl, angry, determined that Owl should lead him now where *he* would. . . .

He blinked and stood under the open night sky, among ruins that glowed blue with spectral fire. This was Uleman's handiwork . . . in Althalen.

Not here, either, he said to Owl, angry and desperate.

Time meant nothing in the gray space. An eye might have blinked in the world of Men; the sun might have risen. He could ill afford Owl's whims, willed him to lead true, and still Owl evaded him, and led him past a line of blue fire, the Line of a ruined palace.

Doggedly he shaped the strong blue Lines of the Quinaltine in his thoughts. He remembered that tangled set of Lines within them, remembered them down to the smell of the incense, the sound of the singing.

He stopped with his foot on a step, and beneath that step was no slight fall. The Edge was under it, and he could all but hear the crack of Mauryl's staff, his stern reprimand to know where his feet were—flesh as well as spirit.

Flesh had obligations, and hazards, and he had risked too much overrushing Owl, thinking he knew where he was going. He meekly wished the bird back to him, and stood patiently until he felt the brush of Owl's wing above his hair.

To the left, or what passed for left: *there* was the place of smoke and incense. He stood where the Holy Father had stood, the last time he had been in this place.

Above him was the roof the lightning had riven.

Behind his back was the hallowed place with the mismatched Lines, the trap for Shadows.

They seethed in a mass here, many, many Shadows roiling in confusion at the intersections of those Lines, Shadows trapped within the vicinity of the Quinaltine, forced over the centuries to endure prayers to gods they did not acknowledge, the gods of those who had usurped their power. Angry, frustrated and frightened, they ran along the rails, down beneath the altar. They flowed away like spots of ink, they skittered into the masonry, and under benches.

There was no sound here until he took a step, the scrape of metal-guarded leather on stone.

Tristen drew a sharp breath, perceiving another presence. Owl flew toward the doors, and up, and up.

And of a sudden a fierce crash of metal rang from the left of the shrine to echo to the heights: a priest in the columned side aisle had dropped a great platter, and fell to his knees, and to his face.

"I came to speak with Prince Efanor," Tristen said, and that priest scrambled up and ran for the outer door.

He had no way to know whether that frightened man would bear his message as he had asked. He had no time to wait. He sent Owl out the opened door, out and around to the high walls of the Guelesfort, to a place midway in the west wing of the palace.

There, there, Efanor slept, closely guarded. It was an easy passage in the gray place, knowing exactly where Efanor was.

And Efanor, unlike his brother, had some slight presence in the gray: his dreams were very much within reach.

—*Prince Efanor, he said. Come to the Quinaltine. Don't delay for anything. Have your servants bring your clothes.*

Efanor leapt into bright awareness, within a gray space he had only skimmed in his meditations.

—*Tristen? Is it Tristen? Gods save us!*

—*Come quickly. I'll not tell you until we meet face-to-face. Come to the Quinaltine.*

Efanor doubted his own reason. Fear and denial colored his presence: good Quinalt that he was, the gray space should not be open to him, or so he believed, and strove halfheartedly to deny his own senses.

But Tristen drew out the little book of devotions Efanor had given him.

—*Know me by this. Come. Believe me. And hurry.*

Efanor believed. Confidence flared. Hope did, and curiosity, and Tristen left the gray space quickly, aware of the hovering Shadows, old Shadows and new ones, hateful and hating. It was no good place to linger, not for the space of a breath. But he knew now that Efanor would come.

Another priest had arrived, and ran back. Then a third, and a fourth, and all fled.

Shadows prowled the confused Lines meanwhile and tested the

strength of them, pressing at the tangle in the wards: Tristen felt their fear and their desperation, and saw the wound in the Lines they made.

He drew his sword and with it traced a Line of his own on the stones, slowly, surely, drawing the Line with the touch of the metal on stone, securing it with the touch of his boots on the floor and the strength of his wishes in the stones.

Past *this* Shadows should not come. This was what they should agree on, this was what they should guard, one Line, one defense. He wished it so, and the ward flared behind him.

The Shadows just at arm's length writhed and seethed, imprisoned in the tangle of Lines that had been, and now so great a panicked number of them pressed against those old wards that one failed at last, as it might have failed under the enemy's assault. The breach let forth a great rush of them.

But they came up instead against the new Line, a moiling confusion that set his teeth on edge. They brought death, and cold, and anger, but his Line held.

He chose the broken Line and dispelled it, freeing more reticent spirits, as easy as a pass of his hand and a wish. He dispelled one misdrawn Line after another, until long-pent Shadows, rushing forward to freedom, found his Line, and knew their boundary, and found a straight path along it. They flowed along that perimeter, and rushed back and forth, back and forth, no few violently trying its strength. But without the crossed lines channeling their anger, those attacks came at random, in isolated areas along the line, and posed little threat. Some, finding order in their movement, *sang* to him, and made the Lines sing, the music of stone, the music of the Masons' making.

Still he brandished the sword up and around until the blue fire of the ward flared along the walls, and up among the rafters, along the threatened roof and down again, past statues in their niches and down again to completion against the pavings.

And those Shadows older than Men, those filled with the greatest anger and contempt, cowered back from that fire, knowing well its potency, and listening to the music.

One Shadow, one of the newest disturbances and blind to magic, challenged the barrier, and battered aside the weaker Shadows, and attempted harm; but it, too, could not break forth . . . a Shadow that held something vaguely of Cefwyn and of Efanor, a strong presence, full of powerful emotions.

Yet it was fear, not anger, that drove it to challenge the barrier.

It feared and fled something deeper and darker, something barriered in older Lines, far back across the floor that now was, that knew nothing of the music—but this Shadow, that had been a warrior and a soldier, and a king, knew the danger there, and tried to rally the others.

There was the real danger in this place. The tangle of Lines he had resolved, and freed the trapped spirits to an easier flow. But there was a reason, deep within, that the tormented Shadows had so persisted at the barrier, a deeper dark where something moved, or many things moved, like so many dark serpents, shapeless and powerful, and unwilling to be confined.

The collective presence in that depth, behind wards grown old and weak, had the coldness and the power of the stone faces, as adamant and as terrible, and what dwelt there was neither resigned to its prison, nor completely contained by the Lines that great Masons had drawn, even before later, lesser, masons had compromised those Lines.

Now, those ancient Lines far back, blue and red, grew weak and sickly at the points of its attacks, and the music faltered.

It did not augur well if that welter of dark breached the ancient barrier and assailed the new Line—if the Shadows of *that* darkness, full of malice, gained power such as the Shadows had at Althalen. Armed men had fallen under the assault of the haunts at Althalen, finding no substance their swords might strike and no protection in their armor or their skill. Only Auld Syes moderated the anger of those spirits, and ruled them.

But she was not here. Only this one Shadow of a soldier. Such was the threat in that depth: all the spirits that Men feared fled it. It was not Sihhë, nor even of Ynefel's age . . . it was older, older, and echoed of his fears in Ynefel's loft, or that night on the stairs, when all Ynefel had creaked and tottered.

And this danger lay in the heart of a sleeping town, at the heart of Cefwyn's kingdom. What precisely it was did not Unfold to him, but he knew it recognized him—he knew it wished him harm, but that thus far it could not press past the protections of his magic.

It hated him as it wished destruction of all that Men had built; and it hated him because he stood with Men, and wished them and their doings well.

It hated him as it had hated him at Ynefel and whispered outside his window.

It hated him as it had striven through Hasufin, but it was not

Hasufin: it had possessed Hasufin, and diverted him from Mauryl's hands.

It hated him because it knew its destroyer had come. And having failed in direct assault, it sought a weakness, any weakness, or an ally that might serve it for an instant—as Hasufin had served, and served more than once.

Here was a battle to fight, within these walls, within the mews. He had a chance here. It was willing to face him here.

But if he failed to be at Ilefínian, *Cefwyn* would surely die. If he failed to be at Ilefínian *Hasufin* would prevail.

A sound disturbed him. He hurtled back to the world of Men, and the outer Lines, and stood by the altar rail, his hands and feet like ice.

Efanor had indeed come as quickly as he had asked, barefoot and wrapped in a sheet, and attended by two of the frightened priests.

"This place is in danger," Tristen said. "I need your help, Your Highness."

"What danger? From the enemy?"

He drew a breath, for there was so much to tell: "The Lord Commander brought Her Grace to Amefel. She's in Henas'amef, with Emuin; Idrys is going back to Cefwyn, in the north. All the south is crossing the river, coming north to Ilefínian, and Cefwyn is coming from the east . . . but so is Ryssand. Ryssand means to kill him. But worse, there's someone who's stopped the messengers reaching me, someone close to Cefwyn."

"A traitor!"

"Idrys doesn't know who. But he's going back as fast as he can, and I'm going north, to deal with Tasmôrden." Owl swept down from some height among the rafters and he unthinkingly lifted his gloved hand to receive Owl's taloned feet. "We can deal with all that. Hasufin is in this. He tried to take Tarien's baby, but we stopped him. Now he's helping Tasmôrden, who's helping Ryssand, and if Cefwyn defeats them, *this* place offers Hasufin a chance to break through."

"*The Quinaltine?* This is holy ground!"

"Henas'amef has a place, a doorway that opens sometimes to a wish from outside. So does Althalen: the Lord Regent wards it, and so does Auld Syes, and I know nothing gets through there. Ilefínian has such a place; so does Ynefel; and this is one, an old place, I think, old as Galasien. Cefwyn says your *grandfather* is here . . . whoever it is, I think all the Shadows here fear what lies beneath this floor."

"Grandfather?" Efanor glanced wide-eyed at the shadows beyond the candles. "Grandfather never ran from anything."

"The wards were never right here. The Masons who raised this building made a mistake and I've set a new Line, but this is still where Hasufin may try to come." He dared no more detailed explanation: he saw the unease on Efanor's face. "I have to go to Cefwyn, to help him. Will *you* guard it?"

"Gods witness I'll guard it!" Efanor declared. "—But how do I do that?"

"You have the gift."

"Oh, no, not I!"

"It waked you from sleep, Your Highness. And you and the priests, gifted or not, must walk this Line, and wish it may hold, wish it with all your hearts and minds. Pray for it! Wish it strong. Let no Shadow break out here, not a single one, or the Line will break and terrible things will come. I've set the new Line on the pavings. Do you see?"

He marked it with his sword, and Efanor came, barefoot as he was, and looked along it, left and right, resolution and wariness in the lines of his face.

"It glows," Efanor said faintly, as if it were a fault to be mended, instead of an indication of its strength and health. "It *glows*."

"It must! Keep it glowing! Walk *here,* Your Highness. Walk this Line continually, and wish it strong, against all the ill it holds back." He sought for some reassurance to give Efanor that would keep Efanor's wits about him and remind him, come what might, of his sole, single-minded duty: and he found it in the little book he had brought, his proof to Efanor who he was, and that they still were friends. He gave Efanor his own gift back again and pressed his fingers about the beautiful little book, even as Owl fluttered up about his shoulders, urging him to leave. "Think on the good, never harm! Think only on the good, and on us living, and your brother being well, and walk the Line and wish it strong. Do you still see it?"

"I see it," Efanor breathed, looking along it.

"Do that for me," Tristen said, "and for your brother." He was sure now that he had made himself understood. He had faith in Efanor, as in no one else in the Quinaltine, and knew Efanor could command the priests as no other in the court could do. And now he felt the place beginning to fade about him. "*Pray,* Your Highness!" That was the magic Efanor knew how to work, and it would have to serve. "Pray and bless the place and think only of good and life! Walk the Line, and make it strong!"

The gray wind whirled about him again, cold this time, and violent. Sounds howled past him, and the gray place darkened around him as Owl flew ahead of him.

Then even Owl seemed uncertain, and took a new direction, and then a third.

Angry Shadows loomed up, old Shadows, those older than Men and resentful of those usurpers, and these Shadows seemed to track him with mindful attention. The dark was their weapon, and they wielded it with a lash of wind to make it more bitter and more biting. They wished to sweep him back again and, by defeating him, to breach the Line he had made, but it was no longer *his* fight, that within the Quinaltine, where Quinaltine prayers went up. The soft tread of feet along the Line resounded among these Shadows like a single repeated chord, over and over, the same thing, endlessly the same thing—yet he could not tell from what quarter. He had lost his way for a heartbeat, he had lost Owl—then thought he saw a light.

He turned that way, then stopped and lost ground, belatedly aware of yet another hostile Shadow, a threat that prowled that region ahead, not behind.

He dared not even think, here. He dared not move. The enemy came as the Wind, both wary and angry, and the Wind blew and whispered to him.

—*Ah, well, here you are.*

He turned away from that Voice. He refused to be afraid, refused to run, but he would not deal with it, either, not now, not yet.

—*Mauryl's mistake walks on two feet. Mauryl's undoing . . . all his efforts wasted in you.*

It could not tempt him to argument. He was concerned only with the way out, and he searched for it.

But the Wind came near him, tugged at his cloak and his hair.

—*I banished Mauryl as he banished the lords of Galasien. Was that not justice?*

Questions. He would not answer, would not look, but his heart seemed apt to burst. He ran the loft stairs, he hid in the dark, and the Wind came and scattered his birds.

—*Banished him, and I shall banish you. Make your wards. Seal your gates. I know the way to your heart, Barrakkêth. I know your name and you know mine. Say it. Say it, and summon me. Do you dare face me?*

—*Nothing at your word,* Tristen said, *and caught after a thickness in the air of the gray space. It was Owl, who settled to his* hand, and fought, rowing with his wings, for purchase there against the gale. Nothing ever at your order.

—Ah! Can you name me? So short a step! Declare my name, and let us deal together—let us bargain, you and I.

—I have nothing to do with you.

—Nothing? Not even hate? There is a darkness in you, there is an anger and I know the key to unlock it. I know what lies beneath the wards in that place as I know what lies behind the gates of your anger, Sihhë-lord!

—Leave me! Leave this place!

—Ah, but do you rule here? Threaten as you will, Shadow of Barrakkêth, the hour will come . . . your hour, and mine.

—Not this day.

—I know a secret. Do you wish to know? Does curiosity move you? Ask. Ask the question.

Curiosity was his besetting weakness, and his prevailing strength. Curiosity had led him to good and to bad and guided him through the dark.

But this question was no question. It led him to harm: he was sure of it.

Yet curiosity drew his gaze, even knowing better, and in the heart of the Wind he saw plains made desolate and homes laid waste . . . he saw battlefields and armies striving on them in the sunset, and above all the banner, the Tower and the Star.

So he stood bespelled for the space of a heartbeat, and felt the desolation of that sight creeping into his soul. This, this was his work, and the Wind beat his back like the buffet of vast wings. Owl fought to stay with him, but began to lose his footing: a presence clawed at Owl from the other side, a Shadow hating and hateful, resentful for her lost life.

But subtle as a sunrise, a presence crept up on him, a presence stealthy and persistent and suddenly headlong, an attack against the Wind.

It had opposed the Wind before, that presence. Something of Mauryl was in the heart of it, and something of Cefwyn, and something of Efanor and even of himself—old teacher, old master of unwilling students, old man curbing young mischief and directing eyes always to the sunrise, not the sunset.

—Tristen! he heard Emuin call. **Young fool! Come back here!**

He trusted and he went, while the Wind roared and rushed and buffeted his back.

He went, and sometimes Owl winged before him and sometimes

behind, but he persevered . . . homeward. He was sure now of that word. Home.

And the gray grew lighter before him as he saw two, no, three and four and five and six faint shadows within a pearl gray dawn.

He walked onto solid stone, his hair stirred by the beat of spectral wings. About him was a corridor of gray brightening to a clear blue light, and in those beckoning hands knew Emuin's touch, and Ninévrisë's . . . even Tarien's, frightened and protective as a mother hawk above Elfwyn's sleepy awareness: she was there. There, too, was Paisi, the mouse in the woodwork, skittish and yet purposeful, and brazenly brave for his size.

It was Paisi who all but shouted for his attention now, and ran forward, to his own peril.

—Fool! Emuin cried.

But in that same instant another dared more than that, and forged ahead into the burning blue. Crissand came, never mind his orders and a wizard's will: Crissand had come, with a devotion like Uwen's, as determined, and as brave. Owl flew as far as Crissand's hand, that far, and hovered, and then flew past, out into the world of Men.

Crissand reached him just as Owl vanished from his sight . . . reaching out to take his hand and pull him home.

—My lord, Crissand called him, king though Crissand would yet be. They locked hands and then embraced, and all the Lines of Hen Amas rose up bright and strong around them. Emuin and Ninévrisë and Paisi hovered mothlike above the fire of the mews, and Tarien, too, with Cefwyn's wizard child—they all were around him; and in their collective will, and a wall went up against the Wind, making firm the wards.

Tristen let go his defense then, and trusted Crissand to pull him safely into the world of Men, and there to hold him in his arms, steadying him on feet that had lost all feeling.

He was cold: it had been very cold where he had walked last, a cold almost to chill the soul, but Crissand warmed his fingers to life, and Emuin reached his heart with a steady, sure light, driving the last vestiges of the dark from him, lighting all the recesses where his deepest fears had taken hold.

"Frost," Crissand said, and indeed a rime of frost stood on his black armor. Tristen found his fingers were white and chill as ice. So he felt a stiffness about his hair, and brushed the rime from his left arm, finding cause then to laugh, a sheer joy in life.

"A cold, empty Wind," he said to Crissand, and then cried: "Did I not say wait with Emuin?"

"I *was* with Emuin," Crissand said. "Didn't you say in that place there's no being parted? I never left him . . . or you, my lord! Paisi and Her Grace of Elwynor never left us. Even Tarien. Even she."

And the babe, Cefwyn's son, her son, her fledgling she would not see harmed: Hasufin had bid for a life and now Tarien herself was his implacable enemy, the surest warder against her twin's malice. He knew that as surely as he still carried an awareness within him of the gray place: Orien Aswydd might have tried to drive him aside and make him lose his way, but Orien no longer had the advantage of the living.

Above all else Orien would not lay covetous hands on her sister's child, not while he was in his mother's arms. Tarien rested now, weary from her venture, still seething with the fight she had fought along the wards. She had become like Owl, very much like Owl, merciless in her cause, possessed of a claimant and a Place and let at liberty.

"Never trust Tarien too much," Tristen said on a breath, for he saw danger in that direction; but the danger where he had been was sufficient. "Did Owl come past?"

"Like a thunderbolt," Crissand said, aiding him to walk: Tristen found his feet had grown numb, as if he had walked for hours in deep snow. "He went somewhere in the hall. I don't know where."

"He'll come back," Tristen said, with no doubt at all, and no doubt what he had now to do. "Is it dawn?"

"Close on it," Crissand said. "All's ready. But rest a while, my lord. Warm yourself."

"We'll ride north," Tristen said. "North now."

"My lord, never till master Emuin says you're fit." Lusin had come to lend a hand with him, and supported him on the other side in what was now the downstairs hall, alight with candles and teeming with fearful servants. Paisi was there, and stood on one foot and the other, bearing a message from Emuin, Tristen was sure.

Paisi pressed something like a coin into his gloved hand. "Master Emuin says carry this and ride tonight."

"He's not fit!" Crissand protested, but Emuin's charge was all Tristen needed to reinforce his own sense of urgency.

"I'll be well when the sun touches me," he said, and took his weight to himself, unsteady as he was. "And Uwen expects me. I know him. He'll ride back, never mind my orders to wait at the river. He'll ride all the way back to town if I don't meet him." He found his stride and gathered his wind, seeing the stable-court stairs. "Is Dys saddled?"

" 'E will be," Paisi said, and sped ahead of him, small herald of a desperate, wizardous purpose.

"My lord," Crissand argued with him still.

"They'll kill Cefwyn," Tristen said to all the company around him. "If he falls, Ylesuin won't see the summer and Amefel itself won't stand." It was clearer to him than anything near at hand: all of that was in flux, but the great currents had their directions, clear to anyone who could dip in and drink—and did not Hasufin know these things?

Surely Hasufin knew, Hasufin who was older than he and canny and difficult to trap: he could no longer be sure of Hasufin in any particular, but what he could do, he had to guess that Hasufin could do as well—shadow and substance, they mirrored one another, and Hasufin tried to make that mirroring perfect, and tried to name him his name, and tried to make him all that Hasufin remembered him to be.

Foresight had advantages, he said to himself as he essayed the west stairs, above Orien's walled-up tomb. Foresight was a great advantage, but expecting everything to be as it had been . . . that was the trap, the disadvantage, in Hasufin's centuries of knowledge.

"Mauryl Summoned me," he said to those on either hand, "but it went amiss. Or did it? Was his wizardry not greater than his working? And didn't things go as he wished, in spite of his wishes?"

"I don't know these things, my lord," Crissand said, at his right hand, and Lusin, at his left. "Nor meself, m'lord. And ye ain't in any case to be ridin'."

"I can. I will." They were in the open air, now, and he knew Emuin had heard what he had surmised.

—As he wished, in spite of his wishes . . . all of that, you are, young lord. You're the substance of his wishes, and the sum of his courage. He let you free. He didn't Shape you. He left that to the world and this age. He left you to Shape yourself, young lord, and Tristen *he named you, and* Tristen *you are. Think of it. Think of it, where you go. Never let that go.*

"M'lord's horse!" Syllan called out, and Lusin shouted: "Rouse and rise, there! Rouse out! Horses!"

Haman's lads appeared out of nowhere, and hard on that, Lusin sent a man to the barracks, and another to the gate-guards, and ordered the bell rung that would rouse all the troops.

Arm and out! the bell seemed to say, and within moments men

appeared from the barracks, and horses were led out under saddle. Crissand's men reached the gates, and a boy brought the three standards, the black ones of Ynefel and Althalen, and the blood red standard of Amefel, in a light that began to supplant the light of the torches.

Arm and out! Arm and out! came from the bells, and Crissand's captain rode a thick-legged gray into the half-light of the yard, carrying a furled dark standard to the steps where they stood.

Crissand came to the edge of the steps and took it in his hand, looking up.

"My lord! This one, for the lord of Althalen and Ynefel! This one, with the others!"

"Unfurl it," he said, knowing which standard it was, and in the wind that began with dawn Crissand unfurled the Star and Crown of the Sihhë Kings, the banner Tasmôrden had tried to claim, and now would see carried against him.

One more Tawwys brought and saw spread against the wind, the Tower and Checker of the Lady Regent, until the standards that should go before a great army flew and cracked on the wind. *She* was with him, as she had helped draw him out of the gray space: she sat now by her fireside, wrapped in her own efforts, which were for the wards of the fortress, and for the watch Efanor had undertaken. With Emuin's sure aid she settled herself to watch all the accesses of the place, and nothing might pursue its occupants here, nothing might pass her awareness. She was the Tower, and she prepared to stand siege.

Paisi appeared at the top of the steps, smallish and wide-eyed, and scampering down the steps to the alarm of the horses.

"Careful there," Lusin chided him, and set a heavy hand on Paisi's shoulder, staying him short of the last dive in among the milling horses.

"Master wishes ye know he's watchin'!" Paisi shouted out. "An' bids ye sleep o' nights!"

Tristen waved at him, understanding, but coming no closer, for the men afoot and the horses being brought filled the smallish yard, and those of them that were mounted had to move to give the others room enough. His guard had mounted up, staying close with him, and new men, all of Meiden, carried the standards.

Dys and Cass would join them outside the walls, among the remounts, and Uwen was off on Liss. It was only Gery that awaited them here, and Tristen mounted up and took up his shield from Aran's hands, the red one, with Amefel's black Eagle. But he did not ride alone: Crissand joined him, on a thick-legged, sturdy gray, while his house guard under his captain waited just outside the Zeide gate, where there was room.

"Let us go," Tristen said, and Gweyl, in Uwen's place until they had regained him and Gedd, relayed the order to send the banner-bearers out before them.

They rode out under the menace of the gate into the chill, clear dawn, out into the town. The bell tolled above them, signal to all the town, and it waked every sleeper and brought shutters open and shadowy bundled figures to the streets.

Lord Sihhë! the people shouted, gathering everywhere along the main street of the town, some wrapped in blankets, straight from their beds and into the chill that frosted breath. All the way to the lower gates the townsfolk stood and shouted out, *Lord Sihhë and Meiden!*

So they shouted out for the other lords of Amefel as they, too, turned out with their house guards, joining them from side streets, and so a handful of enterprising boys shouted from the top of the town's main gate as they rode out, a last salute of high, boyish voices: *The High King! The High King!*

So they had shouted. Was it now or then? The High King and the king of Hen Amas!

The banner then seemed green, Aswydd green, and the dragons reared in defiance and threat as they had loomed above him in the hall.

"Lord Sihhë! Lord Sihhë! Lord Sihhë for Amefel and Meiden!"

So the shouts faded, and, beyond the town gate, they turned first on the west road past the stables. They rode over the traces of other riders, past emptied camps. They were not the first, but the last of the army to ride out.

But with them came the signal for all the lords to move, to force war on Tasmôrden from the south—and to save the king.

CHAPTER 7

The army of Amefel moved at the brisk pace of the horses, so that they had progressed well out from Henas'amef before the sun rose above the hills—while signal fires lit on those hills advised all the outlying lands they were called to arms and must converge on the riverside by country trails and back roads and whatever served.

The whole land was now in movement. All the baggage that might have delayed them, even the equipage of the heavy horses, with the tents, all of that had gone to the river, the last of it following Cevulirn's passage, they needed no shelter with Modeyneth's hospitality halfway, and that left the Amefin nothing to do but make speed.

And sure enough, as the sun stood at noon, two riders appeared out of the distance and the folding of the hills.

Tristen had no doubt who it was. He knew Uwen by his riding and Gedd by his company. They came up on one another with all deliberate speed, and as they met, Uwen swung in close with him and Crissand.

"The Lord Commander's on 'is way," Uwen said first, "an' sent us back before he got to the river, but we told 'im all what he was set to hear, an' we come back fast as fast."

"The fires are lit," Tristen said. "I've taken precautions and left Emuin and Her Grace in charge, with Lusin. The Amefin that will march are marching."

"No delays as I can see, m'lord. I rode as far as Modeyneth. Lord Drusenan's gone to the wall, and roused out a good lot of archers to riverside, as ain't been needed yet, thank the gods, nor will be, if Lord Cevulirn's across."

"Good news," Tristen said, for Drusenan had promised archers, and if Cefwyn pressed too hard and fast from the east or if the enemy came south from the beginning without that encouragement, then archers on the southern bridges might serve them well.

But wizardry had now a third place to attack, and that was Idrys, riding hard toward the river . . . while Cefwyn, blind and deaf to magic, knew to watch Ryssand but not men closer to him. Still, the advantages wizardry had in Cefwyn's direction were all too attractive—for it was to protect Cefwyn that Tristen found himself constrained to take actions he would not of his own will take, when his heart told him to cast everything to the winds and follow Idrys to Cefwyn's camp.

He could not go as fast as his thoughts could fly: if magic alone would serve, he could have gone to Ilefínian before dawn, and stood face-to-face with Tasmôrden and the enemy. He could, he was sure, go aside now to the ruins of Althalen and have a way from there. Oh, there were ways and ways to reach Ilefínian, but only one to reach it with an army; and as much confidence as he had in his own strength, it was not enough to fling himself alone into the heart of his enemy's power: the temptation was there, the urge was there, but he trusted neither, fearing traps, not yet seeing enough into Ilefínian to know what he might face.

So he kept his pace at Uwen's side and at Crissand's, and they whiled away the time as they rode with Uwen's account and Uwen's questions, what had they done, who was in authority in Henas'amef and what time they hoped to make. Idrys had questioned Uwen and Gedd very closely, elicited every detail from Gedd, where he had lodged in town, when he had moved, when he had known men were following him and what he had done.

"Yet he gave no names," Crissand asked. "He gave no indication who it might be that he fears."

"Not a one," Uwen said. "Naught that we can do, 'cept by wishin', which m'lord does, I'm sure."

"That I do," Tristen said fervently, "and wish him speed."

"Speed to us, too," Uwen said, and, turning in his saddle to glance back at the Amefin troop he had driven uphill and down, until men and horses alike had grown used to hard moving. "Ho, ye men, not so sore as ye'd ha' been wi'out ye rid through them hills, is 't?"

"No, sir," the answer came back with many voices. "No, Captain, sir."

"Ain't sorry now."

"No, sir. No, Captain, sir."

"'At's the good word, an' gods bless!"

"Gods bless, sir!"

Tristen found himself moved to laughter despite the troubles of the night. So was Crissand. The sun was up, and the banners flew no matter the difficulty of flying them in the steady wind, for there were men on the move and on guard all across the land. To a man, they wore the red badges of Amefel, having no wish to run afoul of their own watchers in the hills.

And true enough, it was not so very long after that a copse of woods gave up two shadowy watchers who stepped out into the road.

"Lanfarnessemen," Crissand guessed, and Tristen was sure of it. The two went in forest colors and gray cloaks, and might as easily fade into the trees where they stood.

He was glad to see them, however, and drew rein where the rangers waited.

"Lord Tristen," the foremost said with all respect, and indeed, it was a man he had seen with Pelumer, once upon a time. "The El-wynim have moved from Althalen, all but a handful, who've raised an archer-tower there. The most have gone toward Modeyneth and toward the river."

Aeself had followed his orders. Auld Syes had culled her flock, he was sure, no less than the frozen bodies in the snow, but having Aeself's men out early and ranging into the rough lands gave him some trepidation . . . not least for Idrys, whose presence within their lines he had not anticipated. He hoped Idrys had gone as he planned, to the river, to Sovrag: but Idrys was a man apt to change his plans on the instant and do things no one foresaw . . . to his hazard, in a province ready to defend itself against Tasmôrden's men.

"The Lord Commander of Ylesuin is on the roads," Tristen said to the two Lanfarnessemen, "and he may take any sort of clothing and go by himself. No one should harm him."

"A number of men with the red cloth rode out on this road and two rode back to you," the silent man said. "There was a dark man of rank, who stayed with the main body, and where they went is under others' watch. We'll pass that word as quickly as we can."

"Nothin' faster 'n the Lord Commander's apt to move," Uwen said under his breath.

"Do what you can," Tristen said to the rangers, who retreated back into the woods, a trickery of the eye the moment they were within the underbrush.

"Gods send he don't run into Aeself," Uwen said. "We told him about the red bands, and I saw to it he were wearin' one. Whether he'll keep it . . ."

That the signal they had agreed on, Amefin colors, a costly dye, none an intruder could find so easily in his pack or a piece of a common blanket: either cloak or coat, pennon or a scrap of cloth about the helm. It was Pelumer's canny notion, and even his rangers, colorless against the land, wore that one bright badge, scraps of red they showed about the wrist, no more, for Pelumer's men counted on going unseen.

"I shan't wish," Tristen said, fearful of intruding on Idrys' choices, whatever they were: he knew how stealthily the Lord Commander moved in the court and in the field, and there was a real chance that Idrys might at any moment change his mind and his direction and his apparent allegiance, either because the boats might not be where they hoped or because Idrys simply rode the currents of his own unmagical wizardry, and chose not even to have friends and allies know what he would do next. The one thing certain about him was that he was Cefwyn's man, and answered only to Cefwyn.

And on that resolution not to intervene Tristen set the company moving at the same steady pace, as much as they could prudently ask of the horses and still keep them fit for days of effort afterward.

If he wished anything, it was that Cevulirn might have the bridge open and a secure footing on the other side of the river, but that was as much as he wanted, and he wanted that very quietly, with the least possible disturbance of the gray space, emulating, as he could, master Emuin, who could go unseen there.

He had learned from master Emuin, how to be curious without wishing any particular outcome, and thereby how to go more quietly in that place. He had learned by comparison to Emuin how very great a disturbance he could make.

More, he realized now, from Crissand and Efanor and others with the gift unrealized, but who touched the gray space with their innocent wishes, that, even before he knew that the gray space existed, before Emuin had shown it to him, he had been a troubling influence within it, boisterous and self-willed and obstinate.

So he must have been to Mauryl as well.

And had Mauryl not shown him the gray place because Mauryl feared his ignorance would lead him into danger? Or might access to that place have *made* him a danger, to himself, to Mauryl, to all around him?

Certainly he would have learned that others existed, and learned how to reach for them, before he had learned restraint.

By all he knew, Emuin had taken him in hand out of utter desperation . . . had shown him the gray place in great trepidation, marveling only that he had never found it for himself—and then Emuin had immediately retreated to the peace of Anwyfar, distant enough in Guelessar to watch him unseen. Baffling and painful as Emuin's desertion had seemed to him at the time, now he understood how Emuin's close presence would have tempted him into more and more dangerous exploration. The world of Men had been his distraction, discovery after discovery unsettling his understanding, leading him by small degrees, not great ones, and keeping him always uncertain of his balance.

Flesh as well as spirit.

The world of spirit had always been easier for him to explore—easier, but infinitely more dangerous and less confined. Watch his feet, Mauryl had tried to teach him. Learn caution in a realm where the rules were simple, where if one stepped off the cliff edge, one fell to a predictable death—

Caution had been Emuin's wish and Emuin's hope for him . . . when he set free one who might know no bounds.

Win his friendship, Emuin had said to Cefwyn, regarding him, and on this ride it came to him what two things Emuin had wished to do in giving Cefwyn that advice: first to disarm him of the danger he posed to Cefwyn, to set any random wishes he might make to Cefwyn's good, not his ill; and secondly, to distract him with the questions of Cefwyn's material world and keep him occupied with that, out of the gray space.

The gray space might have been quieter before he came. It was certainly more silent in those days when Emuin had been at Anwyfar: the Aswydds had surely been aware of him and cannily held themselves remote.

Remote as Hasufin, too, had kept himself remote: Hasufin had shown no desire, past that first encounter at Lewenbrook, to come at close quarters with him.

Wizards of all different sorts had kept their distance, wary of his ignorance, wary of his disposition, wary of his power, but mostly, he believed now, wary of his lack of wizardry . . . not his lack of power, but his lack of the most basic rules wizards knew.

Wizards depended on those rules to work their magic; he did not.

Wizards planned all they did according to those rules.

He had none. He learned the art only to know what his friends and his enemies might do, or expect. But at the last, he did not find it of use.

In the world of Men, he traveled now to be where Cefwyn appointed him to be, assured that that was the one rule it was wise to follow, but constrained by the rules of the realm of Men as he was not constrained in the gray realm. His options were limited: Tasmôrden could anticipate his moves and guard against them, using the constraints of the land.

But that wizards could not similarly predict his options had made his greater enemy lie quiet, waiting, perhaps, for him to reveal his limitations . . . or his intentions.

More unsettling to their wishing ways, they could not wish *him* to move in certain ways.

Mauryl had indeed despaired of him; Emuin had dealt with him only at safe distance; Hasufin had attempted to use Aséyneddin and his entire army, but then abandoned that hope, and still lost. Hasufin had hoped again in Tarien's child; but Tarien had come home to *him* to bear Cefwyn's son, come to return the Aswydds to their Place in the world. As good fling a stone into the sky: down it would come. Back the Aswyddim had come, even to perish and join the Shadows in the Zeide's stones, and the whole world sighed with the release of a condition that could not have persisted, the separation of the Aswydds from Hen Amas . . . were there not other needs that strained at the fabric of the world, and was not one Crissand, riding with him? And was not one Orien, within her tomb?

And was not one another wizard, born in Amefel?

He had advised Cefwyn to cast the Aswydds out; and so it had served, for the hour of Hasufin's assault at Lewen field, but only for that hour. After Lewenbrook, it was possible *Hasufin* had wanted them apart from him, as much as he wanted them away from Henas'amef—until Hasufin had taken Cefwyn's son . . . but the Place itself had its conditions, stronger, it appeared, than those of Hasufin or himself, and by one means and another, the stone fell to earth, water ran downhill, birds came to their nest, and the Aswydds came back to their hall.

He, however, had no such Place, at least, that he had yet discovered: he only had persons. He had Crissand; he had Cefwyn; he had Ninévrisë of Elwynor and now Cefwyn's two sons.

But he himself felt no inclination to rush to earth. He found no downhill course. He had no direction, other than the needs of those he loved.

Was he himself a hill down which those who knew him, who trusted him, must flow?

And was that the danger inherent in him? That when stones did fall, when water did run downhill, they might wreak havoc in the world?

He was not *like* Crissand, not *like* Cefwyn, nor Ninévrisë, nor like Mauryl nor yet like Emuin, and he was not like Uwen, or Idrys. Nothing *like* him existed or had existed—not even his enemy.

The Lanfarnessemen had not remarked on the banner among the other banners: it was not their place to remark on it, but surely they knew what it signified, and perhaps even knew how they had come by it—Pelumer's men, though camping to themselves in scattered bands, had uncommonly thorough knowledge of what had happened in Henas'amef and elsewhere.

Without doubt, they knew *why* it flew.

Tasmôrden would know.

How northern men would see it he could well guess.

Prudence would have bidden Crissand furl it, or better yet, not to bring it at all; but it would go. Like the Aswydds returning to Henas'amef, that banner *would* go with him—it belonged to him. Cefwyn had known, had *given* him the arms, less the crown, even when he himself failed to know it was, should be, must be—his.

It was not a territory of land that banner claimed; but the rights *of* the land; it was not a town or a capital it represented, but a Place. A Place for him to exist . . . a Place that *was* himself.

He was as he was, in a year which had turned to a new Year, in a land wherein spring much resembled autumn, brown grass, bare trees, a welter of mud, hillside springs gushing full into gullies and turning any low spot to bog.

He had come full circle, but everything was changed. And he was changed. Owl, that mysterious haunt of last year, flitted sometimes in view and came and went in the patchy trees . . . guiding him, confirming him in his choices, no longer ambiguous, but no prophet, either, of the outcome.

And for very long they went, he and Crissand and Uwen, in the silence of men who had exhausted every thought but the purpose for which they went: sharing that, they had no need for words, only the solidity of each other's company, from the ranks forward. They discussed the condition of gear, the change about of horses, the disposition of a water flask, those things that regarded where things were and how they were, but not where they were going or what might happen there: the one they knew and the other no one could speculate.

It was toward late afternoon when they reached Modeyneth and when they saw the traces of many men in the muddy fields, and the safety of the houses as assured as before, they were glad of the sight, and men began to talk hopefully of a cup of something before they moved on.

Drusenan's wife came out to meet them before they had even reached the hall, treading carefully on a walkway of straw that crossed the hoof-churned mud. Her skirts were muddy about the hems: it was not her first such crossing of that yard; and she came with her sleeves girt up and an apron about her, and it well floured and spattered and stained.

"Lord," she said, "welcome! Will you stay the night?"

"We'll press on," Tristen said, "but an hour to rest the horses, that we can spare, and food for us if you have it."

"Stew and porridge, m'lord, as best as we have, but the pots is most always aboil and nobody knowing when the men's comin' in, we just throw more in, the more as comes to eat it. And there's bread, there's always bread."

That brought a cheer from the front rank to the rearmost, and they were as glad to be down from the saddle as they were of the thick, simple fare in the rush-floored hall, with the dogs vying for attention and the women hurrying about with bowls and bread.

Bows leaned against the wall, near the fire, near the cooking tables, near the door, with quivers of arrows, all the same, all ready, and no man's hand near them: it was the women's defense, if ever the war spilled across the river and beyond the wall.

He was determined it would not.

They sat with Drusenan's lady, for a moment paused in her work, and heard a brisk, fair account of every company that had passed, its numbers, its condition, and the time the women had wished them on their way.

"A tall, dark man, among the rest," Tristen said, for that aspect of the Lord Commander there was no hiding.

"That one, yes," the lady said, "and no lingering. Took a pack of bread and cheese and filled their water flasks, and on they went, being in some great hurry . . . we didn't mistake 'em, did we? Your Grace isn't after 'em."

"Honest men," Tristen said, "without any question, on honest business."

"It's comin', is it?"

"It won't come here," Tristen said. "Not if we can prevent it, and if the wall can."

"Gods save us," the good woman said, and was afraid, it was no difficulty to know it . . . afraid not so much for this place, but for Drusenan and the rest. "Gods save Amefel."

"Gods save us all," Uwen echoed her.

"And you and yours," Crissand said quietly.

"We should move," Tristen said, for by her account Idrys' band was early on its way and Cevulirn would have his request to cross and camp. "They won't linger and we shouldn't."

There was not a man of them but would have wished to linger the rest of the hour, but it was down with the remnant left in bowls, and here and there a piece of bread tucked into a jacket, a half cup of ale downed in a gulp, against a hard ride to come, and no sleep but a nap along the way.

Drusenan's lady brought them outside into the dark, she and all the women and the girls, some of them down from the guard post, with their bows. The women saw them onto their horses, with only the light from the open door.

It was muddy going, for the dark and all, and now they had the banners put away and their cloaks close about them. The horses were reluctant, having been given the prospect of a warm stable and that now taken from them: Dys was surly for half an hour, and Cass farther than that, while Crissand's horse and the guards' were entirely out of their high spirits and the horses at lead, those who had carried them all day, plodded.

"Now's the time we look sharp around us," Uwen said to the guards, "on account of if any man's movin' we're the noisiest."

"The Lord Commander will have told them we're coming," Crissand said, meaning the guard at the wall.

"Beyond any doubt," Tristen said, and now in the dark he did resort ever so gingerly to the gray space, listening to the land around them. He heard a hare in a thicket, a fox on its nightbound hunt, both aware of the passage of horses on the road.

And Owl was back, with a sudden swoop out of the dark that startled the foremost horses out of their sulking.

"Damn," said Crissand's captain.

"Men are ahead of us," Tristen said, for he gathered that out of the insubstantial wind: indeed men were moving in the same direction, toward the wall. "Don't venture," he said quietly to Crissand, for Crissand had wondered, and fallen right into the wizard-sight, easy as his next breath. "Someone might hear."

"My lord," Crissand said, and ceased.

It was a fair ride farther to the old wall, where Aeself's archers might be, and a dangerous prospect, to come up on archers at night, and with their badges invisible.

Idrys would have come there ahead of them, at least while the light lasted, and indeed forewarned them. But now there were two groups on the road, and Tristen set a moderately quicker pace, chasing that presence of many men in the dark, one a presence he knew.

It was right near the wall he knew that the other presence in the dark was indeed Drumman; and in that sure knowledge he let the gap close. The men ahead had heard them, and slowed, and stopped; and waited warily.

"Owl," Tristen said, and, rarely obedient, Owl obliged him by a close pass, and by flapping heavily about his shoulder. He lifted a hand to brush Owl's talons off his cloak, and drew a little of the light of the gray space to his hand, and to Owl, who flew off, faintly shining, here and there at once.

A murmur arose in the ranks behind, and even the Amefin blessed themselves; but Owl vanished among the trees and came back again, and all the while Tristen had never ceased to ride at the same steady pace.

Drumman knew, now, who commanded Owl, and waited, a line of riders in the dark beyond a small woods, as Owl came back to him, and then found a perch above.

"Lord Drumman," Tristen said.

"My lord duke!" Drumman said. "Well met. I'd feared you were intruders."

"None have crossed that I know," Tristen said, and took Drumman's offered hand. "But Aeself and his men are along the river, and Cevulirn should have crossed to the Elwynim side. I need you and your men to hold the camp on this side."

"And not cross!" Drumman protested. "We're light horse, well drilled, and well set."

"Then come with us," Tristen said. He had withheld from the lady of Modeyneth their greatest concerns, but to Drumman he told all the truth of Ryssand's action and Idrys' fears as they rode, and by the time the wall darkened the night sky, Drumman understood the worst.

"Beset by his own," Drumman said, as harshly as if he and Crissand's house had never courted rebels or conspired against Cefwyn at all. It was honest indignation . . . so thoroughly the sentiments of

the Amefin had shifted toward the Marhanen and the Lady of
Elwynor.

"By his own, and planning to divide Elwynor between Tasmôrden and themselves," Crissand said. "Which is no good for Amefel.
We know where Tasmôrden's ambitions would turn next."

"Fine neighbors," Drumman said, above the moving of the
horses. "Fine neighbors they'd be, Ryssand *or* Tasmôrden. What are
we to do?"

"Come at the enemy in Ilefínian and reach them before Cefwyn
does," Tristen said, but in his heart was Idrys' fear, a traitor nearer
Cefwyn than the ones they and Cefwyn already knew. Distance mattered in wizardry and Cefwyn being the point on which the whole
eastern assault turned, he had no doubt all the wizardry of their
enemy was bent on his overthrow.

They reached the wall, that reared dark and absolute across the
road, with gates shut and the will of Lord Drusenan to defend it. It
made him think of the maps, and how there was, along the riverside,
the village of Anas Mallorn, and other small holdings scattered along
the wedge of land before the rock, and all that way Idrys had to go,
if he had not found a boat ready and able to take him on the water.

Yet Drusenan's men had long carried on a secret commerce
with Elwynor.

A challenge came down to them as they reached the gates, a
sharp, "Who goes there?"

"His Grace of Amefel!" Crissand shouted up. "Meiden and Lord
Drumman! Open up!"

"Open the gates!" came down from above them.

Then a second voice, Drusenan's: "Welcome, my lord, to our
wall! Welcome to the defense of Amefel!"

There was a brisk rub for the horses, and a welcome cup and
pallets for a nap for the men, but for the lords, no rest—it was
straight to a close council in the restored gatehouse of the wall, warm
and lit with a small, double-wicked oil lamp.

In that place they took their cups of ale, declined food, for that
they had already had, and spread out the map they brought from
Henas'amef.

"The men you sent went through, never stopping but to say you
were coming," Drusenan said, "which is as much as we know, my
lord."

"Was a tall man with them?"

"A grim fellow, yes, my lord."

"And left with them."

"Went with them, my lord, and all of them pressing hard. And they had the bands, every man of them."

There was no more, then, that he could do, and they nursed their cups of ale over small matters of supply and intent until the bottom of the cup, and then a brief, a desperate attempt at sleep and rest.

But Owl was abroad, still, and when Tristen shut his eyes he found himself in dizzying flight, wheeling above the darkened river, where a bridge stood completed, and men crossed by night.

Owl flew farther, and skimmed almost to the water, and up again, where the rocks rose sheer above the river.

Then back again, where a boat traveled under sail, and a dark man looked out from the prow, restless and worried. He traveled alone, that man, having left the guard behind. He was bidden rest on deck, but he could not sleep, and scanned the dark and rugged shore as the face of an enemy.

It was very far for Idrys to travel, even yet.

Owl flew on, and on, and swept his vision past hills to east and north, and Cefwyn's camp was there, hundreds of tents, all set in orderly rows. He wished Owl to turn and show him Cefwyn, Owl veered off across the land, far, far, far, toward the east, Tristen thought, where the Quinaltine stood, where Efanor kept watch.

Of a sudden Owl turned, veered back again in a course so rapid the stars blurred and the world became dark, became the river, dark water, and cold.

Something was abroad in the night. Owl fled it, and that was never Owl's inclination. For a long time Tristen had nothing in his sight but the ragged, raw cliffs and stony upthrusts of the hills, and then the gentler land of shepherds and orchards, laid bare of snow. The enemy hunted, hunted, pursued.

Fly, he wished Owl, for what stirred northward was aware of him, now, and turned attention toward him.

Well and good. Best it come to him. He *wished* it to turn to him, see him, assess what he was, with all the dangers inherent in the encounter. He abandoned stealth. He challenged the Shadow to the north, taunted it, all the while with fear in his heart . . . for in that way he had learned there were things older than himself, this was, indeed, older.

This *was* Hasufin, but it was more.

It was the Wind, and a dark Wind, and it had carried Hasufin and carried his soul still, but it was more than that; it had always lurked behind the veil, and now stood naked to the dark, the very heart of menace.

For a long, long while, his heart beating hard, he stared into that dark, having lost all reckoning of Owl.

But then something flew very near, and Owl called him urgently, reft him away as the thin sound broke the threads of the dream.

He plummeted to earth, aware of his own body again, and Drumman and Uwen sleeping beside him.

But on his other side Crissand was awake, at the very threshold of the gray space. Crissand had felt the danger, and tried to oppose it.

—*My lord? Crissand whispered.*

—*Be still, he said. Be very quiet.* **Something's looking this way.**

—*What? Crissand wanted to know, and then turned his face toward the danger.*

—*Back! Tristen ordered him, and snatched them both from the gray winds before it could come near.*

"A wizard," Crissand said in a low and tremulous voice.

"I'm not sure," Tristen said, knowing in his heart it was nothing so ordinary, that long ago something had entangled itself with Hasufin Heltain, as Hasufin had attempted to ensnare Orien Aswydd, and Aséyneddin in Elwynor.

Then it Unfolded to him with shattering force that this was indeed so, and that Mauryl himself had feared it.

This . . . *this* was in Hasufin's heart.

It was not dispelled at Lewenbrook. It had not been dispelled in hundreds of years. It had only retreated. It was in the depths of the Quinaltine. It was in every deep, dark place the Galasieni themselves had warded, and Hasufin had bargained with it, listened to it, welcomed it in his folly.

He had no choice but draw its attention to himself, now, for Cefwyn's only defense was his blindness to magic and wizardry alike . . . and blindness was not enough, not against something with such ready purchase in Ryssand's heart.

"I wish Idrys may hurry," Tristen whispered into the dark, hearing Owl call again, and a third time, magical three. "I wish the winds behind him, and I wish he may come in time."

"So all of us wish," Crissand said, and fear touched his voice. "I saw a Shadow. Does it threaten the king?"

"It threatens everything," Tristen said, and could not bid Crissand avoid it: could not bid any one of his friends avoid it. It was why they had come, why they pressed forward, why they had gone to war at all, and everything was at risk. "But sleep. Sleep now, while we dare sleep at all."

BOOK THREE

INTERLUDE

Morning came gray and pale across hills not so different than Elwynor. Maids stirred about the fireplace, made tea, presented a breakfast of which Ninévrisë only wished a little bread, no honey in the tea. Afterward she sat in the warm middle of the room gazing at the pale light of the window, asking herself whether the bread had been wise at all.

Perhaps, instead, it was fear that churned inside her—fear and the wish never to have left her husband . . . not a wise wish, to be back with him, but the wish of her heart, all the same.

She was aware, on that level far beyond awareness of the hills and the tea and unwanted breakfast, of Emuin, half-asleep in his tower bed, an old man and increasingly frail; and of the boy Paisi, who made Emuin's breakfast.

Paisi was worried, too, worried for the old man: *loved* him, an unaccustomed thing for Paisi, and more than a little surprising to the boy, who had loved few things and fewer people. He was not sure what to call those feelings, but Paisi was a fiercely protective soul, and set all his gifts to caring for the old man who had roused them in him.

He was suddenly aware of her eavesdropping on him—gifted in that way to an amazing extent, and not knowing anything he could properly do with that ability, either—and stopped and looked her direction in the gray space like any boy caught at anything. He truly disliked to be stared at or made conspicuous in any way, met such stares with hostility—but he regarded her differently, not with the unthought respect of a commoner for a lady, but a far more personal sense of connection.

He hurried about his last morning duties for Emuin, waked the old man, saw him safely seated at his breakfast, and then slipped out of the tower room and down the stairs from the tower to the lower hall.

Up, then, the central stairs.

She knew when he would arrive, knew that he suffered a sudden blush of awkwardness just outside her doors, his brash, common effrontery brought to an adamant halt by her guards.

Why had he come? He pursued his own curiosity, his own sense of duty. He had come to find her and to learn what she meant to that other concern of his, who slept with his mother in yet another room, with a baby's untaught awareness.

She rose, went to her door, and opened it to find a gangling boy with wide dark eyes, face flushed with the vehemence of his argument with her guards.

"Lady," he said, never once abashed, but with a quick bow.

"This is my ally," she said to the guards. "He doesn't know it yet, but he is." She swept the boy inside, and the guards shut the door. All her attention was for a boy her heart told her defended a sleeping baby, for reasons unclear to the boy himself, and defended him even against the babe's own Aswydd mother. It seemed to his loyal heart that the baby had had no defenders; and he had grown up with none but an old woman, and so he took it as his duty, himself, when no one else cared, to care for Tarien's baby. All of that passion was in him, all at once, and for the babe's sake.

In Tristen's absence, he was here at her door—no accident.

And no boyish curiosity had brought him to her, but a wizard's lively attachment to all the world around him: she felt it as she had felt her father's curiosity about the world and never known it was uncommon: Paisi had the same tone of mind and heart, as if she were in the heart of her family again. They faced one another, and at the far remove of his tower, Emuin had stopped his breakfast, and had stopped it for a full several breaths, now, slowly grown present enough that they both knew.

" 'E ain't sayin' anything," Paisi said faintly. " 'E ain't upset wi' me, but 'e knows. The old man knows ever'thin' 'at goes on."

"A very great wizard," Ninévrisë said, "as I never shall be." All her little wizardry had been bent to the north, in earnest hope of a whisper in the gray space, and now this boy distracted her from her watch and made her aware how constant it had been. It both gave her second thoughts, this potent distraction the boy posed, and made her question her own wisdom and her own fate in this war of powers.

It was a small fate, it might be; or a greater one. She had always thought of it as *her* fate—but seemingly now her fate had become wrapped about the child, her child, Cefwyn's child. She had been proud, had commanded in the field, come close to power, and seen all her power over her fate unexpectedly involved in this union with Cefwyn. Now she saw it devolving upon their child, changed in direction and inevitable as the stoop of a hawk—to that extent she knew she had failed of all she purposed, and had failed in it even if she should rule in Elwynor. Neither Cefwyn's rule nor hers, she foresaw, would suffice to settle the border or make a lasting peace. They became forerunners of one who might.

And this boy . . . this all-elbows, tousle-haired boy . . . this self-appointed warden of Cefwyn's other son . . . he came to her to know what she was, and found himself too abashed to look her in the eye.

"Were you always with Emuin?" she asked, a more answerable question.

"No," Paisi said. " 'Is Grace sent me to 'im."

"And do you like Emuin?"

Paisi blushed and looked abashed. "May be."

"And how do you regard Tristen?"

"It ain't for me to say about 'Is Grace," Paisi said in a breath. " 'E just is, is all."

"Yet you do like him."

"Aye," Paisi admitted, with all his soul in that answer.

"And Lady Tarien?"

Silence was that answer.

"Do you love the Aswydds?" Ninévrisë asked. "Or not?"

A shake of Paisi's head, a downward look, and a half glance. "Lady Tarien ain't as bad."

"And her son?"

That drew a look up, so direct and so open it held nothing back. " 'E's a babby, is all."

"No," she said, "not all. Never all."

"Then what 'e is . . . 'e ain't, yet."

"All the same, he has a friend," she said in the deep silence, for that was how she judged Paisi. "He has one friend; and that friend is a wizard, or will be. And when my son sees the light . . . will you love him, too?"

Paisi's eyes darted hither and thither, as if he sought to see some answer just past her; but when he looked at her, and again she could see all the way to the depth of him. "I ain't sighted," Paisi said. "I don't know, lady."

"Yet will you wish him harm?" She asked for half, since she could not immediately have the whole. And seeing every certainty of her own life overturned and changed, she fought for her son's certainties. "Or do you wish him well?"

"I ain't ever wishin' anybody harm," Paisi said with a fierce shake of his head. "Master Emuin says a fool'd wish harm to anybody, on account of it's apt to fly back in a body's face an' do gods know what, so, far as I can wish, I wish your babby's happy."

"So do I," Ninévrisë said, and the bands about her heart seemed to loose. *This boy,* something said to her, *this boy* is worth winning. "I wish peace, and good, and all such things."

Most of all she wished Cefwyn might see both his sons, and might come alive out of the war. She wished that more than she wished herself to rule; but for Elwynor itself she never gave up her wishes to see it become again what it had been.

She had lost confidence herself . . . had lost it the morning Tristen left, and did not know where to find it again in Henas'amef. She was out of place here, and regretted with all her heart that she had not ridden with Tristen, but she felt the presence of life within her and knew what dire thing their enemy had tried to do with Tarien's babe. She would not chance that for her own son, Cefwyn's son, the heir of two kingdoms.

"Do you think Lady Tarien will see me?" she asked.

"I don't know she won't," Paisi said.

What Emuin thought of it was another matter: caution flowed from that quarter, for down in the depths, not so far away, was a tightly warded fear, one so closely bound to Tarien it gave Emuin constant worry.

But all the same she gathered the boy by the arm and went to the door and out, where she swept up half her Amefin bodyguard and walked up the stairs to the hall above.

There was a guard of state at Tarien's door, too, and now Tarien Aswydd knew she had a visitor, and met that notion warily. They were not friends. They had never been. But she came with Paisi, and Paisi knew the old woman who stayed with Tarien, knew her as if she were kin of his, as for all Ninévrisë knew the old woman might be.

Only now she and Emuin and the elderly earl whom Tristen had left in charge of the town were the only authority; and she used hers to pass the doors of that apartment.

The place smelled of baby, and the gray space there was close with protections and wards that tingled along her skin and over

Paisi's. She could see them for a moment, a flare of blue in the foyer, and at the sunlit window beyond, and about the door that let them in.

They were not against her, but against any wizard who came here; against anyone who might wish to invade this small fortified and enchanted space. And at the very heart of it sat Tarien, tucked up with quilts in a chair by the fire, and in her arms her baby, and her attention was all for the child, nothing for her visitor.

So Tarien defended herself, and wove her little spells around and around her, like a lady spider in her den.

Ninévrisë found herself not even angry, the spells were so small and so many and so desperate . . . made of fear, every one.

"Good day," she said, "Lady Tarien."

Tarien did not look up, only hugged her child against her, her prize out of all that had happened. Tarien knew who visited her, and inasmuch as Tarien was aware of anything but her own child, knew there was another son, the son of two birthrights, when her son had no claim or right of even one.

They had no need to speak. She had no need to have come here, except to enter the center of Tarien's attention instead of wandering its peripheries. She had nothing to gain: it was Tarien's child who entered the world a beggar and hers who owned it all.

She felt an unexpected compassion for the two of them. And perhaps Tarien knew it, for she did look up, on the sudden and with an angry countenance.

"I offer you no spite," Ninévrisë said. "No threat to your son. May I stay?"

Tarien turned her face away, but without the anger, only seeking escape.

"Then I shan't," Ninévrisë said. "But may I see him?"

Tarien unfolded the cloth about the baby's face and shoulders; and it was a tiny, wizened face like any newborn, harmless to see him, but oh, such possibility of calamity, or of fellowship for her son.

She let go a sigh, and would have offered her finger to the baby's tiny fist, but Tarien turned him away and hugged him close.

Cefwyn's son. Elfwyn, he was named, like the last High King, and half brother to her own babe, when he was born.

She might summon her guards, exert her power, seize the baby, bring him into her own care, for good or for ill, and Tarien's history made her think that might be a wiser course . . . wiser for them all, Tarien's welfare discounted.

But her father had dinned into her the principles of wizardry, if not the practice of it, that action brought action, that an element out of Place strove until it found that Place. Striving was not what she wished from this child, only peace, and in peace she was willing to leave him, with only a parting word to his mother.

"He has one hope besides his mother's love," Ninévrisë said with all deliberation, "and that will be his father's grace."

"Cefwyn will die in Elwynor," Tarien said fiercely. "Lord *Tristen* will be my son's protector. They hail Tristen High King. High King! And he favors my son."

She had not intended to be nettled by the lady, or to take omens from anything the lady said or threatened; but that claim struck too near the mark, far too near.

Paisi quietly tugged at her sleeve. "Master Emuin'll have me hide for bringin' ye here. Come, lady. Come away."

"The lady deceives herself," Ninévrisë said, both in anger and in utter, steadfast conviction, and it occurred to her to say more than that, that Cefwyn would come alive out of the war, and that Tristen would keep his word, and that nothing the Aswydds had ever done had helped them: all this generation of Aswydds had done brought one long tumble of fortunes toward Tarien's solitude and imprisonment.

But her father had taught her to say less than she knew, so she gathered up her dignity and her freedom and left with them.

It was not a movement of her own child she felt in the doorway of that place, but his presence at least, an awareness of a life within her, and a life bound to all the events on the river and northward.

"Lady!" Paisi cried. Emuin himself had roused at the malice Tarien flung, wizardous malice, and he struck it down, with the firm intent to take Tarien's babe from her care.

—*No,* Ninévrisë *said, steady in her place.*

But guards clearly had their orders. At that outcry they had moved. Ninévrisë pressed herself against the wall as armed men rushed the room and from then matters went from bad to worse, wards flaring, wizardry striking, wizardry countering wizardry, Emuin's, hers, Tarien's, even Paisi's, and the guards oblivious to all. Tarien's shrieks pierced the very walls, stirred the shadows in the depths, rang through the very stones—a mother's cries, a mother's curses, that lanced through to the bones of another woman with child.

"Have a care!" Ninévrisë cried, as in her witness a guard wrested the child from Tarien's hands, and another pulled Tarien away toward the window. Ninévrisë reached for the child herself, as Paisi did, and to her arms the guard yielded the infant.

The baby moved and cried, upset amid all the anger. She held the small bundle, and looked at Tarien's white face, pitying, finally, after her fright and her anger: pity, against Tarien's grieving rage.

"No one will harm him," Ninévrisë assured her. "Be still. Be still! You may yet have him back. Only wish no harm, yourself. Hush."

With great breaths Tarien grew calmer, and reached for the child, which she would have given, but Emuin would not, and the guards would not, and Tarien struck at them with curses Emuin turned.

"I'll call Gran," Paisi said. "She ain't far."

Indeed there was an old woman aware of the child, and already on her way, out of breath and distressed. Ninévrisë turned away hugged the unwanted and crying child close against her, trying to stop the strife within the room and within the gray space, with Tarien's cries still in her ears.

An old woman arrived, the nurse, to whom Ninévrisë willingly ceded the child, and that alone seemed to quiet Tarien.

But the gray space quivered with wrong and with grief, and if a mother's just grief alone could rend the wards of the fortress apart, Tarien attempted it.

"The nurse may have him here to be fed, while the guards wait in the foyer," Ninévrisë said; it was the only mending of the situation she could think of. "And the nurse may care for him next door. If you mend your wishes, Lady Tarien, perhaps you can win more. But make your peace with Emuin, not with me. Ask Tristen when he comes. Don't cast away all your chances, only to spite me and Cefwyn."

"He will *die*," Tarien said.

"No," she said, more than determined, "he will not."

They both wished, each roused the winds in the gray space and, parting company, did not part. There was battle joined, harm with help, and Ninévrisë walked away with her child still her own.

Tarien, however, could not say so . . . and warred against them now. The wizard-threat from the north had turned away from her, and she might have won compassion. But jealousy would not let her accept charity from a rival: nothing had ever prepared Tarien Aswydd for kindness, and she resented it as she resented all things exterior to her own will.

By that she set a course and nothing would divert her.

CHAPTER 1

Ｆrom the height of Danvy's back Cefwyn cast a long look on the Lenúalim, a view that included Lord Maudyn's long-defended bridge and water running higher than he had ever seen it, dark, laden with mud and debris from the unseasonable thaw.

But thank the all-patient gods and whatever friendly wizardry intermittently supported his own plans, the rains had stopped, the debris had not damaged the pylons and the high water had not delayed the installation of the bridge decking. His fast-moving couriers had bidden Lord Maudyn start that process early, well before his arrival.

The last section was in place as of yesterday. Lord Maudyn had immediately enlarged his camp on the far side of the river—a camp he had had in place for months, placed and supplied by small boats and rafts, to be sure of that far bridgehead.

And as late as this morning when the main army had arrived, the far bank had still produced no hostile action against that camp, which now was due to enlarge.

To Cefwyn that far shore remained a mystery of ancient maps and his wife's best recollections, a land veiled in brush and scattered woods—Ninévrisë had assured him the land was much the same as the land this side, rolling hills, a north shore rugged with cliffs which were the same as the high banks on the south.

That was the troublesome spot, those cliffs to the west of this bridge. There the Lenúalim ran deep and turbulent, and bent sharply around in its course through the stony hills as it turned toward Amefel. What tantrum of the all-wise gods had split that great ridge of rock and sent a river through it he was not certain, but on the

292

hither side of that ridge two moderate-sized rivers flowed into the Lenúalim's current . . . one from the Elwynim side of the river, and the other here, their own tame Assurn. The northern river entered as clear water. The Lenúalim was usually murky green and the southern Assurn a pale brown stream. The colors habitually stayed distinct for a time until they merged into the Lenúalim's flood . . . so Lord Maudyn informed him, Lord Maudyn sharing a scholar's curiosity about such things.

And on any other venture, even his skirmishes in the south, he would have been curious to see whether the melt and flood had left any vestige of that three-colored joining . . . but he had grown grimly single-minded since he had kissed his wife good-bye.

That he now fought a war against his own side as well as the enemy had not so much divided his attention as sharpened his wits and made him scour up the good advice he had had from counselors now absent . . . advice which, ironically, he might have been less zealous to follow if they were with him. He became responsible for himself, alone in a host that took his orders and offered him protection. But Ryssand's influence went into unexpected places.

Mindful of that fact, wary of Ryssand's spies, he kept his ordinary guards close to him . . . men in the scarlet of the Dragon Guard, men sworn to protect his back from any assault. If he was horsed and watching the river, so they were. If he dismounted to go among the troops, they dismounted and went close to him, in case some man of another lord's guard had some unguessed connection to Ryssand and his allies.

But they had come this far without incident or assault, and with remarkably few delays. This morning he watched the collapse of the last tents, and the movement of carts within the lines of last night's camp gathering up the bundled canvas in neat order.

Even yet there was no motion from the enemy, but he kept a wary eye toward the far bank. The last information Lord Maudyn relayed to him had Tasmôrden still enjoying his victory at hapless Ilefínian, and taking no action toward the steady enlargement of Lord Maudyn's forces . . . but Tasmôrden could not be ignorant of all that was happening here: Ryssand would not *permit* Tasmôrden to remain ignorant, by what he suspected.

So was this Elwynim earl an utter fool, lazing in Ilefínian, or was he a man trying to make his enemy commit himself too far, too fast?

He sat Danvy's restless back, with his guards around him. He watched, wishing above all else that Ninévrisë were here to see this morning, the fulfillment of the hotly argued marriage treaty and most especially of his personal and far more tender oath to her. He wondered, since wizardry accounted for so much that mere Men called coincidence, whether by some remote stretch of the imagination she might know where he was at this moment.

And if she did know, he hoped she knew he thought of her.

Finally, he said to her in his imagination. *Finally, and in spite of all their objections, your banner is here. Your people will see it.*

A sudden redirection of his guards' attention alerted him to a rider coming from the road beyond the camp, a courier, as it appeared: the red coat was faintly visible even in the dawn, even at this range.

But as the rider came closer it was the red of the Dragon Guard, and the horse well mudded, as if it had been hours under way, this early in the dawn.

"From the capital, perhaps." It might be a courier from Efanor. Gods save them from disasters . . . or some move of Ryssand there.

As he came closer still, the rider's fair hair blew from under the edges of his silver helm in a very familiar way.

"Anwyll!" he exclaimed to his guards, who were moving their horses into his path to prevent this precipitate approach. "No, let him come. This is a man I trust."

The guards all the same arrayed themselves a little to the fore, but Anwyll it indeed was, and the junior captain he had sent with Tristen reined his weary horse to a slow and respectful pace as he approached and moved in among the guards' horses.

"Your Majesty," Anwyll said, out of breath as he drew rein. Dust and weariness made him look shockingly twice his years, or perhaps service under Tristen had aged him in a single winter, but the eyes were still bright and undaunted. "I went to Guelemara first, Your Majesty, thinking you'd be there, but His Highness said you'd gone on. And he sent this message." Anwyll pulled a flattened, hard-used scroll from within his coat, and leaned in the saddle to offer it, but one of the guards intercepted it and passed it on instead, a document heavy with a prince's red wax seal . . . and a white Quinaltine ribbon. *That* was odd. Was Efanor lacking red ones?

"Lord Tristen sent, too," Anwyll said. "But would commit nothing to writing. He bade me say . . ." Anwyll caught his breath: he was sweating under the spattering of mud. "He bade me march quickly from the river . . . with the carts . . . which I did, and they are coming, Your Majesty, but behind me. My company . . ." He pointed to the south, the road by which they also had come. "A day behind. To save the horses and the axles."

"What did my brother say? What did *Tristen* say?" Cefwyn asked sharply. Everything Anwyll had done he was sure was well done, but Anwyll had a way of telling a superior everything but what he wanted most to know, getting all the small details in order.

"His Highness wishes Your Majesty the gods' favor. His Grace of Amefel says that Tasmôrden has claimed the High Kingship, that he holds court in Ilefínian." For two things Anwyll found breath, then a third. "And says beware Ryssand.—Your Majesty, I saw his banners an hour back."

"Ryssand's? Where? The north road?" About an hour back was where the north road came in to join this one, at least an hour back as hard riding might set it; and that was indeed the road by which Ryssand and Murandys might both arrive, inland but more direct than the winding riverside track from the fishing villages.

"A road comes in . . ." Anwyll began to describe it with his hands.

"I know the road! The rest of Tristen's news, man. Spit it out, never mind the niceties. Is it his wishes for good weather—or is it possibly news I need?"

"His Grace did also wish you good health, and said he hoped for good weather—" Gods save him, he saw how Anwyll had always to remember things in order, a damnable fault in a messenger.

"Then? Say on, man! What else did he send you to say?"

"He sent Cevulirn to the river, to my camp, to my former camp, that is, and he himself, His Grace, that is, he of Amefel—will join Imor, Ivanor, Lanfarnesse, Olmern and forces out of Amefel, and cross to receive whatever force of the enemy Your Majesty drives toward him. Most, he begs Your Majesty be careful of Ryssand."

"A very good idea, that," Cefwyn said, desperately frustrated in his hopes for something more current and more than the damning echo of all his instruction to Tristen. If Tristen, obeying his orders, stayed out of the fight, and sent no better than this, it greatly concerned him—and if ever Tristen should violate his express orders or chase off after butterflies, he wished it would be now.

But clearly his message had not reached Tristen before Anwyll had left . . . let alone Ninévrisë: Anwyll was greatly delayed, having gone to Guelemara before setting out in this direction. It was a memorable ride—small wonder he had mislaid a detachment of Dragon Guard and a train of carts between here and the capital.

And Anwyll's spotting Ryssand near him redeemed all possible fault.

"Take a fresh horse," Cefwyn said, and drew off his glove, red leather with the Dragon of the Marhanen embroidered in gold on the back. "Use this for authority, take what you need, and join me across the river."

"Thank you, Your Majesty, but my men . . ."

"Will follow Ryssand. We'll not wait. Go!" Cefwyn reined Danvy around and rode along the shore, taking his guard with him and leaving the exhausted captain to follow as he could.

His rapid course along the riverside drew attention. The tents were each folded down by now, precise parcels of canvas awaiting the wagons to gather them. The men were saddling their horses, and the officers looked sharply toward him. In particular he spied Captain Gwywyn of the Prince's Guard, where the regimental standards of the Dragons, the Prince's Guard, and the Guelens all stood with the few banners of the middle lands.

He rode up to Gwywyn in a spatter of loose earth, and with a sweep of his arm indicated the bridge. "The companies and the contingents to horse, now, and across the bridge. No delay."

There was no question of the readiness of the bridge to bear the carts. The Dragon standard of the Marhanen was flying bravely across the river, from the other end of the bridge, along with the banner of Panys. Lord Maudyn waited for him, had established himself visibly on that other side and indulged himself in no luxury: it would be a camp to use as a base, to move on in another day: those were the orders.

"Sound the trumpets!" Gwywyn shouted out to the heralds. "Advance the standards! All the army to follow!"

"The carts to follow Osanan!" Cefwyn shouted, riding past the quartermaster. "And wait for no one else! On to the bridge! One cart at a time, sir! If that bridge fails us, best you be on it!"

The trumpeters gathered themselves into a ragged, then unified call to standards. The banner-bearers set themselves immediately to horse, to ride past and claim their regimental and provincial colors. Officers were up, and ordered their men.

His guard was around him. The banner-bearers thundered past him at a good clip, a moving bright curtain of the Marhanen Dragon and the Tower and Checker of the Regent of Elwynor preceding the colors of Llymaryn, Panys, Carys, Sumas, and Osanan, banners which flowed back to their regiments. The Dragon and the Tower went where he rode, and ahead of him, with the sergeants behind him bawling out orders and cursing the laggards.

Officers shouted, horses protested, and the oxen that moved the baggage train lowed in their yokes. Disorder overtook the laggards, companies mounting up with only half their tents set into the carts, which thus would wait for the quartermaster's men themselves to gather up the bundles, and those carts thus would fall behind the column as the whole army unwound into a line of march as quickly as companies thus surprised could fall in behind their standard. Carters cursed and soldiers hastened their horses as if devils were after them all the way to the bridgehead, onto heavy, safe timbers whereon five riders could go abreast; and by now the expectation in every heart must be of Elwynim descending on the camp from ambush—could anything else bring such precipitate orders?

They had not their full load of baggage: a good deal of it he had sent out to Lord Maudyn ahead of time, and all winter long, in the lack of carts, Maudyn had moved it by repeated trips, tempting the enemy to reach for it . . . but no such thing had happened.

So, indeed, now he committed them to the other side, and tempted fate and the gods twice by leaving his quartermaster to manage the crossing: trust the drivers not to hurl themselves and their teams into the river by too much haste, and his quartermaster not to crowd up on the bridge—he knew his quartermaster, a steady officer of the Dragons: that man was no fool, to bring more than one heavy wagon onto the bridge at a time, and would not, not if pikes had to prevent it. To cross in haste to defend Maudyn was a contingency they had foreseen: that the Elwynim enemy was not the reason of their crossing was beside the point—the man would not fail him.

And as he came off the bridge and onto the soil of Elwynor, he had clear view of the banners of Ylesuin and Panys set among the rocks and the height that bordered the road.

"Ride on!" he ordered Gwywyn, just behind him, and he drew himself and his bodyguard aside from the road, keeping view of the bridge, reassured in the orderly progress of disciplined troops, the Dragons setting the example and the quartermaster's guards marshaling those who came behind into a calm, rapid order.

It was the lords' contingents that worried him: there were the men who might grow anxious and press forward. An armored man that fell into those deep, cold waters was a dead man, no question about it; and he had worried for the provincial musters if they came to any trial at arms about this crossing. His cleverness in setting the army across and leaving Ryssand behind his cart train could bring disaster on them if some unit panicked.

But for the foremost hazard of their crossing, he was just as glad to move at speed: if ever Tasmôrden had a real chance at a hard, early strike at them, the best chance for him was during their crossing. He had needed to be very sure of Lord Maudyn's scouts to have camped as they had, with the army in sight, but Lord Maudyn's men in reach. He had expected an attack to come on Lord Maudyn in the winter, or again when the decking went on. He had most dreaded an attack at their arrival, but last night, when they had camped with Lord Maudyn on one side of the water and himself on Ylesuin's side, there had been no threat and they had seen no reason to press a crossing and encampment into the dark.

The forces of Ylesuin would have had the leisure to straggle onto Elwynim soil at a stroll had they wished. That in itself prompted a leader in opposition to question his own perceptions and Tasmôrden's qualities as a leader of men.

Dared they trust, as Maudyn reported, that Tasmôrden indeed still lingered among the plundered luxuries of Ilefínian, his troops ranging the wine shops, so dissipated they could not field a squad of cavalry?

Or dared he think that Tasmôrden's lack of response was because Tasmôrden chose to let Ryssandish and Guelens fight a war of their own . . . that he delayed in hope of Ryssand's arriving forces.

"Your Majesty."

Anwyll had found a horse and crossed among the Dragons, a man at loose ends, lacking a command and lacking orders.

"Stay close." Trusted men were rare, and by conscious decision he trusted Anwyll at the same level as he trusted his own guard: if there were perfidy in this man, he counted on Tristen to have smelled it out and never to have trusted him with messages. That was his first thought.

But his second asked whether Tristen was infallible. Had Tristen not sent him that precious lot of Guelens, and the head of the Amefin Quinalt, who had wreaked such havoc?

Then he recalled Efanor's letter, unregarded in his possession since Anwyll had brought it to him. He had tucked it into his belt, another abuse of the scroll, and when he drew it out he found its parchment and its seal alike cracked but not yet separated, a small roll almost overwhelmed by the honors of its seal and binding . . . no question of its origin as he pulled the ribbon frcc, for hc knew the seal as he knew his own, Efanor's authentic seal, with a deliberate imperfection in it, a flaw at the edge, as his own gillyflower seal bore a small mark in one petal.

But why a white satin ribbon, the like of which the Holy Father used, and why was it not the red of the Marhanen?

He broke the seal and unrolled the little scroll in the stiff wind that came down the river.

I take the captain for a reliable man, Efanor had written, *and send him on with the carts which I fear now are too late to serve. Tristen has been here in Guelemara and has banished some sort of darksome unpleasantness from the very altar of the Quinaltine.*

Tristen in *Guelemara,* Cefwyn thought, dumbfounded and dismayed at once. Had Tristen marched for the capital? And *darksome unpleasantness?*

. . . Neither I nor the Holy Father fully understand the means of his visitation, but he pursued some irruption of evil influence daring the vicinity of the altar, and established a line of defense which he drew on the stones. He said that I must guard this place and walk this line and pray continually . . .

There were several wonders in this cramped, tightly written letter . . . not least of which others was the word *pray* within Tristen's instructions. *Pray,* was it, now?

And Tristen had not marched in at the head of an army, either, if that failure to *understand the means* meant something magical.

Flitting hither and thither like the irreverent pigeons?

To Guelemara, was it now?

Then why not here, friend of my heart? Come to me here! Oh, gods, could I wish you by me!

And where have I sent Nevris? To what care?

But he had no magic, no wizardry: Emuin's most careful questions in his boyhood had found not a trace, not a breath, not a whisper of wizard-gift in him. The Quinalt and Teranthine gods were the only recourse of a magic-blind man, and he had no faith Tristen would hear him *or* the gods.

Yet Tristen had flitted his way into the Quinaltine, had he? And surely Ninévrisë was safe with Emuin in Henas'amef, if Emuin had not taken to flying about the land in his company.

And *praying*? If it were not his brother who had written that word, he would not have believed the letter, but it was, and freely so, Efanor's cursive hand.

This I do, Efanor had written, *continually, with the Holy Father and a number of the priests on whom we rely. I fear to say in this letter all that I understand and even more so do I fear to say all that I suspect. Against what enemy we contend we remain largely uncertain. I fear this lonely watch exceedingly and at times feel there is indeed some looming threat behind that Line, although my eyes can plainly see the holy altar beyond it.*

I ask myself whether the hallow here—if hallow it be—might have to do with the untimely death of the late Patriarch, so bloody and recent in these precincts.

Well enough, Cefwyn thought to himself: Efanor dared not lay in writing that they had knowingly hanged a corpse for another man's sin; and for that reason might the old Patriarch be looking for his killer? Shadows, Tristen had called them.

But at other times, Efanor wrote, *I have worse fears and recall all that I have heard regarding the events at Lewen field, as if this presages some attempt at sorcerous entry into Guelemara, at this holiest of sites, and some threat against the capital and the Holy Quinaltine itself. I have hesitated to write to you, knowing the immense concerns which face you in your undertaking, and indeed, you left me to attend such matters, as within my competency. I pray you know I shall continue to stand my watch.*

Yet to advise you of these things should I fall, which gods forbid, I have my one opportune messenger at hand and dare not keep him. I have learned to trust my doubts and to make friends of them, and of all courses before me, I am most uneasy with the thought of remaining silent regarding Lord Tristen's instruction and his actions here, whether by magic or wizardry or whatever agency. If wizardry comes against us here, we believe our task is to prevent it.

Meanwhile I have heard nothing from Ryssand nor of Ryssand.

The good gods bless you and Her Grace. The gods attend your steps and guide you day and night. The gracious gods bring you success and honor.

I send you my devotion and my love.

The last was crabbed into a bend around the edge of the parchment . . . Efanor had made the message scroll itself as small as he could, so that Anwyll might tuck it away unseen . . . remarkable, Cefwyn reflected . . . remarkable and shameful, that they were brought to this pass of secrecy, all for Ryssand and Ryssand's daughter.

Wizardry, Efanor said. Wizardry. Tristen in *Guelemara,* when other and reliable reports, even Ninévrisë's dream, he remembered now, though for a moment he had forgotten it, had said he was in Henas'amef.

What in hell was he to think?

"Did His Highness mention anything to you of Lord Tristen coming to Guelemara?" he asked Anwyll, and saw Anwyll's surprise.

"No, Your Majesty, no such thing! It was Lord Tristen's intent to go to the river."

"To the river, but on the other side of that cursed rock," Cefwyn said half to himself, for it was that impassable barrier which kept him from going aside to Tristen's camp and making one their plan of assault on Ilefínian. Weathered knolls of barren stone and deep pockets of earth bearing tangled brush in the crevices made it land unfit for goats, let alone any hope of joining their forces either side of the river, not until they were most of the way to Ilefínian, which sat at the point of that spear of a ridge.

And had Tristen indeed followed his silly pigeons over *that* and appeared to Efanor in the capital?

Efanor had surely dreamed. Had a vision and convinced his priestly supporters. Tristen was on the other side of that great range of hills; and Ninévrisë would confirm Tristen in his plan to go to the river and cross and bring him whatever support he might need . . . to Tasmôrden's extreme discomfiture. Pray for *that*, brother!

If there were that much force to this wizardous threat Efanor named, surely then Ninévrisë would have read it in her bespelled scrap of a letter and told him so: it was, then, nothing so extreme— only one of Efanor's dreams, that before now had set him to religious excesses. The kingdom was in danger and his brother, with all his other excellent qualities, saw visions.

So whatever had happened in the capital, whatever unholy threat Efanor foresaw, whatever the truth of visions . . . he left that to priests as out of his reach and beyond his advice. What he had more to fear in his vicinity was the equally unholy union of enemies, Parsynan and Cuthan, Ryssand and Tasmôrden, all conniving together, and now Ryssand coming up behind him.

There was the thought to make him anxious. He very much doubted Ryssand would do anything so overt as to attack his own king's baggage train, and it was equally difficult to think that Ryssand could plan anything so reckless as an assault on his back . . . but it was not impossible to think.

Ryssand had buried a son, dead at Cevulirn's hand in this exchange of rancor and wedding proposals. Artisane still fluttered around Efanor and had still hoped, so appearances were, down to the day the army marched.

But considering how Ryssand came chasing after the army with his own muster . . . his own very large muster, which might have with it not only Murandys but Nelefreíssan and Teymeryn and all the northern lands . . . did not fill him with confidence.

Could they all, *all* the north intend to strike at him? Did they conspire together, so blindly hateful of his rule that they would gamble on Tasmôrden's often-bartered promises—or was Ryssand, even Ryssand, innocent and coming to the defense of the realm?

He watched the last of the Guelen Guard come off the bridge, last of the standing regiments, and saw the first of the provincial forces, the contingent with young Rusyn, ride after . . . no great number of foot, except those Panys had brought.

The army he had fielded after all was, as Tristen had once advised him, nearly all horse. It was not near the number of men the lords could have raised in the peasant levies, if they had called in the infantry, as they had planned—he had foregone that, at the very last, had overset long-held plans as the carts delayed and their information from across the river painted him a mobile, smaller enemy than Aséyneddin had led against him. The army he had gathered still would not move as fast as the light horse Tristen and Cevulirn alike had recommended, but they would move and regroup faster than heavy infantry.

And if thanks to Ryssand they had now to abandon all but a few tents in favor of rapid movement into Elwynor, so be it and damn Ryssand: the weather was tolerable and they could manage. They could forage. Without Ninévrisë, he no longer hoped overmuch for a great rising of folk loyal to her banner: their best information portrayed a land cowed and beaten by conflicting warlords, no man daring raise his head. But all the same he carried her banner aloft and hoped to receive some support from the locals, if only in their declining to face him for Tasmôrden.

And at the worst of Ryssand's treachery, they still could survive long enough to reach Ilefínian, against every principle of Guelen warfare that declared the baggage train had to set the rate of march and that they must not leave it vulnerable to attack. For what he did now, he cast back to older models, to Tashânen, to Barrakkêth himself: they must not extend themselves so fast and so far from their lines they lost control of the roads on which they marched and the supplies which moved on those roads, but they had to risk the tents . . . there was no kingdom to go back to if he retreated now, and no hope of victory if he enmeshed himself in Ryssand's schemes. Defeat Tasmôrden, and he would have a far more tractable Lord Ryssand to deal with. Fail to defeat Tasmôrden . . . and he would die here. That was the truth.

And the less visible truth was that the few carts they had and Lord Maudyn's extensive, well-set camp were neither one the most reliable source of supply. No, in fact: the most reliable road and the supply he knew beyond a doubt they could count on was not what he played hop-skip with in evading Ryssand and not what he had spent a winter laying out. It was (granted Tristen had not flitted off with his pigeons) the supply *Tristen* had established on the other side of what he had come to think of as that damned rock.

In Amefel. That was where Ninévrisë was, that was where Tristen was, that was where Emuin was.

It was where Cevulirn was, and Sovrag, and Pelumer, and gods, even that poker of a man, Umanon of Imor. They were the same company as had stood against the Shadow at Lewenbrook. There was supply at Anwyll's former camp, and *that* he did not doubt.

There was the solid support he could trust.

As for the wagons and the carts and the pack train he had . . . he sat his horse at Anwyll's side and watched that line of men and carts across the river, hastening about its business of gathering up the camp and following the army.

"You said Ryssand was at the north road," he remarked to Captain Anwyll. "Approaching this road, or already on it?"

"Approaching, Your Majesty. I saw his banner at a distance."

"His and no others?"

"That was all I saw, but there were very many men, Your Majesty."

That Ryssand had been still in the distance when Anwyll passed, that was good news.

He sat his horse watching and watching as group after group crossed the bridge, and in good time Lord Maudyn rode up to find him, from his camp where they might well have been expecting for some time to receive him and to pay him some courtesy of welcome.

Instead Lord Maudyn, good-hearted man, had ridden to him.

"Your Majesty," Maudyn said, and Cefwyn was glad to see him, and offered his hand across the gap between their horses.

"Well done," he said to Maudyn Lord of Panys. "Very well done. Did you hear that Ryssand is coming?"

Maudyn's countenance assumed a bleak quiet, and then Maudyn cast a curious look toward the bridge, where the first of the baggage carts waited to cross, behind Osanan.

"The baggage train will cross, one by one," Cefwyn said. "Which may be hours, to move all that. And Ryssand can wait. My baggage has to stay close with the army. If he's late, so be it. We'll be moving on to the next camp; there'll be no settling here."

He was satisfied now that the carts were beginning to roll. Ryssand would arrive too late to join the crossing of the provincial contingents. He would have to wait, he and those with him, until the last of the baggage train had rolled across the bridge, and that could be very slow, where it involved ox teams, and axles heavy-laden with canvas and iron.

It was time for the scouts to move out and be sure of their night's camp, that much closer to Ilefínian.

Ryssand could cross today and spend his next hours getting *his* baggage train across. Ryssand might overtake him today. He might not.

It was time to give the orders to the scouts, and to look to where they would stay this night, in weather fair enough to enable a camp without the tents. It was graven in stone that Guelenmen camped under canvas and made a solid camp at night, that Guelenmen moved at a deliberate pace dictated by the slowest oxcart in the baggage train: Ryssand would not expect this.

He might simply unhitch the teams and let the carts stand on the road, such as it was, completely filling it, so that the forces trying to pass them must struggle through the brush and limbs that fringed it. Perhaps amid the trees and thorn vines, Ryssand might gather he was being slighted.

More to the point, so might the lords with Ryssand see where Ryssand's leading had gotten them, and then weigh how angry they were willing to make their king, in enemy territory, when Ryssand was being outmaneuvered by oxcarts.

Let them ask themselves then in a second moment of sober reflection how far they could trust Tasmôrden to do what he had promised and to refrain from attacking them: Tasmôrden's promises and representations might ring somewhat hollow in their ears once they found themselves chasing their king deeper and deeper into Tasmôrden's reach.

One outraged, angry man might be a fool far quicker and far longer than his contentious allies.

That was what Cefwyn hoped, at least, as he turned Danvy to ride between Maudyn and Anwyll.

"We'll go on," he said, "gain as much ground as we can."

"Prudence, Your Majesty," Maudyn said.

"Do you trust your scouts?"

"To report what they believe, without question. But—"

"Do they believe the way is clear?"

"Yet to push ahead, against a walled town, Your Majesty, so precipitately, and without the preparation—"

"You've made the preparation. We have a camp, do we not, on this side of the Lenúalim?"

"Absolutely so, Your Majesty."

"Dug in, canvassed, well set, and provided with a rampart."

"So we have, Your Majesty."

"Then the gods for Ylesuin and devil take all traitors! These are horses, are they not?"

"Indubitably, so, Your Majesty."

"And capable of setting us closer to the enemy faster than the oxen could."

"But without preparation, and wearing down their strength—"

"We'll rest in time. I've had a letter from my brother and one from Amefel, and I'll not wager our lives there's not *wizardry* in the stew—wizardry helping Tasmôrden deceive our scouts, make foul seem fair, right seem wrong . . . no disparagement of your scouts, none! Lewenbrook showed us all what wizardry can do on the field, and gods send we don't see the like of *that* again."

"Gods save us from that, Your Majesty."

"But it's a possibility. *Something* went on at Lewen field, something beyond Aséyneddin's wizardry, that Emuin never has told me . . . Tristen, gods save us, tried to explain, but he doesn't seem to know either, and *that* worries me."

He had never been so frank in council, not with the good Quinalt lords pricking up their ears and ready to bolt. But to Maudyn and to Anwyll, who had served with Tristen, he delivered the truth that, before, only the inmost circle of his advisors had dealt with. And Lord Maudyn heard it in attentive silence.

"Mauryl died," Cefwyn said, "and sent Tristen in his place. Tristen was there at Lewenbrook, but neither he nor Emuin seems to know what was *in* the cloud that rolled down the field. Tristen said he went to Ynefel during that battle—I don't know the truth of that. Emuin was lying abed in Henas'amef, and has no idea. And all along, everyone's assumed because we came off that field alive that Aséyneddin was the center of it all: that he's in hell and that's the end of it. I wonder."

"Lightning struck the Quinaltine," Maudyn said.

"That it did."

"A Sihhë coin turned up in the offering," Maudyn said further.

"*That* was a damnable piece of trickery! And it obscured the real fact."

"Which was, Your Majesty?"

"That *lightning* struck the roof of the Quinaltine! . . . and robbed me of Tristen, of Emuin, of Cevulirn, ultimately, all of Ryssand's connivance."

"The lightning surely wasn't Ryssand's doing," Maudyn said.

"That's the point, isn't it? The lightning was something Ryssand couldn't manage. But it happened, and damned inconvenient of it to hit there and not the Bryalt shrine, wasn't it?"

It was too far remote from the lives of ordinary men. Lord Maudyn regarded him as if willing to agree with his king, but unsure to which proposition he should agree.

"I suppose so," Maudyn said.

"It stole Tristen from me. Emuin would warn me that was no accident. Do you think Tasmôrden can move the lightning?"

"I have no knowledge of Tasmôrden himself, except as an earl of Elwynor, a traitor to his lord . . ."

"Exactly! Exactly so. No knowledge of the man except as an earl among other earls, a traitor among other traitors, no special gifts, no repute, no great allegiance among the Elwynim, would you say?"

"He pays his troops. He hires brigands."

"The Saendal. And pays them with the goods they loot from *Elwynim* they've attacked. Is this a man to inspire loyalty? Is this a king?"

"I would say not, Your Majesty."

"I would say not, as well. No king, no great man, no man loved by the people . . . would you not say a wizard, if he devoted himself to lead his own people to war, might not . . ." Cefwyn waggled the fingers of his off hand, Danvy's reins lying in the other. ". . . *conjure* better?"

"Master Emuin hardly fits the model."

"Ah. Master Emuin. Mauryl. Leave aside Tristen. He's his own creature. But wizards, now!"

"I don't follow Your Majesty."

"The Sihhë-lords ruled. Ruled, with an iron hand. But do you see ambition in Emuin? Did you see it in Mauryl Gestaurien?"

"Kingmaker, they called Mauryl. And Kingsbane."

"But did you see him rule?"

"I saw the man not at all, Your Majesty."

"You see?"

"I don't see, Your Majesty."

"He didn't rule. Nor would Emuin. Gods, you couldn't persuade him to be king if you tossed in a shelf of books and a wagonload of parchment . . . when would a wizard practice his craft, if he ruled?"

"The Sihhë ruled."

"But that's just the point. The Sihhë don't have to study. *Tristen* doesn't have to study." The conclusions poured in on him like a fall of stars from the heavens—or levin bolts on a priestly roof. "Wizards spend their whole lives at it. So if Tasmôrden's sotted in Ilefínian and has to hire his soldiers, because the peasantry's run to Amefel and the other lords are in hiding, such as survive—is this wizardry? If I were a wizard, I'd do better than hire my troops. I'd bespell them to adore me."

"Yet does Emuin, Your Majesty, improve Ryssand?"

"I don't think it occurs to him to improve Ryssand."

"I think he would do what he could."

"Yet what he can do is limited by what he *will* do, and what he *will* do is bounded in the stars, and books, and charts, and seas of ink. He's the greatest wizard left alive, and I'd have him improve Ryssand, yes, if Emuin would, or could. On that score I know something, and the answer is that he can't, not really, not directly, not so a man couldn't rise up and march contrary to wizardry, else what chance would we have stood at Lewenbrook? Can you riddle me that?"

"I daresay," Maudyn said in a quiet voice, and by now they were coming among the tents of Maudyn's settled camp. "I daresay Your Majesty understands more of that than I do."

"Take it for the truth! There was no going into that shadow if a man didn't believe he could, and did, and those that went under it, died; but those that faced it never could have faced it except that cold iron and shed blood do avail something, sir, I swear they do. And I know by all the signs I see in the sky there's more than cold iron at work against me. I'm not mad. I see the trouble among us, and I see the lords who served my father acting like fools, and believing a man who can't charm his own peasantry into taking the field for him."

"I don't understand," Maudyn said.

"Wizard-work doesn't rule. Mauryl was King*maker*, not a king. Emuin doesn't rule. Wizards *don't*. What they want is something more than earldoms."

"And what is that, Your Majesty?"

"That's the question, isn't it? What do they want? What does Emuin want?" What did Mauryl want when he sent me Tristen? That was the silent question, the one he failed to pose for Maudyn and Anwyll, the one he posed himself alone: *Tristen* himself was that puzzle, Tristen who could scarcely fend for himself, now at the head of the southern army.

Tristen armored in black, on a black horse, his gift, and attended by that damned bird and a flock of pigeons . . . what did *he* want?

That was one thing. What Mauryl might have wanted was another matter: Mauryl was an ally of convenience and a wizard's evident frustration with his Sihhë allies . . . or that thin blood to which the line had dwindled.

To prevent this *Hasufin Heltain* having any success: that was the evidence of Lewenbrook. He had no illusions it was any love of the Marhanen or fear for his continuance.

And what had happened, but this damned bolt of lightning that had sent Tristen from him, by his own order.

Cevulirn had gone.

Then Nevris . . . and Idrys. And now he was alone, between these two, Maudyn and Anwyll, good men, both; alone, with his guards. Alone, with the lords of the north . . . and Ryssand.

Mauryl had sent Tristen, Emuin had received him.

And what did this conspiracy of wizards want? What had it ever wanted? Something with which Tristen would agree?

If it was the calamity of the house of Marhanen, he much doubted Tristen would consent to it.

He was aware of silence around him, silence of his companions as well as his guards.

"You wonder what I *do* think?"

"If it please Your Majesty to say."

"Tasmôrden's no wizard, but I'll lay odds someone is, within his court, someone who doesn't care a fig for Tasmôrden, whether he lives or dies." Tristen's fortified the Quinaltine, he thought to himself, with a little chill. He expects something: bloody hell, half a year ago he said there was something wrong about the place.

Aloud he said, to Maudyn and Anwyll: "And if wizards are in it, we've wizardry on *our* side. Amefel and all the company of the south is at our left hand, if only we both ride past that wedge of rock that divides us one from the other."

"To join with Tristen, then," Lord Maudyn said.

"To join with the south if we can. If our enemy stands back that long." It came to him while he said it that the moment advantage shifted to one strategy or the other, wizardry would incline itself to use that advantage: if he tried to meet Tristen, then opposing wizardry would attempt to prevent him . . . and where it worked, men might bleed for it, in great numbers.

"And if not, Your Majesty?"

"If not . . ." Cefwyn looked at Anwyll, who as an undercaptain had offered not a word during all of this. "What do *you* think,

Captain? You've dealt with the Lord of Amefel, latest. What do you expect of him?"

"That he will not desert Your Majesty," Anwyll said, and seemed to hold thoughts back, in diffidence or perhaps in knowledge of Tristen. What he held back seemed likely to exceed what he said.

"And does he remain true to us?" he asked Anwyll.

Anwyll's gaze flashed to him, wary as a hunted creature's.

"Does he?" He did not doubt. He refused to doubt. "I think so. I think so." He set Danvy to a quicker pace. They passed beyond the camp, and he relayed orders to Maudyn. "Your men to hold this ground, come what may."

"Shall we let Ryssand pass?"

There was the question, the question whether one province of Ylesuin should fight another. And that was, indeed, one answer to the challenge: set Maudyn as his rear guard, against his own troops.

"Let him pass," Cefwyn said. "Let him have his way for now. There'll be the day, not so long from now."

They had passed the camp and led on, so that all the men and vehicles behind them would follow.

They were on the march and would proceed a day's march north and west, with the blind hills to their left and a traitor at their backs.

"Ryssand can stew and fret," he added, "but it won't get him past the ox teams in the woods."

CHAPTER 2

Wind tore the morning's white clouds to ragged gray rags by noon, rain threatening but never falling. *Wizardry?* Crissand asked silently, with a worried look, knowing Tristen wished them fair weather, and Tristen refused to agree or disagree: whatever power willed storms to oppose his wishes seemed less mindful opposition than a negligent contrariness, a surly, preoccupied opposition in the north not even caring that it spilled into the heavens for all to see.

Worse thought, that power husbanded its self-restraint, not its strength, as if to hold back and shape its force was a greater effort than to loose it.

Emuin struggled with times and seasons and nudged, rather than commanded, his designs into the grand flow of nature. Emuin moved by knowledge and plan.

Hasufin had learned of Mauryl, before he turned to self-will and attempted to overthrow nature. Mauryl was a wizard. What he could teach was wizardry: all Mauryl's charts, all Emuin's, all those notes, calculations and records . . . that was wizardry.

This, he began to fear . . . this negligent, careless force . . . was not.

They moved through a last descent of hills toward the river, wending down a last terrace of that gray stone so frequent in the district, and then the road tended generally down a pitch that, around a hill, would bring them to the site of what they had used to call Anwyll's camp, on the river.

They were in the district of Anas Mallorn. And of that village and of all the villages of the district, they saw occasional traces as they rode, the droppings of sheep, the stray bit of wool at the edge of a thicket, but they never caught sight of flocks or shepherds: Tristen had noticed that fact and had pondered it even before Uwen remarked on the vacancy of the land.

"Not a sheep from here to the river," Uwen said. "So's the shepherds has the smell o' war, an' ain't havin' their flocks for soldiers' suppers, no. They've seen too much comin' an' goin' of armies hereabouts in recent years."

And Crissand, whose own lands depended primarily on the herding of sheep, nodded. "They'll be high in the hills," he said, lifting his eyes toward the rugged land to the east, that obdurate rock that had no easy passage except the river . . . and how even the Lenúalim had won its passage down to the sea was a distracting wonder.

Had the mountain split for it?

Had ancient magic made a way . . . or Efanor's hitherto silent gods commanded it?

His mind even at this time of urgency hared off onto such tracks, and followed then a forbidden course, wondering how Idrys fared.

That, he would not wonder, not when he had been thinking of their enemy.

The gray space risked too much. What came and went there flitted, skipped, was there and gone again. The gray clouds that had appeared tore to wisps in the heavens and went to nothing with disquieting swiftness. The men noticed, and pointed aloft.

Not a wizard: his thoughts flew back to that uncomfortable suspicion.

Even sorcerors worked a sort of wizardry. Such had been Hasufin Heltain, such he still was, if anything still survived.

But if it was within a wizard's ability to so disturb the weather as this, it was not possible for a wizard then to ignore it as trivial, or to change his mind and change the weather to something else.

Did Emuin know that this force existed? Had Emuin known that something this swiftly-changing opposed them, and never told him?

Mauryl had failed a contest with his own student, Hasufin, and the long-ago folk of Galasien had fallen under Hasufin's rule for a time . . . until Mauryl had made the long journey north to the ice, to the Hafsandyr where the Sihhë dwelled. The tales were not, as he had heard, that Mauryl had Called the Sihhë south, but that Mauryl had gone to them to persuade them south.

And what lay there, in the frozen reaches of the mountains that Mauryl must respect, but magic: and why had only five met him, five sole occupants, as legend said, of one fortress? He could all but see those walls, black and severe against the mountains and the ice.

And where were the fields and the crops, the sheep and the people in this vision?

Had the Sihhë-lords not wives and children and homes to leave?

He could not remember. He could not gather that out of the mists of memory even with effort, whether there had been women, or children, or what had sustained the Sihhë in that frozen, high keep.

Yet Men said that *he* was Sihhë, and he bled, and feared, and did other things that Men did.

He did things, however, that Men and wizards did not do, and saw things they did not see, and had read the Book, and knew he had written it, though it was Barrakkêth's own hand, the first of the Sihhë-lords. It had wanted wizardry and cleverness to read that mirror-written writing . . . wizardry, but not all wizardry; trickery such as Men used, but not all trickery: a mirror and the light of the gray space. In that much . . . had not he done what any wizard could do?

Nothing was simple: wizardry and sorcery and magic commingled, and two of those three depended on times and seasons; the second was the perverted use of the first; the third was innate in those who had it—

And if wizardry had a dark mirror . . .

Might *magic* have one?

Why had Mauryl *gone* to the north rather than speaking to the Sihhë at a distance, as he was sure Mauryl had known how to do?

And how had he gone? By roads? And if by ordinary roads, fearing the ascendancy of his enemy, *why* had it taken five Sihhë-lords coming back with him to overthrow the rule of one mere student of Mauryl Gestaurien—Mauryl, whom all the Men he knew called the greatest and oldest of wizards?

What indeed had Mauryl and the five Sihhë had to face in the south?

Hasufin? The might of old Galasien arrayed against Mauryl?

"Strays is apt to end in stewpots," Uwen was saying, regarding sheep and pigs. "Even wi' the best of soldiers . . . and there's that ragtag lot that's come 'mongst Aeself's lads, who ain't themselves come with wagons nor supply. It ain't sayin' there ain't some Elwynim up in the hills even now, bands not wantin' to join Aeself's lot, not desirous of goin' home, neither. The war's gone one way an' another in Elwynor, and that don't lead all the captains to be friends of one another, nor to trust comin' into Aeself's camp, even if they wasn't ever Tasmôrden's men."

"I don't see any there," Tristen murmured, for to his awareness the hills rising in the east were barren of men and sheep, the same. "The people have fled, if they were able, farther to the south. It was hungry men that came to raid Aeself's camp, and the Lady of Emwy didn't let them in.—But Aeself's moved," he said, for his awareness of the land flared dangerously wide for a moment, a lightning stroke of a wish that lit the landscape all around him. In fear he stifled that vision and made himself see the land between his horse's ears, the road in front of him, the company on either side.

"Gods bless," Uwen muttered. "Moved, ye say?"

"I sent Cevulirn's men by this road," Tristen recalled, "while we visited Aeself: I haven't been this far toward the river since Cevulirn and I traveled this road . . . and all the land is empty now. The people have gone to Drusenan's wall, or they've gone to the south, none toward the river, none toward the hills."

"They wouldn't," Crissand said somberly. "The hills to the east are for bandits and outlaws."

"There aren't any of those there, now, either."

"Taken hire wi' Tasmôrden," Uwen said. "*There's* a sorry way t' clean th' land of bandits."

"Taken hire with Tasmôrden right along with the Aswydd servants," Crissand said. "Every outpouring of Heryn's court is over there, and every common cutthroat from our woods. It's our sins that wait across the river."

"And Elwynor's," Tristen said, for it seemed to him that was the case . . . that the timid had fled and the strong had chosen sides, the strong good men being beaten time and time again and pulled this way and that by successive claimants to the Regency, until this day, that the best men were a small band in Aeself's hands and the worst were an army sacking Ilefínian.

"And Elwynor's," Crissand agreed with him, and added, a moment later: "Gods save Her Grace."

"Amen to that," Uwen said. "As she won't have an easy reign when she has 'er kingdom."

Crissand said nothing to that. The gray space was troubled for a moment, and troubled in the way not of a wizard thinking secret thoughts, but troubled as it grew troubled when words rang wrong. And everything Uwen had said suddenly rang wrong, out of joint with what was now in motion. Crissand had not meant *gods save Her Grace* as a benison, only as a commiseration, as if their positions were equivalent . . . it seemed, suddenly and for no reason, true.

How? Tristen asked himself. How was Crissand's state balanced

with Ninévrisë's within things-as-they-were? That they both were bereft of fathers?

—That they both were, in a sense, heirs to thrones and kingdom,
but not crowned?

Therein, perhaps, the Unity of Things that wizardry so loved and
through which it found its power.

Unity of Things, Unity of Direction, Unity of Time . . .

The three were all met, in those two. And a piece of the world
as it ought to be went into place like a sword into its scabbard, a
weapon ready to his hand.

But in the beginning, Mauryl had called down five Sihhë to help
him, not one.

And Mauryl had overthrown the last faint trace of a Sihhë blood
dilute with generations among Men, finding in the last of them, as
in the first, no model of virtue.

Mauryl had set a Man in power, the Marhanen, to bridge the
gap.

But in the right season, consulting the heavens, Mauryl had called
him into his study, born of fire and a wizard's wishes—Mauryl had
declared him lacking, and sent him forth into the world, all the same.

What had Mauryl calculated he would be . . . that he had not
been?

All Mauryl's papers and parchments had fallen prey to the elements and the vagrant winds at the last. There was no record

And if he had been Barrakkêth, why did it not Unfold to him
what that enemy was, and what it was called, and how to defeat it?
He cudgeled his mind, battered at its walls, but, seeking a name for
his fears, he could think of nothing at all, it was so opposed to all
he understood. He could not go near it. It was as if he could grasp
it, he would inevitably contain it and be changed by it, and he could
not, *would* not accept it within himself . . . nameless it remained
and it would not Unfold to him.

Five Sihhë, without wives, without children . . . without fields or
flocks: it was no kingdom such as Ylesuin: it was contained in one
fortress, a gathering of those with magic inborn, having nothing to
do with Galasien or Mauryl, nothing at all . . . except Mauryl's
appeal to magic, where wizardry went awry.

And whatever might have moved the Sihhë-lords to gather their
resources and come south, abandoning all purpose but one? What
lure but curiosity could move them?

Surely something greater than curiosity had drawn them south
to change the world.

He tested all around the edges of that idea, to see whether there might have been more than five Sihhë, or even whether there might still be, but all that seemed in any sense to Unfold to him was a surety that five was the sum of them, that the Hafsandyr had raised a fortress against some great ill, and that there was enough of Men in the nature of the Sihhë that they had left children in the world.

But where had they gone, one by one? Had they died as Men died?

Or had they wandered across the Edge in the gray space and joined the Shadows that way, as Uleman of Elwynor had gone? Was *that* the darkness he recalled at the foundation of everything?

If he had ever died, the memory of death eluded him. If he had met defeat, he had never recalled it. If he had loved a woman of the race of Men, he had no memory of it. There was danger, he suspected, in slipping too far back, and remembering too much, and becoming bound to it.

Yet there was danger in not knowing, too, insofar as he had weaknesses. Of harm he had dealt with since Lewenbrook, he suspected it was Hasufin who had moved Cuthan, and Orien. It was Hasufin who had attempted to steal his way among Men, and it was surely Hasufin's wizard-work that had moved the archivist, for more than any other thief, principally a wizard would want to know the things hinted at in Mauryl's letters, would seek after any ragtag piece of knowledge, something that might fix only one date, one hour, to make clear all the others, and find a way into Mauryl's workings to threaten him. Indeed, wizardry could harm him, as wizardry had Called him.

But to him, what were hours and times? To him and, he thought, to all the Sihhë, the whole of the world and the life within it flowed like a river, and moved with a sure power he felt rather than knew. What he did was no matter of charts, and plans: it was like sliding on the snow, like that glorious morning when they had come out of doors and men had gone skidding on the steps. That was the feeling he had when he tried to move the weather. So many things changed at once there was no time to ask what had changed: he simply changed more of them, until for one glorious moment he had his balance . . . that was what it was to work a great magic. The little changes just happened, wordlessly, soundlessly, fecklessly; he shed them as he shed raindrops, and such, he feared, was his enemy.

He knew to his regret how great a fear he had evoked in master Emuin at first meeting; he knew how he must still drive Emuin to distraction . . . and he deeply regretted all along having made the old man's calculations so difficult. He had never completely understood what a trial he had been. Now he did know, and knew how brave Emuin was, and how very, very skilled, to have kept him in close rein. With all his heart he wished the old man well . . . wished well all the company that rode behind him, continually, as the sun beat down on them and the world went on as orderly as its folk knew how, in spite of the mischief magic might do.

And of all those near him, only Crissand was completely aware of the frantic racing of his thoughts, and did not interfere or question or pursue him, was not appalled at him—only bore him up with the wings of his selfless, reckless will. It was love that made Crissand a safe companion for him, and adoration that kept Crissand staunch and unquestioning in his tumble of thoughts and this reckless exploration of the world. And that gave him courage when his own courage faltered and when that Edge seemed all too close.

—*I'm here, Crissand said, when he no more than thought of him. I don't understand all the things you say. But I'm here.*

—*I've never doubted, Tristen said. I don't doubt you. Nor ever shall.*

So he said to Crissand as the descent continued around that long hill, and in that moment they had had their first sight of the river and of the camp to the left . . . such as remained. Where once rows upon rows of tents had stood on that flat expanse was now a flat scar of bare, trampled earth. Where Cevulirn and the lords of the south had camped, five tents remained in that trampled desolation, with a handful of horses.

But the bridge that Tristen had last seen as a ruin spanned the dark flood of the Lenúalim with stout timbers and the substance of Cevulirn's good work.

"Nary a soul stirrin'," Uwen muttered at the sight, "nor any boats in sight. Which should be good."

Beyond any doubt of his, Cevulirn had crossed the river and set up camp on that far side, a base from which they might advance north.

But whether Idrys had found one of Sovrag's boats to carry him east was still in question.

They left the road and set out across the bare earth toward those remaining tents, but before they had reached them a handful of Ivanim came out and stood waiting to give them all courtesies.

"Is Lord Cevulirn across the river?" was Tristen's first question, from horseback. "And have you seen the Lord Commander?"

"Our lord and the army have their camp just the other side," the seniormost Ivanim said cheerfully, a man with a scarred chin and gray in his hair. "And the Lord Commander's sailed on with Sovrag's men, upriver, on account of your word, Your Grace, as we hope did come from you."

"It did." Idrys was a man hard to refuse, and might have given Cevulirn himself qualms in his haste to be on eastward, but that Idrys had found passage and was on his way to Cefwyn was a vast relief.

Yet the instant he said that, and thought that Idrys was safe, an uneasy feeling still ran through the gray space, the flitting of a thought that passed him in the same way he was aware of creatures in the woods and men around him. It came to him that he had not seen Owl for some time, and that they were at an edge, of a kind, here on the river shore.

Here was where the war began, and here was where he committed himself and other men to reach Cefwyn and keep his pledge to Her Grace.

Most of all . . . for a moment he could not draw his breath . . . ahead was the reason Mauryl had called him into the world, and he was sure now as at any Unfolding that a rebellious student was not the enemy that had driven Mauryl to the Hafsandyr or the Sihhë to leave their fortress in the high mountains.

He did not detect the danger as near them, nor was it the sort of threat that would have had him order shields uncased and the warhorses saddled. But danger there was. Their camp was on the other side of the river, and what he felt urged him to move on and quickly. It Unfolded to him not as a Word or a slight illumination but as a stroke of lightning across all the heavens, the ultimate reason for all Mauryl had done.

"Good day," he remembered to say, however, recalling Men and their courtesies and their due with the same awkwardness he had felt in Cefwyn's court. "Thank you."

Then he turned red Gery and rode at an easy pace toward the bridge, with Uwen and Crissand close on his heels and the company falling in behind them. The banners streamed past on the right as the bearers sought to get them to the fore just before the three of them rode onto the bridge, and when they had climbed up the slanting approach and onto the rough, newly planed logs, the horses went warily, looking askance at the broad current of the Lenúalim and the height of the span, the like of which they had not met. The wind blew unrestrained here. The thunder of so many riders behind them, even slow-moving and deliberate, drowned the rush of the river under the wooden spans.

"Never crossed the like in m' life," Uwen put it, "nor's Gia. This is a grand work, this."

"Grand work, indeed," Crissand said.

And at the end of the bridge, before they were halfway across: a handful of men stood forth from the woods, occupying the end of the bridge, waving to them, seeing the banners and signaling them, if they had failed to ask at the camp, that it was Lord Cevulirn's men on the far side.

"Welcome!" they said. "Well come, indeed. Go on, go on, our lord will expect you!"

They passed from that meeting into the woods, on a road long unused until the recent passage of oxen and horses. Last year's weeds, brown and limp from melted snows, lay trampled into the mire by shod hooves and pressed into the ruts left by cart wheels. Small brush was crushed down and broken, while the new track deviated around the occasional stout sapling that had sprung up in the old roadway, and others were hacked half through at the root, bent flat, so the carts could go over them.

And at the end of that course was the first of the gray-stone hills this side of the river, wooded and brushy and guarded by some furtive presence atop it: Tristen felt it rather than saw.

"Lanfarnessemen," he said to Uwen, directing him with a shift of his eyes, and Uwen looked up at the nearer hill. At that, the presence ebbed away, shy as any deer: it was a danger not to them, but to their enemies.

Just beyond that stony, forested outcrop, the brush gave way to brown, grassy meadow, and there white canvas had bloomed into a sizable camp, yet a discreet one, too, a surprise to come upon just past the forest and between the hills, and warded by watchers on the heights.

And still that presence on the hill tracked them, watching not them, perhaps, but any action that might oppose them. Intruders under any strange banner would surely have met arrows flying thick and fast: Lanfarnesse rangers seldom used presence-betraying canvas—but they were there. Their Heron banner flew with the Wheel of Imor and the White Horse of Ivanor and the Wolf of Olmern in the heart of the camp, announcing the presence of Pelumer with Umanon and Cevulirn and Sovrag in this gathering . . . welcome sight.

A man ran ahead of them, and told an officer, and that man hurried into the centermost tent as they rode up the aisle of this gathering of tents. Cevulirn came out with Umanon, and Pelumer came close behind, all cheerfully welcoming them in.

"His Grace's banners wi' the rest," Uwen ordered the banner-bearers, and smartly then the banner-bearers dismounted and with manful efforts drove the sharp iron heels of the banners deep into the soft earth, one after the other, until the Eagle and the several standards stood with the others, the Tower Crowned and Crissand's among them.

Tristen dismounted, and of a sudden a night without sleep and the long day in the saddle caught him unawares, sending the world to shades of gray and causing him to hold his saddle leathers a moment as his feet met the ground. He tried to wish his sight clear again, but it was as if the gray insisted, and closed around him, a chute down which it was easy to fall.

But Uwen was there, a hand to his elbow, and Cevulirn named a man to guide the Amefin to their tents, which were pitched and ready for them, and a hot meal besides, while Crissand's voice in Tristen's left ear assured him he would personally see to the guard.

"Go in, my lord, rest."

"There's no rest," Tristen said, and drew a breath and managed to see the camp again, how it stretched off into the trees beyond, the horse pickets out under the branches, under the watchful eye of the rangers . . . he could not miss that presence, as he was aware of every heart that beat within the camp, the converse of men-at-arms, low and wondering at his lapse.

There was nothing so wrong with the place, Tristen said to himself; it was simply fatigue. Indeed the offer of a good meal and a rest from riding came very welcome . . . he might rid himself of the armor for a brief while . . . might sit with friends, a privilege rare in the world, and rarer still on the edge of losing everything. So much . . . so very much he loved; and it all seemed fragile at this moment, on the edge of the enemy's attention.

He drew a breath. He summoned his faculties away from that brink, and steadied himself away from Uwen's supporting hand. He gathered up the threads of things he had meant to say, and walked, and gathered strength with every step

"The Lord Commander," he was able to say to the other lords as he ducked through the tent flap, "brought Her Grace to Henas'amef, for safety's sake. Did he tell you why?"

"Not two words," Cevulirn said, "except it was your bidding . . ."

Another presence had joined them, filling the tent door when Tristen turned about, and that was Sovrag himself.

"Aye," the river lord said. "And all full of mystery he were, an' if the wind hadn't served, why, damn, he'd have driven them lads to row 'im there. What's toward?"

"Cefwyn's in danger." Words poured out of him, and he wished to sit down, but found nowhere. "One of Ryssand's men is beside him and Cefwyn doesn't know."

That brought somber looks.

"Gods save the Marhanen, then," Umanon said. "And a good wind to the Lord Commander's sails."

"So I wish," Tristen said in all earnestness. "And wish it twice and three times. Ryssand's coming to the muster, but he means no good to Cefwyn. Tasmôrden's promised him part of Elwynor for his own if he takes the crown."

"I should have stayed at court," Cevulirn said. "I might have stopped this."

Tristen shook his head. "Wizardry's in question. It reached past all of us."

"We can't reach him," Umanon said. "Gods speed the Lord Commander, indeed."

"Aye," came from Sovrag and Pelumer, with a nodding of heads.

"What says Amefel?" Cevulirn asked, grim-faced and with his arms folded. "If it's to ride this hour, we're ready."

"I'm less and less sure I know," Tristen said in utmost honesty, for Owl was not to be found, and had shied from him—yet he knew nothing to do but forge ahead with the plans they had. "But we have to move. There's no time to sit here."

"Late afternoon now, but men and horses well rested," Cevulirn said. "We can give the order."

"To march at night?" Umanon asked dubiously.

"To move as far up the road as we can," Tristen said. "I can wish winds on the river, but stone is stone and the hills won't move for us. We have to go closer. Tasmôrden surely won't rely only on Ryssand."

"No one should rely on Ryssand," Pelumer said.

It was true. And it was true, after all, that the hills might move, but they were stone and sluggish things and could not change precipitately. Tristen drew in a breath, suddenly apprehending a power rising out of the land and a power rising within him, different than the weary body that housed it. He felt he could scarcely move, scarcely draw breath without breaking lives and men, and yet the ones he would strike . . . were not in his reach. Only friends were. A shield stretched across the north and the west, subtle, and containing men, but it was not men. It was their enemy Tasmôrden, but Tasmôrden was not all of it.

He felt an opposing magic, felt it slip like a step on ice, one matched against the other, and like a third lightning stroke he knew he had met the enemy, met, and slid aside, unwilling to engage.

"Ilefínian," he said on a breath. "*Ilefínian!* That's his place of power in this world, and from it he draws his strength. The closer he is to it, the stronger he will be."

"Tasmôrden?" Pelumer asked him.

"Yes, Tasmôrden. But that's not all." He must sit down, or fall down, and groped blindly after the tent pole, but met instead Uwen's arm, and Crissand's.

"My lord," Crissand said. "What's wrong?"

Owl. Owl was in danger, winging through the woods, diving from left to right, through the trees, with something streaking after him, dark, and broad, and filling the woods.

"Sit, sit down, my lord."

He obeyed, calling Owl with all his might, and Owl heard him. Owl came, through a place of blue light and rustling wings. Owl came as he had come to the hall at wintertide, and burst back into the world again. A tilted view of tents came to him, an evening sun, and he swayed where he sat, then let go the vision.

"Good lovin' gods!" Uwen said, for Owl flew through the door in a buffet of wings, dived past Cevulirn, and hit the canvas wall in a flapping lump that slid to the floor.

Owl gathered himself immediately and fluffed his feathers into order.

A narrow escape, Tristen said to himself, and offered his arm. Owl ducked his head, gave a great flap of blunt wings, and managed to reach him, to settle on his arm, ruffling and settling his feathers.

There was silence all around. Tristen looked up at a circle of dismayed faces.

" 'E all right?" Uwen asked, in that deep silence of the lords of the south.

"He's well." Tristen stroked Owl's breast feathers, and caught a resentful look of two marigold eyes at close range that held his gaze. He knew what Owl had fled, yet had no idea in what words to tell the rest of these men, even Uwen.

"Let him rest," Crissand said.

"Break camp," Tristen said. He saw Uwen's unhappy look, saw the worry on Crissand's face and others'. "There's no rest here."

"Then we break camp," Cevulirn said. "Do as he says." To another man, one of his guards, Cevulirn said, "Food and drink for all these men, and Lord Tristen, whatever we can provide until we get to horse."

"Is it a fight comin'?" Sovrag asked, perplexed as the rest. "Give me what'll yield to an axe, an' I'm ready."

"There's a great deal that will yield to it," Tristen assured him, and reached out for all the rest of them. "I may not ride with you all the way. I don't know. If I can't be there when the time comes, I set Cevulirn in charge. Our enemy won't make the mistake with me he made at Lewenbrook. What comes won't be just at us. It's not one enemy."

"Is it *that* one?" Cevulirn asked in dismay. "The ghost at Lewen field?"

"More than that," Tristen said, uneasy in naming entirely what Unfolded to him, as if by never saying it he could dispell it. Yet he must say it. "It wasn't only Hasufin who brought down Ynefel. And it wasn't only Hasufin who drove Mauryl north to find the Sihhë-lords." Even as he said it he saw icy mountains and a wizard much younger in those days, riding through trackless snow. He saw a great black height, and a fortress of dark stone, and a hall without servants. He felt the cold, and recalled the clean sting of the north wind on his face and the icy stone through the soles of his boots.

He had known the battlements, and all the chambers under his feet; and he had known before Mauryl came what Mauryl would say . . . all these things, all at once. He longed for Mauryl's face, the word, the kindness . . . he watched that lonely figure leaning on the wind beneath his walls, and yearned with all his heart to give the old man at once what he had come to find.

But that was now. *Then* he had foreknown the quest itself, and the middle-aged wizard at his gates.

He knew the peace of the ice, and the company of his fellows. They were only five, five who bore the gift and the curse of magic, and foreknew this wizard's seeking them.

He drew a deep, ice-edged breath, and saw through the years.

" 'Ere, m'lord." Uwen had his arm.

"Ale," Sovrag said. "The lad's seen a haunt, is what."

He was no longer in that place of black stone. He sat beneath a canvas roof, with canvas under him and the lords of the south serving him with their own hands. Uwen set his hands on his shoulders, saying, "Brace up, m'lord, there's a lad, come, take a sip, take a breath."

"I saw the Hafsandyr," Tristen said in the breath of a voice he commanded. "I saw the Fortress of Mists." He did not know how he knew its name, but that was the fortress the Sihhë had held in the far northern mountains, the Qenes, in the language they shared with Mauryl, far, far from Elwynor. He found Unfolding to him a host of things nameless and thoughts unthinkable in the language of Ylesuin and Elwynor, things his hand had written in that small Book he had given to the fire, the night before Lewenbrook.

As now . . . he recalled the north, and the black peaks crowned with ice, and the rap of a wizard's staff against the gates.

Once.

Twice.

Magical thrice.

He ceased to breathe, and then must, and saw all the faces of his friends as strangers' faces, perhaps enemies' faces, even Uwen's.

Had he known these folk? Had he foreseen them?

Then he was mortally afraid, and reached for Uwen's hand and gripped it as Uwen gripped his, until bone ached and flesh turned white-edge. He looked into Uwen's grizzled face and dark eyes and saw a Man, and a good man, and the one above all others whose voice could Call him.

"Speak to me," he begged Uwen. "Say anything at all."

"Ye're me dear lad," Uwen said. "An' my lord, and I'll have no other. Steady. Take a breath. There's a lad."

"I'm here," he said, for those threads bound him to safety and let him draw breath. "I am here."

He knew Uwen would do his best to make sense of half answers, and he fought to leave that other place, to be unequivocally in the world of Men. He wished to make Uwen at least understand, and then Uwen would tell the others.

But another hand took his arm, and a faith as clear as the morning sun shone in that face, and out of those eyes.

"My lord," Crissand said, the aetheling, the foretold, and the long-remembered.

"I know he'll strike at Cefwyn," Tristen warned him. "And he'll strike at you."

"Tasmôrden?"

"Tasmôrden?" For a moment, the name was only sound, a sound bearing no relation to his fears, and once the name did achieve meaning, he shook his head in denial. Then on the next breath he realized: "Possibly. It's well possible, if Hasufin had his way about it, isn't it? Hasufin moved Tasmôrden so long as Hasufin was enough to move him. Whatever houses our enemy . . . it might be Tasmôrden, but more likely . . . more likely our enemy has no Shape in this world. Hasufin dealt with him. Hasufin brought him to Ynefel . . . but such Place in the world as he's claimed now, is never far from Ilefínian. Uleman didn't know the enemy's presence there. He only saw the rebels that rose against him. Orien didn't know he was speaking to her. She only heard Hasufin. I didn't know what brought down Ynefel. I only heard the Wind, as I heard it behind Hasufin, when he killed one of the birds; I only saw the Dark, when it rolled down on Lewen field."

"So we all saw the Dark," Uwen said. "Gods save us, this Wind and the Dark . . . Is that ahead of us?"

"It may be. It may. But Hasufin is a shell for it. He's all hollow, behind. Mauryl knew what Hasufin had listened to. That's why he called down the Sihhë to deal with it . . ."

"What d' ye say, lad?" Uwen had his hand on his shoulder, and pressed it hard, that voice, above all voices, commanding him to make clear the things he saw.

He struggled with words. But he found several. "Old. Very old. Hasufin listened to it in Galasien the way Orien listened to Hasufin in Henas'amef, with no better result."

"Summat *else*, ye say."

"Before Mauryl. Before Galasien's towers stood." He was aware of his gaze fixed on nothing, on darkness and deep, on the depths of Ynefel's foundations, the work of the master Builders, and the Masons who had laid the Lines. "They weren't content to observe the seasons, these old ones. They shaped Lines to master the Shadows, and make Seemings stand in the light of day." It too aptly described *him*. He was not unaware of the irony of his struggle against this darkness that Mauryl had fought. He had ridden so far and set all this in motion, mustered all these men, and now that he was called to ride for the very purpose of Mauryl's Summoning him, did he fall down in trembling and weakness? He was angry with himself, and afraid for the outcome for these men he loved, and took one deep breath after another until the shapes of the world came clear to his eyes, at least as far as a huddle of pale gray that hovered about him.

He clung to that sight. He sought to leave the reckoning of things insubstantial and the maze of gray that wanted his attention, and to shape that maze in substance, of lords of Men who stood for powers on the earth, and men-at-arms of flesh and bone who stood for the earthier, more common magic of hearth and fence and field.

Men ruled the earth now, and the Shadows obeyed the stones that Masons laid in rows on the land.

"I must face him," he said, for *him* was as apt as any word. It thought. It moved. It wished and worked and willed, and the Qenes stood *against* its wishing and working. He was sure of that. The Qenes, the work of master Masons, the home of Shadows and the fortress of the Shadow-lords: there all the powers within the earth held a Line that must not be broken.

He drew a calmer breath. Shadow-lord. *That* was the thing he was. That was *who* he was. The knowledge was no blazing noon of clear understanding. It was a moonrise in a still, cold night, gathering shadows into shapes, and Shadows into power.

—*Auld Syes, he said to the Queen of Shadows. Faithful lady. Cross the water. I need you. Come.*

"Tasmôrden?" Crissand asked, and he realized he had lost the thread of speech. "Is it Tasmôrden you mean, my lord? Or is it something less substantial we face?"

"Tasmôrden, if we can reach him in time. And Ryssand. Ryssand will be the hands and the feet of this attack. Should Cefwyn die, the army would break apart and fight each other, Maudyn against Corswyndam and Prichwarrin, on Elwynim soil. What then could we win?" Owl spread his wings, rowed against the air, settled again on his wrist. "But others must stop Ryssand. Idrys must stop him." And with that realization, the acknowledgment that he could not be in both places, the fatigue settled in full. "I'll sleep an hour, until we ride. Is there a place?"

"Here." The lords might regard him with misgivings, the one who had summoned them who now nodded like a man with too much ale, and after speaking nonsense, began to slip toward dreams. But one quiet, sure voice drew him with its slight wizard-gift, and gained his wide-wandering attention. "Rest. I'll attend the breaking of camp."

"Sir." He knew the name, then, in his distance from the world: Cevulirn would watch over all that had to be done and Uwen and Crissand would care for him, and so he let the two of them draw him to his feet and guide him.

"He ain't taken ill," Sovrag said in troubled tones. "He ain't fevered nor any such."

"Tired," Uwen said out of the gray mist in which the world of Men proceeded. "An' hearin' summat we don't hear. He's a'ready fightin' the fight we ain't come to, your lordship, an' scoutin' ahead of us, don't take it for aught less, beggin' your pardon."

"Gods bless," Umanon said solemnly, but seemed not to condemn him; and Pelumer's presence flitted close and offered comfort and a sense of stealth that Unfolded in all its skill.

. . . Like Emuin, who studied at his charts in Henas'amef, in his tower . . . subtle, and present without even paying close attention to him. Emuin was always doing something else, but he did many things constantly. It was very hard to evade him.

Ninévrisë was a whisper in the gray space, listening, Tristen thought, and wary of what was within her, and wary of that third presence, and the fourth, and the fifth and sixth, Tarien's son, and Tarien, and her sister Orien pacing the Lines of her confinement, as their brother continually attempted the greater Line of the lower hall.

The Aswydds would take any alliance that opposed their confinement. They would steal Elfwyn away with them if they could: that was always a risk, for as long as Tarien lived she had that tie to him . . . but Elfwyn seemed protected, loved, held.

In seething confusion the living mingled with the Shadows, all through the fortress at Hen Amas. Far to the west, within the Lines of Althalen, another Power quietly knew his daughter's presence in the land, knew, and welcomed, and waked to the growing danger of his people.

"My lord!" It was Crissand, returned from the rows of tents and men, aware of his drifting at the edge of the gray space. Crissand's concern flared brightly in the mists. Uwen was there to caution him, however, and Cevulirn steadied him, and the flame that burned so dangerously bright slowly ebbed to a flickering candle.

There was a guide, should he need one, a guide who could fly through any confusion.

. . . Owl swept close, a shadow across his sky, and winged past him, directing his attention northward. Here, Owl seemed to say. This way!

And with the crack of Mauryl's staff, he heard: Pay attention, boy!

Ilefínian . . . there was his battle. Owl drew him there, to where the enemy waited, urged him to leave the battle of Men to men, and abandon Cefwyn to his fate.

And in that mere wisp of an outcry against that notion Tristen knew he exposed his weakness to his enemy, and showed that enemy most clearly the way to his heart, if ever it had doubted it.

It was folly to have followed Owl here, utter, dangerous folly. He drew back from that place, to that flickering candle that was

Crissand's presence. He refused Owl's urging—for the first time in his presence in the world refused what his guide asked of him.

No purpose of wizards was worth Cefwyn's life. Nothing in the world was more precious to him than that. Cefwyn had banished him, severed him from the court, but entrusted him with all that was most precious to him: never had they been closer friends than now.

And could he knowingly ignore Cefwyn's peril? He could shake the mountains and the hills and will them to future courses . . . but he could not gain Cefwyn's attention, could not warn him, could not reach him, not with magic enough to shake the earth.

Cleverness, perhaps, would serve where magic failed.

His battle was joined now, in this very moment, and now he and his enemy alike drew back to consider one another, to reason out what was the feint and what was the true intent.

And Owl urged him northward, constantly northward, as if there were no other course.

As if there were no other course.

Back! he bade Owl, and: **Away!** he bade all advice from wizards, even Emuin, even Mauryl's Unfolding spell. Neither wizard had defeated the enemy. Mauryl had never seen clearly, never understood how little of Hasufin remained, how small a soul still yearned for life and worked at the edges of greater, more terrible ambition: he had had the knowledge to seek powers outside wizardry to repair the breach, but he could not himself repair what Hasufin had done.

Mauryl or Emuin singly or together could not win past what Hasufin had loosed, only delay its ascension.

Emuin would have had him learn the way of wizards, that being what Emuin understood, but, his greatest wisdom, Mauryl being Mauryl and not suffering foolishness easily . . . Mauryl had simply wished him to be, grow, learn . . . become what he could become. And that was the greatest spell of all.

He was not through. Not yet.

He knew, if he fell, Cefwyn would fall. If Cefwyn fell, it was for Emuin to steal Elfwyn away, cloak him in his subtle grayness, and carry on in whatever way he could.

And if he should fail, it was for Emuin to live as long as Mauryl, and learn what Mauryl had known, and Summon him from a second death . . .

—**No!** he heard Emuin protest, far and faintly. But from the Lady of Elwynor came a promise, a vow, a resolution that would fire the coldest heart.

"Time to move, lad," Uwen said, touching him, which even Crissand feared to do.

He opened his eyes on both sober faces and hoped, for he dared not wish, that there be no more to Unfold to him, no more revelations of the sort that opened the Qenes to his memory, and gave his heart the chill of lasting winter.

"The others is summat afraid," Uwen said, "seein' how ye was overcome. They'd take better heart if ye can rouse up an' hear a man, lad."

"I do hear," he said. His heart beat as if he had run Emuin's stairs . . . or the height of the web of stairs in Ynefel itself. But that beat was a comfortable feeling, and that remembered fear he understood. It was the creaks in the dark and the crack of thunder in the afternoons. It was the gray wash of rain and the perfect green leaf that blew and stayed against the stone.

It was hanging perilously from the parapets of the old tower and, stark naked and without shame, viewing the limits of the world upside down.

It was riding through the gates of Henas'amef, and meeting the aetheling, the Sun King, the Lord of Noon, as he was Lord of Shadows.

And he reached out and seized Crissand's hand in his, as he had held the aetheling once before from kneeling, as he had known—not only his friend, but his complement in the world of Men, a Man, and sighted in ways that Men knew. Crissand *saw* things, and had no magic in him to move the sunlit world to do as it ought . . . while *he* only learned the world of Men through others, and moving through the Lines on the earth, had the magic to overturn kingdoms.

Together . . . together they had a unity that only the enemy could challenge.

"That bird's scairt the men," Uwen said, "an' ain't let anybody into this tent, so's ye know, m'lord."

"Contrary creature." Tristen gathered himself to his feet, and found the weariness fallen away from him, not in any natural sense of having rested. His body had become lighter than his spirit, as if one held to the other very lightly. He was aware of Owl, just outside, and aware of creatures winging their way above the road, above the forest, not far, silly, fleet birds with the sheen of violet and green and gray about them, the colors of storm and twilight.

Go! he wished them in a sudden rush of strength. Fly!

Owl would not obey him, but these would, the vain, silly tenants of the ledges. They flew, and wheeled away toward the east.

"We shan't do what he wills," he said to Uwen and to Crissand. "He'll threaten Cefwyn. That's where he'll bring all his power to bear. So must we go there."

"Not to Ilefínian," Crissand interpreted him.

"Not to Ilefínian." Of a sudden his heart was as perilously light as his body. "Let him have his Place so long as he can hold it. I know mine."

And it was not a Place, as wizards understood a Place to be. It was the Oath he had sworn and the banner he had raised and the Men that surrounded him. Suddenly the tactics of the enemy were clear to him, to divide him from these things.

"North and east," he said to his friends, and strode out the door of the tent as if an hour before he had not fallen fainting before them all.

CHAPTER 3

Ere's that pesky bird!" Uwen exclaimed as a shadow passed them, and, indeed, Owl glided past, a petulant, difficult Owl, who had flown behind them and now was ahead, and off to the right hand again, off toward the hills, granting them only a brief sight of him.

So Tristen's own thoughts ranged out and abroad, following Owl for a time, searching the near woods. Owl was put out with him, perhaps, after he had refused Owl's leading, yet Owl still guided him, still spied out the territory ahead . . . Mauryl's, Tristen was convinced, a wisp of the Ynefel that had been, still bespelled and hard to catch and hold: direction, to urge him toward one purpose.

But he did not need Owl to move him forward, did not need Owl to extend his awareness in the world. He felt every small watcher and every bird aloft as if they brushed against him, and was reassured to feel that there was no hostile presence broken out in their immediate vicinity.

He thought he knew now where Cefwyn was, as the wedge of hills drove toward Ilefínian: he was to the east behind that stone barrier.

More, he knew where the enemy was, and knew with more and more certainty that the attack would come not at his magic-defended force . . . but at Cefwyn. If only Cefwyn would hold back and let him come at Ilefínian and deal with this threat as he could, but no, the Guelen lords must have their honor . . . and Cefwyn was deaf to magic as to wizardry, Cefwyn had sent away his one advisor who knew a wizard-sending when she heard it and knew when to regard what Uwen called premonitions. There might be others with minor gifts that might at least feel the currents of the gray space and mutter to their comrades in arms that they had this or that worry, but the question was whether their lords would believe . . . whether Cefwyn would if they brought their premonitions to him. It lent a Man a certain peace of mind, Tristen supposed, to ride through threats and terrors unhearing: it even lent a man a certain real protection, for he could not hear temptation and bad advice to be swayed by it, but it was no protection at all when power reached out with tangible results and brought down the lightning.

So it was his to make what speed his force could, without tents, the wagons left behind at the camp with a garrison of Imorim, Olmernmen, and a dozen Lanfarnesse rangers, men set to assure they had a bridge open if they needed to retreat. That was prudence, for the sake of the men he led, if matters went utterly wrong. Some might make it home.

But for the rest, down to the Imorim, even Umanon had resolved to bring his men along Ivanim-style, each man with his warhorse and his relief mount, his shieldman and packhorses, each man with his own supplies: beyond the habits of Guelenfolk: they came with only muted complaint, learning new ways, foraging in the meadows at their rests, making progress through woodland with their heavy horses and heavy armor faster than any heavy horse company had ever moved, so Umanon swore in his pride in them.

So Tristen rode, and so did Uwen, both of them armed after the Guelen fashion, in brigandine and plate. Dys and Cass, who were accustomed either to their paddocks or their exercises of war, were not accustomed to a long journey under saddle, and after their first burst of anticipation and high spirits, sulked along the brush-encroached road, the same as the Imorim horses. Owl's swooping appearances invariably drew a sharp lift of both massive heads, a flare of nostrils and a bunching of muscle, but Dys would give a disgruntled snort and Cass another, learning to disparage the sudden apparition out of the trees.

In the same way Crissand and his guard and the Amefin Guard, lighter-armed, rode sturdy crossbreds of Petelly's stamp, while the Ivanim light cavalry, near the rear, fretted at a far slower gait than their hot-blooded horses were accustomed to keep. With them, sore and swearing, rode Sovrag and his handful of house guard, armed with axes—intending to turn infantry the instant a fight was likely, and sore, limping at every rest: they endured, being no woodsmen, either, and accustomed to a deck underfoot, not an overgrown road, and not a saddle. The Lanfarnessemen, however, moved as they always did, which was to say no one saw them at all. Lord Pelumer, who rode a white horse among his light-mounted house guard, said they were both ahead and behind the column . . . out as far as the hills and as far south as the river and across it.

On that account no one, Pelumer swore, would surprise the column on the way, and because of them Tristen himself dared reach out a little farther than he might have dared: Pelumer's men were indeed within his awareness when he did so, furtive and quiet as the wild creatures of the woods, the badger and his like, who also knew their passage and themselves served as sentinels.

Their enemy waited, that was the impression he gathered, the breathlessness before storm, but to an unwary venturer there might appear nothing at all opposing them. And it hid something, he was not sure what: it hid something as Emuin could hide things, by creating a fuss elsewhere, by simply being silent.

That was the subtlety of what they faced: for as he apprehended now it was magic they faced, he could only think it was something like himself, whether cloaked in flesh or not . . . and increasingly, thinking of Orien's example, he asked himself how Hasufin had turned from Mauryl's student to Mauryl's bitter enemy.

He had met Hasufin. He had driven Hasufin in retreat, not without cost, but not so that he feared him in any second encounter. He had seen all his tricks, dismantled his wards, and of Hasufin he was not afraid.

Of what he had suspected in the Quinaltine . . . of that, he had been afraid.

Of what nameless fear had chased him through the mews, he had been afraid.

Of the wind at his windows, he had been afraid, the insidious Wind, against which he had warded the windows of the Zeide, as Mauryl had warded his, at Ynefel, warning him to be under the roof when darkness fell, when storm raged, when the wind blew.

It was not of rain and wind that a wizard of Mauryl's sort needed be afraid.

All along it had been something else whispering at night against the shutters.

And it was even possible Mauryl had not known what to call it, except as it turned Hasufin against him, and took his teachings and turned them, and took Hasufin's heart. Mauryl might not have known all he faced, but his remedy, to bring Galasien down, to bring down the Lines . . . and to invoke magic from the north . . .

More, to *gain* that help, which he did not think had come to everyone who sought it . . .

. . . to bring down the walls and the wards and the Lines, so that nothing of any great age persisted in the world . . . what did Mauryl think to do?

What were the faces in the walls of Ynefel but a sort of Shadow, bound to the Lines and the wards, protecting what became a fortress, from which Barrakkêth had ruled . . . had redrawn its Lines, made them to stand against all its enemies . . . but not everything had Barrakkêth redrawn. He had laid down the Lines of Althalen, built the Wall at Modeyneth.

But Men called the Quinaltine hill their own, and defended it, war after war, until a great fortress grew there, and all those Shadows went into the earth.

He drew a great breath. For a moment to his eyes he could see Ynefel as it had been. He could see the land as it had been when there was no Ylesuin and when Elwynor's name was Meliseriedd, and a chill breathed over his nape.

He led Men not all of whom were deaf: Cevulirn and Crissand were very close to him no matter where they rode, the one half their column distant and the other at his very knee, no difference at all. They maintained a quiet, wary presence, learning, but not, perhaps, apprehending all he feared. They were in the greatest danger, and it wrung his heart that he could find no words that would both tell them and restrain them from the curiosity that would plunge them over the brink into a fight they could not win.

All the friends he loved and most regarded were in danger. Every one of them was in danger of his life; but the wizard-gifted went in peril of their souls and their honor . . . and for them he was increasingly afraid.

Go back now, he might say; and he might try to face it alone. He might survive. He might drive it in retreat.

But to take this army back left Cefwyn with no help against the Men that had joined this Shadow of magic, and collectively, if they did not fight the Shadow and win, then none of them would wish to see the rule that presence would impose. *He* was the only barrier against the attention it wished to pay the world: Mauryl and the Sihhë-lords had stood against it as long as anyone remembered, and now he did, and he knew now beyond a doubt that this contest was for his life and its existence.

And oh, he loved this life, as he loved these men, as he loved the world and he would not yield it while there was any will left him, but when the battle came, he knew how far it would take him. Knowing how thin the curtain was that divided the gray space from the world, and on how thin a thread the present order of time itself was strung, he cherished the voices around him and the creature under him. Knowing everything could ravel and fly away from his grasp, he savored every scent in the air he breathed, from the damp forest earth to the smell of horses and leather and oiled metal, the scent of the woods and the meadows as they woke, waterlogged and cold, from winter. He found wonder in the light on Dys' black hide and on the bare boughs of the trees. He looked out at the subtle grays and browns of the forest, finding shades as subtle as a wren's wing and evergreen dark and stubborn at the woods' edge—and there, oh, like a remembrance of summer, an unlovely sapling had half-broken buds.

Everything he loved was around him and he loved all he saw, the kiss of a chill breeze and the warmth and glitter of a noon sun, the harsh voices of soldiers at their midday rest, the soft sound of a horse greeting its master, the voices of friends and the laughter of men who knew the same as he did that these days of march together might be all that remained to them in the world.

One heart was not enough to hold it all. It overflowed. It required several. It required sharing. He pointed out a squirrel on a limb, and Uwen and Crissand, as different as men ever could be, both smiled at its antics. He heard Cevulirn and Umanon and Sovrag talk together as if they had always been good neighbors; and Pelumer joined them, doubtless to tell them how things had been before they all were born. Strange, he thought, to hold so many years in memory: it was strange enough to him to hold a single year and know that, indeed, he had lived into the next, and found new things still to meet.

He enjoyed the taste of cold rations and plain water, for in the dark whence he had come there was nothing at all, and he might go back into that dark again without warning, for the world was stretched so thin and fine the enemy might rupture it, as he might, unwittingly rending what was and what might be. In the gray space, time itself was not fixed: nothing was fixed or sure: he had been in the mews. He had held a boy's hand, and carried out a newborn. He had slept in Marna Wood, and felt a presence coming through the woods, which was his own.

He adjusted a buckle at his shoulder with particular concentration, thinking he could not leave things until a further moment, and the closer he moved to Ilefínian, the more he could not trust the next moment to remain stable and fixed . . . though he willed it: he willed it with all the magic he could command. Every glance at the woods was a spell, every breath a conjuration.

"Ye're uncommon quiet, the both of ye," Uwen said, as if he had taken Crissand, too, in his charge. "Not a word to say?"

"None," Crissand said with a small, brave laugh. "I was thinking about the lambing."

"M'lord'll like the lambs," Uwen said. "Havin' not seen any but half-grown."

"I look forward to it," Tristen said. He clung to Uwen's voice as to life itself: for if all in his thoughts was gray and uncertain, Uwen's voice gave him back the solidity of earth, the rough detail of a gray-stubbled face, the imperfect beauty of eyes lined with long exposure to the world's bright suns. Uwen made him think of lambs, which he imagined as like half-grown sheep, but smaller . . . but that might not be so, thinking of Tarien's baby, and how little Elfwyn looked like a grown man.

It was spring. The world still held miracles. The forest around him did. About them he wove his spells.

Desperately he asked, with a glance aside, "What tree is that?"

"Hawthorn," Uwen said.

Hawthorn, ash and oak, wild blackberry and wild currant. Everything had a name and kept its separate nature. With all the flux in the gray space, the earth stayed faithful and solid under him, and the buds on the trees held an event yet to come, the promise of leaves, and summer yet unseen, precious promise, full of its own magic, an incorruptible order of events.

He embraced it, held it, bound himself to it with a fervor of love.

"There's blooms to come," Uwen said. "These little scraggly 'uns'll surprise ye, how they shine. Ye don't see 'em all summer when the great old oaks is leafed. Then you just curse 'em for bein' brush in your way, but they'll bloom to theirselves come the first warm days an' be pretty as maids at festival. Same's the blackberry vines, as ain't pleasant to ride into, or to catch your feet if ye're chasin' some stray sheep, but they dress fine for spring an' give ye a fine treat in the summer . . . ain't never complained about 'em, meself, if the thorns catch me unawares. As I was a boy, I knew all the patches 'twixt my house an' the hills, an' me mum'd bake up cakes . . . ain't had the same, since."

"I know a few patches," Crissand said. "I'll have my folk send you some."

"Oh, but ye have to pick 'em yourself, Your Grace, and eat a few as they're warm in the sun."

"Then I'll show you where they are," Crissand said, and the earl of Meiden and the captain of Amefel made their plans, as they said, to go blackberrying in the country, so only half the berries might reach the kitchen.

Their idle chatter, their plans—they held promises and order, too, and Tristen wished with all his heart to go with them and taste the blackberries.

And about that thought, tenacious as the vines, he feared he had begun to weave a more perilous magic: he had thought of the three of them together, after the battle that was to come, and he had wished, and that wish coming from his heart had as much power as he had bound between himself and the earth. The more he decided not to wish that day to come, the more easily it might not, and the more easily one or all of them might perish beforehand.

Bind Crissand and Uwen's fate to his, for good or for ill, and set the integrity of the world at issue in that simple, homely wish of friends to eat blackberries . . . dared he? Had he done such a fatal, reckless thing?

That was the peril and the strength of Sihhë magic, that it worked so easily, and fear of what he had done sent him to the threshold of a tortuous course of half-doing and half-undoing that Emuin himself could not riddle out, Emuin who labored over his wizard-work and consulted charts and stars and seasons to which he himself was not bound. The plain fact was that he *could* wish it, and halfway in and halfway out was an untenably dangerous position.

Flesh as well as spirit, had not Mauryl said it? He was *both*.

"I wish it," he said suddenly, aloud and with all his heart. "Pray to the gods, if they hear you: we may need it!"

"My lord?" Crissand asked, alarmed, but Uwen, who was a plain Man, said, quietly:

"M'lord's worked a magic, an' wants help in it; and if prayer'll do it, why, I'll dust mine off and do my best, m'lord, that I will."

So they rode, after that, sometimes silent, sometimes in converse, talking on things that, like the blackberries, assumed an unaccustomed seriousness.

In this, perhaps Uwen even more than Crissand and Cevulirn understood how grave the crisis had been in him, and how dangerous the choice he had made. Cevulirn rode up the column to join them a time, not a talkative man on a day less fraught with consequence, and now seeming content to be near them, a presence at the edge of the gray space, as they were to him . . . perhaps after all Cevulirn had felt more of what happened than seemed likely, and offered his strength, such as it was. They had become friends, beyond that meeting Auld Syes' had foretold; and friendship was its own reason now, three of them, their touch at each other in the gray space as solid as their sight of each other in the world, with Uwen to support them all.

"Getting dark," Crissand remarked. "We may have to camp in this wood."

Tristen shook his head, for he had the sense of a place farther on, where water ran, where one of Pelumer's men waited. He hoped so, for as they passed into the wood beyond a small ruined wall, shadows ran like ink deep among the trees, and the wood grew colder, the branches seeming to rattle without a wind.

"Shall we stop?" Uwen asked.

"No," he said. "Half an hour more."

A glance upward through bare branches gave the only proof day still lingered, and conversations grew quieter, until there was only the crack of dry branches, the scuff of hooves on old leaves, the steady creak of leather. Shadows began to move and flow, Shadows indeed, Tristen thought, and caught Crissand's sudden turn to try to see one. Cevulirn, too, looked askance, and Uwen took alarm from them.

"Nothing harmful to us," he said, though he was less than sure, wary lest the Shadows turn prankish or become more aware of them than they were. As it was, they tended to be harmless: but he reminded himself it was not Amefel, and these were not Shadows he had met before. He had no idea to what authority they did answer, or whether they had any dealings with Ynefel, to the south . . . or worse.

Something else, a wisp of something, begged his attention, but was gone when he tried to ask what, and it seemed to him that neither Crissand nor Cevulirn had noticed it. He almost thought it was Ninévrisë, and that thought greatly worried him, as if something might have gone amiss at Henas'amef, something he dared not pursue. He had to trust Emuin for that: he had to remind himself he could not be everywhere, informed on everything at once.

So they rode a moment more in the silence that followed; but now the trees were thinning to a last curtain of scrub before a meadow, and they crossed a rill that wended its way through the last of them, not to a soggy water-meadow as they had found at their last rest, but by the last of the light, onto grassy dry ground.

And there one of the Lanfarnesse rangers sat waiting on a flat rock, expecting them, having spied out this place.

"Safety for the night," Pelumer rode up to declare, and so it seemed, under the fair evening sky, under the first stars. So Tristen felt some of his fear depart.

But he cast a glance back at the dark wall of the wood. Strange territory in every sense, and strange musings lurked under those bare branches: Owl had not joined him, and he was anxious, still ahorse, while men waited, looking to him to dismount first.

He settled the reins and stepped down from Dys' tall back, landed squarely and looked back a second time, as if he could surprise a Shadow, or Owl, watching him.

"Is something amiss?" Crissand asked.

He shook his head. "Disturbed," he said, and the truth came to him as he began to speak it. "Troubled, but not against us. Still, better here, than among the trees. Better to be who we are. Tasmôrden's men would fare very badly here, if they came."

"They haven't," Cevulirn observed.

"They have not," Tristen said, but with a sudden dread. It was suddenly sure in his heart that indeed Tasmôrden had moved from where he had last felt his presence, that the main force of the enemy army had moved the other direction from Ilefínian, away from him. That conviction lent a chill to the evening wind, one that made him gather his cloak about him, and wish Cefwyn every protection he could offer.

"M'lord?" Uwen asked, distracting him. And he felt now pulled in two directions at once, one the desire to bid them all ride on—that was folly: they would defeat themselves if they wore themselves with a further march. And he wished to go back into the woods and learn what moved there, but that, too, was folly. They were well out of it, and lucky, Uwen would say, because with the sinking of the sun, the Shadows gathered in this land to which they were strangers and intruders, and he wished safety on the rangers, that they, too, might go against their habit and come into the camp tonight.

By twilight the carts creaked and squealed their way about the weedy meadow on the lines of a camp in formation, dumping off tents as they went. Tents already distributed went up like white mushrooms at the edge of an unculled, brush-choked wood in the fading light. Groups of men dug bare earth patches for campfires . . . not for every man, in this overgrown area, but sufficient: Cefwyn had no wish to burn the wood down to give notice of his presence, but there was no persuading Guelenmen to camp like the Lanfarnesse rangers, and fight on cold rations, either. And there was no concealing the approach of an army that moved with carts. But not every man had a tent tonight, and fewer would have them on the following night. They shed canvas like a snake its skin, and hereafter trusted a handful of carts with the most essential supplies, but every man would carry dry rations, and every man had a good woollen cloak, the king's gift, that was blanket, litter for the wounded, and windbreak at need. The Guelen book of war insisted the baggage was everything, and that if they lost their heavy gear, the army was doomed; but Guelenfolk nowadays were no longer invaders far from home, and he saw how even his grandfather had relied on old wisdom. Tristen urged otherwise, their feckless lord of shadows and cobwebs, as Idrys had been wont to call him: but not feckless on the battlefield, far from it, and not feckless now, leading an army northward in support of him. Tristen had spoken against carts and baggage and a long wait until spring; and he had gone instead on his own advice, to the very brink.

Now that things went astray it was Tristen's advice that guided him, and it was huntsman's economy he meant to practice: that was how he explained it to lords who had never ridden Ivanim fashion to war. Maudyn was dismayed to hear he meant to abandon the careful fortifications he had made, and worse, to make every individual man responsible for his own food and warmth hereafter. All day long the line of carts on a narrow, perilously forested road had kept Ryssand at his tail, for Ryssand had not been able to maneuver past.

Ryssand had surely taken the point, for Ryssand had not sent so much as a messenger forward to hack his way through the brush and seek converse with his king. The carts having gotten onto the bridge ahead of Ryssand's forces, and the army having moved past Lord Maudyn's camp without stopping, and some of *those* carts having maneuvered into the road, why, there they were, all day long, moving through wooded land well suited for scattered ambush by archers, but utterly safe from large movements of cavalry such as Tasmôrden commanded. If an army of fools was bound to quarrel in enemy territory, it was an area as forgiving of folly as he could hope for . . . for this one day.

After this, dissent became deadly, but he did not count on Ryssand to care overmuch. He did hope to make as much of a fool of Ryssand as he could manage, and be sure the others that might follow his leadership at least knew how recklessly Ryssand conducted himself.

Now the last contingents arrived: now Ryssand came, with, indeed, Murandys and Nelefreíssan. So the banners declared, as contingent marched in from the wood-girt, well-manured road.

It was the first look he had had at Ryssand's forces, and to his mild surprise, indeed, they all came with more than their household guards: they brought all the peasant muster he had once asked for and which he had now as lief not have trammeling up his battle plan . . . and with those men, they could not keep up with the cavalry as he meant to press them.

Nor could the Ryssandish peasantry avoid heavy losses in what he was sure their lord meant to do, a certainty that drove all vestige of humor from the situation. There were dead men, very likely not even in Ryssand's concern. There were men about to make their wives widows and their children orphans and their farms a fallow waste.

Damn, he said to himself, seeing the trap of his own making. Here were men that should have been left in camp: here were men who should not have advanced farther than Maudyn's first camp, and who certainly should not march from this one. Here were the innocent, no matter that they were Ryssand's. It was Ryssand and Ryssand's house guard on whom he looked blackly, and beyond them, indeed, Ryssand's own baggage train would come hindmost of all: clearly, once it had become a race for the bridge, the traditional force Ryssand commanded had not a chance of crossing in time, not without deserting his infantry.

So Cefwyn stood with arms folded and his guard around him, under the red-and-gold Dragon Banner of the Marhanen. Lord Maudyn, too, came from the edge of his notice and joined him, leaving his sons to deal with the camp-making. He was touched by that sensible loyalty, not disappointed in Maudyn's common sense to see a situation and act, no matter how strange his king's orders throughout the day.

But, gods, he missed Idrys in what would ensue in the next few moments. He wished Idrys could have the satisfaction, for one thing, and missed that wry, acerbic, and critical counsel that reasonable men learned to respect.

Idrys was not here to impose his chilling presence, and so he met these would-be traitors not with his accustomed smile but with Idrys' own black stare.

"Late!" he said, before Ryssand could get a single, carping word out of his mouth. "Late, and out of the order of the camp!"

"Surely Your Majesty knew we would not fail your orders," Ryssand countered.

"Did I? Am I a wizard? I think not!" Cefwyn spared a glance at Prichwarrin and the lord of Nelefreíssan, and settled a second, baleful stare on Ryssand. "On the other hand, wizards advise Tasmôrden!

Does Cuthan, perchance, give you *their* advice? Have you brought him? We can begin our war with a hanging. *That* for a start!"

"Your Majesty." Murandys' dismay at this wide-ranging attack was no pretense, Cefwyn was sure: Prichwarrin was too cautious a man and Ryssand too grossly affronted to say what he would wish to say. It was too early for them to launch a rebellion; it was possible that Prichwarrin himself was ignorant of what Ryssand planned and Ryssand might not want him to know it. And by the gods he was of no disposition to smooth rebels' feathers.

"Have you brought him?" he repeated his question regarding Cuthan, and used his grandfather's temper, nothing held back. "*Parsynan,* perhaps, the hero of Amefel. Do I see him in your train?"

"No, Your Majesty," Ryssand said in cold formality.

"A pity," he said with sudden and equal coldness. "Set your tents in what space you can find tonight. I trust after this debacle there'll be no tardiness on the field."

That, imprudently, perhaps, he sent straight to the heart of Ryssand's intentions, but Ryssand never blanched.

"No, Your Majesty."

On that, Cefwyn began to turn away, allowing them time to show their real expressions, and suddenly spun about and measured one after the other sour face with a long stare, ending with Ryssand, at whom he gazed a long, long moment.

Then he said in unfeigned disgust: "I need you. *Have* I your observance of your oaths?"

"Yes, Your Majesty," Ryssand said for all the others, with never a blink or a glance down in shame, but Ryssand's eyes burned.

"Heavy horse to the center," he said. "Your infantry to guard the camp."

"Your Majesty,—"

"To guard the camp, I say! And your horse to the center! I've a notion where I'll meet that blackguard, if I can rely on my maps . . . if you have better, provide them."

"I've received no such information, Your Majesty. Nor have any of us, save from Cuthan, of course, in whom Your Majesty has no confidence."

Damn you, he very nearly said. The effrontery was at the surface now, the other barons standing well behind, obscure in the twilight, perhaps asking themselves how far indeed Ryssand was prepared to go. Corswyndam's temper had almost leapt into flame. It smoldered, it very clearly smoldered. So did his.

But they were neither of them utter fools.

"Then expect an encounter tomorrow or the next day," Cefwyn said shortly, "depending on Tasmôrden's speed on his own roads. Have your men in order. No drunkenness in the ranks tonight, and early to break camp tomorrow. Here's the redemption of our differences, sir. Make me your friend. I can be courted."

"Your Majesty." Three heads bowed. Three lords backed as if they were in the throne room, despite the informality of a martial camp, and withdrew to their own counsel.

He remained with Lord Maudyn and with his bodyguards and Panys', and told himself he had been laudably calm throughout the encounter, remarkably cold-blooded. Now he found tremors of anger running through his limbs and asked himself whether he should order Ryssand's arrest and execution tonight.

It might bring Nelefreíssan and Murandys into line. It might be the prudent thing. He might survive the action, and Ylesuin might.

Or might not. Dared he do that, and then lead the army into battle with questions unanswered and regional angers broken wide open? He could not answer what Murandys and Nelefreíssan might do . . . and that might rest on how much evidence they feared might come to light if he came home again. He had no idea, that was the difficulty.

March home again to settle matters, his war unfought and Tasmôrden glorying in a temporary victory . . . that was a mouthful he could not swallow. Ylesuin had not wanted his war, but Ylesuin would come asunder in regional and religious bickering. Ryssand had his supporters among the clergy even yet, and as yet he could prove nothing of his charges against the man but his illicit traffic with Parsynan and the fact he had lodged Cuthan and taken messages from Tasmôrden. Both offended the king's law, but the fact that Cuthan had betrayed his brother lords in Amefel was nothing at all to Guelenfolk, who detested the Amefin.

But if Ryssand died, he had, gods help him, Artisane, and whatever man besides his brother he found to sacrifice to that marriage: if Ryssand was a brigand, Artisane was a lying baggage who with a duchess' title would lie louder and with more credible virulence.

Two heads at the Guelesfort gate might bring a wholesome silence, vacate the duchy, and take the consequences of unrest and claimants to vacant lands.

And for a moment Ryssand's life trembled on the knife's edge of his temper. But it was wise to consider who would stand with him: Osanan, who had joined them, had been Ryssand's man in most questions: the lord of Osanan had always inclined himself that way in matters of regional import, the questions of fishing rights and the doctrinist Quinaltines. Where would Osanan stand if he killed Ryssand?

Or would Osanan and many another simply lack enthusiasm to advance in the battle, and retreat at the first reverse on the field? Every man for himself it would be if that sentiment took hold in various units.

Sulriggan? The lord of Llymaryn was no hero. If the army began to break, Sulriggan would trample the foremost riding to the head of the pack, and take his men with him.

Maudyn would stand. Panys. And the Guard.

No. He had laid his plans during this long day's ride, he had settled what he would do with Ryssand, even how he would shape the battle so that units like Osanan could make their choice and units like Panys and the Dragons and Guelens would have their honor.

Let Ryssand fold or hold, as he planned matters: the outcome would be the same. And they would *still* push Tasmôrden back to Ilefínian, with Tristen, he fondly hoped, coming from the other leg of the triangle, to catch Tasmôrden from the other side—the last of the pretenders to the Regency, with an army large only because it was the scourings and the survivors of the long struggle. Honest men had taken to the hills. Bandits took Tasmôrden's hire. And if they pressed Tasmôrden back and if the Elwynim saw Ninévrisë's standard, Tasmôrden would find no support among the commons. It was Ninévrisë's hope and it was his, that one defeat would shatter the pretender's army and honest Elwynim would rise out of the thickets and the hills.

Trust Tristen, that if wizardry could arrange it, Tristen would be there, where he needed him, no blame, no recrimination: Tristen was coming, with Cevulirn and Pelumer and all the south, where he should have placed his trust from the beginning.

And of all unexpected things, a flight of birds soared above the wood's edge and turned.

Pigeons, for the gods' good sake! Pigeons. He stared after them amazed.

When did pigeons become forest-dwellers? They were not. They never had been, not these birds.

Tristen was there, he was surely there, just the other side of this cursed ridge.

Captain Gwywyn, of the Prince's Guard, and in Idrys' absence over the Dragons and the Guelens as well, approached him from the side, bringing a practical and immediate question. "The west for the latest to camp, Your Majesty?"

"The west and north," he said, for there was room in the meadow on that side, and while the petty notion occurred to him to move the horse pickets on the east and let Ryssand and his allies pitch on that soiled ground, the same as they had marched on it all day, the peasant levies did not deserve it, and he did not indulge the whim. "I'll cool my anger. Bid them join us at supper."

"As Your Majesty wishes."

"Advise all the lords to join us at supper. We'll settle our marching order. Hereafter we have the enemy to quarrel with, not each other."

Gwywyn went aside on his mission. Lord Maudyn, who had walked with him, gave him a questioning look and a blunt question: "Will Your Majesty inform Ryssand of *all* the plans?"

"We have to stand on the same battlefield and face the same enemy," Cefwyn said with a sigh. "We'll leave no lord out of our councils. I've no wish to expose the men afoot to risk of their lives: gods know they're not at fault, and I'll not face the widows." He walked a few steps farther in the lord of Panys' company. "But you and I have somewhat to say together. Perhaps we won't tell Ryssand everything."

"I would be easier in my sleep," Maudyn said, "if Ryssand knew less."

"I'm very sure," he said. "To tell you the very truth, I have more doubt of Prichwarrin's courage to defy me than I have of Ryssand's, and that alone frets me: I don't know what the man may do. Ryssand, on the other hand, has courage; but he doesn't give a damn for his servants, his staff, his men, or his horses, not when he sees what he wants. His sworn men and his peasants have no worth, save as they serve him: *I* pity them. He doesn't, and no few will die."

"Then I pray Your Majesty arrest him. Others stand with the Crown. No honorable man could misunderstand."

It was exceedingly comforting to hear Maudyn say so, and he wished he knew it was true. It was almost like hearing Idrys' voice saying: kill Ryssand.

And when he recalled how often and why he had denied Idrys that satisfaction, he became quite clear in his own thoughts.

"No," he said. "No, my dear friend. Much as I wish it . . . much as I regard your advice and your wisdom . . . no. Let him at least do what we accuse him of. Let it be clear beyond even Murandys' ability to find excuses. They think him simply clever at going to the brink. *I* know how far he'll go, but they don't believe it yet."

"Stand by and let him bring a sword against my king's back?"

"That's not what I expect of him."

"What, then?"

"Oh, he'll run—and not he, no, never say Ryssand bolted. Some unnamed man of his will turn and start a panic, and the officers will turn and the company will run, leaving the peasants to face Tasmôrden's heavy horse and leaving the rest of us to the slaughter. And if it's found out later, blame will fall on some poor wretch of a lieutenant, but mark me! Ryssand deals with Tasmôrden, makes a treaty, and marches home with clean hands. *Therefore* I set him in the center. Remember I said so beforehand, and report it in the court later, but say not a word of this even to your sons. I fear I can't help Ryssand's peasants. But the rest I can deal with."

Maudyn gave him a look of intense distress. "Surely—"

"He'll retreat. We'll advance," Cefwyn said. "Trust in me, sir. And *hell* take Ryssand."

Owl called, in the world, and Tristen opened his eyes on stars above him, aware of Uwen sleeping on one side, aware of Crissand not so far away with his household guard and the Amefins all around: aware of the Amefin, the Ivanim, the Olmernmen, and the Imorim, with a handful of Pelumer's rangers tucked away to the side, in their own group.

That awareness went on to all the camp and the lay of the land. Horses slept. Almost all the camp slept.

But the woods did not.

A second time Owl called. And Tristen gathered himself to his feet, feeling the stir of a wind out of the woods, a wind that smelled of rain and green things, a wind that rushed at him and blew and blew, and yet Men slept. Uwen slept. Only Crissand and Cevulirn waked, and roused to their feet as well, seeking shields and swords and helms, for they had simply loosed buckles and slept in their armor.

So indeed Tristen had done, but what he perceived was not a threat that would stop at leather and metal, nothing a shield could turn: Shadows moved in the woods, and with a thought of that Elwynim force left dead in the snow near Althalen, he felt the hair rise at the nape of his neck: *he* would not fall to it, but he was determined his friends would not perish: Uwen would not perish, nor would the men who came here trusting him.

The horses grew uneasy: to have them break the picket lines was a disaster they could not afford, either: the beasts smelled danger, but except for the three of them, and a slight stirring here and there across the camp, no man roused out of sleep.

Peace, he wished the Shadows, and was instantly confident they heard him, instantly reassured, for out of the wood came a whisk of wind that flattened the meadow grass in the starlight, and there skipped a child, blithe and happy and as perilous as edged iron. She skipped and she played in the starlight, and beyond her, around her, came other streaks in the grass, and other children that laughed with high, thin voices, distant and echoing as in some far and vacant hall.

Seddiwy, he named her, and looked for her mother in the shadows.

So Auld Syes came, a white-haired woman as he had first seen her, in homespun and fringed shawl, like any grandmother of the town; and as he had first seen her, the shadow-shapes of peasant folk came following her, the inhabitants of some village, he took them to be, but dim even for starlight.

Then he recognized an old man, and another, a lame youth, and a chill came over him, for they were the folk of Emwy village, dead since summer, young and old.

"Auld Syes," he said to the old woman, and in the next blink saw banners among the trees, a sight that alarmed him for an instant, but Auld Syes turned in slow grace and held out a hand toward those that came. It was the Regent's banner, and the men with it were Shadows as that banner was a Shadow itself.

It was Earl Haurydd, who had died facing Aséyneddin at Emwy Bridge, Ninévrisë's man, and her father's; and with him were others of that company.

And there was Hawith, one of Cefwyn's men, killed at Emwy, and there . . . there was Denyn Kei's-son, the Olmern youth who had stood guard at Cefwyn's door, Erion Netha's young enemy turned friend.

He saw his own banner, the Tower and Star, and the shadowy youth bearing it, and felt the deep upwelling of loss, for it was Andas Andas-son, who had joined him so briefly to carry that banner at Lewenbrook. The dark had rolled over the boy, and he had gone bravely into it, and never out again.

He trembled at the sight, he, who was no stranger to Shadows, but it was not fear that shook him, rather that he felt his heart torn to the point of pain. It was not harm the Shadows brought with them, but their loyalty, their fidelity, faith kept to the uttermost.

"My lord," Crissand whispered, having moved close to him, and Cevulirn arrived at his other hand.

"I know them," Tristen said. "I know them all."

But it was not the end of visitations, and at the next the brush rattled and moved to the presence of living men, and a handful of peasant villagers appeared, ragged lads carrying spears and one of them a makeshift standard.

Then from another quarter, from the road, appeared a handful of men on horseback, and them with well-made banners, and one of them the Tower Crowned.

Aeself was one of them, and slid down from his horse and walked forward as sleeping men began to wake to the commotion, hearing sounds in the world. Men leapt up, seizing weapons and shields, and calling out in alarm.

"Friends!" Aeself called out. "His Grace's men!"

A third time Owl called, and the Shadows all were gone. More and more men came from out of the wood, men on horseback and peasants afoot, and a scattering of banners among well-armed and lordly folk.

Aeself went to one knee, and so did the others. "The King," Aeself said, and so the others said, one voice upon the other, "the King."

"There *is* a king," Tristen protested, but there were more and more of them, spilling out of the trees, while the wood could in no wise have concealed all of them and he could not have been so deceived about their presence. They arrived like the Shadows, as if they had risen out of the stones and the earth, and a wind skirled through the clearing, startling the horses, lifting the banners half to life.

And Aeself rose, foremost of the rest, while Ivanim and Amefin, Imorim knights and Olmern axemen, and a scattering of Lanfarnesse rangers stood utterly dismayed, no less so than their lords.

Auld Syes arrived in their midst like a skirl of wind, fringed shawl flying like threads of cobweb, gray hair shining like the moonlight, and her daughter danced, holding her hand and skipping about her skirts.

—King in Elwynor, King Foretold: deny nothing! The aetheling has found his King, and peril to deny it!

He hoped with all his heart none of the men heard. He wished Auld Syes' aid for all of them, and by no means rejected Aeself or the Shadows . . . how could he turn from Andas Andas-son and Earl Haurydd or deny the outpouring of so many wishes? If Men could

347

bind a magic, he found himself snared in it, caught in their wishes, their long, faithful struggle in what he feared was his war, always his war . . . but now theirs, as well.

"My name is *Tristen*," he said to them all as he had said to Hasufin Heltain. He said it as a charm and as the truth which anchored him in the world. "My name is Tristen. Nothing else."

"King of Elwynor!" some cried, among the living, and the Amefin cried, "Lord Sihhë!" But he shut his ears against it, and turned away, and in doing so, met the faces he most dreaded to meet: Uwen, as Guelen as ever a man could be; and Cevulirn, steadfast in his oaths; and Crissand Adiran, Amefin, aetheling, *king* of Amefel . . . all his friends, all with claims impossible to reconcile, one with the other.

"Lord Sihhë!" the Amefin all shouted now, and so the Elwynim took it up: "Lord Sihhë! Lord Sihhë! *Lord Sihhë!*"

That was the only truth he heard. He turned again to confront Auld Syes, but in that moment's distraction the very light had changed to earliest dawn: there were no Shadows among them to answer, there was no lady and no child, only the shapes of trees and the shapes of Men still indisputably among the living. He knew what he had seen, but he could not believe that every man in the company had seen the same, and could not reconcile what he knew and what they knew, or reason out how much they had heard. They shouted for him: they wanted him with such a fervor it shook him to the heart, and yet he wanted nothing of it, nothing but Cefwyn's safety.

And in hailing him, they turned from Cefwyn. The Elwynim and the Amefin hailed another king: they made him their lord, and would hear nothing else, while the southern lords who had followed him at risk of life and honor stood dismayed, not knowing what to do at this sudden turn of loyalties on the borderlands.

Tristen held up his hands, begging silence, and it was difficult to obtain, in the dim gray light that only hinted at the dawn.

"Lord Sihhë I am," he said. "Lord Sihhë I am willing to be." The cold dark seemed to gape beneath his feet, threatening to drink him in, and yet he strained to see their faces, in that hour that stole the stars. *But no more than that*, he wished to say . . . yet all along he had listened to Auld Syes, and was not sure she was wrong.

"Cefwyn is my friend," he said, difficult as it was to speak at all. "Her Grace is my friend. *Crissand* is the aetheling, and Amefel has a king, the king of the bright Sun! But *my name is Tristen!*"

And with that he could bear nothing more, and turned away, past Crissand's reaching hand, past Cevulirn's grave face. Only Uwen went with him in his withdrawal, and his guard shadowed him until he had found a refuge at the edge of the horse pickets, where Dys and Cass stood and offered mute comfort.

He had left confusion behind him. He had left Aeself and Crissand and Cevulirn with wizardry unexplained. He had left the lords of the south with their understanding challenged. He thought he should have done better. But he could not find how.

He was aware of Uwen's presence, of his new guards, Gweyl and the others, and at this moment he sorely missed Lusin, who would stand by Uwen come what might. He ached heart-deep with what he feared, and what was laid on him to do, with no choice of his: it was what he was made to do. He apprehended at least that Auld Syes was not in charge of him, nor beyond mistakes, only charged with truths as she perceived them. He could refuse.

And his heart cried out against their expectations. It was not Cefwyn's doom to fall. It was not his own to sit in a hall signing and sealing and rendering judgments, when this single judgment was so difficult.

He drew a deep breath when he knew that, as if bands had loosed about his heart. He looked up at a sky in which the stars had all perished, and at Uwen's sober, stubbled face. Love shone there, brighter than the dawn; and he opened his arms and embraced Uwen, for all that Uwen was; in his heart he embraced Crissand, and Cevulirn, and the lords of the south, too, and Aeself, who had come by no ordinary road to find him, whether or not Aeself understood what company he had had or how unnaturally he had arrived.

He heard Owl complaining of the sun. He stood still, cold to the very heart of him, as if his very next breath hung suspended between day and dark.

Lord of Shadows he could be. *That*, more than Lord Sihhë, he might be. He knew the gray space: it would open for him, and he could draw power out of that realm, hurl the hapless dead against the dead that Hasufin summoned until between them they laid waste to the gray space as well as the lands of Men. The last struggle had imprisoned Shadows within the walls of Ynefel and brought down the towers of Galasien. Between them, Mauryl and Hasufin, they had done that: Mauryl, wielding wizardry, and Hasufin, wielding wizardry, had not seen the consequences of the struggle. But he saw that it would not last. At the last, Mauryl had seen the wards falter, he was sure of it: Galasien had perished in vain. It did not hold.

And Efanor and a small band of priests walked a perilous Line in Guelessar, as Emuin and Ninévrisë warded the south and Ninévrisë's father and Drusenan's Wall held the border of Amefel.

It was to keep those barriers strong that he had arrived on Mauryl's hearth.

"I dreamed," he said to Uwen, who most knew the youth who had come to Amefel. "Such, at least as I do dream . . . that there's something behind Hasufin, and the Sihhë-lords fought it, all those years ago."

"Lad, such as I couldn't tell."

"This is true." He could no longer bear to wait, not for the men who stood in doubt and debating among themselves what he had said, not for the disturbance in the wood where Shadows hid for the coming day. He would not be the king Auld Syes foretold. He was never suited to it: it was not—he was as sure of it as of the coming day. "Mauryl didn't Summon me to sit on a throne," he said. "Cefwyn hates it . . . but he's a good king. I'm not what he is. None of us is what he is."

Uwen was silent, in what mind he could not read.

"You don't ask me what I am," he said, curious, for curiosity was always his fault, and he could never understand the lack of it.

"Ye don't rightly know, do ye?" Uwen answered him with a wry smile. "Nor me. Nor do I need to. Ye're my good lad."

"Uwen is what you are," he said, "and the captain of my guard, and my right hand." He reached out to Uwen's leather-guarded shoulder, as much to feel his solid strength as to reassure Uwen. "Set us to horse. Make these men move. Cefwyn needs me. *That's* what I know."

"Aye, m'lord," Uwen said with relief.

That was Uwen's answer.

And for his own, when he went back to Cevulirn and Crissand, he took their hands, and embraced them in the murmurous hush of the army. He embraced Sovrag's huge shoulders, and Umanon's stiff back, and Pelumer's thin and aged frame: he opened his arms to Aeself, when Aeself would have cast himself to his knees, and made him stand and have that, and not a lord to worship.

"My lord," Aeself whispered.

"You can't make me King," Tristen whispered back. "Mauryl didn't, and you can't. But Sihhë, yes, as the five were, that I do fear I am." Ice came to him, as strong a vision as if it had Unfolded for the first time, ice, and the fortress of the Qenes, a dizzying long view, a dizzying long remembrance, for memory it might be. He did not know where he had begun, but he knew what the boundaries of the world should be.

"Yet," Aeself said, "others will join us, my lord, if only they see there's hope: they'll come as these men have come—not for me, not even for my cousin, gods save her: they'll come to the name of the King."

"Then believe there is such a King," he said, for he drew that certainty out of his heart, breathless with the urgency with which he knew it. "He'll be born: Ninévrisë's child, and Cefwyn's. And Crissand aetheling will sit the throne in Amefel. But my banner is not the High King's."

Loyalty that so yearned to bestow itself somewhere worth its hopes shone in Aeself's eyes. "Then whatever that banner is, I am your man, and so are the rest of us. The forest brought us here. The earth poured us out. I don't know how we came, but we've come here, and nothing frights us after this."

"Auld Syes brought you. She may bring others. Until there *is* a King, I *can* say what is and what's to be, and I set you in charge of all the Elwynim that come to my banner."

"I am no experienced man—"

"I say what is."

"*Yes,* my lord." So Aeself said, and Tristen turned to a clearing filled with men and horses, and more men and horses within the trees. Their company had become an army, between dark and dawn.

"We go on!" Tristen said. "Everyone to your horses! Cefwyn needs us!" And turning from Aeself, he encountered Crissand, and pressed Crissand's arm, for he saw confusion on Crissand's face: the dawn showed it to him, a silent, but heartfelt distress.

"Auld Syes said it: aetheling. King of Amefel. —But Uwen I keep for myself."

"My heart you keep, my lord! Have no doubt of it!"

He clapped Crissand on the arm. In the next moment he heard Uwen shouting at the men:

"Arm an' out, arm an' out, you lads, and get them horses ready. We're off to give Tasmôrden 'is comeuppance."

It was a voice to give courage, a voice that had soothed his night fears and his darkest hours: give Tasmôrden his Comeuppance . . . there was a Word that by no means Unfolded to him, and yet did, as an outcome wider and more true than justice a king might deal out . . . it was justice for the Shadows that had joined them in the night, justice for Crissand's father and Cefwyn's messenger, for the old archivist and the soldiers dead at Emwy and on Lewen field . . . justice for very many wrongs: not a justice of death for death—rather the settling of balances back into true and the world back to peace.

Men moved, horses snorted and pulled at their tethers: the whole clearing seethed with an army setting itself rapidly in an order of march.

So Tasmôrden had moved, carrying the threat against Cefwyn, to deal hurt where their enemy could, to gain an advantage, a hostage, a distraction.

The five first Sihhë had retreated to the ice to avoid this very conflict as long as possible: had met it once in its ascendency and brought down Galasien. In its slow working, in retaliation, the enemy had seized Althalen . . . and lost it, destroyed Ynefel, and lost it.

Now it bided the second assault against its domain, beneath all the movement of armies and threat of iron: five Places in the land, where Shadows seethed, a Working of wizardous sort: five points of attack to confront five Sihhë-lords who afflicted it. Ynefel was last to fall to this onslaught: the old mews in the Zeide was the next to last, where now Emuin and Ninévrisë stood guard over Orien's restive spirit. The third was Althalen, where Uleman now warded the way; the fourth he had set Efanor to watch, to shut the very first door it might ever have used . . .

All these ways it had had once at its command, and one by one he had denied it use of them, if the wardens he had set in place could hold firm the Lines.

All but one was shut, that in Ilefínian's fortress, the way Crissand had discovered, when Tasmôrden had lost his banner.

And it Unfolded to him with the breaking of the dawn that their enemy might have arranged them to come to this conflict: but equally they were here because of what they were. There was no turning back now. The Sun King and the Lord of Shadows had come together to set the world and the gray space in balance as best they knew how, while their enemy meant to confound it entirely, and they had no choice. Whatever the grief it brought either of them, whatever the loss or the pain, they had come to do what neither wizardry nor magic yet had done, and not, this time, be held in check, one power with the other.

Halfway had not sufficed, and Mauryl had surely known it when he Shaped him out of fire and Shadow.

And he had known when he looked the first time at the aetheling, that he had found something essential to what he was. Mauryl's spell had finished its Summoning, and he was here, finally, where all along he had needed to be, wizardry and magic opposed to the Wind that had torn Ynefel's stones apart.

CHAPTER 4

The hills that had been only knowledge on a map became a forbidding rampart of stone and bristling evergreen distantly visible on the left hand, a rough land out of which small bands might come to spy or to harry the approach of an invader on the road that led to Ilefínian. Cefwyn had scouts out well ahead looking for just such a force, but they reported there was no sign of enemy presence.

It was troubling not to meet opposition: leaving unexploited the advantage that rocky ridge posed to its native lord was certainly not what Cefwyn would have done, were he defending Ilefínian, but then, Tasmôrden had failed all along to do those things that a prudent commander would have arranged—first of all not having a force at the bridge to have hindered their crossing, and archers in the woods to make their advance far slower than it had been for two days now.

And in that consideration Cefwyn heard the reports of the scouts and frowned, wishing his enemy would do predictable things that had to be fought: the man's brutal dealing with the villages was a terror to Elwynor. Pretenders to the throne and the Regency for a time had been thick as the leaves in this land. It was worth remarking that all the other pretenders were dead, including Aséyneddin, who had perished at Lewenbrook, and that this man was at last report among the living.

That argued that the man was not the easy mark he had seemed all winter, and it suggested that taking too many of Tasmôrden's gifts too recklessly might lead to the one gift an opponent should not have taken.

On the other hand, Tasmôrden might have a distraction from the other side of that ridge. Cefwyn hoped so. He imagined Tristen's army approaching from that quarter and making Tasmôrden's sleep entirely uneasy. Tasmôrden might have expected a Guelen army to move far slower and diverted resources to the western flank of that ridge to deal with Tristen and Cevulirn, who would come up from the south with the speed of light cavalry. That would trouble Tasmôrden's dreams, if there was wizardry in question. So it was possible, Cefwyn said to himself, that he was simply that lucky.

But he refused to rely on it. He kept looking for the traps. He traveled as quickly as he could, strewing baggage behind him in one camp after another, against every rule in the Guelen book of war, following the will-of-the-wisp of Sihhë tactics and accepting the tactics he had refused when he had had Tristen at hand to advise him. No, he had said repeatedly, and now he followed that advice headlong, constantly aware of Ryssand at his back and Idrys gods knew where . . . too far, for his comfort; but Ninévrisë was safe. Against all likelihood of success, he had persuaded her away to safety and left himself free to fight . . . if he could only find the enemy in front of him.

His reasoning and his thus far fruitless expectations of what Tasmôrden should do to prevent him of course supposed that Tasmôrden owned the land through which they marched, and that was not necessarily the case. Those previous pretenders had dislodged the honest peasantry, rent the country asunder in civil war, and left men outlawed, bandits both by trade and by necessity ranging the countryside at will, so Maudyn reported to him.

And if he were a bandit leader, instead of Tasmôrden, he would sit up in the hills in the rocks and watch all the armies come and go, siding with the winner whenever that came clear. At the very least a heavy-armed cavalry was no likely pickings, at least until there had been a battle.

Above all else he kept waiting for the blow to fall. He expected no deep thinking or strategy from hungry outlaws, but he did expect it from a man who styled himself High King and heir to the Sihhë kingdom. He counted it possible that Tasmôrden could raise no support in the east, where all along Ninévrisë had maintained she had the loyalty of people too frightened and too weak to fight Tasmôrden on their own. But he had seen no Elwynim, either, come out of the brush to rally to the banner he flew at the head of their advance, and by now he doubted he would see any until he had at least damaged Tasmôrden. In a practical sense, he doubted Tasmôrden had much fear of scattered peasants.

They came on a village, mere shells of houses, which the scouts reported vacant, and it was clear by what they saw that the people who had lived there had reason to stay low and quiet if they lived, perhaps hiding in those hills yonder . . . or gone across the river to Tristen. It was no recent ruin. Vines overgrew one charred doorway. Weeds grew in the street.

"Gods know which pretender did this work," Lord Maudyn said.

"Shame on him, whoever it was," Cefwyn said, and added, with a chill in his blood and a thought of his own land: "*Here's* the sad end of a civil war: vacant streets and fallow fields. Who had the good of this work?"

"Not the sheep and the shepherds," Maudyn said.

A courier rode up beside them, presented courtesies, advised him Osanan was slowed by reason of a cart and a loose wheel.

Slowed by reason of Ryssand's courtship, Cefwyn suspected uncharitably, but he acknowledged the report.

The lords with him and those with Ryssand had all been uncommonly courteous one to the other when they met in council in the evenings. They had pored over maps together in frosty amity and heard reports of the scouts. Ryssand's partisans asked why Tasmôrden had not confronted them, and then the pretense had slipped aside ever so little as he looked straight at Corswyndam Lord Ryssand, to see whether Ryssand himself seemed to know the answer to that question.

But he had not caught Ryssand looking as if he knew: he was forced in marginal charity to suppose the consultation between Ryssand and Tasmôrden was somewhat more distant.

He had pretended forgiveness once Ryssand had joined their line of march, Ryssand had pretended contrition, and so they got along, and spread out the maps by lanternlight and pretended to have reconciled, though he doubted Ryssand believed it, for he surprised dour looks from time to time when Ryssand was thinking, and when he himself presented the half of his plans to draw Tasmôrden out of his walls and meet him at a brookside near Ilefínian.

So he did plan, if Tasmôrden did not march out sooner and fall on their marching column before they cleared the end of the ridge, or if arrows did not begin to hail down on them from the heights, a natural archer's advantage. He had in fact dispatched a squad of the Prince's Guard to hold that position and warn him.

But the meaningful councils had been of himself and Lord Maudyn, with Gwywyn and Anwyll and the Guard officers, when he had sent out that squad to take the heights just before dawn yesterday.

Maudyn and Gwywyn were his most knowledgeable advisors,

men who had spent their lives at such questions as supply and the lay of the land. They laid their plans in event of this and that ambush, on maps Ninévrisë had corrected, her own handwriting, her own blessing on the maps, as if she continued to advise him even though absent: her notes were on the backs of the stout parchment, and wedged between the representation of a forest and that of a brook.

But unlike Tristen's magical letter it could not speak to him with her voice and advise him what to do next.

It could not unfold the true sight of the ridge, for instance, to inform him how high and sheer the sides of it; or how deep the forest, or whether trees screened them from the rocks, trees that might stop arrows, or whether they would be exposed to fire if that squad failed its mission.

The map of this land was what he had to rely on, while he asked himself continually what in the gods' sweet name he could do if Tasmôrden turned out to have wizardry to help him.

Give him an open, flat field and a fair fight, that was all he asked, but he doubted Tasmôrden would oblige him. Chase Tasmôrden all the way to Tristen's army . . . that was his fondest hope, so he might catch Tasmôrden between the hammer and the anvil and be sure of him.

The bandits, the Saendal, who served Tasmôrden, would fight: here were men who would hang if they were captured. And since pretenders had succeeded one another, each killing the best of their enemy's men, there could scarcely be a remnant with Tasmôrden much better than the Saendal bandits.

It did not encourage surrender, if the tide turned: they would fight like rats in holes, escape if they could, but his own plans were to provide no hole through which they could bolt: the land had troubles enough of the sort that had made that village a weed-grown desolation. He intended to tame this unruly land to bring it gently to Ninévrisë's hand, a wedding gift, a gift—the thought was still new to him—for their own heir to come.

The bloody Marhanen, as the south called him, would earn the name twice over before this war was done; well, that was nothing new. But his lady of the violets would not start her reign dealing with Saendal bandits.

That, however, was skinning the deer before the hunt. There was Ryssand yet to deal with . . . whose betrayal might not come off if Ryssand saw the war going against Tasmôrden, and he did not intend to provoke tension if it were avoidable. It was sure Ryssand would be no truer to one lord than to another, and if they looked to sweep

Tasmôrden before them, why, Ryssand might discover he was loyal after all.

Yet Ryssand might be the true reason Tasmôrden forbore to attack: that they awaited a place and a time Ryssand would strike.

And if Ryssand did strike, it would be in such a place Ryssand thought he could escape if things went badly.

Closer they marched, and closer still to Ilefínian, to solid walls, and to the friend and patron of Parsynan and Cuthan.

Closer to a refuge at need . . . and an assurance of safety for a traitor otherwise in jeopardy of his life.

If Tasmôrden were sure of Ryssand and Ryssand had never told Tasmôrden his king had suspicions of him, there was another reason Tasmôrden need not stir out and put himself to great effort: the war would come to him and the victory fall into his lap almost without bloodshed.

There was the reason, Cefwyn said to himself the farther they went without sight of the enemy. There was all the reason: Tasmôrden did not put himself to great trouble because he counted on the army of Ylesuin tearing its own throat and opening its veins quite obligingly on his doorstep. If things went completely his way, Tasmôrden might watch from the walls and enjoy the spectacle.

Ask whether Tasmôrden had the mildest suspicion that a man who would lie to his king would lie to him in his absolute assurances: if Tasmôrden were at all wise, Tasmôrden would ask himself such questions and doubt Ryssand's character.

That was the difficulty of being a scoundrel, he supposed: that to a lord of bandits and mercenaries, Ryssand and Murandys seemed so ordinary.

All day he waited for some sign of the enemy.

At evening they made their third camp, canvas going up like white flowers in the sunset, and after the bawling of oxen and the clatter and squeal of the oxcarts laying down the few essential tents, and after the quick dispersal of the evening's cold, fireless provender, quiet settled over the camp, the quiet of men ready, after a day's march, to settle close around the small fires. They had not the luxury of bonfires and a camp under canvas, but canvas strung up for windbreaks and spread as cover for essential gear, and as warm as the days had become and as warmly as the sun beat down on a helm, there was still a winter nip in the air at night and enough damp to soak in.

And with the men settled to their evening's occupation, the lords of Ylesuin set to their own pursuits, a sparse and plain supper in one of the few tents they had brought, with small ale and a session of politeness between enemies who eyed one another what time they were not putting on placid faces: but tonight Cefwyn brought out his second-best map in plain view and laid out the plans for encounter.

"Here," Cefwyn said, laying a pen across the map at the ford of that brook, a broad trail of ink, and annotations as to depth and direction. "The long hill, first, and this brook between us and Ilefíni- an's outbuildings. Our battle line will be heavy horse to the center, excepting Sulriggan, you, sir, to the right wing. The brook is not above hip deep to a man at flood, save only there may be holes, needless to say; good bottom, so there's no fear of fording it if we find no bridge there. But I don't wish to cross it, nor shall we, unless you hear the signal from me. I'd rather let Tasmôrden have his back to the water."

There was doubt they could draw Tasmôrden across the bridge to encounter them on their chosen ground. So did he doubt it, and he little liked to practice the acts that might tempt a lord out of his citadel: burning fields and forests would not serve the peasant farm- ers they hoped to save, nor would it leave anything at all worth stealing after the bandits had had their way in the countryside. He did not say that he hoped for help when he crossed beyond the ridge. He never mentioned so curious a thing as a flight of pigeons in the wood.

But he went to his cot when the conference was done having had at last a satisfactory session with his entire command—and having had even Sulriggan, not the swiftest wit in the company, comprehend what he was to do, and what the signal was that would prompt him to advance. He had Sulriggan to the farthest right wing, Osanan to the left with Panys, and himself in the center . . . with Ryssand.

He had not anticipated to be so well pleased in dealing with Ryssand. He had been grudging with Ryssand, then enthusiastic; he thought it a masterful use of persuasion. In the end, he hoped Rys- sand had believed desperation had made them allies, and that if Rys- sand was the traitor he thought, Ryssand would lie abed tonight smug in the belief he had gotten what he wanted and that revenge for his ox of a son was not so distant.

Cefwyn had not expected to find it so, but with the council dis- posed of, under the weight of thick blankets, under canvas in com- fort, while many of the men slept triple and quadruple in their tents, and with the day's difficulties past, he heaved a deep sigh and found himself freed of his concerns of time and place and treachery. He let his imaginings drift southward and west to more pleasant thoughts and safer places.

He wondered what Ninévrisë thought tonight and whether she was asleep . . . whether the gift she had could make her aware of his thinking of her. Some claimed to know when a loved one was in difficulty, or when some great thing had happened completely over the horizon—so the peasants thought, at least, and them good Quinalt men.

Could not a true wizard-gift manage as much?

I love you, he said to the dark.

She was with Emuin, and master grayrobe would have his ear to the earth for very certain: his ear to the earth and his eyes to the sky for portents or whatever wizards looked for. If there was a magical breath stirring in the world, Emuin might know it, and pass it to Ninévrisë. He himself might be as deaf as his horse to such whispers out of the winds. But in the Zeide wizards and wizardry were constantly aware what went on. The old man likely knew exactly where Tristen was tonight, and where he was: that he was deaf to wizard-work might not *help* a wizard find him, but it had never seemed to hinder the ones he knew, either.

Had Ninévrisë met Tarien Aswydd? Almost certainly. He ached to think how she would have to face his cast-off lover and an unacknowledged child.

And when Ninévrisë and Tarien had met, had there been warfare? He imagined it, at least, but told himself Emuin would mute the quarrel and keep knives from the midst of it.

Might Ninévrisë forgive her? There was a question, too. He thought she might, for Ninévrisë could be astonishingly generous, but he feared that generosity.

And *was* Ninévrisë with child? He was sure of it as he was sure nothing else would have persuaded her to leave him. She was with child . . . gods help them both . . . for nothing wizards had a hand in could proceed without convolutions and calamities.

Her child . . . Tarien's son . . . both his. He deserved the consequences of his own folly, but he had never thought a bastard or two mattered; he had never counted on loving the woman he married, or loving the offspring he had—how could he have planned on it? The mother of his son was supposed to have been Luriel, and that *Luriel* might take exception to his sleeping elsewhere had simply been a quarrel to save for the right moment in the perpetual warfare of a state marriage.

He thanked all the gods he had escaped Luriel of Murandys.

And he wished to the good gods he had not taken to the Aswydd twins to spite Luriel, to set her in her place as one woman among his many.

Folly, folly, utter folly, and the result of it reached Ninévrisë, at Tristen's sending, of all unlikely sources. When he had gotten Tarien Aswydd a son he had not even known Tristen's name, nor met the woman he would truly marry.

And on that thought he heaved himself onto his other side.

An object slid atop the bedclothes.

He blinked, eased the covers off his arm, and reached for it.

His hand met a well-worn hilt, a scabbard, and a small roll of some sort attached to it.

His heart skipped a beat. Whatever it meant, it was not his, and it likely was not his guards'.

Who had come so close while he drowsed? How had a sheathed dagger gotten atop his covers while he lay protected by four trusted guards, one at each corner of his tent?

It was stealth bordering on wizard-work, but he could not account for it. If Ryssand or one of Ryssand's men had gotten in, why should they forbear killing him? In the battle there was far less certainty.

Whatever it was, there was not a light to be had in the tent; and he rolled out of bed and went out to his guard. "Bring a torch," he said, and waited with his hands on that leather-bound hilt and the small tight roll of paper. The hilt was cross-laced. It came to him even as he held it in his hands that he knew this dagger, having seen it day after day.

At Idrys' belt.

And was Idrys back? And was this some ill-timed jest at his expense?

Where are you? he asked the unresponsive air. Damn you, what game is this?

Surely, surely Idrys had left him this grim gift, and no enemy had done it: no one could have taken it from Idrys, surely not.

But if Idrys was back in camp—why not stay for questions? What in very hell was this nonsense of daggers and messages?

The guard brought a torch to the door, not inside, beneath the canvas. But even at that range the light confirmed what his fingers knew, that it was Idrys' dagger.

He had to step outside into the full torchlight to read the crabbed small note tied to the hilt.

My lord king, it began, and that was indeed Idrys. *She is safe. The south has crossed the Lenúalim. Keep your own counsel. Ryssand is not the only danger. Someone within the inmost circles, yours or mine, intends to betray us. Be sure I am near, but say nothing regarding me. I fear lest we make this person desperate.*

Is that all? he asked his Lord Commander in silence. He was indignant, wildly angry with the man.

· Standing at the door of his tent, blinded by the torchlight, he looked outward into a circle of bleached canvas, all of which informed him nothing, none of which revealed a traitor in his councils.

Was it one he had already excluded? Or was it one he still trusted?

Is that all you can say, crow?

Gods, give me more than this!

—Oh, gods, what have I said in council—and to which of my trusted officers?

CHAPTER 5

They marched, an army now, and gathered scattered bands from woods and hills as they came. "The King!" the newcomers shouted, undeniable in Auld Syes' declaration and the witness of the Shadows that moved with them, a waft of wind, a chill and a movement in thickets.

Two boys, Elwynim peasant lads in ragged clothes, armed with makeshift spears, joined them from across a meadow, knelt briefly in the grass to profess their allegiance, and ran to join the beckoning troop that marched beside the lords' guards: Aeself marshaled them, an unruly mob in some part, but Aeself's men rode in order, and instructed the newcomers, nothing more than how to stand in a line if they brought shields or pikes or instructions to shoot from the woods if they brought bows: most of all Aeself instructed them to respect the red bands and make no mistake in it.

Tristen had refused the honor they gave: to Crissand and Cevulirn and Umanon, riding beside him, he said, "I don't wish it. But I fear wishing against it . . . I daren't. Can you understand?"

Umanon blessed himself with a gesture, a Quinalt man, and solid in that faith, like Efanor, clearly wishing not to think about it.

Cevulirn said, "Auld Syes has always told us some form of the truth. But that, you'd know better than I, Lord of Althalen. And I'd not go against her."

No longer did Cevulirn call him Amefel: he had made that Crissand's honor, and given that banner and the Amefin Guard into Crissand's command, while he took command of all the army—not because he wanted it, but because if magic favorable to him was flowing that direction, he dared not refuse it. "I wish Cefwyn well," Tristen said under his breath, with as much force as he could put into the wish: for he felt an abiding fear now, the sense that something weighty resisted him. He wished Cefwyn well hourly, when circumstances allowed him; he did it mindfully and fiercely, but all the while feared making Cefwyn so evidently the center of his thoughts . . . and that . . . that was a dangerous fear in itself. Magic worked to advance Tasmôrden's cause, but magic resisted his own will as nature never had: it was wild and unpredictable, shifting its center moment by moment, as if he contested right of way with someone in a narrow hall. Every move found a counter. It was like swordwork.

It was not like Hasufin at all.

This other thing reached into the world . . . not everywhere, but at Ilefínian; and, if he sent his senses abroad, from several other discrete points in the map, south and west, and over toward Ynefel, and south toward Henas'amef, and east again, toward Guelemara, and the altar he had set Efanor to ward . . . he felt not a scattered assault, but a simultaneous one, as if something vast struggled to escape. Force skipped and thrust against those scattered portals, a force changing direction by the moment, able to do this, do that, change footing, no consulting its charts and awaiting its proper moment.

In the haste and confusion of Unfolding world he had not early on noticed a difference in the effort it took him to do things, or known why some things worked easily and some eluded him with unpredictable result. It was like Paisi, whose young legs darted up stairs without thinking: it was easy for Paisi, so he did it: but Emuin, aching in every bone, planned his trips on the stairs carefully and begrudged every one.

Magic was easy for him. *Everything* had been easy for him in Ynefel. Think! Mauryl had had to tell him. Flesh as well as spirit! Don't let one fly without the other!

Mauryl had pinned him to earth, and made him do things the slow, the thoughtful way. Emuin had taught him to reckon his way through difficulties, how to govern Men without wishing them capriciously one way or the other . . . how to deal with friends, and how to have Men of free will about him: that was the greatest gift, greater than life itself.

What must it have been for a wizard like Mauryl, bound to times and seasons, to try to teach such a creature as he was? *I never know what you'll take in your head to do,* Mauryl had complained to him, and now he understood that saying, that it was not just running naked in the storm on the parapet, but willing and wishing and having his own way.

What must it have been to try to teach one ready to wish this and wish that, a dozen spells in a day, and power Unfolding to him by the day and the moment, events tumbling one over the other? A passing moth had been as fascinating to him as a lightning stroke, and when he wanted something, tides flowed through the gray space that he had not yet perceived existed: to him in those days, the world had drowned all his senses in color and taste and noise.

Flesh as well as spirit, Mauryl had taught him . . . and that spirit in him was a perilous spirit, and able to do things Mauryl could not possibly prevent, breaking into utter, reckless, joyous, ignorant freedom.

But could magic work harm?

Oh, easily.

He wanted advice. He wanted someone to tell him the right way.

—*Auld Syes,* he called, for he dared not reach to Emuin. He reached out in an instant of fear and uncertainty, and a blast of wind came up in their faces and out of nowhere. Dys came up on his hind legs. Horses shied off from it.

And when Dys came down on all fours and danced forward, a gray old woman walked between him and Crissand.

"Grandmother," Crissand whispered to her.

"Auld Syes," Tristen said. "What *is* this thing in Ilefínian?"

Auld Syes was gone before he had quite finished saying it, but streaks ran through the meadow ahead, and in the gray space a storm broke, sweeping the pearl gray cloud into slate-colored strands.

There Auld Syes stood, assailed by the winds, and attempting to hold her place.

There Owl flew, scarcely maintaining against the gale.

—*So, said a voice that sent shivers of ice through the air.* **Mauryl's Shaping. So, so, so, come ahead.**

He had never met the like, and yet it seemed he might have dreamed it, long, long ago, a Wind that rattled the shutters and set the faces in Ynefel's walls to moaning.

—*Mauryl's enemy, he surmised.* **Not Hasufin this time.**

—**Hasufin,** *the Wind scoffed.* **Hasufin the bodiless. Hasufin who has no shape, nor life, nor wit. I've missed Mauryl, and lo! He sent me a surrogate.**

A presence flew near him. Owl settled on his shoulder. Auld Syes, her substance streaming gray threads, arrived on his other side, his guides, the defenders of wizardry and magic.

—**You were at Ynefel,** *Tristen said.* **And you are not Hasufin.**

—Oh, names, names, names. Names have no power. Places have none. I have many Places.

Mauryl had despaired of his Summoning's actions, and warded the windows, and warded his dreams and nights as well, with especial care.

—Feared you? the Wind mocked his thoughts. **Oh, with great reason Mauryl feared you. Afraid, are you? Afraid to draw breath? Afraid you'll break these fragile things?**

In his unfettered anger was the terror of any soul who could rend its protectors and its home apart. He posed a fearful danger to those he loved. And Mauryl had held him, restrained him, taught him, and kept him out of the world long enough, as long as Mauryl's strength lasted.

—And what have you done since? the Wind asked him. **Wished this, wished that, turned a king of men to your bidding, all to bring you here, to me? Do you value him? I think you do.**

—Leave him be!

—Can you bid me? I think not. Hasufin thought he could bid me. Mauryl brought the Sihhë out of their retreat, and last of all brought you . . . only one, this time. The old man was at the end of his strength, and Hasufin's become a shell of a creature . . . both mortal, in the end. I wish another such, I think . . .

It tried him. It reached for Crissand, and for Cevulirn, nearest to him, but Tristen was as quick and they were wary, so that instantly the gray space cleared, and Auld Syes stared at him, her gray hair all disordered, her eyes dark as cinders.

—The same kind, Auld Syes said, *but not the same.* **King thou art. Take up the sword!**

"What is it?" Crissand asked, and Cevulirn, silent, stared grim-faced toward the north.

But Tristen found no Name for it: he perceived only the sweep of winds toward an abyss out of which that Wind had come.

"Magic," was the best Word he could find. "*Magic* gone to sorcery. Not Hasufin. It was Hasufin opposing us, but he's gone. This remains."

He could only think of the cloud in the gray space, pouring continually over the Edge. And the gray space continued to pour out its force, as if magic had no limit and the flood would never cease.

"What's amiss?" Uwen asked, looking from them to the north and back again. The horses were restive, disturbed by the streaks in the grass. "Summat's goin' on."

"He's gone," Tristen said again. A *magic* gone amiss: in the precise way Men parsed words he found no words for it. Sorcery was wizardry turned askew. What could Men know of what he had felt opposing him, its power and its grip on the elements?

If it existed, it was nameless, unless someone had bidden it into Shapeless existence long, long ago; it owned no master now, and it was by all he perceived every other creature's enemy. What it wanted, it willed, and what it willed, it willed without a thought to any creature but itself. It was magical, and it was free, and set no limits on itself such as Mauryl had continually dinned into him. It had learned no patience with frustration such as Emuin had taught him.

And to wield magic after that unfettered fashion when there was only oneself with that power . . . that was inconceivable to him: what if there were no Mauryl, no Emuin, no Uwen or Cefwyn? What if there never could be for him a Crissand or a Cevulirn?

Lord Sihhë! the people cried in the streets of Henas'amef. Lord Sihhë, the word had gone through an army discouraged from calling him King.

But what was this thing?

And what was he?

Sihhë? And what was that?

That was the question of all questions, the one question no one of his friends could answer. He was not sure even Mauryl could have answered it completely—although Mauryl had known to call on the Sihhë to deal with the threat Hasufin posed.

And did that not inform him something? Mauryl had known that magic would stop Hasufin, when his student Hasufin turned. So Mauryl *had* understood: Mauryl *had* known the source of Hasufin's wrongdoing.

Mauryl could not defeat this magic without help, and then had defeated only Hasufin, and that not completely. Not even the five Sihhë-lords had completely overcome this threat, for through Hasufin this threat found its way into Althalen after the five were gone.

The question began to gnaw at all confidence . . . it came as an assault, an opening thrust from the enemy.

What was he?

Lord of Shadow, with the Lord of the Sun. His blade was Illusion and Truth, dividing one from the other.

"Where," he asked those with him, "where do you suppose the Sihhë came from?"

"The north," Uwen said. "As they say."

"But before that?"

"It was never recorded," Cevulirn said. "Not in any account."

"They were not good," Tristen said. "It's nowhere recorded that they were *good,* only that they were strong."

"Barrakkëth was the friend of our house," Crissand said.

They wielded magic; they lived together under one roof and rode and fought together in the south. But they were not all kind, or good, or gentle—in fact the histories recorded the opposite: yet they had never wielded their magic to seize all will from their subjects, never turned it to have their own way from each other, fought no wars within the five. They had that much wisdom.

Only five, and no children, no women: could such as the Sihhë arise by nature . . . or were they something created, as he was created, creatures of less than a lifetime?

There were no tombs such as Uleman's, no trace of their passing. It was never recorded that they died, only, the records said, that Barrakkëth passed the rule to another, and that was all.

He felt cold in all his limbs, the chill of earth and darkness. His gloved fingers maintained their grip on the reins. His eyes maintained a hold on the sky and the horizon: he would not slip into that dark, would not go over the Edge, where the Wind alone held sway.

Lord of Shadows, Lord of the Sun: without shadow and light, there was only the gray space, forever and ever, changeless change, never settling.

"Speak to me," he begged those with him.

"M'lord?" Uwen answered, that potent, commanding voice that brought the land and the day and the war back to him. And Uwen, experienced of such demands, heaved a great sigh and remarked how fair a day it was: "As there's a good breeze, ain't there? Which wi' the sun beatin' down on armor is a good thing, ain't it?"

"A good thing," he said desperately. His heart was hammering against his ribs. He breathed as if he had run a race. He had met the enemy. Crissand and Cevulirn gazed at him with alarm.

But he looked to the horizon, where trees met meadow . . . where still more stragglers, peasants and battered men-at-arms, survivors of lost battles and defeated lords, came to join their march. They had flowed to him since last night with the currents moving in the world, and after what he had seen, he knew that all things opposed to what sat in Ilefínian must flow to his banner . . . all that was Elwynim, all that was the south, whoever would, he could not deny them now. Auld Syes was the voice that spoke for them, but the summoning magic ran through the land and the woods and hour by hour the rocks gave up fugitives such as Aeself and his men . . . he felt presences far and wide; he felt their moving through the land, though to the east he was blind . . . a veil he himself drew over that one force his heart yearned to see, with all that was wrong in it.

"The Sihhë ruled for hundreds of years," he said, thinking of Cefwyn and Ryssand. "They never fought each other."

"It's not recorded that they did," Cevulirn said to him, and, perhaps thinking of the same conflict: "Wiser than we, it seems."

Restraint ran between the lines of all that Barrakkëth had written in his Book . . . he remembered. Line after Line Unfolded to him, not alone the nature of magic, but the Shape of the world, the restraint that let the world Unfold in its own time.

He had burned that Book to keep it from other hands, and now it seemed to him that he might have possessed and destroyed that for which the junior archivist had murdered his senior: that not only Men had yearned to find among those mundane letters and requests for potions the very thing he had had . . . and destroyed.

Knowledge of the enemy was there.

The fount of those words was in himself, but now that he inquired of it, he found of all the words that Barrakkëth had ever poured onto parchment, the two true ones were written on opposite sides of his sword: Truth, and Illusion.

"They never fought each other," he said aloud.

And the truest thing of all was the Edge between the two, the dividing line, the line of creation and destruction, dream and disillusion. There had to be both, for there to be movement at all in the world.

In his heart he could all but hear Mauryl's voice saying, Boy! Boy, listen to me! Pay attention, now! This is the crux of the lesson!

"Ye're woolgatherin'," Uwen observed. "Lad, are ye with us?"

He drew a deep breath. He smiled at Uwen, who alone of them could wake him to the ordinary world.

"You still have that power," he said to Uwen.

"What power, m'lord?"

"To call my name." He glanced solemnly aside at Crissand and Cevulirn on the other side. "I obey Uwen's voice as no other," he said, "and I gave him the calling of me. It's a magic he can do. Wherever I wander, Uwen can always find me."

"As I'd follow ye to hell, m'lord," Uwen said. "Ye know that."

"I'd rather you called me out of it," he said. He had no true knowledge what the Quinalt meant by it, but he knew where he had fared when he faced Hasufin Heltain.

He knew where he would go now when he faced the enemy.

"Guard Uwen," he said to Crissand and Cevulirn. "Make sure he's safe."

"That's the wrong way about, m'lord, them guardin' me."

"Yet that's His Grace's word," Crissand said.

"A Man," Tristen said. "And my friend, and wise as wizards."

"Oh, that I ain't!" Uwen cried.

"Trust Uwen," Tristen said to his friends, and in his mind's eye he saw Barrakkêth's Book, its pages curling as it burned.

When he had cast the Book into the fire he had been armed as now, ready to ride against Hasufin: so he was now, astride Dys and armed and with Uwen beside him.

He used great care when he let anything in that Book well up out of the dark: its answers informed him there was much of illusion in what he loved.

Past and present and time to come mingled in the old mews, and in Ynefel, and in those other places: had been and might yet be were interchangeable in those places: they were the easiest path for magic, and his enemy had found a toehold in each and every one.

He found the meadows and woods gone dim around him, and the light gone to brass.

He saw a child dancing across the dry gold grass before them. A wind blew the grass and followed that child, and that wind suddenly smelled of storm.

"That's odd," Uwen said. "Smells like rain an' the sun's shinin' and the sky is blue. An' I swear that's a cloud just come above the ridge."

"I wish it mayn't rain," Tristen said, but spent little strength to wish it. He still saw the child, but no one else did, not even Crissand or Cevulirn.

Troops of Shadows seemed now to follow the child, Auld Syes' daughter, who had lived once, he was sure, and danced in the meadows, a long, long time ago: as there had been nothing ordinary about Emwy village, where Auld Syes had seemed to be in authority. Men had died, and thereafter Emwy village had perished, lost, perhaps not for the first time.

In magic, time itself came unhinged, and Emuin's Great Year governed the progress of the world only so far as to say that strange appearances were easier than at other times.

Mauryl had brought the Sihhë from the north. But who had Summoned them? And out of what?

He looked at the sky, looked at the bare trees and at the sun on Dys' black mane. The world was so beautiful, and there was so much of it: he could gaze forever at the wonder of leaves and not see them all: could inhale the wind and not smell all its scents, hear the sounds of men and horses and not hear all the sounds of the woods, and taste the thousand flavors in stale water and still find it wonderful . . . because it was not darkness.

The darkest night in the darkest room in the world was not that darkness which was behind his first memory of Mauryl's fireside. And that was not the worst that might befall.

He would fight to live. He knew that now. He would fight to keep these things, aside from all reasons Mauryl had Summoned him. He had gathered his own reasons, and was not, now, Mauryl's creature.

Barrakkëth, some said, even his dearest friends.

But he said *Tristen*, and he said it with every breath he drew.

The dagger rested concealed in Cefwyn's boot, for if Idrys had come by stealth, Cefwyn thought it wise to keep the secret, and hid that weapon which some eyes might recognize. He rode Danvy at the head of the Dragon Guard. Anwyll's contingent being newly joined to the main body, Anwyll was close by him; and he ordered the Guelens to bring up the rear and the Prince's Guard to hold a place at the middle of their line of march, lest any surprise attack should try to split the column of less experienced provincials.

The land was roughest here, so the maps had indicated and so it was. Rocks encroached from the left and the trees spilled down off the heights and across the road. Weeds had grown here during more than one summer, legacy of Elwynor's civil conflicts.

It was the third day, and from Ryssand and his allies as yet he had had no dissent, possibly the longest period of peace with Ryssand he had known since he had come to his capital. Knowing that Ryssand was about to be a traitor was a distinct relief from wondering what Ryssand was about.

But now there was more worry, which had arrived with the dagger and the message.

A traitor near him. A traitor to whom he might have confided all his plans, when plans were hard come by, and hard to change.

Unfair, he said to Idrys, scanning the trees and the rocks and wondering whether Idrys watched the column from that rough outcrop or from the depths of the woods. He was vexed with Idrys, not an uncommon thing in dealing with the Lord Commander, but no signal he could give would order Idrys in.

He needed advice on a matter far more important than Ryssand's treason and Ryssand's conspiring with someone he trusted.

We have a war to fight, have you noticed, perchance, master crow?

Should I care that one more of my barons would put a dagger in my back? I am not destined to be a well-loved king, but thus far and somewhat by my own wits I am a live one. Come in! Stop this skulking in the bushes . . . it ill behooves a commander of the king's armies.

Damn, he said to himself as birds flew up, startled from a thicket.

He found he was anticipating attack, not attack from one of his barons, but attack out of the woods that were no more than a thin screen between them and the ridge . . . not enough to prevent archery lofted over and down, if Tasmôrden were so enterprising. He had sent his scouts ahead to investigate the heights he had sent a squad to occupy, indeed, but the essential trouble with scouts was that they had to come back to report what they saw. A man with critical information might not be able to come back, might be lying dead with a dozen arrows in him.

So might Idrys, if he went poking and prying into the woods ahead, if he had his attention all for the barons and none spared for the enemy.

And which of the barons, or which of the officers, was a traitor to him?

He refused to suspect Maudyn or Maudyn's sons: Sulriggan's turning on him would be no news and no loss. He had never been sure of Osanan.

He led the rest, not reckoning any one of them a potent threat, not reckoning Murandys would dare cross him: that alliance of Murandys with Ryssand was lately frayed; and Murandys was not a man to take rash and independent action.

Anwyll was never suspect, either. Complicity could not possibly lie in that face, in those forthright blue eyes. There was never a man less given to conspiracy: Anwyll always expected honesty of the world, was indignant when he found otherwise; and for the rest of the officers, they had served Ylesuin in his father's reign and served with honor, no marks against any of them.

An owl called by daylight, and drew alarm from the men nearest. Maudyn laid a hand on his sword. But then a true owl took to the air and flew off across their path, so Maudyn laughed, and no few of the men did.

Then a horseman came from around the bend of the road and toward them at breakneck speed.

Attack came: there was no question—and they had not reached the chosen battlefield. Cefwyn's heart leapt and plummeted, seeing the guardsman rode perilous in balance, the dark stain of blood on his red surcoat, an arrow jutting from his back.

"Form the line!" Cefwyn shouted, and already the banner-bearers halted and spread out across the meadow: they wanted all the open land they could take, the devil and Tasmôrden take the woods where heavy horse could not have effect.

They might have met the ambush attack of some bandit, some startled peasant farmer; or it might herald the presence of an enemy whose surprise was spoiled.

The scout came riding up, scarcely staying in the saddle, and managed his report:

"Enemies in the valley next, a line, a camp . . ." The man had used all the wind he had, and sank across his horse's neck.

"Tend this man!" Cefwyn ordered, and shouted orders next for the banners to advance and compact the army again into a marching line spearheaded by heavy cavalry. "Panys!" he shouted at Lord Maudyn. "Take the left as we come through." They had a barrier of woods yet to pass to reach that place the scout described, which by the condition of the scout might mean hidden archers on either side of the road. "Shields! Lances!"

Here was the battle he had come for. Tasmôrden *had* come out of his walled town, fearing, perhaps, that its surviving population was too hostile, its secrets were too well reported; and so they were: Ninévrisë had told them to him in great detail, and swore, too, that such townsmen as still lived could never love this lord, of all others.

The sun was shining, the hour toward noon: there was no impediment to the fight they had come for . . . and Tasmôrden came out to fight, relying most on traitors to do their work.

So Cefwyn instructed his Guard: "Watch my back!" They knew from whom to guard it; and there was no more time for musing. A page brought his shield and another his lance, young men themselves armed and well mounted, young men whose duty now was to ride with messages, and so he dispatched them down the line to advise the hindmost to arm and prepare, and the baggage train to draw up and bar the road with the carts, save only a gap through which they might retreat if they had to ride back through the woods: an untidy battle if it came to that, but the saving of some if the encounter went badly, the saving of part of an army that might come home to Ylesuin, to Efanor's command . . . if it came to that.

He took the precautions, but he had no intention of losing. His grooms brought Kanwy up, his heavy horse, and with the groom's help he dismounted from Danvy and mounted up on a destrier's solid force, settled his shield, looked on the descent of a low hill and the strand of woods that ran from the road to the left slope, screening all the land in that direction, away from the ridge: they had climbed gradually for two days. Beyond this, his maps told him there was one great long slope before they reached the end of the ridge, a long ride down to the valley where he most expected Tasmôrden to meet him, beside what his best map, Ninévrisë's map, warned him was wooded land.

He had fought in worse land, on the borders. They had come downhill out of the brush into a Chomaggari picket barrier, and had had to climb over it. Such hours came back to him, and with the high beating of his heart, the confidence that the Elwynim, aside from their bandit allies, were not disposed to such ambushes: it was heavy horse they were bound to meet ahead, lines that mirrored their lines: the shock of encounter and the skill of riders to carry through.

The king of Ylesuin, however, did not carry the center of the charge, not today.

Leave that to Ryssand and Murandys.

CHAPTER 6

One moment Tristen's company crossed a wide meadowland in the bright sunlight; and in the next, slate gray ribbons of cloud raced across the heavens, broader and broader, until, rapid as the drawing of a canopy, the sun gave up a last few shafts.

"Gods!" Crissand said, for it was not only the gray space which changed so easily, but the world itself which had shifted, and Men and horses faltered in their march, dismayed. From the confidence of a world that could change but slowly, they had entered a territory where magic met magic and the sun itself was overwhelmed.

A sudden gale buffeted the foremost ranks, and lightning cracked and sheeted across the hills. From ranks behind them came wails of dismay: seasoned veterans and country lads who had run to the banners of the High King met hostile magic and wavered in their courage as the lightnings gathered alarmingly above their heads.

Tristen flung up his hand and willed the lightning elsewhere. It took a tree on the wooded ridge to their left: splinters flew in a burst of fire.

Owl came winging to him, and swung a broad, self-satisfied circle, on a light breeze.

—*Well, well, said the Wind. We are quick to seize the advantage, are we not? And confident?*

—*Owl! Tristen would not distract himself in debate with his enemy. He let Owl settle on his fist, and sent out one burning message through the gray space to all he loved and trusted, nothing reserved now: Ward yourselves! Let nothing in or out!*

"Damn!" Uwen said on the heels of the lightning strike. "That were close!"

374

"Do you hear it?" Tristen asked him, and then thought, foolishly, no, of course not. Crissand and Cevulirn might have heard the Wind speak. But Uwen did not. The army stood in ignorance, blind to its real danger, its confidence shaken by the lightning.

One rider came up from the ranks in haste: Aeself drew his frantic horse to a halt and pointed to the horizon ahead.

"Ilefínian!" Aeself said. "Just beyond the hill, my lord! The end of the ridge!"

"Then move ahead!" Tristen said, for when he ventured to know what Aeself said was there, he felt the truth of the threat in the gray space, a tightly warded opposition, so wrapped about with magic it was hard to see at all as that near him. He set Dys in motion, and reached out in the gray space for Crissand and Cevulirn both, settling his own protection on the likeliest targets of hostile magic. Such as they knew how, they warded him, and Uwen, too, while Owl lofted himself again and flew outward and back, a long gliding passage that ended on Tristen's outreaching hand as they crested the hill.

Here the stony ridge ended in a long, forest-girt plain, and a last outrider of that ridge, a hill rose within the valley. On that hill, towers and town walls rose from skirts of winter-bare pasturage and fields.

Lightning sheeted across the sky, a wall of brilliant light, west to east, and against it that distant fortress stood clearly to be seen, above its strong town walls. It was a Place as Ynefel was a Place, ancient and deep-rooted, and in the fire across the heavens it unveiled itself in all its power. Tristen felt it and shivered in the crash of thunder.

Far to the south, the Lady Regent herself knew they had come to her capital.

To the west, Efanor, at his prayers, knew.

And in the ranks, the Elwynim behind them knew, and raised a shout that drowned the thunder.

"The king!" someone cried, and other voices shouted it: "The High King and Elwynor!"

But others shouted, "Lord Sihhë!"

And clearer to him than all the voices was a sense of foreboding presence beyond the ridge that pointed like a spearhead toward Ilefínian, the knowledge of lives at risk the moment Men and horses set themselves in motion.

Cefwyn was in danger, Tristen thought in anguish. He had brought his army where he wished, to the end of the ridge, and in sudden clarity he knew Cefwyn was on the other side, he knew the enemy lay in wait, where he could come at them from behind, but he could not turn aside. Cefwyn was in reach of Tasmôrden's forces, in peril from his own men . . . but worse—he was within reach of Ilefínian, where the danger was wrapped not in iron edges, but in an ageless, malevolent will.

"It has to fall!" he shouted to those nearest, to Uwen and Crissand and Cevulirn, and pointed toward the fortress on its hill. "We cannot go to the east! We have to break the wards of that place, or Cefwyn will die. They all will die!"

The carts went into place, a line between the rocks and the woods, men hauling gear off the carts in feverish haste—casting anxious looks at the heavens, for a pall of cloud flowed from over the ridge, west to east, and all across the horizon what had seemed hazed blue sky proved to be gray. Lightning raced across the heavens and thunder boomed from off the heights, and now men looked up from their work in fear.

"Form the line!" Cefwyn ordered his forces as lightning cast white light over all of them, once, twice, thrice. "Form the line, Ylesuin! We've beaten wizards before! *Forward, the banners!*"

He let Kanwys have rein, wary of the woods that fringed the road on the right . . . on the right, where shields were on the left. Those woods slanted away rapidly toward the right as he moved past the trees into meadow, and there the hill arched away downward, while on the left the ridge descended with it in a tumble of rocks the size of peasant huts. He knew his maps: this was the dizzyingly long, broad downslope which both his grandfather's maps and Ninévrisë's warning had told him was a long, long highland . . . but gods! All the subtle rise of the land over two days came downhill at once, grassland pasturage spread out for a long, long, uninterrupted descent to the cultivated plain. The view captured the eye, distracted the wits, suddenly beset with the scale of that descent, while the sky flickered with no natural storm.

But the Dragon Guard advanced, men who had stood before worse than this. The Prince's Guard moved, and so did Ryssand and Nelefreíssan and Murandys, earliest ready, a wall of iron to shield men still preparing.

Were it not for the courage of the scout the army would have had no warning until an assault disorganized their line of march. "Bear east!" Cefwyn said. "Dragons! Ryssand! Hold center! Panys to the right! Bring the blackguards out in the open!"

Messengers sped and banners moved outward under the flash of lightning. As Panys' line formed, light midlands cavalry probed the border of the woods—and rapidly fell back before a howling outrush of motley armed men.

Irregulars, the Saendal, armed with axes and pikes and bows, and the force with which they charged was considerable even across the slope and on the uneven ground. Brigands, hirelings, hill bandits who regarded no law but gold, hire, and murder . . . with them Murandys' stolid peasant infantry proved of some use, standing for a first taste of battle largely because they did not regard the trumpet signal that called them back, and for a moment there was a sharp contest, before some of Maudyn's forming right wing alike began to give backwards, disengaging in the distance across the hill.

"Hold fast!" Cefwyn shouted, chafing to have the rest of the heavy horse move up from behind. He chosen to engage the brigands' ambush quickly on this eastward fringe of woods, to keep the enemy from harrying their flank. Two of his allies, Sulriggan and Osanan, were still behind the lines, equipping their heavy horse to bring them forward, please the gods, at some convenient time: damn Sulriggan's lackluster drills!

Ryssand, however, had moved with dispatch, and so had Murandys, spreading their forces behind the immediate deployment of the red-coated Dragon Guard and the company of light horse who went at the ready.

And granted Ryssand's naive peasants who had gotten in the way of the Guard and trammeled up their advance, those peasants still had made a line, a line they must hold long enough for the heavy horse to set itself in order. He was sure now Tasmôrden's main force lay closer than that streamside he had planned to have for a battlefield, never dreaming Tasmôrden would give him the advantage of the higher ground, but knowing it had its disadvantages, too, in the very momentum it gave them.

Traps were more than possible.

"Guelens, Maudyn, damn it, *Guelen Guard!*—Tell him so, boy! Ride!"

If Ryssand's and Murandys' peasant farmers yielded more ground on the flank, where they had crowded together, he had to trust the Guelens, the city troops among them, would account the skirmish with the Saendal their sort of brawl. And as he shouted the order another messenger of the Guard scrambled to horse and was off behind the confused wing to reach Lord Maudyn.

The embattled Dragons, too, under Gwywyn, bore toward the tangle of the peasant line, not where he wanted them situated, for this attack he was certain was meant to create as much confusion as it could, pouring downhill at the back of his right wing if he had formed early, at very least keeping him from coming onto that slope unreported to the enemy.

"Majesty!" Now, *now,* there was a general movement of Sulriggan's heavy horse from out of that screen of carts and forest. Cefwyn settled his shield and stilled Kanwy with his knees, putting him to this side and the other to settle his restless forward impulse. That would be the difficulty, with all the men: the impulse to charge downhill. Discipline; discipline: a peasant army could not restrain itself; veterans could scarcely restrain themselves when tumult surrounded them and deafened them to signals.

"Lance!" he shouted at his pages, and the solid ash arrived within his grip. His guard had gathered around him, and now others of his house guard had arrived, the heavy-armed center of the Dragons and the Prince's Guard, Gwywyn's ordinary command, solid heart of Guelen force. Panys' younger son, near him, caught away from his father's command, had his grooms fighting to further tighten a cinch, the horse wild-eyed and resisting.

And in the skirmish with the lad's recalcitrant horse, one of those cursedly ridiculous incidents that precede battle, for some reason, no reason at all, he found himself in high good spirits, all the strictures and obligations of kingship fallen away from him.

"Dragons!" he shouted out, sending Kanwy on a restrained, restless pace near Anwyll's command. "Trumpeter, sound out! Form the line! Banners! Form and stand! By the plan!"

Banner-bearers spread out, signaling men where their companies should be. And, unraveling the chaos that had threatened the right wing, the veteran Dragons answered quickly to the trumpets and the movement of the banners and set position on the left.

Osanan drew his men into line: that was the centerward edge of the left wing; and Panys and the Guelens maintained the skirmish on the right wing, while Sulriggan's company moved in feverish and wasteful haste, crossing to the fore of the Prince's Guard, not the rear as he ought—damn the man! Cefwyn thought, but it was ineptitude, not treason.

More slowly, with laudable precision, Ryssand, Murandys and Nelefreíssan, heavy horse and the center of the line, took their place and stood firm.

In the distance Maudyn's trumpeter sounded out another call that called the right wing to desist pursuit: the engagement there, which Cefywn could not see from the left wing, had become a downhill rout it was not Maudyn's choice to pursue: gods knew whether the peasant infantry remembered that trumpet signal, or knew theirs from Tasmôrden's.

More precise than the trumpets, the banners were a constant signal; and three more king's messengers hovered close at Cefwyn's side, awaiting orders that would send last-moment changes to the line, to answer whatever surprises Tasmôrden had contrived.

There was a moment that the army was poised, prepared. Everything they had done toward this moment came to the test.

The wooded ridge was to their left, a steep, brushy range of boulders that spilled away in a wedge downhill; a narrow band of woods played out to their right and gave way to meadow and a broad plain below, curtained close at hand on the left by the ridge.

But out across the plain and under the shadowed sky, all but obscured by the ridge, a keen eye could make out the regularity of cultivated land . . . it was a moment before Cefwyn was sure what he saw, but once he saw, there was no mistaking it.

It was the cultivated border of a town, its sheep walls and winter brown barley fields. This slope met the end of the cursed ridge that had kept them from joining forces with Tristen and their southern neighbors.

And at the very bottom of the slope, all but obscured by the downward fall of the hill, the massed forces of an army.

Tristen, he thought at first, seeing black banners. But Tasmôrden had claimed the High Kingship; and those lines held nothing of the bright banners that should be with Tristen, nothing of the White Horse of Ivanor, the Heron banner of Lanfarnesse.

No. It was not Tristen.

"He is there!" Cefwyn cried aloud. He had good eyes, better than most, and he pointed for those who might see once they looked. "Tasmôrden's waiting for us below! We've come to Ilefínian, *and we've met our enemy!*"

"Ilefínian!" Anwyll of the Dragons took up the shout. "The gods for Ylesuin!"

"The gods for Ylesuin and the Lady Regent!" Cefwyn shouted back, and loyal men of the Dragons echoed him.

The skirmish over by the woods had surely been a signal, messengers fled back to Tasmôrden, warning of their arrival, a light-armed force that carried word what they were, and in what numbers, and perhaps, essential to one who relied on traitors, word whether Ryssand's banner flew among the rest.

It did, and if Tasmôrden's men had lingered to report how they ordered their line, why, it flew centermost, where he had ordered it to be, foremost of Ylesuin's defense, after all.

Tristen rode in the world at a steady, ground-consuming pace, with all the south at his back, while the gray space grew violent with lightnings and that black Edge appeared which had appeared at the Lord Regent's death . . . so vivid a sight Tristen had difficulty knowing what was the world of Men and what was the other place. Chill wind blew out of that gulf and threatened to sweep them all away into it: at one moment and in the white fire of lightning he felt the whole world tilted and sliding, and yet when he made himself look squarely between Dys' black ears it was no different than the world had ever been.

"Do you see anything?" he asked those about him, and yet knew it was foolish of him to ask. "Do you feel the cold?"

"The cold, yes, my lord," Crissand said: Uwen did not answer, but Tristen doubted any Man without the gift had perceived what he saw or felt. He hoped they did not, for the cold was bitter and the view unsettling to the heart . . . but courage, these Men did have, to face what came.

The town rose before them, veiled by fire-blackened orchards, its gates shut, and more than shut, warded. He felt the strength of it even here, warding that might admit those blind to it, but not him. He sent Owl out, as far as Owl dared go, to try to find a way for him, but Owl turned back suddenly as if he had met a barrier, and suddenly the horses went as if they trod on eggshells, sniffing the wind for what no one could see.

Yet the shadow of a little girl appeared walking before them down that lane of burned orchards . . . gone for an hour and two and now back again, under the sky laced with lightning and muttering with thunder. Then, with her, hand in hand, Auld Syes appeared, looking like some country wife walking with her little daughter.

"There's the child," Crissand said in wonder, as if he could not see the mother. And Cevulirn said nothing, whether he saw or not.

Then Sovrag rode forward, swearing there was winter in the air again, and he had seen sleet on the wind, though the smell in the air was rain and burned wood.

Immediately behind him came old Pelumer, with little fuss, only silently joining them. And last came Umanon on his great destrier, with his guard. They all were to the fore now, all the lords.

"Shall we ride up to the gates and ask politely?" Umanon asked. "Or where is Tasmôrden, do you suppose?"

Umanon asked, and Tristen looked back at the stony ridge that spilled downhill behind them in a tumble of great boulders that ended with abandoned orchards and weed-grown fields, and the question wrung his heart, for after so long and hard marching they had come almost within reach of one another . . . almost within reach, but not in reach at all, and not within his protection.

There was Tasmôrden, he thought, and forgot to say so, his wits were so distracted with the threat aloft and the threat of the walls before them.

"I see the child," Uwen remarked in surprise. "Walkin' wi' someone, she is."

The light dimmed as if a dark cloud had gone over the sun, then dimmed further. Tristen looked up at a slate gray pall that streamed over the tops of the charred trees at their left. In the next moment a gale blasted through the trees, tearing the banners sideways, throwing Owl tumbling. Horses turned from the gale and riders fought them back to a steady course as the trees shed a sleet of broken twigs.

Shadows gathered out of that orchard, not the shadows of the overwhelmed sun, but Shadows from out of the depths of ruin, Shadows that flowed like ink in the gust-torn brush, with wafts of cold air. Thunder muttered above them, and lightning sheeting through the clouds whitened the black trees, but did nothing to relieve the flow of darkness seeping from woods and rocks.

"Something's beside us," Crissand said anxiously, and cries of dismay arose from behind them.

"Ride," Tristen said, urging Dys forward, for what swept about them felt to be neither friend nor foe, only the outpouring of magic reaching into dark places and drawing out all the Shadows imprisoned there. He swept them up, urging them also against the walls where the enemy had his citadel.

The heart of all that was wrong was in Ilefínian, and how they should pass its gates, he did not know.

Lightning chained across the sky, setting all that was bright in unnatural clarity against a darkened sky, and thunder cracked above the army's heads. A warhorse broke the line and charged forward, fighting his rider's signals, prompting other horses to break forward only to be turned back, and Cefwyn reined Kanwy about to shout at the Dragons to stand fast, no matter the wrath of heaven or the folly of horses.

The trumpeters sounded out loud and long, king's men, experienced and sensible, calling out for attention; and men heard that, through ears half-deafened by thunder, those who could not hear their king's voice. The line that had wavered steadied.

Cefwyn rode Kanwys out to the fore, riding across the slope in front of the red ranks of Dragon Guard, the black of the Prince's, and shouted out, over and over, "The gods for Ylesuin! The gods against sorcery! Gods save Ylesuin!" while the men, encouraged, shouted back,

"The gods for Ylesuin! Gods save the king!"

They had men enough armed, now, and the line was formed. The enemy had not come upslope after them, only prudent; but neither had they taken their greatest opportunity, that moment of confusion in the Saendal's assault on their flank. If sorcery helped Tasmôrden, in whatever balance it warred with Emuin and Tristen, at least it had not helped Tasmôrden come over that hill in time to catch them unprepared.

Tasmôrden waited instead in the valley, prepared to receive a cavalry charge.

But traps were possible, trenches and stakes and pikemen and other such unpleasant means to turn the charge of heavy cavalry into carnage: for that reason among others Cefwyn would not give the order to rush headlong downhill, letting his troops slip prudence and outrace the trumpet signals and the reach of couriers. He saw with satisfaction that Maudyn had completely crushed the attack from the woods.

And he had recovered his men from the panic charge they might have made. It was harder to go deliberately, to measure their advance, but he relied on his veteran companies, and had sent out messengers sternly advising the line to prepare a moderate advance . . . gods keep the peasant levies steady.

He gave the signal and led, keeping Kanwy tight-reined. Behind him, the veteran companies that were the stability of Ylesuin's line held their horses to the pace he set, allowing the peasant line to keep up. He could see the center, Ryssand's forces; and the right wing, Maudyn's, stretched out to indistinction against an unkept woods which had already sent out an ambush. They advanced, keeping their ranks, never quickening the charge. It was a game of temptation: Tasmôrden tempted him to a mad rush downhill: he had his own trap in mind.

"They aren't facing untried boys!" Cefwyn shouted at Anwyll, with the Dragons, where a little too much enthusiasm from Anwyll's lot crowded up. "Steady pace!"

Ryssand and Nelefrcíssan and Murandys to the center, the Dragons, Osanan and the Prince's Guard in the left wing with him, while Maudyn commanded the right wing: Panys and Llymaryn, Carys and the other eastern provinces, with the Guelen Guard, as they had settled among themselves. At the very last, their heavy cavalry had to screen their far fewer pikemen, who would be slow as tomorrow getting to the fray, and in peasant order, which was to say, damned little order at all . . . likely to arrive only for the very last action if the cavalry once lost its good sense and plunged downslope.

Yet it was always Ylesuin's habit to have the pikemen for support, and Cefwyn asked himself a last time was it folly on his part to have declined to summon the Guelen and Llymarish levies into this, not to have had the double line of pikes that had distinguished his grandfather's successful assaults.

It was far too late now for second thoughts. Kanwy fought him for more rein and jolted under him like a mountain in motion, plate-sized feet descending a steep slope in deliberate, uncomfortable strides that made it clear Kanwy wanted to run.

For a guard at his back he had those who had defended him for years; and for a man at his right he had young Anwyll, lately from watch on the Lenúalim.

Where are you now, master crow? Taking account of this? On the ridge watching?

I know where all my enemies are. I've dealt with it, thank you, faithful crow. I could use your shield just now. Anwyll's a fine young man. But he hasn't your qualities.

The horizon flashed white, then dark, and the foot of the hill gave up a sudden movement of dark banners with a white device that shone like the lightning itself.

It was the heraldry of the Sihhë High Kings carried before him, in the lines of the enemy, the black banner of the Tower Crowned.

And before Ylesuin's line, beside the red Dragon Banner of the Marhanen kings, shone the Tower and Checker of the Lady Regent, blue and white and gold, bright under the leaden sky.

"Hold!" Cefwyn said, and reined in, to allow his line to assume a better order: the wings had begun to stray a little behind. "Let's see if they'll climb to us!"

The line drew to a ragged stop, re-formed itself in an even, bristling row of lances.

He sorely missed the Lanfarnessemen, archers that would have taken full advantage of this height. From the right wing issued a thin gray sleet of arrows aloft, archers from Panys' contingent, the best they had, and likely to do damage with the higher vantage.

Back came a flight from the other direction, uphill and short, a waste of shafts.

A solitary horseman rode out from the halted opposing line, rode back and forth, shouting something in which Cefwyn had no interest at all, except the mild hope that an arrow would do them a favor.

There, he said to himself, seeing the glint of gold encircling that helm, there was Tasmôrden at last, taunting them, wishing the king of Ylesuin to descend into the trap he had laid.

He would not shout back, would not give way to anger. He set Kanwy out to the fore at a mere amble, rode across the center and rode back again, gesture for gesture, leisurely as a ride through his capital. Arrows attempted the uphill shot with no better effect than before. Arrows came back down the hill, and the dull thump of impact below echoed off the rocks to their left, with satisfying out-cries of anger from the enemy below.

In the same leisure Cefwyn rejoined his wing, rode to Anwyll's side, and pointed to a stand of brush somewhat past Tasmôrden's line. "When we do charge, we will meet Lord Maudyn there, behind his line. Bear somewhat left. We shan't be in a hurry until the last."

"*Left,* Your Majesty . . ."

"Left, I say. Out and around his flank. There may be trenches. But there we meet Lord Maudyn, and come back east again. No driving into Tasmôrden's center, where I most think he's fortified. That honor is Ryssand's."

"Yes, Your Majesty." There was grave doubt in Anwyll's voice.

"Relay that to Captain Gwywyn."

Anwyll rode off at a good clip, met with the captain of the Prince's Guard, who stood in Idrys' place in general command of the king's forces, and came back again in haste toward him, to take his place as shieldman.

"*Sound the advance!*" Cefwyn cried to the trumpeter, and as the trumpets sounded, gave Kanwy rein to resume a measured advance.

Only when he was close enough to the foot of the long descent did he let the pace increase, and set himself not in the lead, as he had done in other wars, but back with the line: his guard was around him, the Dragons beside him, and the forest of ash wood lifted at the heavens now began to lower as the ranks closed.

He lowered his own visor, lowered the lance, took a good grip for the shock to come; and hoped to the gods the veteran Dragons evaded the brush where he wagered stakes were in place: they were too expert for such traps.

And his leading was not to ride full tilt into the lines that offered; they evaded the rows of brush that skirted the center and met the shock of heavy horse that swept out from the enemy's line to prevent that flanking move—met it with a crack like a smith's hammer. Horses went down, fewer of theirs than the enemy's, and they slid by—doing nothing to attack the entrenched line of brush-hidden stakes and pikemen. They went past the flank of the cavalry, and the heavy horse of Tasmôrden's center, seeing the gap they had left, charged past them, going uphill, unchecked.

Ryssand had buckled, had retreated.

And Tasmôrden's riders plunged up and up into that pocket of retreating men, blind to the sweep from either wing that now turned behind them.

Cefwyn took down an opposing pikeman with the broken stub of his lance, sent Kanwy through a last curtain of infantry, and saw Maudyn's banners coming toward him from the east, to meet him behind Tasmôrden's line.

More, he saw Tasmôrden's banners in the heart of the remaining pikemen, and saw the cluster of mounted heavy horse guards that betokened a lord's defense, between him and Maudyn.

"With me!" he shouted at Anwyll and whatever of his own guard could keep up, and, sword in hand, he rode for that gold-crowned man in the heart of the enemy.

The pretender to the High Kingship failed to see his approach; he shouted in vain after his charging troops, who by now had chased halfway up the hill in pursuit of Ryssand's retreat.

"Tasmôrden!" Cefwyn shouted, and the man turned his face toward him, a dark-bearded man in a crowned helm, in black armor, bearing the forbidden Tower Crowned on his coat and his shield.

Kanwy went through the guard like a bludgeon, scattering unready pikemen, shouldering horses aside as Cefwyn laid about him with sword and shield; with a shove of his hindquarters as if he were climbing a hill, Kanwy broke through the last screen of defense, trampled a man, kept going. The clangor of engagement was at Cefwyn's back: his guard was still with him, shouting for the gods and Ylesuin; and the crowned man, realizing his danger, reined full about and swept a wild blow at Cefwyn's head.

Cefwyn angled his shield, shed the force of it, and dealt a blow past the opposing shield. Kanwy shouldered a horse that hit them hard, bit another. Cefwyn cut aside at the encroaching guard, veered

Kanwy full about as he bore, in time to intercept another of Tasmôr-den's attacks, this one descending at Kanwy's neck.

The sword grated past the metal-guarded edge of his shield, scored Kanwy's shoulder. Kanwy stumbled, recovered himself against another horse, and blows cracked like thunder around them. One numbed Cefwyn's back, but as Kanwy regained solid footing he had Tasmôrden in sight and drove his heels in, sending Kanwy over a fallen rider and through the mistimed defense of two pikemen who tried to prevent him. A pike grated off Kanwy's armor. A man cried out and went down and Kanwy bore him past, and up against his enemy.

Tasmôrden flung up his shield, desperately choosing defense: but Cefwyn's strike came from the side, with Kanwy's impetus behind it on a wheeling turn. The blade hit and hung, needing force and a twist of the arm to free it, and when Cefwyn freed the blade, Tasmôr-den toppled from his saddle, helmless, a black-bearded and bloody face disappearing down into a maelstrom of horses and men.

"Majesty!" Cefwyn heard a man shout, and saw Lord Maudyn across an ebbing rush of Tasmôrden's forces.

Suddenly the air thickened. The hairs of his head and Kanwy's mane alike stood up.

Wizard-work, he thought. A trap.

And force and light and sound burst from the heart of the enemy.

Lightning broke above the towers, ripped across the sky, and even at a distance the air shivered with it. "Gods bless!" Uwen said, yet to Tristen's knowledge not a man behind them turned back.

The child and the Lady still went before them, and still that inky flow ran along the edges of the woods, but the lightning flash had for the blink of an eye seemed to illumine men and horses, gray as morning mist, that moved where the darkness flowed.

"I see men," Crissand said, while above them and near at hand the towers of Ilefínian now seemed to flow with inky stain in the cracks and crevices. The darkness flowed, too, in the ditch beside the road, and between the stones of a ruined sheep wall. It wound itself among the thin, straggling branches of blackened, bare trees, and drifted down like falling leaves, to coalesce and run like dark fire along the ground.

It became footprints, and the next flicker of the heavens showed ghostly riders in greater numbers.

"Haunts," Sovrag said, and Umanon blessed himself. Ahead of them all moved the lady of Emwy, but now it seemed banners had joined theirs, banners in great numbers, and a handful of ghostly gray riders, heedless of the trees, paced beside them toward the looming gates.

"Lord Haurydd," Aeself said in a muted voice, and Tristen, too, recognized the man and the banners, dim as he was under the flickering heavens. The walls of the town seemed manned, but it was uncertain whether with living Men or Shadows.

Behind his banners, the Elwynim, the Lady's sparrows, had come to take back their town; and the south of Ylesuin had come to defend their land against Elwynor's wars of succession.

Tristen turned in the saddle and looked back over the host that had come to this place, men who had left their own lands for a comfortless camp and the risk of sorcery out of the stones of walls that had known too many wars. The earth itself seemed to quake, and the gray place held no comfort.

—At my very doors, the Wind whispered. Mauryl's precious hatchling. Have we known one another at some time, disagreed, perhaps?

He swung about. It was not only that voice. There was another presence, far more familiar, that drifted around the perimeter, one that taunted and mocked him and still dared not come close.

He recalled the courtyard at Ynefel, and Mauryl's face within its walls, as all the others had been imprisoned, all the lost, all the defeated.

So might Ilefínian stand, as haunted, as wretched in its fall.

"The gates are barred," he said to Uwen, for the Wind told him so.

—Ylesuin's down, it said. Folly. Great folly. Will you help him, I wonder?

In the unstable clouds of the gray space he saw a field where lightning had struck, and the dead lay all about, men and horses, and Cefwyn . . . yet alive, within reach of him, if only he reached out to rescue him.

He turned his head suddenly and looked up at the walls, seeing the lure it cast him, its intention to have Cefwyn's life and his as surely as he turned that direction, and he would not do as it wished.

He struck at all of its presence he could reach within the gray space, he struck desperately and hard, and failed. His hold on the world weakened. His strength ebbed. It was the wards that drank it away from him.

"Uwen," he said, "I have to go in there. I have to open the gates."

"Not alone," Crissand said. "No, my lord!"

There was no debate. The way was plain to him for an instant, the blink of an eye, and he cast himself into it, alone, knowing only that there was within the fortress of Ilefínian a room where a banner had hung.

And that his enemy, bent on destruction of all he loved, invited him.

Lightning had hit, and only the fact he remembered that told Cefwyn that he had survived. He remembered Kanwy falling sidelong and pitching him to shield-side. He recalled the impact on his shield against a carpet of metal-clad bodies, and after that was uncertain whether Kanwy had risen or not: all the world was a noise in his ears and a blinding light in his vision, so bright it might have been dark instead.

He lay an instant winded and uncertain whether he felt the sword in his hand or whether it was, like the fall, only the vivid memory of holding it.

But his knee moved, and his elbow held him off his face.

And if he would live, his father had dinned it into him, no matter how hard the fall, no matter the pain, if Ylesuin would survive, he had no choice but cover himself and find his guards and his horse.

He gained one knee, levered himself to his feet with his sword, proving he did indeed hold it. He stumbled erect into a blind confusion of wounded men and horses, a morass of tangled bodies and shattered lances that turned and shifted underfoot, to a second fall and a third.

A distance along, his eyes began to make out moving shadows, but he thought others must be as dazed by the bolt. No one attacked him, no one seemed aware of any color or banner, and he had no idea at the moment where the lines were. He had lost his helm, his shield was in two pieces, and he shed it as an encumbrance, staggering on uneven ground, but aware at last that downhill was not the direction of his own men.

In front of him a fallen horse raised itself on its hindquarters and began to gain its feet, like a moving hill rearing up before him: his gloved hand found its shoulder and its neck and he seized the reins and tried to hold the stirrup, but the dazed horse tore away from him and veered off on its own way across the field, trampling the dead and the dying in its course.

Damn, Cefwyn said to himself, holding an aching side and recovering with difficulty from the blow the horse had dealt him. A second time brought to a standstill and having no other sense to help him, he listened past the roaring in his ears, trying to make of the sounds he heard any known voice, any sign of his own guards or any surety of his enemies. Men moved and called to one another near him, voices lifted over the distant clangor of battle, but his ears could not distinguish the words from sounds that might be wind or thunder.

It was a predicament, beyond a doubt, and he felt his father's disapproval of all he had done. Headlong folly had set him here afoot and alone.

But by the good gods, the battle plan had seemed to work. On a deep breath he recalled the successful sweep of two wings around Tasmôrden's flanks, while Tasmôrden's center charged uphill and Tasmôrden cursed his own men helplessly from the bottom of the hill.

Now he recalled the encounter with Tasmôrden. Now he recalled that he had come within sight of Ilefínian, and remembered that the enemy no longer had any semblance of a king or a leader. Orders would no longer come to them. Captains must direct such fighting as remained, and for hired captains, there was no more source of gold, no reason to linger.

But then another realization came to him . . . that in the bolt that had overthrown him and obscured Tasmôrden's fall, there was no coincidence—none he accepted since he had stood on Lewen field—none, since he had claimed Tristen for a friend. The hand of wizardry was beyond a doubt in that bolt, and *he* was still alive—inconvenienced mightily, afoot, half-deaf and three-quarters blind, but alive, while Tasmôrden was lying somewhere below.

He could in no wise say whether it was his wizards or Tasmôrden's who had just set the heavens afire and brought down the hammer of heaven on the battle with Tasmôrden, but they had called the lightning on the Quinaltine roof, and he began to suspect the answer lay in a wizardous tug of war.

Yet whatever magic had aimed or pulled the bolt this way or that, it had not hit *him,* and in that fact, he saw Tristen's hand.

He paused in that astonished thought, gazing toward the town his hazed vision could no longer find. At least he had seen it before the lightning fell . . . all his promise to Ninévrisë, all the ambition of his grandfather, all wrapped in one. That, and his enemy.

But if it was folly to have charged after Tasmôrden himself, it was greater folly to stand gawping in the middle of the carnage. He could not find a horse, or his guards: he began to realize he would not find either wandering here. From the mere effort to see, his eyes streamed tears. His very bones ached, his skin felt the first instant of scalding, endlessly maintained, and he doubted any man in the vicinity of the lightning could have fared much better. He recalled a field of dead men where he had waked, and told himself he had used all the luck that wizardry had parceled out to him on this field: he could not count on it twice.

And if downhill was the direction of Ilefínian, then he recalled the lay of the land, the spill of boulders that curved down to the flat where he had engaged Tasmôrden. That had been on the right: he knew by that which direction was east and west, where Tasmôrden's men had been tending; and knew now where he might find a place against which to set his back and live long enough to regain clear sight.

Determined, then, he went toward the west, where the ridge advanced outcrops of rounded stone and brush, and went unchallenged except by one wounded man nearly as blind. They hacked at one another, neither with great success, and blundered by, both shaken, both content to escape, the common soldier having no notion, perhaps, that he had engaged the king of Ylesuin.

His dazed wits wandered: he had caught buffets like that from his father in his day: had sat down with one ear near deaf in the practice yard. He was confused from moment to moment whether it was the practice yard or the battlefield, but after that encounter his ears began to make out sounds that informed him it was no practicce, and when he reached a haze of gray winter brush and crashed against a sizable boulder, he was content only to sink down beside it and catch his breath.

Sight began to come to him, alternate with dark.

Uphill, his banners and Ninévrisë's still flew. Uphill, a band of moving red had swept around the blue ranks of the Elwynim.

It was his design. Ryssand's retreat had done exactly what he had hoped it would, and the Dragons had not perished in the lightning: they had lived, and charged back uphill. Ryssand in his compact with his Elwynim allies had started a panic retreat in his center, intending the army to break apart in confusion . . . but Cefwyn rejoiced to know his own plan had driven the wings both full tilt downhill instead, downhill and around, while Tasmôrden's men had chased uphill into the pocket Ryssand gave them . . . breaking their line, losing contact with their own wings: too much confidence, too fast an advance. They had chased their own ally's retreat between Ylesuin's left wing and right, sure they had won the encounter down to the moment the jaws closed.

And Tasmôrden, who had let his troops slip his hand, could only stand behind them and curse, seeing disaster none of his men on the hill had been able to see.

Now the remnant of Tasmôrden's center was caught in a tightening noose, for surely in desperation, Ryssand's peasant muster had held its line better than the cavalry that had deliberately started the rout, and now the Dragons and the men of Panys, coming uphill, had the Elwynim in a bottle from which there was no escape.

And gods knew whether Maudyn was alive, or Gwywyn, or who of all them was giving orders up there. Gods forfend it was Ryssand . . . who might just have assumed the crown was within his grasp.

On that thought, Cefwyn staggered away from the rocks that had upheld him, began to climb the hill to reach his troops, picking his way past the dead and wounded at the edge of the brush and the rocks and finding this part of the hill woefully steeper on the climb up than it had ever seemed going down it.

CHAPTER 7

*T*he clouds of the gray space flickered with lightning the same as the clouds of the world, but it was not only the sight of the clouds that chilled Tristen's heart: it was the sight of the Edge, over which a cataract of cloud roared and vanished, endlessly.

—**Come inside,** the Wind said, a mere thickening in that stream . . . a curl amidst the cloud.

And in the blink of an eye and half without his will Tristen found himself indeed inside Ilefínian, inside its fortress, within that room where the banner had hung.

More, Crissand was at his back, and four archers confronted them with bows bent.

He stepped back to escape. Then he realized a trap indeed, for the escape at his back instantly seemed to be the old mews. *That* former retreat was the path his thoughts most easily held and that was the path that his own will by mischance opened, not only to them, but to the enemy.

"Get to safety!" he wished Crissand, for they both stood within the mews. He felt Emuin's startled presence, and Ninévrisë's, almost within hail of his voice. He turned to remake the wards, as a vast Shadow poured after them.

The wards held against it, but a lesser Shadow slipped past to find its master a way in, through wards it well knew: Shadows waked within the Zeide's walls as the ragged remnant that was Hasufin breached the new defenses: a shriek ran through its stones as if iron bent, and a rumbling resounded through its vaults as if stones moved. A crack raced up the several chimneys of the tower.

Tristen knew his ground and held it against all distraction: he had Crissand beside him, and the mews for the moment sealed itself fast, walling out the attack that came from Ilefínian's heart.

But their enemy's servant raged on in his own search. It was still the child Hasufin sought, and as Tristen reached to prevent him, he realized the child was not with Tarien: *Ninévrisë* had Elfwyn, had seized him in her arms at the first alarm from the mews and held him fast.

The Shadow in the burned cell clawed at the stones, flowed between them into every crevice of her prison, frantic in her search for a way out of the wards, trying to find the least small crack that might open. In the shriek of iron and the echoes of the deep vaults she called to Tarien Aswydd as the smell of fire tainted the gray space . . . *Sister, sister, my twin, my other self . . . call me out! Call me out of this prison . . . aetheling, aetheling as we are, queens of this land, sister . . . is that not the dream? Can you forget?*

It was a bond more magical than wizardous that extended through the stones, cords of a sister's anger and a mother's yearning that plunged Tarien's head into her hands, knotted her fingers into her hair, and sent a silent cry of anguish through the stones, for in the moment of choice, it was Ninévrisë she upheld, not her sister. It was Ninévrisë who had taken her child and Orien who had governed all her life . . . and the moment she denied Orien's voice the shock went through the gray space, a wail resounding through the stones.

—Stand fast! Tristen urged Ninévrisë.

Allies embraced, rooms apart. Two women held close, Tarien's eyes shut tight, heart clenched tight about the child she ached to have in her arms again, the infant that Ninévrisë promised, protected, warded for her with all her strength.

Above, in the tower, the crack in the chimney jolted wider and Emuin's shutters flew open: a draft howled from the lower hall to the tower height, and Paisi, his arms full of parchments, dived beneath a table at Emuin's feet, striving to keep the wind from tearing the charts all away.

All of this happened in a heartbeat . . . all the fortress leapt in one instant into clarity, as blindingly swift as the Shadow seeking that reciprocal crack within the wards.

With another jolt the crack in the wall raced downward, opened across the ceilings of the lower floor and let a winter-cold gale blow into the old mews.

Beneath a horn-paned window, beneath a rough sill in Ynefel's upper tier, ruin had begun from a single crack. The stones had fallen, beginning from there, until Ynefel stood in ruins, overthrown.

So Althalen had gone down in blackened timbers, stones fallen, the Lines sleeping and broken.

Until, *until,* Tristen thought fiercely, Lord Uleman had held it for his court. Next Auld Syes' sparrows had spread their tents there, reclaiming it for the living. Aeself's battered folk, lasting through the bitter snows, had raised a wooden tower that creaked and swayed in the winds. The scattered sparrows had built themselves a shelter that, though it leaked in the rains and admitted every draft—yet was home.

So Althalen had risen from the ashes. Wind there scoured the stones, flattening the grass that grew where the palace once had stood; above it all the wooden tower stood, Aeself's work, where lightning threatened and wind tore at the sheltering canvas . . . the women who held that post cried out in terror of the storm, and the tower quaked and swayed, but Tristen willed Aeself's tower to stand against the wind. With a sweep of his arm he willed the lightning away: it was *his* land, *his* lordship, and if he gave it to Crissand, still, he warded it against the enemy. He willed all who were in the place safe, and bade that tower stand.

Owl flew past, a brown streak, and wheeled away on a gust, a skirl of dust that, out of the grass of the ruins of Althalen, became the shape of a man . . . bits of grass and dust formed all the substance that Hasufin Heltain could command now. He had failed his master, failed his bid for the child. The man of dust had reached after Owl, but fell asunder, no more at last than dust and chaff.

Tristen lifted his hand to recover Owl, who lighted on his arm as lightning chained across the heavens.

He stood in Ynefel, amid shattered timbers, the ruin of all the wonderful stairways that had run like spiderwebs up and up to the loft.

He stood in the courtyard, where Hasufin had been the haunt.

But not the only one.

Dust and leaves blew across the pavings, encountered the cracked wall . . . and fell, a mere scattering of pieces. Hasufin could not return, not now. His strength was spent.

But the Wind came stealing softly through the open gate. Or had done. Time was always uncertain here, and the Wind came and went unpredictably, like Ynefel's other visitors.

—*Well, well, well, said the* Wind, *here, too, brave prince of Shadows.*

—*Still here, Tristen said in the foreboding hush.*

—But not there, are you? Not in that land where your allies need you . . . are you, Lord of Ghosts?

Fear touched his heart, fear for Crissand, and for the army he had left to others' leading—but he was not, as Emuin called him, a fool, to glance aside and distract himself with his enemy's chatter. He kept one thing in mind, and the threats and the gusts could not shake him.

—Can I not? Can you not fear me? Others do.

He suddenly had that feeling he had had of nights when Orien's dragons loomed above his bed: and at once he was flung into the gray space in a swirl of cloud. The Wind wrapped about him like a cloak and spun about and about and down.

It left him facing the Edge, where cloud poured like rain down a roof.

—Look in, it said. Do you dare?

And without his bending at all the Edge seemed to open before him. He stared into a dark that reflected shadows and light, and was the image in a rain barrel, no more than that.

It was his own image it cast back, all dark hair and shadow, with the sun at his back, as he had seen himself when first he tried to know his own face.

He drew back in the instant the Wind sought to push him over the Edge. He turned, sword in hand, and faced it with the question he himself had wished to answer:

—Who are you? Do you know? Do you dare look at your own reflection?

—I dare. A Shape formed itself out of cloud, a young man, mist for a cloak, storm for raiment, and shifting haze for armor. It was a mirror of himself, of Crissand, but neither shadow nor sun: a nameless Shaping of grays and magic, out of its seething clouds of the gray space.

And the challenge it posed was magic, a power breaking free of all law that had ever constrained it, all the wizard-work, all the Lines on the earth, all the bindings ever bound. It breathed in, and on its next breath it might carry all the world away.

And the weapon to counter it was not alone the sword and its spells: it was even more than the Lines of Ynefel's wards, or the Zeide's, or Althalen's, or any barrier of stone laid down in the world: it was all the work of all the wizards and all the Men that had lived their lives in constraint of power and the habit of order.

The Wind gathered force, and gathered force, all for one great effort . . . it Summoned all who had ever fallen to its lure, all who had ever gone deep within its embrace and lost themselves, not alone Hasufin Heltain, not alone Orien, or Heryn Aswydd or the hundreds of others without name. It lacked Shape, so it cloaked itself in his likeness, all grays, living magic, the third force, balanced between Shadow and Sun.

—*Barrakkêth*, it whispered, but he would not own that name.

—*I know you*, it said, as Hasufin had said, but he would not be limited by what it knew.

Instead he recalled an age of watching the suns above the ice, raising the stones of a great, solid fortress to hold the Lines of the World against the ceaseless change of magic.

He recalled the gathering of those who could answer a wizard's call when it came, for a barrier was breached. The unthinkable had happened. Time itself circled around and around that moment, around those few who could keep the gray space in check.

—*Five who failed*, the Wind taunted him: it was a willful creature, and destroyed without a thought: it changed and made change: that was what magic did. It slid, and shifted, like a step on ice.

—*You can only reflect me*, he answered it, the untaught truth, for it had Shaped itself in the image of all it knew, all it saw outside the gray void where it existed . . . it was the changing mirror of all it met: the Book had said these things. That was the dark secret, the one that would not Unfold to him. He saw the gray force, the middle one, the force in the breach.

—**Hasufin wanted that knowledge so**, mused the Wind. **He wanted that Book to know what he had done. He thought there was a way to bind me. He was mistaken. The Sihhë failed. He was doomed.**

—**No**, Tristen said, for in a leap of fear he saw the danger it posed in its accommodation to his Shape: it reasoned in his own voice and he had begun to listen to it. In its gray reflection of himself he saw the chance to learn more and more and more of what he was, and to find what the Shape withheld from him.

But it would gather him in if he listened to it. Yes, it would answer the questions. It would mirror all the world, and bring all his desires within his reach, all encompassed, all answered, all perfect, and complete.

But the world he loved was less orderly, less perfect.

The world he loved defied him and caused him grief, and contained the warmth of the Sun and the voices of friends. It held the smell of rain, the taste of honey, and the softness of feathers.

A throng of foolish birds, a scramble after bread crumbs.

Owl's nip at his finger.

Emuin's frown. Crissand's smile. Cefwyn's wry laughter.

—**No**, *he said a second time, shaking his head. And,* **No,** *a third time, and with a sweep of the sword he drew a burning Line between Truth and Illusion.*

He stood in the pouring rain on the parapets of Ynefel in the next beat of his heart. The Wind rushed over the walls at him, edged with bitter cold, and tried to hurl him down.

He Called the wards of Ynefel and they sprang up in light . . . the Lines not only of the fortress, but Lines alight all through Marna Wood, all along the old Road, all along the river shore: *Galasien's* Lines rose to life, and Lines spun out and out through the woods, the shape in light of the ancient city, recalling what had been, what could not now be.

"Crissand!" Tristen cried, realizing the danger of that slide backward. He hurled himself into the gray space, to go back to all that he had left at risk . . . but his attempt careened off into the winds. He Called further: now Althalen's wards leapt up, and the blue of the Lines rose up and raced on and on across the land.

At Henas'amef, the Zeide flared bright as a winter moon, and all the Lines of the town and its walls leapt to life. The light of Lines raced along outward roads like dew on a spiderweb, touched villages, touched Modeyneth. Light ran along the foundations of the Wall that Drusenan had raised. Blue fire touched Anwyll's camp, and raced along the bridge, and across the river to the camp, and on to the trail of the army, through woods and meadows.

He had no Place, and had every Place. The lightning chained about him, and the light of the gray place ran along his hand and into the tracery of silver on his sword. He had no wish to do harm. He had no wish to end his existence.

—*Pride, pride, pride, the Wind mocked him. It was certainly Mauryl's undoing. So do you inherit his mantle, Shaping? You think you can keep me out?*

—*You invited me in, he reminded the Wind. I hold you to that.*

It disliked that. It strengthened its wards against him. And for the second time the Wind gathered Shape, reflecting him, as if a young man wrapped himself in a cloak of shifting shadow, and glanced mockingly over his shoulder.

—*Do you like what you see, Mauryl's creature? Question, question, question everyone, but never the best question . . . what are you? Mauryl's creature? Mauryl's maker? Come, be brave, ask your-*

self that question. I'll give you this: we aren't that different, you and I.

He could never resist questions. Questions led him, distracted him, carried him through the world forgetful of his own substance and fearful of what he might find.

But among those questions he remembered the fabric of that cloak . . . a roiling of shadow and smoke beyond a railing. Then he asked a different, unasked question: why now? Why not Lewenbrook? Why come through Hasufin, until now?

Then he knew what had changed since Lewenbrook. Then he was sure whence it had come . . . not out of Ilefínian, where it had now taken hold: but it was never lord there in the Lord Regent's domain. The breach had come elsewhere, magic breaking forth from a tangled maze of shadows, repeated attempts to ward it in.

Lines built upon and rebuilt, until its ally sent the lightning down . . . confounding the Lines that Men had built, breaking a small gap wider. Ilefínian was the second step.

And he had redrawn that Line . . . *there!* Tristen said to himself, and with a thought carried himself to the ward he had traced on the stones of the Quinaltine shrine.

Here he engaged his enemy, and *here* he brought the new Line up in brilliant light, in a place of chanting and incense, and sudden consternation.

"Gods!" Efanor cried, armed and armored, amid guards and priests as he faced the intrusion on his long watch. *"Amefel!"*

"Stand fast!" Tristen said, for the gray space broke forward, rushed at the Line: and when it could not cross that barrier on the new stones, spilled upward like smoke, spiraling up to the rafters. The Wind tugged at the heraldic banners between the columns, rising up and up toward the gap that had once been there, a mended gap that suddenly and with a rending of timbers opened to the sky.

"Amefel!" Efanor cried as timbers crashed like thunder among the benches, splintering wood, resounding on stone. "What's happened? Are we lost?"

"Not yet!" Tristen wheeled the sword about, struck a clanging blow to the Line on the stones, and called the Shadows up and up, until blue fire leapt from the blade to the rafters. Shadows rushed into that breach in the roof, a rift in the wards that had let the gray space rip wide, a Line straight to Ilefínian's unprotected heart.

Owl made a swift passage behind the columns about the shrine, routing a last few Shadows, and rose up, up on the draft.

"Stand fast!" Tristen asked of Efanor, and hurled himself through the gray space, seeking to breach the wards the enemy had made.

But the mews began to remake itself about him, glowing with blue light, row on row of perches, Shadows that raised ominous wings and battered the air, defying him, defying the Lines that now existed, ready to rend and destroy.

But Emuin, besieged in his tower, wind-battered, waved a bony arm and wished him on his way north, as Men measured the heavens.

"The Year of Years, young lord! This age is yours! You, young lord, *you* claim it! *Do as you must! Go!*"

A flock of birds started up at his passage, wings brushing the gray space: his frail, silly companions of lost hours . . . he was startled by their rise into the mews, and seeing them so frail and foolish against the Shadows, he spread his magic wide to protect them on the wing: he wished them up, and through all hazard—for a way out was what they sought.

The winged ghosts of the mews rushed up as well, but his flock turned in a wide sweep, wings flashing against the roiling dark, by his wish evading the killers. Owl rushed by like a mad thing, losing feathers, himself nearly prey.

—Fly, he wished Owl. And Crissand. And Cefwyn, and all the wizards of Men who had ever drawn a Line against this thing. He followed Owl, tried to thread the needle through the wards of Ilefínian . . . and found himself instead flung to the Edge with his back to the brink.

The mirror-youth faced him, the gray space flashing with storm.

Tristen stood fast, going neither forward nor back, calling the light of the gray space into his sword until the silver on the blade burned blinding bright. Truth, one side said, and Illusion, the other, and the line between the two he aimed at the heart of his enemy.

—Shaping of Mauryl, it taunted his defense. Bind me, you upstart? Banish me, do you think? Go back into the dark, foolish Shaping, until you learn my name!

—For him I bind you, Lord of Magic! For Mauryl! And for Hasufin, when he was Mauryl's friend!

The Wind roared over him, an outraged wall of gray, and the force that attempted to form about him, to Shape itself about his shape, sundered itself on the sword's edge, and lost all form. He could not see its fall, or if it fell, but behind him there was nothing but the Edge.

. . . or the reflection in the rain barrel.

. . . or the endless rush of wind and cloud into the void.

The wards it had woven, threads stretched from the Quinaltine and wound about Ilefínian . . . collapsed like a wall going down.

"M'lord," he heard from a great distance. "M'lord, we could truly use your help, if ye hear me."

Thunder cracked. He stood in that hall in Ilefínian with Crissand at his side, and the archers loosed arrows as Crissand gave a wild cry and charged them . . . battered them with shield and sword all the way to the door, where Crissand stood, sword in hand, glancing out into the hall.

Then back. "Which way?" Crissand asked.

"I've no idea," Tristen said in astonishment, feeling that time had one certain direction now, and that it moved indeed as he willed it. His knees felt apt to give way; and he took two steps, helpless as a child and apt to faint, except he had the echo of Uwen's voice ringing in his ears: it seemed to him now that Uwen had been calling for some time.

Crissand meanwhile had two shafts hanging from the bright sun on his shield and a lively challenge shone in his eyes. Between two heartbeats, it might have been, the loosing of an arrow and its strike.

"Downstairs," Tristen said, remembering the town gates that lay far downhill of the fortress, and suddenly knowing the limits of flesh and bone—that they could not gain the gates by wishing themselves there.

"More are coming," Crissand said at a racket of footsteps on some distant stairs. "Shall we hold here a bit?"

Lord of Althalen, he was, Tristen said to himself. Lord Sihhë he accepted to be.

"Owl!" he called.

Out of thin air and the stones of the wall, Owl flew, and flew past Crissand, out the door.

Where Owl flew, there Tristen knew he should go. Strength came back to his limbs. He settled his grip on his sword, and heard, distantly, not the crash of thunder, but the boom of something battering the doors downstairs.

Sweat ran beneath the helm and streamed into Cefwyn's eyes as he climbed the hill that had been a long, long slope down. The fighting on the hill above him swam in a blur of red mingled with that pale blue that always in his thoughts was Ninévrisë's.

The black banner no longer flew. He was sure of that. He thought that that was indeed Ninévrisë's standard up there with the Marhanen Dragon . . . but he could not be sure; and to lose the battle now, for want of officers up on that hill, that possibility, he refused to bear: to see Ryssand escape him, he refused; and he drove himself despite the haze of his vision and the ache in his bones.

Black coat on a rider that turned his way: Tasmôrden's man, he thought in alarm, but black was the color of the Prince's Guard as well; and with a pass of a bloody glove across his eyes he confirmed that it was one of his own who had seen him, one of his own who turned toward him, across the corpse-littered field.

More, he knew that blaze-faced horse: it was Captain Gwywyn who came riding in his direction, leaving the battle above, and the fact that Gwywyn came personally reassured him that loyal officers were indeed in command up there, that the fighting was all but done.

With a great relief, then, Cefwyn climbed, using the rocks to help him on his right, though Gwywyn's horse gained ground downslope far faster than made his weak effort climbing at all worthwhile. Gwywyn quickened his pace . . . then reined back hard, in inexplicable alarm, gazing up.

Cefwyn turned as with a grate and a scrape of stone and metal a heavy weight slid down from the rocks . . . a man landed afoot in front of him as Cefwyn lifted his sword in defense: an armored man in black, and likewise armed, and familiar of countenance.

"Master crow?" Cefwyn said, forcing his unused voice. "Damn you, you're late!"

"If my lord king hadn't led me a damned downhill chase," Idrys retorted, "I'd have been in better time." A glance gestured back toward Gwywyn, who, Cefwyn saw, had come to a baffled standstill. "That, my lord king, is no rescue."

"Gwywyn?" Cefwyn blinked and saw in Gwywyn's bearing and in Gwywyn's unsheathed sword suddenly not his defense, but a threat, the substance of Idrys' warning of some nights past . . . Gwywyn: his father's Lord Commander, his father's right-hand man. And if Gwywyn had turned traitor . . . or if Gwywyn had always been Ryssand's . . . the three of them were far enough from the rest of the army that no one up there might hear or see what happened in these rocks.

Why should Gwywyn pause? Indeed, why should Gwywyn have doubts in approaching his king, seeing the Lord Commander?

Then Cefwyn saw a reason for Gwywyn to wait, for from the side of the slope nearest the ridge appeared two more men. Corswyndam was one.

"Ryssand," Cefwyn said, with a longing to have his hands on

that throat, and a fear that he might not have the chance. "Have you help, crow? We may need it."

"I saw from the heights," Idrys said. "And could not reach that far. But men of mine are aware of him."

"Aware of him!" Cefwyn cried in indignation. "They daren't see either of us leave this field alive!"

"Gwywyn did seem likeliest as a traitor," Idrys said. "I wasn't wrong."

"You might have told me!"

"I had my eye on him."

"Your eye on him, damn you! *How long have you known?*"

"That he was Ryssand's man? Messages went astray, such as only a handful knew. Lord Tristen informed me of several instances . . . whence I deemed it a matter of some haste to reach my lord king—and not to make myself evident to the traitors at the same time. I had no evidence."

"No evidence!"

"No more sufficient than had my lord king, since my lord was clearly still temporizing with Ryssand. I spied over the situation. I was never far.—Her Grace, by the by, is well situated in Amefel and sends her love."

"Gods bless!" He was all but breathless, stung to life by the thought of Ninévrisë and unbearably angry at the prospect of dying on this hill, nearly in possession of all he dreamed to have. "Could you not have told me you suspected Gwywyn?"

"I also suspected the captain of the Guelens . . . who does seem innocent. I'd not ask my lord king's good temper to face one more known traitor in his councils. The half dozen my lord king already knew about seemed sufficient to suggest caution . . . and I consulted with men of mine, each night. They have their own orders: if Ryssand retreated, he was not to leave this battle."

"*That* is Ryssand, crow. He's left the battle! Where are these men of yours?"

"Uphill, doubtless, where my lord king should be, except he chased downhill and engaged in combat, scattering my men behind him . . . 'ware, my lord! They're about to charge."

Gwywyn had joined Corswyndam now, and they came ahead: three scoundrels, Cefwyn thought, regretting his shield. He took a solid grip on his sword and reckoned the threat of Ryssand's horse, which was not Kanwy's equal: a heavy-footed, bow-nosed creature he liked no better than its master.

"What was the lightning down there, by the by?" Idrys asked him. "Wizard-work?"

"Hell receiving Tasmôrden," Cefwyn said with a deep breath. For a moment he felt scant of wind, felt the ache in his arms, and then found his spirits rising, for his shieldman was beside him, and that was the most help he had had in days. "I give you your pick, crow."

"I'll take my own traitor, then, and my lord king can have his." "Done."

Lances lowered. Horses gathered speed.

There was a difficulty in attempting to run through wary opponents, ones who had seen wars before this one, and who had their backs against a barrier neither horses nor lances could pass. Cefwyn waited, waited, and he and Idrys went opposite directions at the last moment, when lances had to strike or lift.

Ryssand tried a sweep of the lance to catch him: Cefwyn flung himself past its reach. Ryssand spun his horse about, its iron-shod feet about to overrun him; but Cefwyn had fought the Chomaggari, with their breed of infighting, infantry half-carried into battle by their cavalry, in among the stones and brush of the southern hills. Ryssand kept turning his horse, his shieldman trying for position, but Cefwyn laid hold of the tail of Ryssand's surcoat and held on, pulling Ryssand sideways, down on his back and under his own horse's hooves as the horse backed from its rider's shifting weight.

The horse dealt the telling blow. The second came on the sword's edge, and Ryssand's head parted his body.

With an anguished shout Ryssand's shieldman forced his way past his lord's horse and rode down at him, and in a moment stretched long and clear as if by magic, Cefwyn turned on his heel and kicked the butt of the fallen lance into the horse's path.

The horse went down, the rider spilled, and lay unmoving when the horse gathered itself dazedly to its feet.

Cefwyn caught a ragged breath then, and lurched half-about toward Idrys, who engaged his predecessor on foot in a noisy bout of swordsmanship, Idrys the younger man and the quicker, but Gwywyn a master years had proved.

Gwywyn knew, now, however, that he was alone, and he began to retreat, perhaps fearing some ignoble blow from the side.

He erred. He died, in the next instant, and Idrys shook the blood from his sword.

Cefwyn proffered him the reins of Ryssand's destrier. "Catch me the guard's horse. I'm too weary to chase him."

"Majesty," Idrys said, between breaths. It was rare to see sweat on master crow, but it was abundant. Idrys looked as if he had run miles, and perhaps he had, but he took the offered reins, and mounted stiffly on Ryssand's bow-nosed horse.

And now four Dragon Guard and two Lanfarnesse rangers came sliding down from the height of the rocks.

"Damn you!" Cefwyn said to the Lord Commander.

"*They* were engaged," Idrys said smoothly, from horseback. "I hurried to my appointment, my lord king. I think more may arrive shortly.—By your leave."

He rode out. In a moment he had caught the guard's horse, and led it back.

"My lord king," Idrys said calmly, handing him down the reins, and by now, indeed, several more rangers stood on the height, and the fighting uphill had come almost to a standstill, a last few of the enemy seeking safety in flight, which Idrys indicated with a flourish of his hand. "Lord Maudyn seems to hold the hill; we have these rocks and several score men of my choosing from place to place along the ridge. I think between us the enemy has met his match."

CHAPTER 8

The battering of the doors gave way to a crash of wood, a clump and a clatter on the stairs, and a worried shout.

"M'lord!" Uwen called, and came running up the steps, shield scraping on the stones, his face white and sweating: it was a far run in armor, but up he came, with Tristen's guard and Crissand's thumping behind him, onto the upper floor of the fortress.

"It's gone," Tristen said, meeting him in that unfamiliar hallway, and such was the relief he felt in saying it that the sky outside the windows seemed lightened. Crissand was beside him. There, too, was a glad reunion, Crissand with his father's guard and their captain.

"The lightnin' cracked an' the sky was blowin' somethin' fierce," Uwen said, out of breath. "But then we said that you was in there an' b' gods them gates was comin' down."

Just so he could imagine Uwen saying it: those great, well-set gates.

"With a ram," Crissand's captain said, "since there was this great old tree gone down in the wood's edge. The lads spied it and we had the limbs off it and up and took it against the gate."

"But the guards at the gate was confused in the banners," Uwen said, "Tasmôrden claimin' the same device. They fell to arguin' amongst themselves whether it was Tasmôrden back again rammin' 'is own gates, or what it all meant . . . which he's outside the walls, m'lord, somewhere! But Aeself's goin' through the town, street to street, now, tellin' all the folk that it's yourself, m'lord, that it's Amefel come across the river, and they should hunt out the black-guards that's left."

There was a sudden tumult of arms within the halls, some-where close.

"Our own," Uwen said pridefully. "Them bandits o' Tasmôr-den's is goin' t' ground an' hopin' for dark. They're outnumbered by far."

The gray space was open again. It was as if with the passing of the Shadow within the fortress that the sky and the land had light-ened and spread wide, and Tristen could both hear and see again within the gray space. And the lords of the south he perceived. And the skirmish in the hall he perceived, and the living folk in the town, with Aeself among them. Cefwyn's forces he perceived.

But Tasmôrden he could not find.

"Cefwyn's east and south of us," he said. "We have to tell him we're here." He led the way down the stairs, down to the lower hall of a fortress he had never entered by its proper doors. Its walls were stone unplastered in its upper courses, and its floor pavings smoothed more by age than art.

And the wooden doors stood ajar, the bright wounds of the wood and a bar standing askew attesting how force and a stone bench had gained entry for his men.

He set a hand on Uwen's shoulder, grateful beyond measure, and they went outside, where Lord Cevulirn stood on the steps with Umanon of Imor Lenúalim, directing riders who occupied the walled courtyard.

"The lost are found," Cevulirn said, seeing them, and Tristen came and embraced the man, embraced stiff and proper Lord Uma-non as well, and then had the dizzy notion that hereafter he truly did not know why he lived, or what he should do, or where he belonged. It was as if all that directed him had left, and when he stood back from Umanon he looked outward across the open court-yard, to the open doors, and the walls of houses of a town he had never seen.

He was still lost. Owl had flown up when he came out the doors, and settled now on an absently offered wrist as he gazed over all this motion and tumult of men who took his commands and sought his advice.

But Cevulirn and Umanon knew the governance of a people far better than he knew; Uwen knew the ordering of soldiers in far more detail than he. Crissand knew the needs of the countryfolk far better than he. He looked out across the square and saw Sovrag of Olmern with his men, and Lord Pelumer with him, saw all this array of martial power set now amid a town that had been in the grip of a bandit lord, and saw what appeared to be the common people venturing to the gate, to look inside and wonder what had come on them now.

He knew where he did not belong.

—*Emuin? Master Emuin?* *he asked, anxious for the old man, for Paisi and Ninévrisë and Lusin and all he had left behind; and an answer came to him, at least that master Emuin's charts were in an irresolvable muddle and that baskets and pots and powders were strewn everywhere.*

But Emuin was alive, and so was Paisi, and so was Ninévrisë, and they could be here, if they chose. He invited them, if they chose . . . **Leave Lusin in charge,** *he said, and showed Emuin the way.*

"Where's Dys?" he asked, for he longed to find that other heart he could not touch at a distance: he relied on Uwen, and on Crissand, and sure enough, now his guard had found him, Gweyl and the rest, and would not be shaken lightly from his tracks. "Cefwyn's out there."

"Ye ought to send a messenger, m'lord," Uwen said. "Ye ought to sit here safe and send one of these lads."

"But I won't," Tristen said, with the least rise of mirth. "You know that I won't."

"As I ain't the captain of Amefel any longer," Uwen said, "I can shake free an' ride with ye; an' as your guards has to go, though probably ye can call the lightnin' down on any leavin's of Tasmôrden's lot . . . still we'll go, m'lord."

Idrys' men had gone out, probing toward Ilefínian, and came back again to say there was a strange assortment of banners before riders on the road: the black banner of the High Kings that Tasmôrden had claimed, in company with the Tower and Checker of the Regent and the Eagle of Amefel, with two and three others less clear to the observers.

"Tristen," was Idrys' pronouncement, where they had established not a camp, but a staying place on the hilltop, under the open sky, a place for dressing wounds and collecting the army in order. "Did I not say this egg would hatch?" Idrys asked. And Cefwyn finding no word: "What shall we do, my lord king?"

What indeed should they do? Cefwyn asked himself somberly. Go to war with Tristen? Call a battered Guelen army to take the field against the friend of his heart, who had claimed that banner?

"Bring Danvy up," Cefwyn said, looking out and down the hill.

Close after the battle, two of Anwyll's men had found Anwyll climbing uphill with Kanwy in hand and a handful of the company behind him, but Kanwy had a wound and was due a rest: it was his light horse that would serve now, for a short ride and a meeting.

"What shall we do?" Idrys repeated his question, hammering it home.

"Do? I think I shall meet my friend and hope for my lady's safety at his hands."

"Hope?" Idrys echoed him. "Is hope what we have, now? Nothing of faith? The hatchling's spread wings, my lord king, and it's no damned pigeon we deal with."

Cefwyn gave a wry and silent laugh. "A dragon. A dragon, master crow. But he is still my friend."

Idrys said nothing for a moment, only gazed at him as if in reproach. Then: "He was still your friend when he sent me to the Olmernmen. He was still your friend when he marched, and he leads those who are my lord king's sworn men, but now, now there is a question."

"What should I do?" Cefwyn repeated. "If you have any notion, crow, out with it."

"Demand," Idrys said. "Impose. Insist, my lord king. You owe the kingdom that."

"The kingdom." The ache had settled hard into his body. Even drawing a deep breath hurt, and he swept a glance about him, at those who had been faithful, whatever their reasons . . . some even for love of him. He looked at that, rather than the betrayals, but not wholly successfully. "He has the knack of gaining love. That's to envy."

"My lord king has those who love him."

He glanced at Idrys, catching something perhaps by surprise. He did not know why, after all else, he was embarrassed to catch Idrys thus unaware. But he pretended to have looked elsewhere, for both their sakes, and folded his arms. "Horses."

"My lord king," Idrys said, and relayed the order to a page, who called a groom, who called his assistants, for where the king of Ylesuin went was no small number.

Riven trees marked the battle in the elements, a trail of splintered trunks and wrecked limbs, bright wood through the leafless forest; so Tristen saw as they rode. The limbs were bare as those in Marna's depths, where the wood wound around the end of the ridge.

But there color bloomed, the bright red Marhanen banner, and the Tower and Checker of the lady Regent, and so they came within sight one of the other.

Tristen set Dys to a faster pace, and rode ahead of his banners and those who chased after him; so did the king of Ylesuin, and they met under the afternoon shadow of the ridge, slid down from their horses and embraced as friends too long parted.

"High King, is it?" Cefwyn asked, setting Tristen at arm's length.

And it was a question Tristen had to answer, but not in few words.

Ninévrisë had come with Emuin: he knew that while he rode. It was brave of them, but arrive they had, by the old mews, and Tarien with them, for Ninévrisë would not leave Tarien or the baby behind in Henas'amef. There was one Aswydd who ruled there, and it was neither of them.

"Emuin's come," Tristen did say. "And Her Grace. Not by the road, by the old mews. And Crissand's the aetheling, which I don't want to be."

"What *do* you wish?" Cefwyn asked him, and he knew the seriousness of that question, as he knew the significance of the banner he could not set aside.

"To ride with my friends and see the summer again," he said, which was indeed the best thing in the world to him. In the gray space Emuin might say the banner had to fly, and Owl was surly and insistent, winging constantly toward Ynefel, but he was determined not to stay there, nor at Althalen, where the frail wooden tower still stood.

"Come to Ilefínian," he asked Cefwyn. "Owl wants me to come with him, but I won't, yet. There are things I don't know yet. There are things I haven't seen." A crown and the duties of a king were not at all within his longing: rather escape from both was what he plotted, escape for him, and the freedom of the kingdoms and the kings and lords to live in peace. A king over all could be a king in name, but the rulers of the lands had to live there.

A bough had broken its buds, the least small hint of gold and green, recalling whole forests that sighed and moved with the breezes.

Spring and promises: everything was new and old at once. Tristen saw it with wonder and saw the pledge of the summer to come, green grass and gentle winds.

A child danced before them, as they rode back to Ilefínian. Cefwyn and Uwen neither one could see her, but Tristen and Crissand did.

LEXICON

Concordance for the Fortress Books

YLESUIN

Amefel—*southern province;*
banner: black Eagle on red field

Royalty / Lords
  Aswydd Household
    Heryn Aswydd—Duke of Amefel, the aetheling,
      His twin sisters:
      Orien Aswydd—Duchess of Amefel;
      Tarien Aswydd—secondborn
        Thewydd—Heryn Aswydd's man
  Tristen's Household
    Tristen—Marshal of Althalen, Lord Warden of Ynefel
    Uwen—Lewen's-son, Tristen's man, sergeant of Cefwyn's Dragon
      Guard, captain of Tristen's guard
  Tristen's Guard
    Lusin—Captain of Tristen's bodyguard
    Syllan—one of Tristen's guards.
    Aran—one of Tristen's guards.
    Tawwys—one of Tristen's guards
    Aswys—groom
      Cassam, Cass—Uwen's warhorse, bow-nosed, blue roan
        gelding
      Dys, Dysarys—Tristen's warhorse, black, full brother to Aryny
        and Kanwy
      Gery—Tristen's light horse, red mare
      Gia—Uwen's light horse, bay mare
      Liss—Uwen's horse, chestnut mare
      Petelly—Tristen's cross-country horse, a bay of no breeding

Amefin Earls and Their Households

> Edwyll Adiran—earl of Meiden, remotely related to Aswydds; banner: gold sun
>
> Crissand Adiran—son of and successor to Edwyll
>
> Azant—lord of Dor Elen province, which borders the ver orchard district.
>
> > A daughter: widowed twice, once when married only seven days
>
> Brestandin—Amefin earl
>
> Cedrig—elderly Amefin earl living in retirement, owner of room Tristen lodges in, then where Ninévrisë lodges in Henas'amef
>
> Civas—Amefin earl
>
> Cuthan—earl of Bryn, distant relative of Aswydds
>
> Drumman—lord of Barardden, youngest of earls except for Crissand; his elder sister is Edwyll's wife, Crissand's mother
>
> Drusallyn—elderly lord, married local gentry in Amefel
>
> Drusenan—earl of Bryn, successor to Cuthan. wife: Ynesyne, an Elwynim.
>
> Durell—Amefin earl
>
> Edracht—Amefin earl
>
> Esrydd—Amefin earl
>
> Lund—Amefin earl
>
> Marmaschen—Amefin earl
>
> Moridedd—Amefin earl
>
> Murras—Amefin earl
>
> Prushan—Amefin earl
>
> Purell—Amefin earl
>
> Taras—earl of Bru Marden
>
> Zereshadd—Amefin earl

Other Persons

> *Clergy / Clerics*
>
> > Cadell—Bryaltine abbot in Henas'amef
> >
> > Faiseth—Bryaltine nun
> >
> > Emuin Udaman—wizard/tutor/priest, Teranthine, tutored Cefwyn and Efanor
> >
> > Del'rezan—Bryaltine nun
> >
> > Pachyll—priest, Teranthine patriarch in Henas'amef
>
> *Military*
>
> > Cossun—armorer
> >
> > Ennyn—Guelen Guard second in command
> >
> > Gedd—sergeant in Tristen's guard
> >
> > > Aman—gate-guard
> > >
> > > Nedras—gate-guard
> > >
> > > Ness—gate-guard
> > >
> > > Selmwy—cousin of Ness at town gate
> >
> > Wynedd—Guelen Guard commander

Minor Officials

    Tassand—started as Cefwyn's servant, now Tristen's chief of household

    Haman—stablemaster at Henas'amef

Local Gentry

    Ardwys—thane of Sagany, leader of the peasant contingent from Sagany and Pacewys

Miscellaneous

    Auld Syes—witch, in Emwy village, near Althalen

    Paisi—street urchin

    Seddiwy—Shadow, Auld Syes' child

    Wydnin—former junior archivist

Titles, Places, et cetera

    Aetheling, atheling—title, used instead of king in Amefel; royal in their province

    Althalen—old Sihhë capital, where last of Sihhë died, now Tristen's, in ruins, banner is silver Star and Tower on black

    Amefin—of Amefel province

    Anas Mallorn—Amefin village, on riverside

    Ardenbrook—brook after Maudbrook on way to Henas'amef

    Arreyburn—camping spot of Emuin on the way back to Henas'amef from retreat

    Averyne crossing—crossing to Guelessar from Amefel on the way out of Henas'amef

    Arys—district/town, Arys Emwy, Emwy village: destroyed when Ináreddrin was killed; district contains Althalen and Lewen field

    Arys bridge—bridge near Emwy to west, where Elwynor rebels could enter Amefel

    Arys district—near Henas'amef, contains villages of Emwy and Malitarin

    Asfiad—old name for Aswyth

    Asmaddion—place in the province

    Assurn Ford—river border of the province

    Assurnbrook—river

    Aswydd, Aswydds—surname, Heryn's house, also Orien's, Tarien's; there is Sihhë blood in this line

    Aswyddim—of the Aswydds

    Aswyth—a village

    Athel—Amefin district bordering Meiden's land

    Baraddan—Drumman's district, contains orchards

    Bru Mardan—Taras district

    Bryn—Cuthan's estate

    Ceyl, Trys—Trys Ceyl—Amefin village south of Henas'amef.

    Dor Elen—Anzant's district, orchard district

    Drun, Trys Drun—next to Trys Ceyl, village south of Henas'amef

ealdorman, ealdormen—council of Henas'amef
Edlinnadd—old name for Ellinan
Ellinan—a village
Emwy—village/district, see: Arys, Arys Emwy, Emwy village
Emwysbrook—brook near Emwy
Forest of Amefel—near Althalen
Grayfrock, grayrobe—nickname for Emuin
Hawwyvale—village
Hen Amas—old name for Henas'amef
Henas'amef—capital of the province
Kathseide—old name of Zeide, fortress in Henas'amef
Levey—Amefin village, part orchard, part pasturage for flocks
Lewen—brook giving its name to area of battle
Lewen field, Lewen plain—near Althalen, battlefield where
    Hasufin was destroyed
Lewenbrook—brook
Lewenford—area of battle, see Lewen field
Lewenside—area of battle, see Lewen field
Lysalin—Amefin village
Maldy village—Amefin village with crossing to Elwynor
Malitarin—Amefin village two hours from Henas'amef
Mallorn, Anas, Anas Mallorn—Amefin village on riverside
Margreis—ruined village, haunt of outlaws, near Emwy
Marna, Marna Wood—haunted forest
Marshal of Althalen—Tristen's title, bestowed by Cefwyn
Massitbrook—camping spot on way to Lewen field for Cefwyn
    and troops
Master grayrobe, grayfrock—nickname, refers to Emuin,
    wizard/tutor/priest, Teranthine
Maudbrook—on the way to Henas'amef
Maudbrook Bridge—bridge on the way to Henas'amef
Meiden—sheep district; banner: blue with gold sun
Pacewys—Amefin village, sent troops to Lewen field, commanded
    by Lord Ardwys, thane of Sagany
Padys Spring—one hour south of Henas'amef, once called
    Batherys
Ragisar—Amefin village
Raven's Knob—past Emwy on way to Lewen field, Lewenbrook
    near Althalen
Sagany—Amefin village on way to Althalen and Lewen field, sent
    troop to Lewen field commanded by Lord Ardwys, thane of
    Sagany
Sagany Road—on way to Althalen and Lewen field
Tas Aden—town in Meiden
Trys, Trys Ceyl—Amefin town near Trys Drun
Zeide—shortened name for Kathseide fortress in Henas'amef

Carys—northern province

Guelessar—north-central province; banner: quartered, gold Dragon on red, gold Quinalt sigil on black

Royalty

Selwyn Marhanen—Cefwyn's grandfather, king of Ylesuin; banner: gold dragon on red

Ináreddrin Marhanen—king of Ylesuin, father of Cefwyn and Efanor

Cefwyn Marhanen—third king of the Marhanen dynasty, brother of Efanor

Idrys—Lord Commander of the Dragon Guard

Annas—Cefwyn's chief of household in both Amefel and Guelessar. Later Lord Chamberlain

Lasien—senior page at Henas'amef

Efanor Marhanen—His Royal Highness, Duke of Guelessar, Prince of Ylesuin

Gwywyn—soldier, Ináreddrin's captain at Althalen, made captain of Efanor's guard at Guelemara

Lesser Royalty / Household

Alwy—Ninévrisë's maid and one of Cefwyn's former lovers

Brysaulin—Lord Chancellor after Cefwyn is crowned

Cressen—Lady, one of Cefwyn's former lovers

Fisylle—Lady, one of Cefwyn's former lovers

Trallynde—Lady, one of Cefwyn's former lovers

Parsynan—Guelen gentry, Cefwyn's viceroy at Amefel until Tristen's appointment as lord of Amefel

Horses

Aryny—heavy, warhorse, full sister to Dys and Kanwy

Danvy—Cefwyn's light horse

Drugyn—Idrys' warhorse, black stablemate of Cass, Kanwy, and Dys

Kanwy—Cefwyn's warhorse, black

Synanna—blaze-faced black, usually Efanor's horse

Clergy/Clerics

Patriarch—priest, absolute head of Quinalt sect

Jormys—Quinaltine priest, serves Efanor

Benwyn—Bryalt sect, assigned as Ninévrisë's priest

Baren—Quinaltine doctrinist

Neiswyn—doctrinist among the Quinaltines

Udryn—Quinaltine doctrinist

Military

Anwyll—captain of the guard, assigned to Amefel under Uwen

Kerdin Qwyll's-son—Kerdin, second-in-command under Idrys, captain of Guelen Guard, died at Lewen field

Essan—captain of Guelen Guard in Guelessar

Andas—soldier, eleven years in Dragon Guard, Andas' son, Tristen's banner-bearer, was killed at Lewen field

Brogi—soldier

Brys—soldier, in Anwyll's company

Cossell—soldier in Anwyll's company

Hawith—soldier, killed at Emwy, one of Cefwyn's men

Jeony—soldier, killed at Emwy

Lefhwyn—soldier, rode with Cefwyn at Emwy

Nydas—soldier, rode with Cefwyn at Emwy

Pelanny—soldier, Guelen scout, presumed dead or taken by Aseynéddin at Lewen field

Peygan—armorer for Cefwyn at Henas'amef, old friend of Uwen's, married to Margolis

Pryas—king Cefwyn's messenger

Minor officials / Household

Margolis—wife of Peygan the armorer. One of Ninévrisë's ladies

Mesinis—slightly deaf clerk

Tamurin—Cefwyn's accountant

Other Persons

Rosyn—Cefwyn's tailor in both Henas'amef and Guelemara

Places, Titles, et cetera

Amynys—river, old boundary of Guelemara

An's-ford—town, on road between Guelemara and Henas'amef

Anwyfar—Teranthine retreat near Arreyburn

Blue Hall—place, in Guelemara, in palace

Clusyn, Clusyn monastery—Quinaltine religious house in Guelessar

Cressitbrook—town near Guelemara

Crown Wall—Guelenfort's official limit

Dary—Guelen village at first ring road outside Guelemara

Drysham—Guelen village

Dury—Guelen village

Guelen—of Guelessar

Guelenfolk—people of Guelessar

Guelenish—of Guelessar

Guelenmen—people of Guelessar

Guelesfort—citadel in Guelemara

Guelemara—capital of Guelessar; banner: red with gold Castle

His Highness—Efanor

Holy Father, His Holiness—title, highest Patriarch in Quinalt sect

Lyn—soldier, messenger sent from Tristen to Idrys with Ryssand's treasonous letter

Marhanen—surname, Cefwyn's house: Gold Dragon, surname of Cefwyn, Selwyn, Efanor, Ináreddrin

Master crow, raven—nickname, refers to Idrys
Red Chronicle—Marhanen history book
"The Merry Lass from Eldermay"—country song played at
    Cefwyn's harvesttide festival
Wys-on-Wyetlan—Guelen village

Imor—southern province; banner: Wheel

Ruler
    Umanon—lord of Imor Lenúalim, Quinaltine
Places, Titles, et cetera
    Hedyrin—river south of Imor
    Imorim—of Imor

Isin—northern province

Ivanor—southern province; banner: White Horse

Ruler
    Cevulirn—lord of Ivanor, southern baron, Teranthine
        Geisleyn—Cevulirn's man, captain of light horse, from Toj
            Embrel, Ivanim
        Erion Netha—friend of Cevulirn, Lord of Tas Arin in Ivanor,
            wounded at Lewen field
Places, Titles, et cetera
    Crysin—horse breed of Ivanim
    Embrel, Toj—Toj Embrel, Cevulirn's summer palace
    Ivanim—of Ivanor
    Ivor—district
    Ivorim—of Ivor
    Tas Arin—town
    Toj Embrel—Toj Embrel, Cevulirn's summer palace

Lanfarnesse—southern province;
banner: Heron

Ruler
    Pelumer—duke of Lanfarnesse
    Feleyn, Feleyn's—a Lanfarnesscman
Places, Titles, et cetera
    Lanfarnesseman—people of Lanfarnesse

Llymarin—central province; banner:
Red Rose on green background

Ruler
    Sulriggan—lord of Llymarin, cousin to the Quinaltine Patriarch.
      Edwyn—nephew of Sulriggan, attends Efanor
Places, Titles, et cetera
    Llymarish—of Llymarin

Marisal—southern province;
banner: gold Sheaf with bend and crescent

Ruler
    Sarmysar—duke of Marisal; personal banner: lily

Marisyn—southern province;
banner: blue field and blazing Sun

Murandys—northern province; banner: blue field,
bend or, and white below with Quinalt sigil

The Nobles
    Prichwarrin—duke of Murandys
      Cleisynde—Lord Prichwarrin of Murandys' niece
      Luriel—Cefwyn's most recent lover, niece of Duke Prichwarrin
        of Murandys
      Odrinian—younger sister of Luriel, Duke Prichwarrin of
        Murandys' niece
Other Persons
    Romynd—Quinalt patriarch of Murandys
Places, Titles, et cetera
    Aslaney—capital of Murandys

Nelefreíssan—northern province;
banner: pale azure with White Circle

Places, Titles, et cetera
    Nelefreimen—men of Nelefreíssan

Olmern—southern province; banner: Black Wolf

Ruler

Sovrag—lord of Olmern (rivermen), in Olmernhome
Brigoth—Lieutenant of Sovrag of Olmern
Denyn—Cefwyn's door guard, Olmern youth, Kei's-son

Places, Titles, et cetera

Capayneth—Olmern village, traded with Mauryl
Olmernhome—Sovrag's capital
Olmernman—person of Sovrag's province

Osanan—eastern province

Ruler

Mordam—duke of Osanan

Palys—north-central province

Places, Titles, et cetera

Wys-in-Palys-under-Grostan—a village

Panys—northern province

Ruler

Maudyn—lord of Panys, commander of Cefwyn's forces on the riverside
Rusyn, Lord Maudyn's second son

Other Persons

Uta Uta's-son—squire of Magan village

Places, Titles, et cetera

Magan—village

Ryssand—northern province; banner: blood red with Fist and Sword

Ruler

Corsywndam—lord of Ryssand
Brugan—Corsywndam of Ryssand's son and heir
Artisane—Corsywndam of Ryssand's daughter, one of Ninévrisë's ladies-in-waiting

Places, Titles, et cetera

Ryssandish—of Ryssand; also, an ethnic group distinct from the Guelens, but closely tied to them

Sumas—*eastern province*

Teymeryn—*northeastern province*

Ursamin—*northeastern province*

ELWYNOR

The Regency
    Uleman Syrillas—Regent of Elwynor, father of Ninévrisë
    Ninévrisë Syrillas—daughter of Uleman
Lesser Nobles
    Aeself—lieutenant of loyal force
    Angin—companion of Aeself, q.v.
    Tarwyn Aswydd—ancient warrior
    Elfharyn—Elwynim lord, loyal to Ninévrisë, holding throne and regency for her
    Haurydd—Ninévrisë's man, earl of High Saissond
    Palisan—one of Ninévrisë's men
    Tasien—earl of Cassissan, Uleman's man, captain of his army, related to Ninévrisë through her mother
    Ysdan—Ninévrisë's man, earl of Ormadzaran
    Aseynéddin—rebel earl of Elwynor, enemy of Ninévrisë, died at Lewenfield; banner: Griffin
    Caswyddian—rebel Elwynim lord, earl of Lower Saissond, enemy of Ninévrisë, killed by Shadows at Althalen
    Tasmôrden—Elwynim rebel lord, enemy of Ninévrisë
    Uillasan—companion of Aeself
Places, Titles, et cetera
    Ansym—bridge, at border of Elwynor
    Ashiym—place in Elwynor, seven towers, old Sihhë connections, one tower destroyed
    Banner of Elwynor—black-and-white Checker with gold Tower, quartered with blue
    Casissan—Tasien's earldom
    criess—village near Ilefínian
    Elwynim—of the kingdom of Elwynor
    Her Grace—title for Ninévrisë
    High Saissond—Elwynim province, Haurydd's home
    Ilefínian—capital of Elwynor

Lower Saisonnd—lord Caswyddian's province
Melseriedd—old name for kingdom of Elwynor, prior to
    Regency
Nithen—district and hamlet near Ilefínian
Ormadzaran—Ysdan's earldom
Saendel—bandits who served Aseynéddin at Lewen field
Syrillas—surname, Uleman Syrillas, regent of Elwynor, Ninévrisë
    Syrillas
Syrim—bridge at border of Elwynor

GALASIEN

Persons
　　Hasufin Heltain—wizard, possibly a prince of Galasien, enemy of
        Mauryl
　　Mauryl Gestaurien—wizard, Galasieni
Places, Titles, et cetera
　　Galasieni—a lost race
　　Kingsbane—nickname of Mauryl
　　Kingmaker—nickname of Mauryl
　　Nineteen Gods—the unnamed hidden gods worshiped by wizards
　　Silver Tower—at Ynefel, Mauryl's symbol, then Tristen's: black
        banner with Silver Tower and Star
　　Ynefel—Mauryl's tower: Silver Tower

OTHER TRIBES

Arachim—northern tribe
Chomaggari—southern barbarians
Casmyndan, Casmyndanim—far southern tribe on the coast
Lyra—a hill tribe
Lyrdish—belonging to Lyra

SIHHË / SIHHË CONNECTIONS

Persons
　　Barrakkêth—one of five Sihhë-lords
　　Elfwyn—last Sihhë king, a halfling

Harosyn—Sihhë king
Sadyurnan—Sihhë king (ancient) in Hen Amas
Sarynan—Sihhë king
Ashyel—Sihhë halfling, son of Barrakkêth
Tashânen—Sihhë halfling, engineer and strategist, wrote *The Art of War*
Aswyn—Sihhë halfing, youngest brother of Elfwyn, thought stillborn, body inhabited by Hasufin

Places, Titles, et cetera

Arachis—old name, Sihhë connections
Aryceillan—old name, (possibly old tribe with Sihhë connections)
Deathmaker—nickname for Barrakkêth
Hafsandyr—mountains in north, original home of Sihhë
Kingbreaker—nickname for Barrakkêth
Sihhë, Sihhë's—lost race, five Sihhë came down from north to rule in Ylesuin and Elwynor

OTHER

Bryalt—religious sect of Ylesuin, mostly Amefin
Bryaltine—of the Bryalts of Ylesuin
Bryssandin—horse breed, used in breeding Crysin horses
Bathurys—old name for Padys Spring
Far Sassury—proverb: "the back of beyond"
Five Gods—the unnamed gods worshiped by the people of Ylesuin
Ileneluin, Ilenelluin—mountain
Jorysal—a place, an old name in histories
Lenúalim—a river, major border between Elwynor and Ylesuin
Manystys Aldun—philosopher, wrote tome on oceans
Marchlanders—refers to the southern lords and their armies, excluding Amefel
Merhas—truth, carved on one side of Tristen's sword
Quinalt—a strict religious cult
Quinaltine—of the Quinalt
Shadow Hills—area north of Ryssand
Shaping—a creature or person called into being and shaped into flesh by a wizard
Spestinan—horse breed
Stellyrhas—illusion, carved on one side of Tristen's sword
Teranthine—moderate religious cult
Wys—any of a series of villages
Wys-on-Cressit—a village in Ylesuin